Bonded in Death

Titles by J. D. Robb

Naked in Death
Glory in Death
Immortal in Death
Rapture in Death
Ceremony in Death
Vengeance in Death
Holiday in Death
Conspiracy in Death
Loyalty in Death
Witness in Death
Judgment in Death
Betrayal in Death
Seduction in Death
Reunion in Death
Purity in Death
Portrait in Death
Imitation in Death
Divided in Death
Visions in Death
Survivor in Death
Origin in Death
Memory in Death
Born in Death
Innocent in Death
Creation in Death
Strangers in Death
Salvation in Death
Promises in Death
Kindred in Death
Fantasy in Death
Indulgence in Death
Treachery in Death
New York to Dallas
Celebrity in Death
Delusion in Death
Calculated in Death
Thankless in Death
Concealed in Death
Festive in Death
Obsession in Death
Devoted in Death
Brotherhood in Death
Apprentice in Death
Echoes in Death
Secrets in Death
Dark in Death
Leverage in Death
Connections in Death
Vendetta in Death
Golden in Death
Shadows in Death
Faithless in Death
Forgotten in Death
Abandoned in Death
Desperation in Death
Encore in Death
Payback in Death
Random in Death
Passions in Death
Bonded in Death

Anthologies

Silent Night
(with Susan Plunkett, Dee Holmes, and Claire Cross)

Out of This World
(with Laurell K. Hamilton, Susan Krinard, and Maggie Shayne)

Remember When
(with Nora Roberts)

Bump in the Night
(with Mary Blayney, Ruth Ryan Langan, and Mary Kay McComas)

Dead of Night
(with Mary Blayney, Ruth Ryan Langan, and Mary Kay McComas)

Three in Death

Suite 606
(with Mary Blayney, Ruth Ryan Langan, and Mary Kay McComas)

In Death

The Lost
(with Patricia Gaffney, Mary Blayney, and Ruth Ryan Langan)

The Other Side
(with Mary Blayney, Patricia Gaffney, Ruth Ryan Langan, and Mary Kay McComas)

Time of Death

The Unquiet
(with Mary Blayney, Patricia Gaffney, Ruth Ryan Langan, and Mary Kay McComas)

Mirror, Mirror
(with Mary Blayney, Elaine Fox, Mary Kay McComas, and R. C. Ryan)

Down the Rabbit Hole
(with Mary Blayney, Elaine Fox, Mary Kay McComas, and R. C. Ryan)

BONDED IN DEATH

J. D. Robb

ST. MARTIN'S PRESS
NEW YORK

This is a work of fiction. All of the characters, organizations, and events portrayed in this novel are either products of the author's imagination or are used fictitiously.

First published in the United States by St. Martin's Press,
an imprint of St. Martin's Publishing Group

Printed in the United States of America. For information, address
St. Martin's Publishing Group, 120 Broadway, New York, NY 10271.

www.stmartins.com

The Library of Congress Cataloging-in-Publication Data is available upon request.

ISBN 978-1-250-37079-2 (hardcover)
ISBN 978-1-250-37080-8 (ebook)

Our books may be purchased in bulk for promotional, educational, or business use. Please contact your local bookseller or the Macmillan Corporate and Premium Sales Department at 1-800-221-7945, extension 5442, or by email at MacmillanSpecialMarkets@macmillan.com.

First Edition: 2025

10 9 8 7 6 5 4 3 2 1

The purple testament of bleeding war.

—William Shakespeare

Revenge is the poor delight of little minds.

—Juvenal

Prologue

London—Urban Wars

In war, life and death hung in tenuous balance. In war, taking a life in battle wasn't murder, but victory.

And still, death won.

In war, planning the death and destruction of the enemy was strategy.

And still, death won.

Violence, like a virus, spread from city to city. A stray spark in Hanoi kindled a fire in Chicago. A fire set in Berlin burst into a blaze in Tokyo. Wild winds of fury carried flames to New York, to Moscow, to Brazil, to Hong Kong.

And cities across the globe burned.

The human race consumed itself in a conflagration of rich against poor, culture against culture, with some beating the drums of fanaticism, be it religion or politics or the gnawing hate of the other.

And so, death won.

The twelve who gathered in the bowels of the old stone church understood the horrors and miseries of war. They had taken lives in battle, through strategy, through guile and deceptions. And accepted that the blood on their hands would leave a stain.

It seemed peace couldn't win unless death won first.

Though they'd come from different walks of life, war had bonded them. They called themselves The Twelve, and each brought to the war room, in what had been a place of worship, their own skills. Skills noted by the Underground.

They'd been recruited, then trained in other skills.

Killing skills.

Their number included a teacher, an actor, a dancer, a cop, a medic, a young scientist, technicians, a retired soldier called to duty once more, a thief, a mechanic, an heiress.

All spies now, all soldiers in a war that swept through cities around the globe and threatened to leave them in smoking rubble.

Deep under the streets where blood and death had become horribly normal, their headquarters included a large round table, like Arthur's of old. Counters held computers, listening devices, communication centers.

Weapons of war—the guns, the knives, the grenades, the explosives—they stored in racks and cabinets.

A room off the main was set up as a makeshift infirmary and dispensary. The medic treated wounds there when necessary, and dispensed the drugs—locked in another cabinet—for use against the enemy. Hallucinogens, sleeping powders, poisons, venoms.

Though each knew the names the others went by in this time of war, they called the medic Fox.

Another room held wardrobe, wigs, hairpieces, makeup, face putty, and more used in disguises. Though the actor continued to use her name as part of her cover, they called her Chameleon.

Yet another room served as a workshop to make explosives, the wiring, the timers, and the remotes used to detonate.

The teacher, who at the dawn of the wars had dug the broken and bloody bodies of her young students from the rubble of the bombed school, now made bombs. Her purpose, one she'd vowed when weeping over those broken and bloodied bodies, was to destroy those who would murder children.

She'd met the medic that day, the day that had changed her life forever. Out of the smoke and blood there had been a light.

They'd loved, they'd married and created a cherished child.

To keep her safe, they took the child out of harm's way in the care of a trusted friend.

They called the teacher Fawn.

She worked with the retired soldier most directly, the one they called Rabbit.

The others, due to his age and experience, considered him the de facto leader.

He stood now, gray hair shaggy, his face lined with time and duty, and scanned the table. All battle-scarred, he knew. Some physically, and every one of them in heart and mind. But they'd fight on. He trusted them as he trusted himself.

They'd become, over these ravaged years, family.

"Before we begin briefing on this mission, a bright spot. The intel on North America, and this has been confirmed by the Underground and MI6. While pockets of enemy activity remain, the tide's turned. Revolutionary headquarters in several major cities have been infiltrated or destroyed.

"Mole."

The heiress nodded. "I can confirm. My contact in New York reports the city is in the hands of our allies, enemy forces are surrendering. Washington, D.C., reports the same, as does Los Angeles, Chicago, Dallas, and up into Canada—Montreal, Toronto."

She brushed back her fall of icy blond hair. Though studs sparkled at her ears—she'd come from a dinner party—they pretended to be diamonds.

She'd sold most of her jewelry to buy food, medical supplies, weapons—whatever those suffering required. She glanced at the dancer they called Panther.

"My sources also confirm." Her accent came from Eastern Europe, her birthplace, and the birthplace of her illustrious career. "Cease-fires are being negotiated even now."

"Good news, but you wouldn't know it from London." The thief, Magpie, shrugged. His voice reflected his life on the streets.

"Not yet." Under the table, Fox took Fawn's hand. A connection of hope. "But North America stabilizes, Europe will follow, and the world follows that. I've treated more enemy wounded than our own these past weeks."

Like Panther, Fox's accent spoke of his homeland in Ukraine.

"Some are deserting, retreating," Fawn added. "Running out of London." Her hand tightened on her husband's.

"Our baby's fine," he assured her. "If they run, they don't run to fight but to survive."

Because they were a family there, he lifted her hand to his lips. "We'll see our girl very soon. And your sons, Panther. We're grateful you gave us a safe place for our daughter."

"Fawn hid my sons here before London became too dangerous for them. We—we all—look out for each other."

"And the innocent," the scientist called Owl added.

"Always."

The tech called Wasp lifted a hand. "And Italy? I haven't heard from my brother in Rome for more than a week. My wife and my mother in Tuscany can't reach him."

"The fighting is intense in Rome," Panther told him. "I'll see what I can find out."

"Thank you."

"I spoke with my sister this morning." The other tech, Cobra, lit a cigarette. "She says, as does Fox, she's treating more of them than us."

Beside him, the detective constable known as Shark lit his own cigarette. "My intel says the same. On the run, outnumbered. Supply line issues on all sides, but we're used to that. We may not have hit flash point yet, but we're close."

"We'll be closer when we complete our next mission," Rabbit said. "Wasp, if you will."

He rose to man a computer.

"If we could have the map on-screen. Our target is here. Beneath these buildings, evacuated early in the conflict, is Dominion's London headquarters."

A murmur went around the table.

"This is confirmed?" Fox demanded. "Our last intel indicated the West End was more likely."

"Misinformation—likely deliberate." Chameleon pressed her lips together. "I don't like being duped. If we'd moved on it, as I pushed for—"

"Your cover would've been blown." Shark gave her a cheeky grin. "Cooler heads, my lovely."

"Normally I say bollocks to cooler heads, but in this case . . ." Now she shrugged, tossed back her bold red hair. "I can't, yet, confirm the target."

"I saw what I saw, heard what I heard." Magpie spoke up. "And no, I wasn't seen, I wasn't heard. Scavenging, scouting out a new area, and I stumbled on a tunnel that shouldn't have been there. Happened on some air ducts, a handy way to get around. They've got a war room, at least twice this size. Well-equipped, well-manned. An armory—and I was tempted there, but the well-manned discouraged me. Better to report back and live another day."

"We need to go back, get the full scope."

"I got a pretty full scope, Fox, and sent the old SOS to Rabbit." Magpie used his finger in the air to draw an *X* and two *I*'s—the symbol for twelve.

"And that's why we're here. Part of that full scope is a prison."

"In the HQ?" Mole asked. "I've been hearing about a prison in Whitechapel."

"And you hear well and true," Rabbit told her. "Magpie was able to take photos of that building and location while slithering through the duct system.

"The prison is the second part, simultaneous with the first. The first, destroy enemy HQ; the second, take control of the prison and release our people."

He looked at Magpie. "One more trip through for you, mate, photos if you can get them, any additional information. Fawn, Hawk, and I will build the explosives, Fawn and Hawk will place them."

"Team Two—Fox, Panther, Chameleon, Wasp as tech—will hit the prison, using the explosion as cover and as signal to move in.

"Mole and Owl, lookouts for team two. Magpie and Shark, lookouts for team one. Cobra and I will run communications here."

For days they worked on details, on timing, on weapons, approaches, escape routes.

When it was done, when Command green-lighted the mission, they suited up, sat around the table once more for a final briefing.

And Rabbit passed a bottle of whiskey around the table.

"A drink before the war. This is our flash point, the turning point in this long, hard battle. And we will succeed. Tonight we take lives, and we save countless others. Remember what we fight for. Not ourselves, but the innocent."

He looked at Owl.

"Our children."

Then at Fox and Fawn, at Panther.

"Not just for England, but for all. To The Twelve."

They drank, not knowing that one who drank with them was a traitor.

Chapter One

WASP HAD GONE BY MANY NAMES IN HIS LIFE. BUT WHEN HE FLEW FROM Rome to New York in September of 2061, he traveled under the name he'd been born with.

Giovanni Rossi.

He'd retired nearly eight years before, and now spent his days in his garden, enjoying his grandchildren, sipping wine in the evening with his wife.

He'd gone soft in the middle, and didn't mind a bit. Gone was the whip-lean tech, the slippery spy, the reluctant soldier who hated war.

He looked like what he was, a man inching toward eighty and comfortable with his life. There were times, still times, when he flashed back in dreams to when the world went mad.

But he woke beside his wife, safe in his bed, and in good weather—even not such good weather—enjoyed his breakfast on their little terrace as Rome came awake.

Next to his family, the city where he'd been born, had lived for decades was the love of his life.

He would miss waking beside his wife in the morning, and his terrace, and Rome. But the signal had come, and he'd taken a vow that bloody, treacherous night.

He'd packed lightly—if he needed more, New York would provide. So he rolled a small case behind him, and had a bag on his shoulder.

He saw the uniformed driver holding a sign with his name on it, and smiled.

"I am Giovanni Rossi."

"Signore Rossi, let me take your bags. Do you have more luggage?"

"No, this is all."

"Please follow me."

The man spoke with an American accent, and with deference as he asked how the flight had been, and hoped Rossi enjoyed his visit to New York.

Giovanni hadn't expected a limousine, but wasn't surprised. After all, Fox worked for a very important and wealthy man.

The driver opened the door for him, and Giovanni slid into luxury seats of smooth leather, flowers in bud vases, a bottle of wine already opened for his pleasure.

"With traffic, I'm afraid the drive will take about twenty minutes. There's music programmed if you like."

"*Grazie.*"

"Please let me know if you need anything."

Though Giovanni wouldn't have minded company or conversation, the privacy shield slid silently into place.

He poured the wine, settled back to enjoy the ride.

It had been nearly a quarter century since he'd seen New York, and seen it as an operative of Agenzia Informazioni e Sicurezza Esterna.

Interesting times, he thought as he sipped, and looked out the window at the lights sparkling in the city that, like Rome, had come back from a brutal beating.

Frowning, he thought of the message, encrypted, he'd received.

XII
New York
Do not contact me under any circumstances.
Transportation will be waiting at the international shuttle station on your arrival.
Your ticket is attached to this message.
Urgently, Fox

How long had it been since they'd communicated? At least ten years, he thought. How those years flew by. And what could he possibly do, a man of his age, soft in the middle?

But a vow was a vow. And he'd taken that vow with blood still fresh on his hands.

A little sleepy from the trip, the wine, he sat back, closed his eyes. And, drifting just a bit, caught the taste of something in the air, something that wasn't the flowers in the vase, the wine in the glass.

He was a man over seventy, retired for nearly a decade, but training kicked in.

He bolted up, dropping the glass, spilling the wine.

But the window didn't open, the door refused to budge. Levering back, he kicked viciously at the privacy shield, but it held.

It took only a few minutes for him to slip into unconsciousness, barely that much again to die.

The driver took his time, enjoying himself, humming along to the music he'd programmed as he watched Rossi's death on the small monitor. He knew exactly how long the gas took to debilitate a man of Rossi's size, how long it took to kill.

He'd been trained, after all, in the art of war.

For the next steps, he lowered the rear right window a half inch, engaged the fan so the gas would slowly filter harmlessly away.

After it cleared, he pulled into a garage of a house he'd purchased over a year before. His mission required patience, and he'd honed that virtue over decades in a cage.

A cage Rossi had played a part in locking behind him.

He got out of the car, and from the trunk removed a breathing mask. A precaution, as he'd given the gas time to dissipate.

But miscalculations, small mistakes—and *impatience*—had cost him dearly in the past.

He opened the passenger door and studied his work.

Rossi lay crumpled on the smooth leather seat. The knuckles of his hands, still fisted, showed scrapes, bruises, blood where he'd beaten them uselessly against the windows, the privacy shield.

He looked, his killer decided, like a dead walrus with his ridiculous mustache and pouchy belly. And with his mouth open, eyes bulging, appeared to be waiting to have someone toss him a fish.

His killer found that delightfully amusing.

After checking Rossi's pockets, he withdrew the printout of the message he'd sent and placed it in his own.

He replaced this with another, boldly printed on a carefully replicated business card, and this he slid between the index and middle fingers of Rossi's right fist.

HERE LIES THE DEAD WASP.
HE JOINS FAWN, HAWK, RABBIT.
XII ARE NOW VIII.
SOON THERE WILL BE ONLY I.

"They'll come, oh yes, they'll all come."

In the house, in the room designated for disguise, he removed the chauffeur's uniform, the short brown wig. Slowly, a bit painfully, he peeled off the skin mask that, while uncomfortably tight, wiped two decades off his age.

Once he'd removed that, he massaged cream into his skin, all but felt it absorb like a thirsty man drinks water.

He took out the colored contacts, cleaned the makeup off his hands that matched them to the duskier tone of the skin mask.

He changed the black dress shoes with their two-inch lifts for black kicks.

He covered his hair—dyed raven black to remove the gray—with a lighter brown wig long enough for a short tail. He added a few pounds to his girth under a simple T-shirt and casual pants.

He drove east out of the garage.

He carefully drove the limo he'd stolen a week before until he parked it beneath an underpass.

He abandoned it there—such a trick would only work once—and strolled away. He walked easily for four blocks, enjoying the stubborn heat of late summer.

He had a car, a luxury sedan he'd treated himself to shortly after his arrival in New York. He paid the parking fee and drove home again.

After removing his last disguise, he replaced everything, organized, inventoried in the room on the second floor, a room he kept secured at all times.

In the well-appointed kitchen with its river view, he fixed himself a snack. Some olives, cheese, thin crackers. He poured a cognac.

He took the tray into what he considered his parlor, one he'd outfitted with comfortable, streamlined furniture and a large entertainment screen.

As his mood was jovial, he chose a comedy for his entertainment.

He would prize, always, the freedom to eat what he wished when he wished, to come and go as he pleased.

Seven remaining, he thought as he settled in. He still thought it a pity Rabbit had died quietly at home, surrounded by his family. But that didn't mean he couldn't extract payment there, too.

When the rest was done, he could select a member of that family as a stand-in.

Plenty of time, he thought. He had nothing but time, while for the rest of The Twelve, oh yes, their clocks were ticking.

Lieutenant Eve Dallas slept quiet, slept deep in the big old four-poster beside her husband, with the cat curled against the small of her back.

If she dreamed, the dreams stayed quiet, too.

She didn't hear Roarke rise for the day, awakened by his personal internal clock.

The sound of his shower brought a waterfall into her sleeping mind, its waters blissfully warm and as wildly blue as Roarke's eyes.

They swam there together, bodies sleek and naked. Wet, his mane of black hair gleamed in the moonlight, that full moon dazzled on the water, and into the wonderful wild blue of his eyes.

When she swam under the warm, clear water, the sand below lay smooth and pure white.

And when she rose up, he reached for her. Their legs tangled and locked together as their mouths met, and the pleasure shimmered through.

Something bit her ankle.

She woke with a jolt, with her communicator buzzing.

"Damn it. Jesus." She snatched it up. "Dallas."

Dispatch, Dallas, Lieutenant Eve. Report to underpass FDR Drive at Ninetieth Street. DB in vehicle. See the uniforms on scene.

"Acknowledged. Contact Peabody, Detective Delia. Dallas out. Lights on, twenty percent," she ordered.

Then sat a moment, scrubbing her hands over her face.

With a white towel slung around his waist, his hair still damp from the shower, Roarke stepped into the bedroom.

He took one look at her. "Well then," he said.

"Dead body, Upper East Side. Why are you up?"

"It's nearly half-four, and I've a meeting." As he spoke, Ireland weaving through the words, he moved to the cabinet holding the AutoChef. "I'd say it's coffee for two then."

"Yeah. Hell." She started to get up, then frowned at him. Mostly naked, hair wet. "I think I was having a sex dream."

He brought her coffee, strong and black, looked into her sleepy whiskey-colored eyes. "I hope I made an appearance."

"Yeah. You were wet. I was wet." Shaking her head, she gulped coffee. "Then dead body—for real."

She got up, which had the cat rolling over to sprawl. With the coffee, she walked to, then into, the forest of clothes that was her closet.

"Summer's hanging on," he told her. "You'll want to keep that in mind."

She grabbed a white T-shirt—unless it was cream, or oatmeal, or another of the myriad shades of white with stupid names. Gray trousers seemed good enough. But when she started to reach for a gray jacket, all those damn shades defeated her.

Too early for this crap, she decided, and went with a navy jacket.

Black boots seemed like too many colors, and God knew Roarke made sure she had a zillion to choose from. She grabbed navy there, and dressed in the closet so it would be done before he could point out the error of her fashion-declined ways.

And somehow when she carried the jacket out to grab her weapon harness, he already wore a sharply cut gray suit, a shirt in a deeper tone of gray with the slightest sheen, and a perfectly knotted tie with hints of burgundy against the gray.

"I guess when you were stealing your way across the planet, the quick change came in handy."

He smiled. "It didn't hurt. You'll eat something."

"I need to—"

"Are uniforms on scene?"

"Yeah, but—"

"And the victim's already dead. So you can take five minutes for food. Sit. Five minutes."

She sat, but started the countdown in her head even as Roarke handed her a plate holding ham, eggs, cheese tucked into a golden-brown biscuit.

She took the first bite—good!—and glanced at the still sleeping cat.

"Looks like it's too early for Galahad to try to steal some breakfast. What about you?" she asked as he sat beside her with his coffee.

"Just the coffee for now. I may wander downstairs after the meeting and see what Summerset's having."

She only grunted at the name of Roarke's majordomo, father figure, and most usual pain in her ass.

"Brain's waking up, and it seems to me Carmichael and Santiago were top of the roll. Must've already caught one. People are always murdering people in the middle of the damn night. And in broad daylight," she added. "Who's the meeting with?"

"Sydney."

"Sydney who?"

"Australia, darling. I can reschedule if you want me to go with you."

"No. I've got the dead body, you've got the world domination."

"It's good to play to our strengths. Now, about this sex dream."

"I think we were swimming in a river. Why would we be swimming in a river?"

"To be wet and naked?"

"There was that. But other things swim in rivers, like fish and water snakes. And, depending, alligators. I don't see getting wet and naked with alligators."

"They would take the mind off sex."

"So do dead bodies." She rose, walked over to strap on her weapon harness, gather up her badge, her 'link, and all the rest.

After shrugging on her jacket, she dragged a hand through her short brown hair and considered it groomed.

"I've gotta go."

"As do I. I'll walk with you."

"Why didn't they take the vehicle?" she wondered. "Had their own? Can't drive?"

"You'll find out."

Before he made the turn toward his office, he drew her in, kissed her. "See you take care of my cop."

"I got that." She laid a hand on his cheek. "I'd rather be swimming in a river with you."

"With alligators?"

"No. That's a deal-breaker."

She kissed him again, then he watched his long-legged, lanky cop walk away to hunt a killer.

In the car, she programmed more coffee from the in-dash AC, then drove across town. One advantage of driving across Manhattan at not quite five in the morning? Barely any traffic. No hawking ad blimps overhead, advantage two, she decided.

She spotted a trio of street LCs hanging in for one more john or jane before calling it a night. She imagined when they did, they'd hike in their tiny skirts and mile-high heels to the all-night deli a block away for some fake coffee, a bagel and schmear.

Along her way she saw a quartet of twenty-somethings that had obviously put in a full night clubbing. Their voices, laughter—more than a little drunk—carried through her open car windows.

A café for them, she decided. Something with pricier fake coffee—most likely flavored—omelets from egg substitute, sides of pretend bacon that had never been part of a pig.

She drank some of her very real Roarke coffee with gratitude.

The towers and lofty homes of the Upper East took over. She could hear the whoosh of cars on the FDR, but those tucked inside their minor palaces wouldn't.

A few lights glimmered here and there. Early risers—she sure as hell had married one of those—insomniacs, maybe a light left on for someone coming home late.

So many lives, she thought, in so many places, stacked, spread, scattered.

And someone was always taking one, ending one.

For so many reasons.

She guided her DLE to the underpass, where the traffic above came in a muffled roar.

She frowned when she saw the pair of uniforms beside the long, shining black stretch limo.

Unexpected, she admitted.

She got out, turned on her recorder, flipped up her badge.

She got out her field kit before walking toward the limo.

"Lieutenant Dallas, sir."

The cop on the left, male, Black, early forties, had a mirror shine on his hard shoes. He stepped slightly to the side.

"Officer Mitgy. My partner, Officer Blane."

Blane, female, white, about a decade younger than her partner, just nodded.

"We've got the nine-one-one caller in the patrol car," Mitgy continued. "He states he spotted the vehicle, and curious, knocked on the driver's side door, then opened it. Upon seeing the body in the back, called it in. He admits he waited in hopes there might be a reward."

"He's a little stoned, Lieutenant," Blane put it.

"He appears mildly impaired," Mitgy corrected. "We responded at zero-four-ten. Took the caller's statement, then opened the rear door of the vehicle and determined, visually, he is deceased."

"And has your card in his hand."

Eve frowned at Blane. "My card?"

"Lieutenant Eve Dallas. Homicide. NYPSD. Cop Central. Your badge and 'link numbers."

"That's correct. We determined something was printed on the back of said card, but would have disturbed the body by removing it to read fully."

"'Here lies the dead Wasp,'" Blane said. "There's more after that, but we couldn't be sure what."

"All right, let's have a look."

She sealed her hands, her boots, then opened the passenger door.

The victim lay, mouth agape, eyes wide—the white showed streaks of red under the film of death. He had a faint blue tinge to his lips. He wore a light jacket, a collared shirt beneath, tan pants, brown loafers.

He wore a wedding band on his left hand, a ring with a blue stone on his right.

A wineglass lay on the carpeted floor, and the stain on the carpet, a splatter on the door panel looked more like wine than blood.

His hands, fisted, looked as if he'd fought something or someone. The card stuck up between his clenched fingers.

"The victim, as yet unidentified, is male. Hair gray, eyes brown. About . . . five-ten, approximately two hundred pounds. He's got a business card—what appears to be one of my business cards in his right hand. I'm removing it."

She tugged it out, and it took a tug.

"Appears to be my card, but it's not. The paper's thicker than mine. There's printing on the back—all bold, all caps.

"'Here lies the dead Wasp,'" she began, and recording it visually, read out the message.

"Someone wants me to know he killed this guy, and intends to keep at it. Who the hell is the vic?"

She took out her Identi-pad, managed with some effort to turn the victim's thumb onto it.

"The vic is identified as Giovanni Rossi, Rome, Italy. Age seventy-nine. No New York address or U.S. address. Mitgy, check the trunk. Seal up first."

She backed out enough to toss him her can of Seal-It, then her master.

She slid back in, began to go through the victim's pockets.

"Got a passport. And a 'link, a wallet. He's wearing two rings and a wrist unit. Killer didn't bother to help himself. Not even," she noted when she checked the wallet, "to about three K in USD, and, ah, that again in euros."

"There's a suitcase, Lieutenant, and a shoulder bag in the trunk."

"Just came in, didn't you, Rossi? Just flew into New York tonight, from Rome. Limo picked you up. Wasp, what the hell does that mean? Wasp, Fawn, Hawk, Rabbit."

And where the hell was Peabody?

"Blane, run the limo's plates. Mitgy, check international flights, Rome to New York City."

She found the 'link passcoded—not a surprise.

She checked the body for wounds.

"No injuries visible other than the knuckles, both hands."

She frowned at the window. "Looks like a little blood on the glass."

"Lieutenant, a vehicle of this description was reported stolen seven days ago. Executive Transportation."

"A week. Couldn't have it on the street for a week. Had it stashed somewhere. Had adjustments to make."

She climbed out. On the off-chance, she hit the ignition. It purred to life. "He didn't bother to lock the ignition. Didn't bother with the code. Done with it."

She hunted and found the mechanism for the privacy screen, lifted it.

Rounding to the back again, she studied the screen from the victim's side. "Blood traces, and it looks like he tried to kick it out."

She looked back at Rossi.

"You're trapped." She tried to lower the window, and it didn't budge. Tried the door handle. It stayed firmly in place. "Locked in. Pro job, all the markings of a pro. But why the card, my card, the message?"

"TOD, zero-forty-six," she said when she inserted her gauge. "COD, ME to determine. Poison leads my pack. Slow-acting enough for him to try to get the hell out."

"Lieutenant, a flight from Rome landed at the international station at zero-eighteen hours. Giovanni Rossi was on the manifest."

She didn't need to be a math whiz to figure the killer hadn't waited long. Under a half hour from landing? Barely time to get off the shuttle, through Customs, get into the limo, and pour that glass of wine.

She picked up the wineglass, sniffed it before bagging it.

And heard the clomp of her partner's favorite boots—pink cowboy boots Eve had been weak enough to buy for her.

"Sorry, Dallas, sorry. It took forever. Lower West is like a different world from Upper East."

Eve glanced back.

Peabody had her red-streaked black hair in a high bouncy tail. She had a white shirt with thick pink stripes under a light blue jacket.

At least she wore sensible black pants.

"McNab with you?"

"They said vehicle, so we didn't see the point in him coming all the way up here, then back to Central again. Do you need him?"

Eve figured Peabody's man, and one of NYPSD's e-detectives, could slide through the vic's passcoded 'link in minutes. But it could wait.

"No." She bagged the 'link, passed it to Peabody. "Passcoded. EDD will open it up."

She held up another evidence bag, the one holding the business card. "Vic had this stuck in his fist. The killer stuck it there."

"Your card."

"Made to look like it. This is better paper than what we get." She turned the bag around.

"Code, you think? Animal names. Well, a wasp isn't an animal. And Roman numerals. Why leave you a message you wouldn't understand? Unless—did you know the vic?"

"No. He just flew in from Rome. Look, the nine-one-one caller's in the patrol car. Get his statement, his name, contact. Low odds he's in this. I want to contact Morris myself. I can't give a COD on this one. I'll call the sweepers. We're going to need the limo taken in, and taken apart. He rigged it. The killer rigged it to trap the victim in the back."

"I'll take the nine-one-one caller now."

Eve stepped away, pulled out her 'link.

The chief medical examiner answered clothed as Roarke had been—before the suit. He wore nothing but a towel—a black one in Morris's case—hung low on his hips.

His long black hair spilled damply down his back nearly to his waist. He had swimmer's shoulders, and though he only operated on the dead, the hands of a surgeon.

He smiled. "So, we wake to the dead?"

"Yeah. I got a male victim—age seventy-nine, dead in the back of a stolen limo. Only visible wounds his hands—smears of blood on the privacy screen, the window. I got most of a bottle of red wine, and whatever was in the glass, and didn't go in the vic, spilled on the floor. Vic flew in from Rome tonight."

"A poor end to a long trip."

"He had a facsimile of my card in his hand, and a cryptic—you gotta say cryptic—message on the back."

She held it up for Morris to read.

"That would reach the cryptic level. So our victim would be the Wasp. One way to dispense with wasps is poison."

"Yeah, I'm thinking, but can't confirm. He's otherwise known as Giovanni Rossi, out of Rome. I've still got some work to do here, but wanted to give you a heads-up."

"I'll contact the dead wagon for you, and be in-house as soon as possible."

"Appreciate it."

"I assume, until tonight, you were unacquainted with Signore Rossi."

"Don't know the name, don't know the face. Something might jog when I notify next of kin. Maybe I know his killer. He's the one who made the card."

"Well, we love a mystery, don't we? I'll see Rossi soon, and you when you come in."

She pocketed the 'link, then walked back to go through the victim's luggage.

She found nothing out of line. No weapons, no secret compartments. Just the clothes and toiletries of a man on a trip. Along with a photo of the victim with a woman she assumed had put the wedding ring on his finger.

Peabody came over. "Caller's Trevor Stash, age twenty-two. He lives a couple blocks from here. I let him go, Dallas. He was a little high, or had been. Admitted it. Blubbered a little, never seen a dead body before, but he could tell dead when he did see it. Figured the guy had a heart attack or something, and maybe the limo driver went for help."

"Did he touch anything?"

"He says not, and I'd believe that."

"And he was here because?"

"Cut through here after partying with friends. He gave me a list of names, clubs. Then the name and address of the girl he left the last club with, got lucky with.

"Said he was feeling really good, and just tried to be a good person. Thought, at first, maybe the limo had some trouble, then he saw the body in the back. Also admitted he started to just take off, all shaken up, but wanted to do the right thing. And maybe there'd be a reward. Called it in, waited for the cops.

"Comes off true, Dallas."

"Yeah, he's not in it. Vic had jewelry, had cash, it's still there."

Night began to give way to day as she stood, shoved her hands in her pockets.

Who the hell was Giovanni Rossi, and why did he come to New York? What did he plan to do? Who did he plan to see?

More, why did his killer want her on the case?

Chapter Two

THE MORGUE TEAM PULLED IN, BAGGED AND TAGGED THE BODY.

In Morris's hands soon, she thought, and then they'd have some answers.

She waited for the sweepers, had a conversation. Eve didn't expect they'd find anything outside the limo itself, but they'd sweep and scan.

With Peabody, she got back in her car, then sat another minute, studying the scene, and the white-suited sweepers got to work.

"Not a lot of people who'd cut through here, at least not after dark. Still, a risk somebody sees the killer getting out of the car. Even in New York, people are going to notice a big-ass limo sitting here. If nothing else, they're likely to do just what what's-his-name did."

"Trevor Stash."

"Clearly you want the body found, want me called in on it. Don't care about the limo—it's done the job. Had to take some time with it first. Locked down the back seat. Windows are tinted, and that's usual, so people can't gawk at the passengers. Did he scream?" she wondered, and started the car.

"Could he scream? Seems likely enough with the evidence he beat on the glass hard enough to bleed."

"Poisoned the wine, most probable," Peabody put in. "But what if Rossi didn't drink it?"

"Italian guy, after a flight from Rome, sitting in the back of a fancy limo? Odds are pretty good. Not absolute, but good. The killer knew him, or whoever hired the killer knew him. Banked on him sitting back, enjoying a glass of Italian red."

The traffic had kicked up, but Eve didn't mind it. Plenty of early birds on the sidewalks, walking dogs, heading to work, getting in a run or a trip to the gym.

"Not a lot of luggage, so maybe a quick trip. Enough for a few days. You can start checking hotels, see if he booked a room. Limo treatment, so hit the upscale ones, start with the East Side. I'll do the notification. He's got a wife—an almost-fifty-year deal—four adult kids, and eleven grandkids. Somebody ought to know where he planned to stay, what he came to do."

"Coffee, please?"

"Coffee, right. Two. Let's get the vic's 'link and the tablet I found in his shoulder bag to EDD after we check at the shuttle station. The killer wasn't worried about that, either, but you never know. You never know," she repeated, and used the in-dash to contact Roarke.

He sat at his desk in his home office, and lifted his eyebrows.

"Case closed already?"

"Nowhere near. Do you know a Giovanni Rossi, out of Rome?"

"The name doesn't strike."

"Seventy-nine, retired, cybersecurity. Gray and brown, big mustache. Wife—more than four decades—Anna Maria née Adolphi."

"Your victim, I assume, and no. But let me check on retired employees in Rome. Why do you think I know your victim?"

"Just covering a base. He had a facsimile of my cop card in his fist. With a message printed on the back."

Roarke's eyes went hard. "A threat to you?"

"No. It called Rossi the Wasp. Does that mean anything?"

"It doesn't, no."

"Okay. Long shot anyway."

"I'll run that check before I leave for the office. If I find anything, I'll tag you."

"Thanks. Later."

"You mind my cop."

"I already am."

"A good hunch," Peabody said. "He could've done some work for Roarke, and that connects you. Otherwise, it stays weird."

"The other angle's the cybersecurity. Maybe he played a part in sending someone over, and this is a revenge killing. A team," Eve speculated, "of twelve. Which seems like a lot to work a single cyber case, but we'll consider a big one. Maybe busted a syndicate."

"What was it? Fawn, Hawk, Rabbit," Peabody remembered. "Already dead? That leaves the eight. And the message said there'd only be one. Why leave one if you're on a vendetta?"

"The killer, or the one who hired the hit, is the one who'll be left."

"Someone the victim worked with then. Maybe on the take, and the others helped bust him?"

"It's a theory." A reasonably solid one, Eve thought. "Picked him up on the West Side, but drove across town to dump the limo and body. Maybe needed that much time for the poison to do the job. We'll get a look at the security feed, and whoever picked Rossi up."

At the international shuttle station, she left the car, On Duty light flipped on, at the curb. Inside, a group of travelers had the glazed look of red-eye passengers. Others standing in the waiting areas let out squeals, calls of greeting.

People hugged, kissed, and some got teary.

Others in suits or uniforms held up passenger names.

"Could've got the vic that way. Hold up his name. 'Hello, Mr. Rossi, I'm Chuck with Deadly Limo Service. How was your flight?'"

Peabody let out a half laugh. "Or 'I'm Suzanne with Murders R Us.'"

"Yeah, could be a woman. Women go more for poison."

Eve made her way to Security, held up her badge.

"I need to see the feed for disembarking and pickup from the flight from Rome that landed about midnight. Twelve-eighteen landing."

"I'll need to verify your IDs."

The dark-suited male with broad shoulders and a waving gray streak through ink-black hair ran the scanner over the badges.

"Lieutenant, Detective, come with me. Bonnie, I need to go to the hub."

"Got you covered."

He led them through a warren, used his swipe on a door, then through another warren and another door.

Inside, the many screens showed people disembarking, others clipping their way down tunnels for their flight to wherever.

Another screen, and people, looking antsy, bored, or exhausted, shuffled through the line at Customs.

Still others showed people slumped in seats, some sleeping, others scrolling on 'links or tablets.

Other camera angles displayed luggage areas. Shops, bars, restaurants.

"Barry, NYPSD. Need to see security from last night."

"Arriving from Rome," Eve supplied. "Zero-eighteen. We need to see who picked up a passenger." She pulled Rossi's passport photo.

"Take half a sec with face rec."

"I'd like to see him from when he disembarked to when he left the terminal."

"Cover that."

And in about half a sec, she watched Rossi walking up the slope of the tunnel, the shoulder bag on his arm, his wheeled case rolling behind him.

He looked a little tired around the eyes, Eve noted, but she saw excitement in them. More, she thought, than end-of-the-journey pleasure.

She watched him breeze through Customs, give the officer there a cheery smile before he pocketed his passport.

The screen shifted as he came out of Customs.

And there he smiled again. At the man in the black uniform, complete with cap, holding a sign with his name.

"Freeze on the pickup," Eve ordered.

Mid-fifties, she gauged, around six feet, and a trim one-seventy. Brown hair, blue eyes, mixed race. Smooth-shaven, square-jawed.

And obviously not concerned about showing his face on the security cameras.

"Okay, roll it from there."

Without audio, she couldn't be sure of the words exchanged, but she saw no recognition in Rossi's eyes, nothing in the brief conversation to indicate the men knew each other.

Just a driver meeting a client at the airport, taking his wheeled case, shoulder bag, and leading him out.

"We need a copy."

"Cover that."

"The driver. Can you run face rec there? See when he came in, what he did?"

"Gotcha."

In about a sec and a half, Barry had the driver entering the terminal at twenty-three-fifty-six. After a brief scan of the terminal, he walked to the waiting area. He sat, then took a card out of his breast pocket.

He looked directly at the camera, held the face of the card up. Smiled.

No, Eve corrected. Smirked.

"Son of a bitch."

"Want I should zoom in on what it says?"

"I know what it says."

"Got balls," Peabody commented when they left the terminal. "He knew we'd check, and wanted you to see."

"Arrogant fucker" was Eve's opinion. "We'll run our own face rec when we get to Central. Pro or not, he's an arrogant fucker. Arrogant fuckers make mistakes."

"He pissed you off. That's a mistake."

"Yeah, it damn well is."

She sat behind the wheel a moment to let the pissed off fade some.

"Heading to Central. Go ahead and take the 'link and tablet to EDD when we get there. Rossi should have his hotel confirmation on there. If not, next of kin might know. And if not, we start contacting hotels. Or you do. I'm going to dig into the limo. Did Rossi order it? Did the person he came to meet—if he came to meet someone—send it?

"He didn't recognize the driver," Eve continued. "So maybe a pro hit. But I'd bet your ass and mine, if a pro, Rossi would've known who hired the hit. It's personal, and expensive."

"You're thinking whoever got him to come to New York hired the hit."

"It plays. Someone he knew. Someone he trusted."

"And shouldn't have."

"He came alone," Eve pointed out. "That says something, too. Why not bring his spouse? Spend a few days in New York, catch a play, whatever. But he came alone. He looked excited when he got off the shuttle. Business, sure, maybe. But he was happy. Going to see an old friend?"

"Maybe a female-type old friend?"

Eve shook her head. "He had a framed photo of his wife in his luggage. No sex toys, no sex meds. He didn't travel a few thousand miles to bang another woman."

She pulled into the garage at Central, then into her slot.

"Old friend," she repeated. "Or old colleague."

They walked to the elevator. "We're going to do a deep run on the victim. Whoever wanted him dead went to a lot of trouble. Got him over here from Italy to do it."

"You're not in Italy."

"And Italy has cops," Eve said as they stepped into the elevator. "So it's specifically me. That smirk on his face on the feed? Yeah, that was aimed at me. So they had to get Rossi here instead of just sticking a knife in his gut in Rome. Instead, they steal a limo, know enough about mechanics to make the adjustments, or again hire someone who does. Pick him up, have the wine all ready for him. Drive to the Upper East."

The elevator stopped, let a couple of uniforms on.

"It didn't have a scent. The wine, the glass, the spill, the bottle. Smelled like wine. Fast-acting, no scent. Vic's eyes were bloodshot—and they weren't on the security feed. He had a faint, just faint tinge of blue on his lips."

She checked the time as the elevator stopped again. The uniforms got off. More got on.

"He doesn't care we'll find COD. And I bet it won't be usual. Some weird-ass, exotic poison like . . . tarantula venom."

Peabody's opinion was "Eeww."

"'Yeah, I personally squeezed the poison out of this big, nasty spider. Aren't I a clever bastard?' Take the electronics up to EDD."

When she got off on Homicide, she realized the pissed off hadn't faded much at all.

She moved through the bullpen and straight into her office. Into the quiet. And went straight for more coffee.

Needed a minute, she admitted. Just a minute.

So she stood by her skinny window, looking out at New York. The sky trams carried the morning commuters to work, the night shift workers home.

Under the streets, the subways did the same. On the street, maxibuses hauled more.

Everyone had somewhere to go, something to do.

Giovanni Rossi had had somewhere to go, and undoubtedly something to do.

Now he didn't.

Was he dead because of something he'd done, didn't do? Something he knew, or someone?

Fawn, Hawk, Rabbit.

Wasp.

Who were the other eight, and how the hell did they connect to her?

Turning away, she sat at her desk. She'd get the worst over before setting up her board, opening the murder book.

She'd notify the victim's wife of nearly fifty years.

In Italy. What the hell time was it in Italy?

Jesus, she hated the whole planet turning on its axis.

"Computer, damn it, what time is it in Rome, Italy?"

The current time in Rome, Italy, is twelve hundred hours and forty-one minutes.

"Great. Ah, Computer, engage translation program, English to Italian for my audio, Italian to English for receiver's audio."

Acknowledged . . . program engaged.

She made the call.

The woman who answered may have been seventy-five by the record, but she wore those decades well. She had sparkling brown eyes in a face where the lines and creases somehow added an allure to age. Her hair, a waving mane to her shoulders, wasn't white, wasn't gray, but a glorious mix of both.

"Ms. Rossi, I'm Lieutenant Dallas with the New York City Police and Security Department."

The sparkle in those brown eyes went to full alarm. "Gio! Gio is in New York City!"

"Yes, ma'am. I'm very sorry to inform you that your husband was killed last night."

"No, no, no. He only arrived last night! He texted me! He'd be sleeping now. He's to call when he wakes."

"I'm sorry for your loss, Ms. Rossi. His body was found last night, shortly, I believe, after his arrival in New York."

"But no. No." Even as she shook her head, her tears streamed. "My Gio is full of health! An accident?" Her hand pressed to her throat. "There was an accident?"

Eve hedged with the truth. "We haven't yet determined the cause of death. Ms. Rossi, I know this is a difficult time, but—"

Rage cut through shock like a sword. "You say my Gio is dead, and this is difficult? Where is my husband?" And as grief drenched rage, she began to sob. "Where is my Gio?"

"Ms. Rossi, is anyone with you?"

"No, no, no. Gio is in New York. He goes very quickly."

"Can you tell me why he came to New York?"

"He said he must, but couldn't say. Not until he saw his friend."

"What friend?"

"He couldn't say." She covered her face with her hands. "Only that he must go. He'd taken an oath, and must go. He asked me to trust him, and I do, of course."

"Do you know where he planned to stay?"

"With his friend. And he would tell me all he could tell me when he could. He's a good man. A good husband and father. A grandfather. It would only be a few days, and he was happy to see his friend, but worried. I know when my husband has worry.

"Where is my husband?"

"He's with our chief medical examiner."

"Oh, no, but—"

"Dr. Morris is the very best. And he's very kind. I can promise you your husband is in good hands, caring hands."

"They are not my hands. I must come there. I must come to New York and to Gio."

"I can make arrangements for your travel, for a hotel."

"No." She snapped it, then sighed. "You will excuse me, this is kind of you to offer. I know how to do such things."

"If you contact me when you arrive, I can arrange for you to see your husband."

"Yes. I must see Gio. I must tell our children. Oh, how do I tell them? Tell our grandbabies?"

"I can—"

"No. This is not for you. This is my duty. I will do my duty. You are a policewoman?"

"Yes. Lieutenant Eve Dallas."

"You will find out why my husband is dead in New York City?"

"Your husband is my duty, Ms. Rossi. I'll do my duty."

It was the best she could offer, Eve thought, and after the call pressed her fingers to her eyes.

Then rising, she started her duty by putting Giovanni Rossi's crime scene shots on her board.

When Peabody came in, she looked up from her desk and the murder book.

"McNab wasn't in yet—arrived there before I left. But they got the 'link and tablet open. We went through. No hotel confirmation."

"He didn't book one. He told his wife he was going to stay with the friend he came to New York to see."

"Who? We didn't find any communications with New York."

"She doesn't know. He said he couldn't tell her, that he would when he could. That he had to go. He'd taken an oath."

"Well, shit." Peabody glanced at Eve's ass-biting visitor's chair. Opted to stand. "I guess she doesn't know what oath."

"He asked her to trust him."

Marriage Rules, and four-plus decades, required trust.

"She said he was happy to see his friend again, but worried. Conclusion? Either the friend lured him here to kill him—motive unknown. Or the friend's in trouble, and someone took Rossi out before he could help."

Eve pointed to the computer. "I started the face rec on the driver, no hits. Yet."

"Did you do global?"

"There's a reason I'm the LT, Peabody."

"Sorry, it's just . . . Going through his 'link? No contacts in New York in there. No communications, either, like I said. He tagged his wife when he landed. Just to let her know he arrived safe. His sign-off, translated? 'I love you more, my own, every minute of every hour of every day.' And hers? 'And I'll love you more tomorrow than today.' It was so . . . sweet, romantic, true. It choked me up a little."

Did it make it harder or softer, she wondered, that the widow had had that last sweetness?

Because she had to, Eve set the question aside.

"She'll be in New York in a few hours. She'll let me know when she gets here. When I finish the book, I'll see if EDD can monitor the face rec if we don't get a hit. You start a deep run on Rossi. He had a friend, or someone he thought was a friend, in New York. Let's find him.

"When I'm done here, we'll go see Morris."

"I'll get started." Peabody glanced at the board. "He and his wife really had a bond. A tight, loving bond."

When Eve finished the book, wrote up her report with still no hit, she pushed the face rec on EDD.

In the bullpen, the full complement of detectives manned their desks. And Jenkinson's tie of the day struck her eyes like an atomic blast.

It might have represented one, she decided. Just a screaming mass of violent colors without pattern, without mercy.

She dug the sunshades she somehow hadn't lost or broken out of her pocket.

"Peabody with me."

"Half a sec," she said, and took several before she popped up.

Eve bypassed the elevators for the glides.

"I think—don't give me the pooh-pooh."

Eve simply stared at her partner. "The what?"

"You know, the pooh-pooh." Peabody waved her hand dismissively to demonstrate. "But I think, maybe, Rossi was a spy."

"Please note, I'm not saying your incredibly silly word that's not an actual word. Why do you think, maybe?"

"Well, it's all so pat, so ordinary, and then, when you go way back, there's the Urbans, and just a mention of him working with the Underground."

"In New York?"

"In Europe. As a cyber tech. But they had spies in the Underground. And after? He's listed as working for this Italian company, in IT, and in cybersecurity. Way ordinary. And for decades. Same job, same place, and same position. It just seems so pat."

"People live ordinary lives, Peabody. And given his age and tech skills, it's not a shock he was part of the Underground. We're talking forty or fifty years ago, easy, right?"

"Things began going to shit in Europe in about 2016. Started earlier, lasted longer there, in some places, than here. Don't you think his wife would know?"

"If so, we'll find out in a few hours. Meanwhile, we'll keep your spy-guy deal under consideration."

"Maybe he didn't actually retire. It's just a smoke screen."

"Under advisement," Eve said, and they clanged down the metal steps to the garage.

"There are all kinds of frosty vids about spies during the Urbans."

"Vids are vids, not real life."

Peabody got into the car. "The Icove vid is pretty true to life. We lived it."

"Don't remind me. And you know what? You know what the hell? Maybe this arrogant fucker decided he wanted the cops who had a couple of damn bestsellers detailing their cases, and a vid about one of those cases, chasing his ass. So he can prove how goddamn smart he is.

"It wouldn't surprise me a damn bit."

"But that would be his mistake," Peabody pointed out. "Because we're the cops who busted the Icove case, and the cops who kicked Red Horse's ass."

"Yeah, yeah, yeah." Eve zipped out of the garage. "You know Nadine's working on another freaking book."

"The Natural Order investigation. I know. I bet it rocks."

"I worry about you, Peabody. I don't want to, but I worry about you."

"I want two minutes."

"Oh God."

"Two minutes, Dallas. We're spending the weekend in the new house! We bought a new bed. McNab and I splurged, because bed. We're putting the one from the apartment in one of the guest rooms. Mavis and fam are going to spend the weekend there, too. Roarke says three weeks and it's done. But we get a whole weekend! Our office is done, and my craft room, and the main suite. We have a suite!"

Peabody pumped her fist in the air.

"The kitchen. Oh, it's just everything. And we've started outfitting the living room. Oh, oh, Bella's room! It's a dream. And the nursery for Number Two is really taking shape. I'm building that toy box to match the chair you're giving her. She doesn't know. Leonardo knows because he designed the fabric for the chair. We're going to have a party. A big, giant party as soon as it's all done. Which is almost now!"

"That's two minutes, plus."

"I know. But I'm so happy. And you don't mind, not so much."

She didn't really. Not so much. Especially since it was nearly done, and she wouldn't have to hear regularly about tiles, paint colors, refurbished tables.

"And here we are at the house of the dead."

Relieved, Eve pulled up.

"Let's go see what Rossi told Morris."

Chapter Three

INSIDE THE MORGUE, THE WHITE TUNNEL ALWAYS ECHOED. AND ALWAYS smelled of chemical lemons with an undertone of death.

Postponing the inevitable, Peabody paused by Vending.

"I could use a cold drink. I'll buy you a Pepsi."

"Peabody, Morris stocks them."

"Oh, yeah, right."

"You saw the body in the back of the limo."

"Yeah, but it's different on a slab. I don't know why, but it is. I do know why," she corrected as she walked down the tunnel with Eve. "It's because I know Morris has been, you know, in there. Pulling out organs and all that. Cutting into the body and taking stuff out that shouldn't be taken out."

"Taking it out tells us why the victim's a victim."

"You'd think they'd find another way to do that."

"Until they do."

Eve pushed through the double doors of Morris's theater.

He played Italian opera. Eve supposed it suited the moment.

Under his clear protective cape, the medical examiner wore a suit of pale, pale blue with a shirt of crisp white, a tie of sapphire.

He hadn't taken his usual time with his hair, she noted—due to her contact, no doubt. So he wore it in a single high tail that streamed down his back.

The microgoggles accented the almond shape of his dark eyes.

"I think he enjoyed his last flight," Morris began. "He had a late supper of Bolognese with rigatoni, a green salad, a sourdough roll, some cream cake. And about sixteen ounces of Cabernet. Another two ounces of Merlot less than eight minutes before TOD."

"Poisoned?" Eve walked to the body laid out on the slab.

"No. No poison in the wine. In fact, a very fine vintage. He was gassed."

"Gassed?"

"The lab will have to confirm and identify, but he didn't ingest poison. He inhaled it. And he knew."

Morris, in his gentle way, laid a hand on Rossi's head. "He fought. His knuckles aren't just bruised and scraped. He has some breaks. He fought hard."

"Gassed," Eve repeated as she studied the body. "So the passenger area was completely sealed off? And gas . . . through the air vents. The AC?"

"Again, that's for others to determine. I can only tell you his mouth, his throat, his nostrils, his lungs, and so on indicate he inhaled what killed him. My findings indicate it took less than four minutes for him to lapse into unconsciousness, during which time he fought to live. In under five minutes, he lost that battle."

Morris walked to his mini-friggie, took out the cold drinks, and passed them to Eve and Peabody.

"It would've been painful but brief. Otherwise, he was a healthy man for his age. A bit overweight, but not excessively. No face or body work detected, though he had some broken bones during his life, a couple of fingers, a couple of ribs. Well mended. There's a scar—you see there—along his left rib cage. A knife wound most likely."

"I think he was a spy."

Morris smiled at Peabody as she cracked her tube of Diet Pepsi.

"Do you? How interesting. He certainly would have lived through the Urbans, and the knife wound appears to be at least thirty years old, and carelessly tended. A field dressing perhaps."

"Gassed," Eve said yet again. "I'll have the sweepers look at how that worked. A lot of trouble for a kill."

"He was nearing eighty," Morris said. "Overweight, likely out of shape, but strong. He would've had good upper body strength."

"So the killer didn't want to risk going head-to-head. His widow's coming in from Rome. I'll let you know when she gets here."

"I'll have him ready for her. He had good health all in all. Could've expected another thirty or forty years."

"We'll find who took those decades from him. Appreciate the quick work, Morris."

"Your name on a card in his hand? And the cryptic message. I'd like to be updated as you progress."

"All right. Let's hit the lab, Peabody. Gassed," she said yet again. "There has to be a reason to go to that kind of trouble."

Eve rolled it over on the short drive to the lab.

"Who gasses an almost-eighty-year-old man in the back of a limo?"

"Spies."

Eve spared Peabody a glance. "Under consideration. There are easier, less risky, less expensive ways—thinking spies. Bump into him on the street, give him a little jab. They've got shit that'll kill you in seconds that way. And if you're going to all this trouble, why not poison the wine? Has to be simpler than rigging up some toxic gas."

She thought of the smirk.

"Because he didn't want the simple. He's showing off his clever, his skill."

"Maybe he showed off, killed the others he named, and showed off the same way."

"Yeah, we're running a global on like crimes once the lab identifies the gas. He's got a kill list, and there are seven names still on it."

"They could be anywhere."

"If he wants me hunting him, they're in New York, or like Rossi, he'll get them here. If he killed the other three, why leave the card on this kill?"

"Maybe Roarke will dig up a connection."

Eve wasn't sure if she considered that a good thing or not.

In the lab, she scanned the labyrinth of counters, cubes, glass walls. It always made her think of a hive.

She spotted Chief Lab Tech Dick Berenski's egg-shaped head bent over at his station. Imagined his long, spidery fingers at work.

If necessary, she'd bribe him to push on the gas angle.

He'd earned the title Dickhead for a reason, and she figured a couple of box seats to the ball game would do it this time.

As they made their way through the maze, Eve saw him slide his rolly chair from one end of his workstation to the other, then back again.

Something, she decided, had his attention. With luck, she could hold back the bribe for another time.

He looked up, scowled at Eve.

"What the hell you got going?"

"You tell me. Morris said the victim was gassed."

"Like a rat in a hole. What they used it for back when. We've got better ways now for pest control."

No bribe this time, Eve noted because she saw the interest in his dark, beady eyes as he gestured to a screen where she saw formulas, symbols. Something that looked like a three-legged pyramid.

"Okay, what is it?"

"Phosphine."

"And what is it?"

"Jesus, Dallas. It's your freaking murder weapon. Colorless, odorless—for the rats and all, technical grade, they added shit that made it stink. What you got here's a mix of pure phosphine with some CO_2—that agent's to take down the flammability point. The pure shit'll go off. It can self-ignite.

"I alerted the sweepers. Might be more in there, so they need to follow protocol."

He held up a spidery finger, rolled down his counter. "It's bad shit, and got phased out for commercial use over thirty years ago. Planetwide."

"So not something the killer could access easily."

"Hell no. You can make it, yeah, if you know what you're doing and don't mind the risk. Close quarters, like that limo, inhaling it? You're dead pretty quick. But . . ."

"But?"

"If you know how to make it, you ought to know how to make something that wouldn't maybe light you up in the lab. Or in liquid form spill on you and give you a hell of a case of frostbite. Like hydrogen cyanide. The fucking Nazis used that—Zyklon B. Or arsine. Or—"

"I get it. Easier ways."

"And plenty you can get—pest control, right, industrial uses, textiles. I figure you got yourself a mad scientist."

"Wouldn't be the first time. Anything else you can tell me?"

"I gave you the murder weapon. You want more, bring me more."

Berenski looked back at his screen, shook his head. "He's a goddamn loose cannon using that shit."

"What would he need to make it?"

"Balls. That's first because you'd want white phosphorous, and that's a killer right there. Add that to boiling water with sodium hydroxide, and you got phosphine gas."

"The gas was released in a limo."

"You asked. Made a canister, maybe got his hands on one from thirty years ago or whatever. That's your deal. Wouldn't mind knowing when you do."

"What about his clothes?"

"You don't get residue with this—that was an advantage. Harvo'll let you know if different, but with this?" He pointed at the screen again. "Not happening."

Dickhead or not, Berenski knew his science.

"All right. Appreciate the quick work."

Berenski continued to study the screen as Eve moved off.

"Badass, fucker's a crazy son of a bitching badass," she heard him say.

At the moment, Eve's main concern was the crazy.

"He wanted that," she said as they walked out of the maze. "That reaction, Dickhead's reaction. A kind of admiration. A little horrified, but admiration."

She paused, frowned at the hive.

"Let's see how far they've gotten with processing the limo."

They took the interior walkway to the next building, then the elevator down to the garage level.

She badged a tech with goggles around her neck and her hair bundled under a clear cap.

"Spooner brought in a limo early this morning."

"Bay four, and it's on lockdown. Potential toxic substance."

"I need to talk to Spooner, or whoever's in charge of bay four."

The tech, short, curvy, barely old enough to buy a legal drink, stopped herself before she completed a full eye roll. "All the way down." She gestured. "Locked down," she repeated. "You can talk to Spooner through the intercom until it's clear."

"All right, thanks."

Though it echoed here, too, unlike the morgue it smelled—faintly—of bad coffee and someone's spiced-up veggie hash.

At the door to bay four, the NO ENTRY light burned red.

Eve looked through the thick glass, saw a team of sweepers in hazmat suits and breathing masks.

She pressed the intercom. "Spooner, Dallas. Can we suit up and come in?"

One of the team stepped back. The head shook, but she walked toward the door.

"Not yet, and no need. We found a canister, about two hundred and twenty-five grams. Appears to be empty, but it's going to our lab for testing."

"Where was it?"

"Positioned in the ceiling, has a remote trigger. Piped into the AC. Canister's clean as you get, but it's not new, Dallas. It says Phosphine, and some joker drew a skull and crossbones on it, along with the name of your vic."

"His name?"

"And that's recent, but the canister itself isn't going to be. It's dated 2024, and it's an old-school device. So's the remote."

"I need to see it."

"I'll send you a picture, and you'll get the canister when we're done with it. We need to strip the vehicle down, make sure there isn't more. We got a cam, too, one with audio. And that is new. The driver could see and hear what was going on in the back on the dash screen."

"Did it record?"

"Yeah, it did. I'll get that to you asap. Everything in here has to be tested, scrubbed, and cleared before it leaves the bay. That includes us."

Behind the protective shield, Spooner's eyes went hard. "The victim didn't go easy. He went fast, and that's your blessing, but he didn't go easy. Did Dickhead tell you about the chemical?"

"Yeah, enough. Be careful in there, Spooner."

Now she smiled, a little. "Never anything but."

Studying the limo as the team continued to dismantle it, Eve jammed her hands in her pockets.

"So he watched—more personal. He had to feel it when Rossi kicked at the privacy window. Knew what was happening, but he needed to see it, and to hear it. Or have the record for his client to see, to hear."

"Proof for the balance of payment?"

"Maybe. Could be that."

Accepting she couldn't make the sweepers work faster by watching, Eve turned away and started down the corridor.

"But that smirk, Peabody? I can see a pro holding up the card if that was part of the deal. But the smirk? You don't pay for that. Personal," she said again. "And I don't recognize the face. Let's find out if EDD hit a match. I want this bastard's name."

Back at Central, she had Peabody go back to digging into the victim's background. And she went straight to EDD.

Even the crazed mix of colors, patterns, movement couldn't compete with Jenkinson's choice of tie today. She saw McNab, skinny hips rocking in a pair of baggies striped in red, blue, yellow, and orange. His red-streaked tail of blond hair bounced on the back of a red T-shirt with a full moon floating on the back.

The moon had a grinning face with one eye closed in a knowing wink.

She started toward his station when Callendar waylaid her.

Callendar's bibbed baggies hit a green you might get if you fertilized your lawn with plutonium. She'd cut her hair into a kind of wedge. One side ink black, the other plutonium green.

Eve thought: Why? Then let it go.

"We haven't hit. McNab's trying searches with different hairstyles, colors, bald. I'm doing dead guys, in case he tried that angle. Nothing's hit."

"Okay."

"I'm thinking a pro who keeps it down low enough wouldn't hit. But the card he left on the body sure as hell isn't down low. So puzzlement. We could still hit," she added. "We're all over it and back again twice."

"Thanks. I'll let you get back again twice."

As she started out, Feeney came to his office door, waved her in.

In contrast with his unit, he wore brown, a wrinkled shit-brown jacket and pants, a tie the color of shit that had dried out after a few weeks in the sun, with a shirt of sad beige.

She found it comforting.

His wiry ginger hair exploded on his head. His baggy basset hound eyes studied her face.

"We're working it."

"I know."

"I got a program running in here. Not that the kids don't know what they're doing."

"Callendar's running dead people."

"Cover the bases. You got COD yet?"

"Yeah. Not poison—or not the usual gulp down some wine and die. He was gassed."

Frowning, Feeney leaned back on his desk. "In the limo?"

"No question where, and now no question how. Sweepers found a canister of it. In the ceiling, which meant removing the ceiling, installing the canister so it would go through the AC vents, the air vents. Replacing the ceiling."

"Lot of work. Lots easier ways to get the job done. He's a poser."

"Yeah."

Since he was there, the man who'd trained her, taken her into Homicide, made her his partner, she pulled out her 'link.

"Check this."

She showed him the killer holding up the fake cop card and smirking.

"Arrogant bastard poser."

"He installed a remote on the canister, so he could release the gas once Rossi was in and secured. And eyes and ears. He could watch him die on the in-dash."

Nodding, Feeney snagged a couple of candied almonds from the crooked bowl on his desk. "Making sure, maybe. More likely enjoying the show. You gotta connect somewhere. Does Roarke know Rossi?"

He might've been captain of EDD, but Feeney still thought like a murder cop.

"Not offhand. He's checking."

"Something's gotta be there. Or the asshole wants notoriety. Get the Icove cop, the Red Horse cop on the chase."

"Shit. Just shit."

Now he smiled. "It's a damn good vid. The wife's reading Nadine's new book. She's liking it. Could be as simple and stupid as that. Figuring he'll get himself in a book or vid."

"Yeah, yeah. I'm going to check with Nadine, see if he's contacted her or tried to."

"She'd let you know if he had."

"She would, but—"

"Cover those bases. What kind of gas?"

"Something Dickhead called phosphine. Colorless," she began.

"Now, that's something I haven't heard of in a hell of a time."

"You know what it is?"

"Got banned right after the Urbans over here—pretty sure. And mostly because some hotheads, mostly on the other side, used it here and there. Killed themselves as often as not. Bioweapons, supposed to be off the table. But you'll have hotheads."

"The head sweeper said the canister they found was dated 2024."

"Yeah, that was the thick of it. An old canister." Considering, Feeney picked up the bowl, offered it to Eve.

She just shook her head.

"Might be stockpiles somewhere. Not supposed to be, but not supposed to don't mean dick. Military hordes. The just-in-case crap. But . . . They got better, more efficient shit like that. It's old-school."

"Rossi was almost eighty, and he did some tech work for the Underground in Europe."

"Old-school. Might be something to look at."

"And I will."

"You do that, and we'll keep running. If we hit, you'll be the first."

Eve left, and thought Feeney knew as well as she did if they hadn't hit by now, the odds dwindled.

She started to catch a glide when her comm signaled with an order to report to the commander's office.

Word got around, she thought as she changed direction. And Whitney might sit behind a desk, but he had his ear to the ground.

When she arrived, Whitney's admin waved her straight into the office.

Whitney didn't sit behind his desk, but stood at the windows with his sweeping view of the city he served. Broad-shouldered in a slate-gray suit, his hands clasped behind his back, he only nodded when Eve said, "Commander."

"Part of being a cop is finding yourself a target. Or being taunted. And still, I dislike when one of my cops finds themselves in that position."

He turned then, his wide, dark face set, his dark eyes hard.

"Phosphine."

"Yes, sir. Berenski identified the substance. Spooner and her team—"

"I've been in contact with both."

"Yes, sir."

"What do you know, Lieutenant?"

"The victim was an Italian citizen, married—long-term—four adult children, grandchildren. He retired a few years ago from the security company, Rome-based, where he worked since 2027. He has no criminal record, and hasn't traveled to New York in over twenty years.

"Prior to his employment, he served as a cyber tech for the Underground in Europe. There's little to no additional data on that."

Thoughtfully, Whitney nodded. "Cyber techs were valuable tools, key players in the Urbans. If he was any good, and I assume so, he would have made sure there was little to no data. Even after the wars, some key players were targeted, some assassinated."

"I believe his killer is a professional. Whether this is his personal mission or he's working for someone, he's a pro."

"The card."

"Not NYPSD issued, but close. The message might be cryptic, sir, but it's still clear. Rossi was part of a group, and likely from his time during the Urbans, as the use of this particular gas indicates. Code name seems the most likely."

"Agreed. Feeney had one."

"Sir?"

"Unofficially. A lot of us who fought through that ended up with names. He was Hound. He could always catch the scent. God, we were young."

She caught a wistfulness, rarely heard, in Whitney's voice.

"Young and fearless. In any case, that sort of name was common enough."

"If it has to do with the Urbans, Commander, it's a long time to wait."

"A very long time. People scatter. Feeney and I stayed in New York, on the job, but people scatter."

"Rossi didn't. His killer knew where to find him, and what to say to get him here. An oath, he told his wife he'd taken an oath. And that might also connect to the Urbans.

"People went to prison," she added, "some for a long time."

"They did. But many sentences were commuted in the forties. It's something to look at."

"Three others—according to the message—are dead already. Fawn, Hawk, Rabbit. Rossi might not have been the first, just the latest. I'll run like crimes. He may have used the same method, but—"

"He may tailor his kill to the victim," Whitney concluded.

"Yes, sir. Or, it's been a lot of years. And it was war. So the others maybe died in the wars, or from natural causes since. Without names . . ."

"And the widow?"

"I don't think he told her anything, or as little as possible."

"That wouldn't be unusual. He was older, had family. He'd spare them the details to protect them, and himself. I want daily updates on this one, Dallas. If he has a stockpile of that gas in the city, we need to find him. Find it."

"Understood. His widow is on her way here. I'll talk to her again. She may know something she doesn't understand she knows."

"Keep me updated, and watch your six."

"Yes, sir, I'll do both." She walked to the door, then decided not to resist. "Did you have a code name, Commander?"

He smiled and meant it. "Lightning. I could move fast in those days."

She didn't know war, she thought as she worked her way back to Homicide.

She knew battle and the risks of it, understood tactics, strategy, sacrifice, and blood spilled.

But she didn't know war.

However long ago it had been, Feeney did, Whitney did. They'd lived it and survived it. They'd built their lives, their families, their careers despite it.

Maybe, in some ways, because of it.

Now she wondered, however long ago it had been, if Giovanni Rossi, who'd lived it, survived it, building his life, family, career because of or despite it, was yet another victim of war.

Chapter Four

She turned into Homicide, started to signal Peabody into her office.

Jenkinson and his atomic tie snarled.

"Some fucking fuck screwing with our LT. We've got your back, Dallas. We're all in."

She started to shoot Peabody a look, then remembered: Jenkinson. Her detective sergeant heard all, saw all, knew all, almost before it happened.

"I've got it, Jenkinson."

"With respect, Loo, bullshit. Come after one of us, come after all. Especially the boss. Whatever you need, we're in."

Apparently, murder had paused long enough so all her detectives and most of her uniforms were in-house. And every one of them looked at her with fire in their eyes.

"I'm not the one who's dead," she reminded them. Then relented.

"Giovanni Rossi, lured to New York from Rome, possibly through some connection to the Urbans. Gassed in the limo that picked him up. Phosphine gas."

"I know what that is." Detective Carmichael lifted a finger. "I aced chemistry. That's been on the banned list practically as long as I've been alive."

"That's what he used. Rossi, possible code name Wasp, seventy-nine, did at least some cyber tech during the Urbans. This may or may not be connected. The man who killed him, either hired to do so or on his own, is as yet unidentified. EDD's working that. There are, according to the message on the card, another seven targets—also unknown and unnamed. Three others, Fawn, Hawk, Rabbit, are presumed dead. For a total, with the killer or the one who hired him, of twelve.

"Peabody will send you all the data we have. Nobody works it if they have another case. And that includes you, Detective Sergeant."

He just grunted.

"I'm not a target." For now, she qualified in her head. "He wants me in pursuit. I'm going to accommodate him. Now, for Christ's sake, get back to work. I don't, under the circumstances, want to kick your asses.

"Peabody, send the data, then my office."

"Sir."

Trueheart, young, earnest, but not as green as he'd once been, raised his hand.

"Detective."

"They specify you in pursuit, they get all of us. Sir."

Baxter, his trainer, his partner, his friend, just beamed with pride. "Kid speaks truth."

"Fine. That's fine. But any of you catch a case, you pursue that first. You're paid to protect and serve the people of New York, not your lieutenant."

"Can do fucking both," Jenkinson muttered.

"So say we all." This from Santiago.

Eve just walked to her office.

She wouldn't have her bullpen treating her like a victim.

She wasn't. Once she had been. But now she headed a team of exceptional cops, and was anything but a victim.

And yet, she had to appreciate the one-for-all sentiment.

As long as no investigation got the short straw in the meantime.

She programmed coffee, then sat to scan her incoming.

And sitting, she studied the photo of the gas canister.

It looked old, she realized. Like something she'd see in a museum. But, as Spooner had said, very clean. No dents, no rust, no dust, with the skull and crossbones carefully added. And with a more contemporary style remote trigger attached.

An Urbans-era canister of toxic gas with a remote from now.

The killer, or his accomplices, had the skill or training to weaponize the canister, to remove and replace the ceiling of the limo and install it. To fix it so the gas would discharge into the back of the limo.

And only into the back.

Seal the doors, seal the privacy window. Install the ears and eyes to watch the kill. A lot of time, a lot of trouble taken, with the flourish of the drawing.

Personal, she determined.

Peabody clumped down the hall.

"I didn't spill it to the bullpen," she began.

"You don't have to spill anything. Jenkinson has some sort of radar. Which makes him a damn good cop."

"Everybody just wants to look out for you, Dallas."

It only took a look.

"Yeah, you can look out for you, but that's who we are. And who we are comes down from the top. From you. I don't think you should leave them out of this."

Eve spoke with just a touch of frost. "Don't you?"

Peabody's jaw jutted—just a touch. "No, I don't. And I'm hungry. Can I hit the AutoChef? We'll split a pizza. A pepperoni pizza. I'm just saving time," Peabody claimed as Eve's stare could have burned holes in flesh. "You'd have said yes, but it would take time. Plus, I grabbed just a mini breakfast burrito in the subway, hours and hours ago."

It had been hours ago, Eve realized. "Fine."

"If one of us got a message like this," Peabody continued as she programmed, "you'd be all over it."

She couldn't deny it.

"We're cops. We're a family of cops. Oh, and I think you should contact Nadine, in case it's the book/vid thing driving this."

"Which I intended to do before you're pulling pizza out of the AC."

"You can have a slice first. Has Roarke gotten back to you?"

"No, and if he'd found Rossi in his vast herd of employees, present or former, he would have."

"Yeah, he would." Peabody handed Eve a plate, a tube of Pepsi, then sat on the floor with her own. "So that's probably not it."

"Probably not." The pizza, Eve had to admit, smelled amazing. And tasted the same. "The canister's from the Urbans, and the remote's from now. The camera's going to be from now. Code names like Wasp were, according to Whitney, fairly common during the Urbans era. Just a thing—like Baxter's sometimes Horndog—not always an official spy deal."

"It's a spy deal," Peabody insisted, and bit into her slice. "Oh God, this is so good. Anyway, digging into Rossi, there are gaps. They don't look like gaps until you stop and look at them as gaps."

"Which means?"

"Well, I've tracked some travel, back in the thirties, the forties, that doesn't make a lot of sense. Not for a family man. It's listed as business travel for the company, but why is he going to Dubai and Budapest and Dublin and Paris and Prague, like that, when he's basically a cog in the wheel? It's a lot of travel, Dallas."

"Nothing recent?"

"Nothing since he retired. I mean nothing like before. Travel to Florence, to Provence, to his wife's sister's farm in Tuscany a few times—all travel with his wife, or the whole family. But he hardly left home in the last five years. And this is the first solo trip anywhere I found. And the first trip to the U.S. in like twenty-plus years."

"Let's contact his boss or supervisor."

"I've got a call in. Got the runaround, but I've got a call in. I used the translator, but still."

Eve kicked back, looked at her board.

She wanted some quiet time, some thinking time, but for now, she'd bounce off her partner.

"Someone contacts Rossi. Someone he considers a friend or colleague. He's taken an oath."

She thought of her bullpen.

"There's a unity, a bond, so he doesn't hesitate. Come to New York. He makes arrangements. Quickly, according to his wife. He's going to stay with said friend—no hotel. He's happy to reconnect with this friend.

"Someone from the Urbans—that's speculation, but it rings. Someone he served with. That's a tight connection. Whitney . . . He mentioned some things about him and Feeney and the Urbans, and you could feel it. That connection. They were partners on the job, but after that. That's another bond, the partnership."

"But they'd been through a war together. I don't know what that's like, but it feels like it's big. It's like, forever. 'We few, we happy few.'"

"What?"

"It's Shakespeare. I can't remember from what. But about war. 'We band of brothers.'"

"What about sisters?"

With a shrug, Peabody drank some of her diet version of Pepsi. "Well,

Shakespeare, so I don't think women did much soldiering. Anyway, yeah, a tight connection."

"Why do you kill your brother? And Fawn? That sounds female. Why do you murder your fellow soldier?"

"Somebody from the other side?"

"Who's still pissed they lost. Yeah, that's an angle. Somebody who lost, and did some considerable time? That, at least, would explain the gap of decades. The old-school kill, the old canister. The Wasp. Or all that's the smoke screen. Set up to throw us off."

Eve ate more pizza. "Too soon to tell. We need to talk to the widow again. How do you live with someone for four decades and not know?"

"I've got a great-uncle—my dad's side. He was in the Urbans. I've never, ever heard him talk about it."

"I thought Free-Agers were pacifists."

"True, but he wasn't, at least not then. I think it turned him into one though."

Peabody frowned as she nibbled a second slice.

"Summerset worked as a medic back then, didn't he?"

"Yeah." She'd mine there if necessary. "And his friend, Ivanna, did some Underground back then. I'll push there if I need to. I don't see how—"

She broke off when her desk 'link signaled.

"Antonio Rossi. That's one of the vic's sons."

She picked up the 'link. "Dallas."

"Lieutenant Dallas. I am Antonio Rossi. My father is—was—Giovanni Rossi. My mother and I are now in New York."

"Mr. Rossi. Should I engage the translator?"

"That won't be necessary, thank you. I speak English. My mother does as well, but not as fluently. Please tell me, Lieutenant, you are sure this is my father?"

"Yes. I'm sorry. We're very sure."

He looked to be early fifties, with dignified gray at his temples, deep brown eyes that radiated grief.

"We would ask if you'd tell us when and where we can see my father."

"Yes, of course. I'll send you all that information, and notify the medical examiner. Mr. Rossi, I'd like to speak to you and your mother at your earliest convenience."

"This will help you find who took my father's life?"

"I believe so."

"Then we'll come to you. I think this is easier for my mother. To come to you after seeing my father, and beginning the arrangements for him."

"All right. You'll ask for Dr. Morris," she began.

Though his grief pumped through the 'link, he remained polite, restrained, throughout her instructions.

When she'd finished, ended the call, she looked at Peabody.

"Let's hope they know something they don't think they know. Seven more, Peabody. He's an arrogant bastard and a crazy fucker, but he's got a plan. A plan and a kill list."

Peabody looked at her signaling 'link. "It's Rossi's workplace. I'm going to take this at my desk." She scrambled up and out.

So Eve took her thinking time with the rest of her slice.

The method of murder with Rossi. Time-consuming, complicated. Overly complicated, she thought. So a purpose to the method or why bother?

She swiveled around to deal with the stolen limo.

Peabody hustled back in, then dropped to the floor to finish her pizza.

"That was Rossi's direct supervisor. Shocked, upset—genuinely upset when I told her Rossi's dead. She pressed for details."

"Which you didn't give her."

"Which I didn't give her. And she wasn't big on giving me many, either. A lovely man, a good family man, excellent at his work."

"And that work, exactly?"

"Providing cybersecurity for companies and individuals throughout Europe. She said Rossi handled clients remotely or on-site, though in the last few years of employment had requested less travel. And that jibes with the data. She said he was a valued employee, respected, always willing to assist if a team member had an issue, and kept current with tech."

"If he was so good, why wasn't he a supervisor after nearly four decades?"

"I asked, and she told me he preferred working in the field, being part of a team rather than leading one. She asked about his family, and that seemed genuine, too, the concern. She didn't know, or said she didn't know, of anyone who had a problem with him, anyone who'd wish him harm. And said she didn't know anything about a friend in New York.

"I don't think that was genuine. Just a feeling because she never hesitated, looked me straight in the eye. But . . ."

"But?" Eve prompted.

"I felt like there was something under it. I expected the block when I asked about clients, about details of his work. Privacy, confidentiality. And the fact he'd retired several years ago. But it just felt . . . rote. Oh, and she had perfect English. Not just good, perfect. I complimented her on it, and asked if they had clients in the States. She said they just served Europe."

"Okay. Go ahead and do a good, solid run on her. The more we know, the more we know. How old is she?"

"Early fifties."

"So he'd have had other supervisors before this one. She'd have been a kid during the Urbans." Thinking, Eve looked back at the board. "Do that run anyway. If we circle back to her, or any previous supervisors, I'll take it. Boss to boss."

"I'll get started on that." Peabody got up, and like Eve, looked at the board. "I've been trying to find out where he got that scar—the one Morris said was a knife wound. And where the breaks Morris mentioned were treated. I've got nothing."

"Medicals can be tricky, especially from way back."

"Yeah, but I've got some of the usual. Vaccines, standard physicals, a sprained ankle a couple years ago. But nothing on a knife wound, nothing on broken bones."

Eve considered. "Morris can give us a ballpark, but . . . I'll ask him to consult with DeWinter. She's bones, so she'd likely be able to do better than ballpark.

"I don't see how it applies to murder, but—"

"The more we know," Peabody echoed.

"Yeah," she murmured when Peabody left.

She read the ME's report again.

Broken clavicle, two broken fingers, three broken ribs, broken left arm.

A lot of breaks, she decided, for an e-man.

And, so far, no medical report on the treatments.

Assuming Morris was with Rossi's family, she sent him a text.

> When you're done with Rossi's family, can you request Dr. DeWinter examine the body and the scans—the breaks? I'd like to date them as accurately as possible. Just crossing t's.
> Dallas

Probably chasing the wild goose, she thought.

"And that's another stupid saying. Why would anyone chase a wild goose?"

Then it hit her.

"Okay, you wouldn't. So that actually makes sense. Except." When she caught herself trying to wind it around, she pressed her fingers to her eyes. "Never mind. I'm chasing the damn wild goose."

She started a search on the Italian company, Sicurezza Informatica.

From the dates, it looked as if Rossi had gotten in on the ground floor there.

A good-sized company, she discovered, with its base in Rome, satellite offices in Madrid, Naples, Palermo. They offered their security services throughout Europe. Remote or on-site.

The full range, blah blah, for businesses, individuals, corporations, educational facilities.

They maintained a five-star rating.

It looked solid and standard to her eye.

With what was left of her Pepsi, she sat back, put her feet on the desk, and studied her board.

She studied Rossi's ID shot. A nice, ordinary face, the face of a man who looked as if he enjoyed life, and should've had a few more decades of it.

And the crime scene still, of Rossi slumped on the leather seat, mouth agape, eyes red-streaked and bulging. Then the closed fist, the raw knuckles. And the card wedged between the index and middle fingers.

Frowning, she swung her legs to the floor and looked at the ME report again. Was it a coincidence he'd broken those same fingers at some point in his life?

"No, because coincidence is bollocks. You knew him, goddamn it. You knew about those broken fingers, and that means something. Personal, something personal. Using them? Just another little flourish.

"This is hate," she concluded. "It's hate. Not rage, not a kill for gain. It's hate. What did a devoted family man, loyal employee, retired, enjoying his life do to generate hate?"

She put her feet up again. "Wasps sting. Who did you sting, Rossi?"

She closed her eyes a moment.

Hawk—they fly, they hunt. A predator. People say eyes like a hawk, so good vision.

Rabbit? What the hell did a rabbit do? Hop around, eat carrots? But they're fast, she remembered. A suspect rabbits when they take off.

Fawn? Nothing scary about a fawn. A little deer. Pretty if you went for wildlife. Quiet maybe, looked harmless. Was that it—looked harmless?

People ended up with code names, even nicknames for a reason. Three animals and an insect.

And eight more, including the killer.

Twelve. A team of some sort. It had to be, and most likely with its roots in the Urbans. And, also likely, they'd all be over sixty.

Opening her eyes, she studied the photo of the canister.

2024. Thirty-seven years death had waited. Had the killer kept it all that time? Hidden away somewhere until he carefully drew the skull and crossbones, rigged the trigger?

Phosphine = fumigation. Kill rats, pests. Wasps = pests.

"Saved it for you. Specifically you? Like crimes isn't going to hit."

She'd run them anyway, but it wouldn't hit.

Peabody came down the hall.

"The Rossis are here."

"Faster than I figured." She started to get up.

"I thought we'd do the lounge, but she's really hurting, Dallas. So I booked a conference room instead. More private. Maybe I could transfer some of your coffee, the tea you stock for Mira into the AC there."

"That's fine. How do you kill a rabbit?"

"Aw."

"He might've killed the other three he named. A method designed for them. Kill the Wasp—poison gas. Kill the rabbit?"

Peabody worked on the AC transfer. "We used stinky repellents—harmless, but really foul—to discourage rabbit and deer from the gardens."

"He's no Free-Ager, Peabody."

"Maybe poison—bait a trap. Maybe shoot—gun or arrow—like they used to. If he had that canister, he could have illegal weapons."

"Yes, he could. Poisoned bait, a trap, seems more his style than a bullet. Nothing time-consuming or complicated about a bullet."

She'd play with that, but for now, she walked out with Peabody. She recognized the mother and son who sat on the bench outside her bullpen. The mother had her magnificent hair carefully rolled into a bun at the back of her head and wore a stark black dress. The son wore a suit, also black.

As if they were already attending a funeral.

They sat close, hands linked together.

Though Antonio Rossi resembled his father more than his mother, they wore twin expressions of shocked misery.

When Antonio saw Eve, he squeezed his mother's hand, murmured something to her, then rose.

"Lieutenant Dallas."

"Mr. Rossi." She shook his hand. "Ms. Rossi, if you'd both come with us, we have a quiet place we can talk."

"He was very kind." Anna Maria got to her feet. Her English carried a heavier accent than her son's, but there would be no need for the translator. "The Dr. Morris. Very gentle and kind. My Gio was very gentle and kind."

"Come, Mamma." Antonio put an arm around her, led her down the hall with Eve and Peabody. "The medical examiner said we can't take Papà home yet."

"No, I'm sorry. Not yet."

"How long must he stay in that place?" The widow's voice thickened with tears. "The doctor was kind, but that place, it's cold. Gio likes the warm."

"I promise, we'll clear it for you to take him home as soon as possible."

"His mother. I had to tell his mother he was gone. She lost her youngest son in the Urbans, and her husband, Gio's papà, he died young from wounds that had never healed from that time. And now another son, lost. I promised her I'd bring him home."

"She's a hundred and two," Antonio added. "And more frail than we'd like."

"I understand. I hope we can let you take him home soon." Eve gestured them into the conference room.

"We have coffee," Peabody began. "Tea, water, of course, and soft drinks. It's a very nice tea, Signora Rossi. It's soothing."

"Yes, Mamma, you'll have some tea. I would have coffee, if it's no trouble. Black will do."

"He thinks to take care of me." Anna Maria looked up at her son as he led her to a chair at the conference table. "He forgets he's my *bambino*." She clung to his hand a moment longer, and sat.

Then she straightened her shoulders, turned fierce eyes on Eve. "The doctor said you would tell us what happened to my husband, to the father of my children."

"We will. We have questions."

"We will answer your questions. But first, we will know why Gio is gone."

"You said he left quickly for New York."

"Hours after he told me his friend needed him. Have you found this friend?"

"No. Mr. Rossi had nothing on his person, or in his luggage to indicate who asked him to come. An old friend, you told me."

"He says an old friend, an oath taken. He says he will explain it all when he comes home. My Gio would never break a promise. He left to keep one."

Tears swirled in her eyes again, but didn't fall.

"He can't keep the one he made to me, but he would have. I understand who you are, and what you do here. Did this friend kill Gio?"

"We don't know." Eve waited while Peabody set out the tea, the coffee. "We do know whoever killed him knew of his plans, and the quickness of his travel, the actions of the killer indicate his killer knew of his travel details."

Until she got this part over with, Eve knew, she'd get no answers.

"His killer posed as a driver. He had a sign with your husband's name on it at the shuttle terminal. We've seen the security feed and there's no indication your husband recognized this man. He drove a limo, stolen a week ago."

"This is all deliberate. Very deliberate."

Eve looked at Antonio. "Yes. Your father was the target. He was escorted to the limo. And there, trapped inside. The locks were engaged so he couldn't open the doors, the windows. The privacy window between the driver's area and the back seat, also secured, and sealed. The driver released a toxic gas into the passenger area."

"Oh." Shaking her head, shocked eyes spilling tears now, Anna Maria pressed both hands to her mouth. "*Madre di Dio!*"

"He fought. He fought to get out, but it wasn't possible. He succumbed within minutes."

"*Assassino!* Murderer!"

She collapsed against her son, and he wrapped his arms around her, wept with her.

"Alone. Alone. This man who harmed no one dies alone, away from his family, through such wickedness."

"It was wickedness," Peabody said softly. "We're doing, and will keep doing, everything possible to find this wicked person. We need your help."

"Help? What help can we give? He was away from us. No one at home would hurt Giovanni Rossi! He was loved! His family, his friends, neighbors. Oh, the children would flock around him when he went for a walk. He always had a joke, sweets in his pocket for the children. Who does this to such a man?"

"Someone he knew." Eve said it flatly to stop the rise of hysteria.

"No. How?"

"Mamma." Antonio gripped her hand. "How else?" Then he kissed her hand before using an already damp handkerchief to dry her tears. "We'll be strong for Papà now. And help however we can help."

Now he kissed her cheeks, and whatever he said to her in Italian sounded so loving to Eve's ears she felt her heart crack a little.

"Sì, Sì." She picked up the tea, drank. "*Un attimo.* Ah, one moment, please."

"Take all the time you need."

"You are kind. You offered to arrange my travel. Your doctor was kind. This girl who gives me tea is kind. So much kindness. So much wickedness."

She took another sip, and once again squared her shoulders.

"Ask your questions. What we can answer, we will. Then you will find this killer, this wicked devil of a man, and I will look him in the eye. I will look him in the eye and spit in it."

She nudged the tea aside.

"Ask your questions."

Chapter Five

"YOUR HUSBAND RETIRED A FEW YEARS AGO."

"Yes. He enjoyed his retirement. Gardening became more passion than hobby. He had more time for the grandchildren. And to, ah . . ."

She turned to her son, asked something in Italian.

"Putter around," he said.

"Yes, yes." Her lips curved into a trembling smile. "Under my feet!"

"He worked for the security company for a long time. What did he do there?"

"Oh, he made secure the electronics, the Internet. He would find and stop those who used it to cheat or, ah, exploit. He would go sometimes to fix problems or, ah . . . Antonio, my English."

"Is excellent," Peabody said.

"She means to say he would build systems, electronic security systems, and as part of his duties, search out hackers, those who attempt—and often succeed—in conning the unwary out of money. Or attempt to harm."

"As part of a team."

"He liked best to be in a team," his widow said.

"He was part of a team, in the Underground, during the Urban Wars?"

"Yes. He was very dedicated."

"And the names of his team members?"

"I can't answer. He never spoke of them, not by name."

"You never met any of them?"

"I did not. Even before he lost his brother, he sent me—we had Antonio and Katrina, and he sent us to where my sister and her husband had a little farm. In the country, you see. To safety. He wouldn't come with us, though I was weak enough to beg him to come with us.

"He only came when he could, a day or two, a few days at most. Long enough," she said with a smile, "that we began our third child, and then our fourth. But he would never, never speak of what he did. Not then, not after. But . . ."

"Anything, Ms. Rossi."

"I know something happened. After Paolo was born, our youngest. He was different, his voice when we spoke. And I could see it when he came to see us. Something dark inside him, a pain inside him. But he wouldn't speak of it, and I left it alone. He needed me to, so I left it alone."

"Do you remember when this was?"

"Ah . . . After Paolo. He is the twelfth of January, 2026. Gio was with me for the birth and for another week. Then he came back in . . . May, I think. Yes, he came in May."

"May of 2026?"

"Yes. This helps?"

"Everything you can tell us helps. He was wounded in the war?"

"Wounded? No, he did the . . . cyber. Dangerous, yes, dangerous times, but Gio didn't fight. Not a solider but a technician?"

"He has a wound, an old wound." Eve touched a hand to her side.

"Yes, the scar. An accident, a fall from his scooter—yes, that same spring, after Paolo and before Gio comes again. A rainy night, and someone drove too fast and close, wet roads, and he wrecked his scooter. He hurts the ribs, and has the cut. Ah, and he broke these two fingers in the fall."

She held up her index and middle fingers. "They were still healing when he came to see us. And the wound on his side, infected a little. My sister treated it the country way, and it healed. A scar, but it healed."

"And he had other injuries?"

She looked blank. "No. Oh, yes, he sprained his ankle in the garden three years gone. And once, he returns from a trip with his eye blackened. He walked into the wall." She laughed a little. "Up in the middle of the night, thinking home, and forgot where the wall was in the hotel. You mean this?"

"It's helpful" was all Eve said. "What about the Wasp?"

She got the reaction she'd expected. A blank frown.

"In the garden? They will build their nest sometimes. Gio doesn't like to kill them—he says they serve a purpose. But he doesn't want them to sting the children, so he knocks down their nest, and tells them to build a new one but not in the garden."

"Did he ever mention anyone he called Fawn, or Rabbit, or Hawk?"

"No. I would remember such odd names as those."

"How many languages did he speak?"

"Oh, Italian, of course, and English as good as the children's—he insisted they learn to speak English very well."

"He spoke better English than any of us."

She smiled at her son. "He had a gift. He speaks very good French, Spanish as well. Some German, even some Ukrainian. It helps, you see, for his work. He is often sent to places where they speak another language, and Gio is very good with languages."

"How did this friend contact him?"

"I never thought to ask." This clearly distressed her. "I never thought to ask him this."

"Did this friend ever contact him before?"

"He never said. But I think a good friend, *Tenente*, as he spoke of an oath. A promise made, and he left so quickly. I know worried, but also pleased. Pleased to see this friend again. How could he be so pleased if this was his killer?"

"He wasn't a stupid man," his son added. "He may not have fought in the wars, but he worked through them, lived through them, kept his family safe. He worked in cybersecurity, rooting out those who commit crimes."

"I don't for a minute think Giovanni Rossi was a stupid man. I think his killer used his loyalty as a weapon against him. It's possible this contact wasn't made by the friend, but someone posing as his friend. Or, if not, that this person had no loyalty.

"What about coworkers? Do you know anyone he worked with at the security company?"

"Yes, of course. His supervisor the last few years, before he retired. Some of the young ones. Many had, like Gio, retired. And the younger came in. He enjoyed them, working with them, being around them. He said they kept him—"

Once again she looked to her son.

"On his toes."

"*Sì, giusto.*"

"If you could give me some names. Coworkers—the ones who retired, like he did. Some of the others he might have worked closely with. Team members."

"Yes, I can do this, if it helps."

"I'd appreciate it. How long are you staying in New York?"

"Until we take the father of my children home."

"It may be a few days."

"I will not go home without my husband."

Eve met her eyes. "Neither would I."

"So you know this bond. One death cannot break."

"I do. My partner and I will do all we can so you can take your husband home soon."

"I believe you. You have truth in your eyes. I think there's an anger behind the truth. I respect the anger in them. I will send the names."

"Thank you for coming in. Again, we're very sorry for your loss. Detective Peabody will take you out."

Alone, she sat for a moment, playing those questions, those answers over in her mind.

She rose, walked out, and met Peabody coming back.

"They held up," Peabody observed. "It wasn't easy on either of them. They just didn't have the answers."

"They had plenty of them. They gave me the answers because they didn't know the answers."

"Is that a riddle?"

"They didn't know the answers because he never told them, not even the woman he lived with for half a frigging century. He didn't tell them not just because he didn't want to talk about it, but because he'd taken an oath.

"He didn't tell them because he was a freaking spy."

First Peabody's mouth fell open. Then her eyes lit as she pumped her fists in the air. "I *knew* it!"

"No, you wondered it, and you hoped it—because it adds—what's the thing frosty stuff adds?"

"Cachet?"

"Sure, that works. But he was a goddamn agent, at least up until a few years ago. Didn't fight in the Urbans? Got a knife wound and broken ribs, broken fingers falling off a scooter?"

Eve shook her head.

"I figure he was a damn good agent in his day."

"Do you think the security company where he worked is like a front, a front for covert ops?"

"If not, he used it as a cover."

"This is pretty frosty, Dallas."

"Murder's never frosty."

"No, I mean before the murder. The life he led. Frosty. He was a spy, during the Urbans and beyond. He traveled all over Europe, a covert agent posing as an ordinary e-man. And while he did that, he made a family, what seems like a really good family. He not only kept them all safe—removed from his real work—but he kept their lives normal."

"It couldn't have been easy. Keeping it all contained. Contained and separated."

"No, and that's another layer of the frost."

"I'll give you that, but here's what's not frosty. He had enough experience, enough knowledge to understand exactly what was happening, going to happen the instant he felt the first effects of the gas."

Outside of the bullpen, Eve paused.

"The last minutes of his frosty life, with all the normality he'd built into it, ended in pain, fear, and the terrible knowledge that he'd die thousands of miles from home. More, Peabody, he knew, he was too smart not to know, that his killer had seven others on a list."

"It all goes back to the Urbans."

"And whatever happened, most likely in May of 2026. We dig there. Major incidents in significant European cities after the first of the year and before May 2026."

"His data says he worked out of London, not Rome." Peabody hunched her shoulders at Eve's long look. "That doesn't mean he did, because spy."

"Get started there. I'm going to contact Nadine on the off-chance—" She broke off as she turned into the bullpen, saw not only camera-ready Nadine Furst but the young apprentice Quilla.

Quilla sat at a chair pulled up at Jenkinson's desk. Obviously unaffected by the atomic tie, she studied him intently as he wound through some story for her.

The teenager wore black pants that stopped just above her ankles and her purple kicks. The button shirt she wore untucked matched the sneakers. As did the thick fall of bangs and a few scattered streaks through her brown hair.

Nadine, watching them, wore a green suit that matched her cat eyes. Her streaky blond hair, perfectly coiffed, waved back from her sharp-angled face.

Eve caught the fading scents of sugar and chocolate.

Whatever bakery bribe Nadine had brought in had already been devoured.

"Detective Sergeant, haven't you got work?"

"I'm doing it, Loo. You cleared the kid to come in."

She had, Eve remembered. Quilla had completed her story on EDD, and Eve had given her the green light to conduct interviews in the bullpen.

But that was before murder and spies and what she believed could be a decades-long grudge.

"DS Jenkinson said you'd be too busy to talk to me today." Quilla, eyes bright, turned to Eve. "But he and Detective Reineke had some time. Detectives Baxter and Trueheart are in the field, and Detectives Carmichael and Santiago are in Interview."

Eve flicked a glance to the case board. "So it says, right there."

"If they have time later, that's chill. If not, I can come back. I'm going to talk to some of the uniforms. And I really want to interview you and Peabody when you're not busy."

"Don't you have school?"

"This is part of it." Quilla tried for earnest, but couldn't quite hide the smug. "Part of my education."

"You gave her the green light," Nadine said.

"Yeah, yeah. Why'd you bring cookies?"

"As a thank-you," Quilla piped right up. "For giving me the time, and because everyone here protects and serves."

Eve caught Nadine's overtly smug smile. "She's a freaking mini you."

"No, she's all Quilla."

"My office." When Nadine hesitated, Eve offered her own smug smile. "Does she need you to watch her?"

"No. No, she does not."

Pushing off Peabody's desk, Nadine went with Eve. "You cleared her, and it's a major project for her."

"This isn't about that, and what's on my board is off the record. What we're going to talk about is off the record."

"All right."

Just like that, Nadine's agreement and Eve's acceptance of it. Like her victim, Eve thought, Nadine kept her word.

But she turned those cat eyes on Eve's board.

"Giovanni Rossi, out of Rome. Cause of death not yet determined." Then shifted them to Eve. "But it has been, hasn't it?"

"I need to know if anyone's been in contact with you, or attempted to contact you about me."

Nadine's eyebrows winged up. "I have the bestselling true crime book in the country at the moment, and you're the lead investigator in it. Of course people contact me about you. I'm adapting the screenplay for a major film based on that book. The last one won me an Oscar. I talk to the Hollywood people, and you do come up, at least once a week."

"Well, shit."

"That's your card on the board."

"No, it's one whoever killed Rossi made to look like my card."

"And this message?" Nadine moved closer. "The Wasp? I've never seen anyone who looks less wasplike. He looks jovial. What happened to him?"

Eve waved that off. "Any contacts or attempts regarding me from someone you don't know, or didn't check out?"

"No. I get communication from readers, fans of the books, the vid. And yeah, sure, some of them—a lot of them—ask about you. Or Roarke, or Peabody, and so on. I'm careful, Dallas, I can promise you, on how I respond, or have Quilla or my assistant respond. There's nothing personal.

"Are you a target?"

"No." Of that, at least for the moment, she was sure. "But they picked me, specifically, left my card and the message, for a reason."

"And you wonder if it's the notoriety from the books, the vid. It could be. It could be your reputation on the job. It could be you're married to the richest man in the galaxy. And it could be," she added, "a combination of all of the above.

"Which you'd have considered."

"I'm considering."

Nadine pointed at the AutoChef, got a nod.

"If I had to pick," Nadine continued as she programmed two cups, "I'd go with the second, and consider elements of one and three in there. What's phosphine?"

"What killed him."

Nadine passed Eve her coffee, sipped her own. "Like a gas? Toxic gas? It's dated 2024."

She frowned now. "That's nearly forty years. Since I've heard nothing about the driver's death, I'm going to assume he not only survived but is your number one suspect. Not in custody?"

"No. Rossi worked with the Underground in Europe, Urbans era. An e-man."

"Oh." Nodding, eyes narrowed, Nadine sipped again. "2024. That's about the end of the Urbans, isn't it? I'd need to check to be sure, but weren't things largely settled by then?"

"Here, yeah. I did check. In Europe, it took a little longer, and some pockets still had trouble longer."

"You weren't even born yet. Me, either. I'm sticking with choice number two. The killer's challenging you. I can put some researchers on it."

"No. Nobody."

"All right. I can do some research on it. You already are, but you never know. A bioweapon. That's a big risk, isn't it? A big risk with a long, long, ugly history. There'd be a reason to use it."

If a crime beat reporter didn't think like a cop, Eve decided, she wouldn't last long.

"I want to break this when you clear it. Your card left with the victim, so that's a one-on-one, very least. A live on *Now*'s even better."

And if Nadine didn't know how to push, she wouldn't be at the top of her game.

"I'd like to catch him first, and I'd like to do that before there are seven more people on this board."

"He shouldn't have pulled you in, pissed you off. He thinks he's smarter than you, and wants the shine of winning. I have good reason to doubt the first and categorically refute the second."

She lifted her coffee in a toast. "Add, he shouldn't have taken an arrogant swipe at a friend of mine. I'm also goddamn smart and goddamn tenacious. You'll get him, and if anything I do helps, I'll take that shine. And the interview."

"Maybe you're Adult Quilla."

Nadine's laugh held easy delight. "She's a gem, Dallas. Another thing I owe you, for putting her in my sights. She's so fucking bright. And the school? An Didean? What you and Roarke have done there—"

"He did it."

"She's doing so well there. Not just academically, but socially, emotionally. She works hard, but she's made friends. You know she's seeing Jamie."

Eve slapped a hand on her eye as it twitched. "I don't want to hear about it!"

"It's not serious. He's in college, she's still in high school. She wants to do what I do, he wants to do what Feeney does. They both know you can't mix that. But they're good for each other, and I really think they'll stay friends."

"Fine. Friends is fine. Look, I don't want to block her from this project, but I don't know when I can talk to her, or spare Peabody."

"She'll wait. Anyway."

She set down her empty mug. Then heaved a breath.

"Hell, hell. Do you have two minutes? Just two minutes for something completely else?"

"Maybe."

"Jake."

"Oh." Eve had the sudden need to roll her shoulders as if shifting a weight. If there was trouble between the reporter and the rock star, what the hell could she do about it?

"Look, Nadine, if something's gone wrong there—"

"No! Everything's right. It's just so right. It's terrifying, and wonderful. I've loved other men before, but never been in love, and it's different. For him, too. For both of us. Together."

She pressed a hand to her belly. "I get the jitters. Nobody ever gave me the jitters before. I like it. Am I supposed to like it?"

"Maybe" was the best Eve could do.

"I thought it would be easy once we said the word. The *love* word. But once you do, it's right there. Before you do, it's this is fun, it's great, it's interesting and exciting. It's amazing sex."

"I don't want to hear about the sex."

"I'm not going to talk to you about the sex."

"Okay then."

In her sky-high heels, Nadine turned a circle.

"I'm crazy in love with him, and I didn't expect it. I wasn't looking for it. But now I have it, and I want it. I want to keep it. He's moving in with me."

"Oh, well, good?"

"It is, it is." Now Nadine paced in her green spikes. "He was practically living there before. And he's got his place with the recording studio, and he'll keep that. He travels, I travel. Sometimes we can coordinate that, but it's all good if not."

"And the problem is?"

With a hand to her heart, Nadine pivoted. "What if I screw it up? How do you not screw it up?"

"I screw it up all the time."

"Do you? I don't know if that makes me feel better or worse. We're hard cases, Dallas, you and me. Women who've worked their way up to boss because they're smart, determined, they believe in what they do, and they're damn good at it. And sometimes what they do has to come first."

"Yeah. So?"

Nadine let out a breathless laugh. "And strangely a little better. Men like Roarke, like Jake, they're damn good at what they do. And they're no pushovers."

"Who wants to get stuck with a pushover?"

"Exactly." Still pacing, Nadine shot a finger at Eve. "We'd never respect that, and we want to respect the person we're with. They're both strong, smart, and, yeah, damn good at what they do. I don't know half of what Roarke does."

"Join the club. I'm president."

"But he's damn good at it. Jake is a freaking rock star. Literally a freaking rock star. He could have anyone. So could Roarke. They picked us."

"What, like flowers?"

Nadine threw up her hands. "You're right, wrong phrase. Shows my mind's scrambled. They fell for us, like we fell for them. Because of all that. Who we are, who they are. Was it easy for you and Roarke? Did it just . . . slide into place and stick?"

"No. Nothing was easy, and I had a lot to do with that because he scared me. What I felt for him scared me, too."

"Oh, thank God." Nadine stopped pacing. "I needed to hear that. I really needed to hear that. I know it's not supposed to be easy. I know it takes work. I'm smart enough to understand that, and I love him enough to do the work. But I know I'm not easy, and I don't want to screw it up."

"You will. You'll both screw up, then you'll both deal with it, figure it out. You look good together. I don't mean physically, though come on. I mean you look right together."

"It feels right. That first night, that horrible night we met? Everything started changing, even in the middle of that."

She let out another breath. "I know timing, and I know I went way over the two minutes. Thanks. Serious thanks. I'll get out of your way."

She walked to the door, then glanced back. "I know I compared him to Roarke, but the fact is, Jake is more like you."

"Seriously?"

"Yes, seriously. I don't know what the hell that says about me."

Since she didn't, either, Eve just shook her head. Rather than coffee this round, she got a tube of water.

Sitting behind her desk, she wrote up the interview with the Rossis, copied Whitney. Because she felt she was dealing with a kind of madness—a sly, arrogant kind—she copied all the data to Mira.

She'd like the opinion of a shrink, a profiler, a woman whose opinion she respected. Given the time and the amount of data, she requested a consult the next day.

She'd already considered and rejected contacting Homeland regarding Rossi, and/or the security company. She had many reasons, and some very personal, for not trusting HSO.

She considered, then rejected contacting Agent Teasdale. She did trust the FBI agent—and former Homeland agent. But Eve decided to hold her in reserve.

She had another way. Taking that way bent the rules, but it wouldn't be the first time. When dealing with covert, why not use the covert?

She got an incoming with a scheduled consult for oh-nine hundred, plugged it in, shot that to Peabody.

There was one more potential source, and though she tried to find a way around it, it only took a glance at her board. She didn't look forward to this particular consult, but Summerset had served as a medic—and she suspected more—in Europe during the Urbans.

He could give her, if he didn't blow her off, an in-person perspective.

He had a woman friend who'd done covert work. Possibly she could try to tap Ivanna Liski for information. Again, possibly, she would know if the security company Rossi worked for was indeed a front.

Something happened in the spring of 2026. Maybe one of them knew more about that.

A long shot, she thought, considering how many people lived through, fought through, worked through the Urbans. But if you didn't take the shot, it couldn't pay off.

"Might as well get it the hell over with."

She shut down, walked into the bullpen.

Since she didn't see Quilla or Nadine, she figured the interviews there were done. For now.

"That's a smart kid, Dallas. Got a head on her shoulders," Jenkinson added.

"Where else would it be?"

"Plenty have theirs up their asses."

She had to nod. "They sure as hell do. I'm working from home," she told him, then turned to Peabody. "I'm going to talk to Summerset, and Ivanna Liski if possible."

"That's a good angle. They both lived through it. I've got your consult with Mira on your schedule."

"If you get anything more, send it."

"Will do. I figure to see if McNab can dig any deeper than I am."

"Do that. I've got an angle there. I'll let you know if it comes to anything."

She headed out, risked thc elevator first.

Summerset would be looming in the foyer, as always, she expected. She could push there straight off. Too early for Roarke to be home, most likely, so her angle there would wait.

If Ivanna would talk to her, she could go to her, if necessary.

Clearer picture, bound to be, of what was going on in 2026 in Europe than she'd get from any research. Even firsthand accounts were secondhand by the time you read about them.

Summerset had lost his wife during the wars. She didn't know when, only that she didn't survive them.

She knew Ivanna had lost her husband. And had two sons from that marriage.

She knew that in the secondhand way of research once Ivanna moved to New York, and started—was it dating? Not thinking about that, Eve thought, absolutely not.

Renewed her friendship with Summerset.

That settled more smoothly.

When it occurred to her she'd already put in twelve hours and intended to put in more, she just shrugged.

Nadine wasn't wrong. She was a hard case.

Chapter Six

THE RAIN STARTED AS SHE DROVE OUT OF THE GARAGE AT CENTRAL.

Drivers immediately lost twenty percent of their IQs, as if rain just washed part of their brains away.

At least their driving brains.

The wet didn't stop the ad blimps from blasting out about *Step into Fall* sales.

"It's still summer, you freaks! It's eighty degrees!"

She glanced at her dash.

"Eighty-three! That is not goddamn sweater weather no matter what you say."

And they did say it, repeatedly.

She fought her way through knots of traffic, shoving up into vertical twice. Not in a particular hurry, she reminded herself, but had to resist the temptation to hit lights and siren out of sheer frustration.

When her mind wandered to her discussion with Nadine, she nearly gave in just to erase it from her brain.

"Fine, it's fine. I did my job there, didn't I? There are Friendship Rules, too. Marriage Rules, Friendship Rules. Family Rules? Sure there are. They probably vary, depending."

Her world required rules, and she added them on when necessary.

She intended to bend one of them now. Not a real break, but a definite bend by using Roarke's unregistered equipment.

She didn't want the all-seeing eye of CompuGuard, and the eyes behind it, to see her poking into an Italian security company she suspected served as a front for covert operations.

Something specific to Italy? Possibly. Something more broad-based? Maybe Interpol.

She had a contact there, but wasn't ready to tap it.

Covert agents and international police tended to clam right up if outsiders poked in.

She didn't hold it against them.

The rain, steady and gray, dogged her all the way uptown, made the drive a running series of annoyances.

And gave way to sun as she turned into the gates of home.

A rainbow arched like a fairy tale over the castle Roarke built. It shined over the towers, the turrets of glistening stone. And still, after all this time, it could take her breath away.

How could this glory be home? Her home, the beaten, battered, broken child of monsters? What wild twist of fate had brought her here, to this wonder, this warmth, this welcome?

She'd started her day with death—and did so often—and she'd pursue the one who'd caused that death. But for a moment, just this moment, she could steep herself in the beauty.

The sheer miracle of beauty.

She rarely, if ever, took photos that didn't pertain to the job. But she stopped on the long drive where the thick green leaves dripped rain, where the still thriving flowers stood heavy-headed with it. And leaned out the window to take a shot of the house with its rainbow crown.

Maybe, she considered, when things got very bad, she could look at it and remember the miracle.

Now she had work, and it started with Summerset.

She left her car at the entrance, walked through the damp air to the grand front doors. And into the foyer.

He wasn't there. No bony cadaver in black stood, looming, dark eyes cool—and scanning for bloody or ripped clothing. No fat cat sat by his feet.

"What the fuck! The one time."

She turned to the house comp.

"Where the hell is Summerset?"

Darling Eve, Summerset is not in residence.

"Well, shit."

I am unable to perform that function.

"Funny. Is Roarke in residence?"

Roarke has not yet returned. Shall I notify you when he does?

"No. Crap. Where's the damn cat?"

Galahad is in your office, Darling Eve . . . Update, Galahad is leaving your office.

Frowning, she stood another moment. Then saw the cat coming down the stairs.

"Nobody here. You don't count." Then she bent to stroke him when he rubbed against her legs. "You count, but not for this. I've got the whole freaking castle to myself, when I don't want it. I'm going up. You might as well come. Christ knows you can use the exercise."

He didn't seem offended as he jogged up the steps with her.

She went to her office. She could access Roarke's private office and the unregistered. But if she waited for him, he could accomplish more than she could in a fraction of the time.

She'd set up her board, her book here.

"Where the hell is Summerset?" she asked the cat.

He just padded over to her sleep chair, leaped into it, and made himself comfortable.

"He's always here. But today, no. Not here when I actually want to talk to him. I can contact Ivanna. No, no, that's better coming from him."

Annoyed, she began to set up her case board. When done to her liking, she sat at her command center. She opened operations and dealt with her murder book.

And maybe, since it was so damn quiet, she'd take some serious thinking time.

She programmed coffee, angled to her board, put her feet on the L of her command center.

As she did, Roarke came in.

She hadn't heard him come up the stairs, walk down the hall.

The cat's feet were an elephant's compared to Roarke's.

"You beat me home," he said.

"You and everybody. Where the hell is Summerset?"

"It's his day off. I hope he's enjoying it."

And since Summerset hadn't been there to take Roarke's briefcase, he set it aside, then crossed the room to bend down and kiss her.

"Disappointed you missed your daily insults?"

"I need to talk to him. About the Urbans."

Frowning, Roarke looked at her board. "Then this somehow connects to that. To Summerset?"

"To the Urbans, and Europe. I figure he can give me a picture. But of course, he's not here, so I can't, and he can't. I'm in a shitty mood," she realized. "It's his fault."

"Of course it is." Adoring her, he kissed her scowling mouth. "I'm going to get us some wine, and you'll tell me about all this."

"What do you know about Sicurezza Informatica?"

"Not a great deal, I suppose." He crossed over to open the wine cabinet and choose a bottle. "A respected cyber firm based in Rome. It's been around decades with a solid reputation."

"I think it's a front."

He paused in the act of opening a bottle of red. Red, as he thought her mood would lighten with some very nice Cabernet. "For what?"

"Intelligence. Covert ops."

"Is that so? Well now, that's interesting."

"If we used your unregistered, we could maybe find out."

"And still more interesting. We can do that, of course. I'd like you to fill me in first, as it would give me better direction. You can do that while we have a meal."

"I want fries," she decided. "I want lots of fries. Like a mountain of fries."

"All right then."

"Jake's moving in with Nadine. Jesus, Jesus on 'roids! Why is that stuck in my head?"

"Is he? That's happy news, isn't it?"

"I guess. Sure. Why not? Feeney and Whitney both did stuff during the Urbans. You had to figure that—plus, I knew Feeney did. They had code names."

"Those I must know." He handed her a glass of wine.

"Hound and Lightning. Guess which is which?"

"That's no challenge, darling. Feeney would be Hound—he'd have the scent. So Lightning falls to your commander."

"Apparently he used to be really fast. It was a long time ago, Roarke. But I think Rossi died because of something that happened back then."

"How did he die?"

"Toxic gas piped into the back of a limo. Do you know what phosphine is?"

"I do, yes. A very unpleasant death."

"Yeah. Very."

"They found a stockpile—it had already been banned—when I was a boy in Dublin. There was a leak, and several died, others were sickened. I think I was six or seven, but I remember it."

"He used a canister dated 2024."

Rising, she walked to the board with her wine. "I think Rossi was a good man, a loyal friend, and a spy. My victim. His killer put a card with my name on it between his index and middle fingers, fingers that had been broken in the past. And in the spring of '26. I've asked to have DeWinter date the breaks. He had more of them."

"Your card, yes, I see."

When he turned to her, she didn't need the Marriage Rules to know to take his hand.

"It's not about me. He wants me to hunt him, but it's not about me. Read the message."

"I have."

"It's about them. And until I figure out who the hell they are, the seven left, he's got a clear field. He wants them dead. I don't."

"I'll get the meal, and we'll sit. You'll start at the beginning."

"Roarke." She set her glass down, slid her arms around him.

Yeah, she was a hard case, and here he was, loving her anyway.

"There was a rainbow."

"During the Urbans?"

She laughed, and loved him for keeping his mind on her case. "No, when I got home. It rained on the way, then it stopped, and there was a rainbow right over the house."

She pulled out her 'link, swiped it up, showed him.

"Ah now, that's lovely, isn't it? Send it to me, will you? It lifts the day."

"Did you have a hard one?"

"I didn't, no. But it's clear you did. So you'll share that with me over dinner, and we'll do what comes next."

"I love you. So much."

"*A ghrá.*" He drew her in again, kissed the top of her head. "You're a rainbow to me, even in a shitty mood."

He made her laugh, then she squeezed him tight. "I'll never understand that. I don't need to. Tons of fries. What goes with tons of fries?"

He tapped the shallow dent in her chin. "I'd say your mood requires red meat. We'll have a steak."

"Now, that sounds like the right choice. I'll get it. You haven't even had time to take a breath. You can feed the cat."

"I'll do that, and while we're at it, you can start with the happy, and Nadine."

More than fair, Eve thought as they moved into the little kitchen.

"Quilla's doing a report or project on Homicide. She did one on EDD."

"You told me, and you'd had a moment and agreed to let her do the same in Homicide."

"Yeah, a moment. So she's there, and Nadine's there, and I wanted to see if Nadine had anyone going at her about me. The card."

"I follow."

She programmed the meal while he fed the cat, who acted as if he hadn't eaten in days.

"Then she's about this moving-in business. And all jumpy and weird. Worrying about screwing it up. I told her I screw up all the time."

She looked over at him. "You're not disagreeing with that. I don't get: 'No, darling Eve, that's nonsense. You're just perfect'?"

"For me, you are. But you will screw up, won't you? I've been known to do the same myself."

"Damn right. Anyway, she's stupid in love with him, and I think that's good because Jake's solid. He's not an asshole, and he gets her. I did the friend thing. There are rules."

"Of course there are. You must have them."

"I must have them," she agreed, and set the plates on the table. "Rossi had rules."

Nodding, Roarke brought side salads—she'd never think of that—and a basket of bread. "Tell me about him."

So she did, what she believed, what she'd learned from his widow, his son, even from Peabody's interview with his former supervisor.

"So what you see is a good man, a loyal friend, a family man who led a secret life."

"In a nutshell. Why is it a nutshell?"

"They're compact."

She considered, nodded. Cut a bite of steak to go with her French fry mountain.

"Okay. He had a number of old injuries. DeWinter can pinpoint dates there. They're not going to be from wiping out on his scooter."

"I agree with you. Why you? I'd like that question answered."

"I think, from what we have, he wants someone he thinks is good, but he's better."

"He's not."

She shrugged and ate another salt-drenched fry. "I'll run the security feed from the terminal for you. He's a smug bastard. Not Rossi's generation. Maybe twenty years younger, so that's a puzzle. Maybe an enemy's son. Maybe just a pro hire."

"Covert ops, my literal cop. There are ways to make one appear younger, different, to disguise age, race, even gender."

She paused with another bite of steak halfway to her mouth.

"Well, fuck me."

"I'd be delighted to later."

"But it's so much goddamn trouble."

"No trouble at all."

"Not that." But she laughed. "If that's it, he went to all that trouble to look a couple decades younger. I couldn't, and so far EDD hasn't, matched him on face rec. But he leaves a copy of my card, and a message? What's the point?"

She held up a hand.

"To keep me spinning my wheels awhile. To give him time to plan out his next kill. It has to be in New York or I'm out. But maybe he's picked investigators wherever his kills are."

"Not impossible, but why just the one for you? No, Lieutenant, I believe he wants you. You may be right, it's the notoriety from Nadine's books, from the vid. Arrogance wants the best. Wants the shine."

"So New York. But could the rest be here? It's not probable, just not logical. He had to pull Rossi here. Is he—or had he already—done the same with the others?"

Sitting back, Roarke sipped his wine. "I'd want them one at a time. Draw out the pleasure of it, the satisfaction. And the challenge. And yet, do these other seven not know? Don't they keep any sort of watch?"

"And know Rossi's dead in New York? Or know when it gets out here? By tomorrow, I'd think, to anyone paying attention. That's a good thought. That's good."

"So your talk with Summerset, to get a feel."

"Yeah." He'd been, essentially, raised by the man, she thought. And had ways of finding out whatever he wanted or needed to know.

"How much do you know?"

"Not a great deal. I know he served as a medic, and I know—though he's been cagey, and I didn't push—he did more."

"Why didn't you push? Or just look?"

Lifting his wine, he looked at her over the rim. "If he'd wanted me to know, he'd have told me. And to push, or look on my own? Why would I disrespect him just to satisfy my curiosity?"

"Okay. You only know what he's told you, which is?"

"I know he worked as a medic during the Urbans, and met his wife. I know his wife was killed when Marlena was only a baby. I don't know how, and there, again, I didn't push. It's painful for him."

"Ivanna worked covert. Even after the Urbans."

"True enough, but the details are sketchy. Before I was born, or when I was just a lad. Before Summerset took me in."

Watching him, she tapped her fork in the air. "You could've found out more there, too."

"I could have, yes. I didn't. It's, again, disrespectful. Ivanna is his friend, important to him. Summerset saved my life. He gave me a life, and he didn't have to."

Roarke handed her some bread.

"I never pried into his personal life. And accepted what he told me. Why wouldn't I?"

"I don't want to pry, either. I don't need details, just a big picture. And Ivanna may have more. If he'd been home, I'd have this over with."

"He'll give you what he can," Roarke told her. "And we'll find what we can find on this security company. If it's a front as you believe, we'll dig down. And I do think, considering murder, Ivanna will tell you if she knows more.

"They fought as you do, Eve, for the innocent, for the right."

"The fight should be over for them. I just want to say, to you, I'm sorry to bring it back."

"You haven't. Rossi's killer did. After we finish dinner, we'll clean this up, won't we? And go up to the unregistered."

The cat, curious enough to stir himself, followed them up to the secured office. At the door, Roarke plugged in the code, engaged the retinal scan.

"I've upgraded a bit, and as CompuGuard adds layers, so do I."

"CG serves a purpose. I don't always like it."

Roarke gave an elegant little shrug. "And those who want to evade that purpose will find a way."

He opened the door, called for lights on full as Galahad wandered in. He found a leather chair acceptable and made himself comfortable there. A plump, watchful gray pillow.

Here, privacy shields guarded the windows, the sort that would give the equipment and expertise at EDD a lot of frustration.

The vast command center looked the same to her, but then she expected upgrades meant some internal e-wizardry she'd never understand.

Roarke crossed to it, laid his hand on a palm plate. "Roarke. Open operations."

It came to life, a quiet hum like a breath taken. Across the black field, control lights snapped on, gleamed like colorful jewels struck by the sun.

The command center faced an enormous wall screen, but for now, Roarke tapped a control. A screen slid out of a hidden slot on the black field.

"This may take a bit of a while," he told Eve. "Even if they're only what they purport to be, any good cybersecurity company will have their blocks, walls, tunnels, shields, and so on."

"Okay."

"If you've work of your own you want to deal with?"

He used another control, and a mini data and communication unit opened at the end of the counter.

"Upgrades," he said again as she frowned at it. "You can use the mini well enough. It'll require your thumbprint and voice command."

She walked to it, pressed her thumb on the pad. "Dallas."

And it hummed to life.

"I can't use unregistered for reports."

Roarke merely stepped over, pressed a glowing red button. It shifted to green.

"Now it reads as the comp in your office."

Slick, she thought, just slick. And while more a violation than a crime, still.

Still, she decided, she'd think of it—right now—as a tool. A comp was a comp wherever it sat.

Roarke set coffee on the counter for her, then flicked his finger down the shallow dent in her chin.

"You can go to your own office, and I'll bring you whatever results I have when I have them."

"So I not only bend the rules, but I'm a hypocrite about it? This is fine."

"The rules snap back, Eve. If we're honest, CompuGuard's stated purpose is to detect criminal activity, which they do a remarkably poor job of. You don't."

"Detecting terrorist activity . . ." She rolled her eyes at herself. "And they don't do such a hot job there, either. Not anymore."

"Outdated, underfunded, exploitive. So? Continue?"

"Yeah. Do what you do."

"Command, Sicurezza Informatica, Rome, Italy, and satellite locations. Shielded first-level search."

Received, accessing . . .

He took off his suit jacket, rolled up his sleeves. From his pocket he took out a leather tie, pulled his hair back in a short tail.

Work mode, Eve thought, and settled into her own.

Her first step was to read Peabody's report on the deeper run on the vic.

Everything about it said ordinary, blameless.

The ordinary and blameless often ended up on a slab, she thought, but not like this.

While Roarke worked manually, fingers swiping, tapping, sliding, so did she. His occasional voice command didn't disturb her as she dug into 2025 and 2026, Europe.

Something happened, something she believed was big enough, important enough to resonate for decades after—and lead to the murder. The precise and complicated murder.

She found a pair of executions in Athens—ugly, public executions.

Over a dozen dead anti-war protestors, gunned down as they'd marched in Paris.

A group bringing humanitarian aid ambushed in Rome and slaughtered.

A bombing of a building in London, Dominion—extremists, a violent fringe element—HQ, resulting in more than a hundred deaths, scores of injuries.

Beatings of civilians by police in Dublin.

Homes invaded, bombed, burned. Children abducted.

When the back of the wars broke in the early summer of 2026 in Europe, the tribunals and trials. War crimes, insurrection, treason, assassinations.

Some, in that dreary aftermath, had medals pinned on them. Others sat in cages. And others faced execution.

When she sat back, Roarke signaled to her.

"Have a look here."

He used the wall screen now, and on it she saw what she recognized as blueprints.

"Okay, that's the building the cyber firm's in?"

"It is, yes. And you see we have labs, offices, temp-controlled areas, secure areas, lounge areas, a fitness center—small, but big enough—data storage, two conference areas, and so on."

"And?"

"Well now, it's bollocks. Not all, but bollocks just the same. Look here."

He brought up a second set of blueprints.

"This is the building that stood there until the mid-twenties. It was severely damaged in the Urbans, but not destroyed. Then it was razed, as it was deemed unsafe. What do you see?"

"I see there's an underground area. Looks like two levels, and they don't show on the new blueprints. Neither do the tunnels."

"Interesting, isn't it? As it's well cloaked. Also interesting is this building has military-grade shields. Two layers of shields that are regularly upgraded. That's not only a considerable cost for a company of this size, this nature, this profit/loss margin, but inexplicable as—"

"Military grade is for the military, not private companies, not for civilians or civilian companies."

"Exactly."

"Do you have them?"

"Well now, of course, but of my own design, and the expense is built in. We don't have that here—not that shows. The financials are bogus as well, and I'll go after that shortly. Here's one more."

"What's this one?"

"This is the home of your victim's supervisor. This area?"

He highlighted it.

"This also has two layers of shields. I believe if I take the time to pinpoint other supervisory staff, I'll find the same."

"Sometimes you have to work at home," Eve murmured.

"As we prove most every day. Your victim's home doesn't have those shields. But it did, in one area. Apparently removed eight years ago."

"When he retired. So the company is a front."

"It carries on its business—a good business, successful, very competent. But that business doesn't pay for these shields, and doesn't require them. And it defies logic they wouldn't use and have use for those two levels. The tunnels still exist—I've verified that with other buildings."

"Can you get through the shields?"

His impossibly blue eyes met hers. "Darling Eve, you wound me."

"Undetected?"

"Ouch."

She rubbed her hands over her face, laughed. "All right, Ace, go at it. I'm picking through bombings, brutality, corruption, and treason."

"Do what you do," he said, and went back to his own.

Eve worked, drank more coffee. And heard Roarke's occasional mutters, curses, heard the Irish thicken in his voice as he ran into walls.

The cat snored lightly in his sleep. Outside the windows, the city lights glimmered.

"There, bugger you now, I've bloody well got you."

"You got it?"

"I'll need a tourniquet if you keep stabbing my ego."

She swiveled, stared at the screen. "That's a live feed! You got a live feed."

"I can't keep it for you and stay in the shadows. What they have's too good for that. You have ten seconds more."

"Those are the lower levels. There are people working there. That's a goddamn armory! And labs. And—"

"I've got you a still, but that's all we can risk on the live. What you have there, Lieutenant, isn't just a front."

"It's an HQ."

"My guess, AISE—Italy's intelligence agency. Possibly a collaboration with AISI."

"What's the difference?"

"AISE is foreign intelligence, and you mentioned the victim traveled through Europe. AISI is domestic."

"I don't think I want to know how you know that right off the top of your head."

"I can also tell you that the two agencies helped form the Underground. With MI6, the CIA, DGSI—France—and others. It was more formally known as the International Intelligence Agency."

"The IIA disbanded in the '30s or early '40s."

Roarke smiled. "Did it?"

"Huh. Okay, maybe, maybe not. Maybe parts of it are still in operation in places like this, with people like Rossi still working as agents, operatives. Either way, Rossi wasn't just a cybersecurity drone."

She turned away, paced.

"He was born in Rome, worked in Rome, started his family there. In November of 2025, a group of humanitarian aid workers were bringing in supplies—food, water, medical supplies. A unit of paramilitary ambushed them, killed every one of them, stole the supplies."

"I've read about that, yes. It was a turning point. Support and sympathy for the revolutionaries dried up. It's known as—"

"Massacre of Hope. Hope was the name of the humanitarian organization. I read it just a bit ago. The Underground helped track down most of the killers. It took months to track them and bring them to trial. And most of those were executed for war crimes."

She turned back. "This could come from that. Rossi worked for the Underground. He might have helped hunt them down. And this is payment for that."

"The dots connect. It's a straight line."

"I'm going to follow it. In Paris, another massacre—civilians, slaughtered during a peace march right after the first of the year—2026. In London, the bombing of Dominion's secret HQ in May. All contributed to the end of the wars, and fit the time period I'm looking at.

"We can shut down here. I can follow it on regular equipment."

"And the HQ in Rome?"

"I'll push on that if I need to. I had questions, now I've found these major incidents. I can talk to Feeney, Whitney. I still want to talk to Summerset. Ivanna could be a better source."

"I left him a memo."

Summerset found the memo when he came in the house. As habit, he used the house comp.

"Are the children at home?"

He never asked for their location, as that violated their privacy.

Affirmative.

Before Summerset stepped back, Roarke's voice came through.

Welcome home. I hope you enjoyed your day. The lieutenant would like to speak with you when you get in, as a case she has may be tied to the Urbans in Europe. I suspect she'll work near to midnight if you get in by then.

Eyebrows arched, a frown deepening, Summerset looked toward the stairs. The Urbans was an area of deep pain, and strange glory. And nothing he wished to discuss. Particularly since he'd planned to brew some tea and end his day off with a book he was currently enjoying.

But there was duty, and he had to admit, curiosity with it. So he walked to the stairs, and up. Since he couldn't imagine he had anything he could—or would—tell her that would apply to a murder in 2061, he expected the conversation would be brief.

As the majority of their conversations were.

When he stepped into her office, he saw the empty command center—and no cat, who would be wherever they were. Thinking Roarke had talked her into sleep—or something more intimate—earlier than expected, he started to step out again.

Tomorrow would do.

Then he saw the board.

There was pain, sudden and sharp. Shock rushed behind it, just as searing.

And decades fell away in an instant.

Chapter Seven

"JUST ANOTHER HOUR. MAYBE TWO," EVE SAID AS THEY WALKED BACK TO her office. "The killer could be the son of one of the people Rossi helped hunt. Or hired by one of them who didn't get a death sentence. I'm damn sure he's a pro."

"And may be so good at it that his face doesn't find a match. But so good at it, he leaves your card? Drawing you into this?"

"It's stupid," she agreed. "Stupid and risky, but he wants the challenge, the hunt. I can't say why—maybe Mira will figure it. And yeah, I need to find out. I may not be able to put a name to him—yet—but I have to know who he is."

"Not only for Rossi." Roarke understood. "But because he intends to kill again."

"Seven times more. So—"

She broke off as they turned into the office.

Summerset stood, back to them, facing the board.

"Finally. Listen, I just need you to give me some basic—"

She broke off again when he turned around. When she saw his face.

He had, to her eye, a cadaver's face at the best of times. But now? With all the color leached out of his face, with his dark eyes full of grief, he looked like a victim.

Roarke moved quickly.

"You'll sit. Sit over here now. I'll get you some brandy."

"Yes, a brandy if you will."

As Roarke led Summerset to the sofa, Eve followed.

"You knew him. You knew Giovanni Rossi."

"Eve, a moment." Roarke snapped it. "He's dead pale. He's in shock."

"Shocked, not in shock," Summerset qualified. "Yes, I knew him. A friend."

The cat leaped on the couch, moved into Summerset's lap. He stroked Galahad, gently, his grieving eyes on Eve's.

"I knew him when . . . we were young. Why was he in New York? I don't understand."

He took the brandy Roarke gave him, and his hand shook slightly as he lifted the glass.

A victim, Eve reminded herself. You handled a victim differently than a source.

"He didn't contact you?"

"No. No. I haven't heard from him in . . . nearly twenty years? I'm not sure now. Retired. I know he retired."

"From?"

His hand steadied as he sipped again. Something more than grief came into his eyes. "His work."

"Don't bullshit me on this. I've uncovered enough to know he worked covert ops, probably for AISE, out of a cybersecurity company front. I know he worked for the Underground during the Urbans. And the gas that killed him came from that era."

"Phosphine, so I saw. It was banned from use as a weapon even then. And still there were some."

"You worked with him?"

"I was a medic."

Before Eve could slap back at that, Roarke murmured to her, "Easy. Summerset, you can't protect him now. Eve needs to know, whatever you can tell her. His family needs to know who did this to him."

"His family." Now it was fear that shot out of him. "He has a wife, children, grandchildren. They have to be protected."

"This isn't about his family. It's about his team. And Jesus Christ, were you part of that team?"

"I was a medic." Then he shut his eyes. "Old habits die hard. I was a medic," he repeated, "and worked with Gio, and others, for the Underground. In the last few years of the wars, we made a team of twelve. The Twelve, each with our skills, our purpose. We made a unit, forged a bond of the sort nothing, I think, but war can forge."

"What did he do? Rossi?"

"His work was cyber and communications. In the last few years we had a base, deep below a church. Fully equipped and operational."

"Why Wasp? Code name?"

"We only referred to each other by code names. This was our protocol. He was Wasp, as he could find his way through any crack, and sting before you knew he was there."

"You have all the names. Who was Rabbit?"

"Sylvester Farr—colonel, retired. He was the only professional soldier in The Twelve. The de facto leader. He was about the age I am now, so older than the rest of us. He died peacefully. Fifteen years ago. Nearly sixteen now."

"Hawk."

"Leroy Dubois. A mechanic also skilled with explosives. He died in '26."

"Fawn."

"Alice." His hand reached up, drew the chain from under his shirt, and the wedding ring it held. "Alice Dormer. She was my wife."

Eve knew love, and understood, as Rossi's widow had said, it could and did outlast death.

"I'm very sorry. I'm sorry I have to dredge it all up, but I do. Your wife was with the Underground?"

"Fawn, we called her. She looked so gentle, and was, had been. Gentle, harmless. And she was fierce. She was a teacher, and we met when I came to her school, after the terrorists had bombed it. She was hurt, bleeding, but the weeping was done for her. She wouldn't stop, wouldn't stop digging, and pulled those young, broken bodies from the rubble."

Because he needed it, Eve gave him silence, and waited for him to say more.

"We saved some. And some we saved because she wouldn't stop. Her hands, raw and bleeding, but she wouldn't stop. I fell in love with her while we worked on those innocents, in the blood and the stench and the cruelty, we fell in love."

"What happened to her?"

He stared down at his brandy, then lifted his gaze, steady and even now, to Eve. "She died on May 18, 2026, with Hawk—with Leroy Dubois. Heroes, they died heroes. And they died victims of treachery, betrayed by one of us."

"Who?"

"We called him Shark, and he proved well named. Conrad Potter. He was a cop, one who'd been in the military, in intelligence. He was a traitor who betrayed his comrades for money."

"Was?"

"He died. Not then, and not by my hand. Wasp found him first, and broke some fingers fighting him. Was stabbed, had ribs cracked, but like Alice, he wouldn't stop. Gio wasn't a fighter, not a hand-to-hand man, but he found him first."

Slowly, Summerset sipped more brandy.

"He might have killed Potter. Possibly, though he wasn't a killer. But I stopped him. I thought, this is for me to do. It's for me to kill the man who killed my Alice, killed the mother of our baby. Who killed my friend."

"What stopped you?" Roarke asked.

"Alice. In my mind, her voice in my head. So clear, as if she stood with me. 'Let him live, let him live a long life without his freedom. Let him live with the shame, with blood on his hands. Death's too quick. Let him pay, *moya lyubovna*, every hour of every day of every year.'

"She was gentle and fierce, a teacher who became a warrior. So for her, I let him live. They tried him in The Hague, and there were more war crimes uncovered. He had so many deaths on his hands. He died in prison, but after decades."

"When? When and where did he die?"

"On the third of November, 2056, in the prison they call Five Hells, in Manchester."

She'd confirm that, but moved on. "I need to know about the other six. You and six more are still alive."

"Ivanna you know. She was Panther, for her grace, her cunning. We were young together, and had . . . we were lovers. So very young. The dance took her away, and the war made her another soldier. Clandestine. Ivan, you met."

"Jesus, the let's-screw-with-time guy?"

"He was a young scientist then. Not a soldier, or only when needs must. He had no taste for that. A scientist, an inventor. Brilliant. He was Owl.

"Cyril Snowden, Cobra. Like Giovanni, a cyber. He lost most of his family to the war, in the early days of it.

"Boy." Summerset looked at Roarke. "I trust you'll know this name. Marjorie Wright."

"The actress?"

"A long, successful career. Such talent. And she used it, that talent for becoming, for acting, to fight. She was Chameleon, as she changed into whatever was needed. You may know the name Iris Arden."

"I do," Roarke agreed, a little astonished. "Arden Teas. It's more than tea, but that's what built the fortune. But she'd have been very young."

"Barely twenty. Young, yes, and beautiful. She used youth and beauty, and the doors they and her wealth opened, to gather intelligence. She was Mole. And Harry, Harry Mitchell, who was Magpie. A thief, a very good one. Not as good as some," he added with a smile for Roarke. "A small man, agile and quick. He not only scavenged for whatever was needed and couldn't be provided but slipped and slid into places with good eyes, good ears."

"And you?" Eve asked.

"Fox. Sly, I suppose, and I like to think clever."

"You took an oath—eleven of the twelve? After?"

"How do you know?"

"It's my job to know. Rossi would only tell his wife he had to go to New York, a friend needed him. He'd taken an oath and had to go. And he came here, he came right away. He honored the oath."

"We swore. First, before the mission, an oath, and Potter with us. And again after we lost Alice and Dubois, with their blood still fresh before we set out to find Potter, that same oath. If any one of us needed help, we'd come. No matter where, no questions. Nothing would stop us. We would never speak of it, as I am now, breaking that oath."

"You're not breaking an oath. You're helping me find out who killed your friend. A war hero. A husband, father, grandfather. And, clearly, a spy. Retired."

"We would come—that was our bond, to the lost, to ourselves, to each other."

"So you know where they all are, and they know where you are. How to contact each other."

"Yes, but we don't. I saw them all at the funeral for Rabbit. It's the last we all gathered together, the last we all spoke together of those times."

"Are any in New York besides you and Ivanna?"

"No. I know she speaks, not of those times, but sometimes speaks to Mole—Iris—and to Marjorie. But the talk is of grandchildren and personal things."

"I need their contacts. They need to be contacted now."

"I'll contact them. They know me," Summerset insisted. "Yes, they know of you because they would have kept track of me as I have of them. But they don't know you. If I tell them what happened to Gio, and that who killed him wants their lives, they'll believe me."

"First, take a good look at the board, at the face of the driver."

"I have. I don't know that face. He's not one of us. He would've been young when we were The Twelve, but I'd know that face if he were part of us."

"All right. Make the contacts. I can arrange for protection."

Summerset let out a bark of laughter. "Forewarned, they are protection. Wasp had no warning. He had to believe either Ivanna or I called for him. Your board tells me the driver met him and drove a limo. It makes me think he believed I sent for him. Roarke would provide a limo for my friend. So the killer used me to kill.

"I'll contact the others. They'll come."

"It's not necessary for all of them to—"

"They'll come," Summerset said flatly. "We took an oath."

"They'll stay here." Roarke flicked a glance at Eve, watched her struggle with it, then shrug. "This house is secure, as you know. They'll be safe, which is Eve's concern, and yours. And they'll be accessible—to the lieutenant. We have more than room enough."

"I'm grateful—"

"Don't." With some heat, Roarke cut Summerset off. "Don't say 'grateful' to me. I wouldn't be here without you. Use my office, with the secure line engaged. Talk to your friends, and we'll arrange for their travel."

"That's best." Eve nodded at that. "Keep the travel off the radar. The killer might expect it, but he won't know when. They should cover the departure and arrival, and—"

"Lieutenant, we spent years in espionage. They know what to do. Old isn't feebleminded."

"Rossi wasn't feebleminded, and he's dead."

"He had no warning," Summerset insisted. "And no reason to doubt. He would have been worried for me, or Ivanna." Carefully, Summerset got to his feet. "I'll contact them, all of them, and make the travel arrangements. See rooms are ready.

"It helps to have duties, a purpose," he said before Roarke could object. "I was shaken, but I have my balance now. I know you, Lieutenant, will hunt the killer of my friend. And you'll find him. I'm grateful."

"Don't say 'grateful' to me when it's my job."

"It's not a job, but a calling. I know callings."

He walked away, into Roarke's adjoining office, shut the door. The red light, securing it, blinked on.

"I'm going to need to talk to him again, about all of this. Pull out details."

"Not tonight."

"No, not tonight."

"I want them here, Eve. I want him to have the comfort of that. I know it's an imposition."

"No, no, you're right. Safe, accessible. He's got plans, Roarke."

She rose, walked to the board. "He has a plan in place for every one of them. How do you kill a fox?"

"They hunted them, riding on horses, with dogs giving chase, catching the scent. Barbaric kind of sport."

"A chase. Maybe."

"Or a trap. Trapping them. You think the method is connected to the code name."

"Possibly. I need to get the other seven on my board."

"I'll help you with that." He got up, went to her, took her hands. "Then you'll call it for tonight. We'll have a houseful tomorrow. And you'll have these very capable hands full with interviews, I suspect."

"Right. I can't keep this contained, just the three of us and the ones coming in. I have to report this to Whitney, I have to give Peabody the details. And I'm going to need to talk to Mira."

"He'll understand, and if he doesn't, he'll have to accept it."

"You didn't know."

"I knew he'd probably done some covert work during the Urbans, but it wasn't something he chose to talk about. I knew he'd lost his wife during the wars, but not precisely how. I knew she'd been a teacher, but not that she'd worked with the Underground."

"He's going to need to tell me more."

She scrubbed her hands over her face, then shoved them back through her hair. "This is hard on you. Seeing him take this kind of hit's hard on you. It's going to get harder. I'm going to make it harder. So . . . apologies in advance, I guess."

"He's on that kill list."

"Yeah. Gotta be."

He stroked a hand down her cheek. "You'll make it harder, because you'll do everything you can to keep him from being checked off that list. Him, and the others he worked with, fought with. I'll likely have some reactions to your methods."

She actually smiled a little. "You think?"

"Apologies in advance."

"Let's get this done, get some sleep. Tomorrow's going to be a hell of a day."

That night, no one slept well in the house Roarke built.

Once again, she woke before dawn, and woke alone. But for the cat who curled at her back.

"Time display," she ordered, and stared at the numbers on the ceiling: 5:12.

She could try for another hour, but it wouldn't happen, so why bother? Far from rested, she called for lights—fifty percent would do until coffee.

With coffee, she stood at one of the bedroom windows waiting for the jolt to wake up her body. Her mind was already up and running.

Who killed Giovanni Rossi? Who intended to kill six others? Had Conrad Potter had a protégé? A relative, a lover? One who waited decades to strike?

It made no sense. Rossi, and the others, had lived their lives, built careers for those decades while Potter sat in a cage. They'd made families and homes while they'd slipped into middle age, and some to beyond that.

And put, as much as anyone could, the blood and battle in the past.

And was that the point? To wait until it was all distant, almost like another life? When *this* life was precious?

When guards were down?

Rossi's certainly had been.

Was it that best-served-cold business? she wondered.

She downed the coffee, then went in to shower.

Let it simmer, let it cook, let it brew.

The driver/killer. Middle to late fifties. No match on face rec. A pro. Another agent?

There, the smirk bothered her. Why hold up the card, why draw attention? The arrogance of it didn't read pro or covert agent.

A dozen questions, what seemed like inconsistencies ran through her mind as she stepped out of the shower, into the drying tube.

The through-line came clear, she thought as she grabbed the robe—short, silky, and scarlet.

A team of twelve, and one turned traitor. His actions caused the deaths of two of the twelve. And you could call it murder. Now nearly four decades later, another murder, another of the team of twelve.

Her card stuck between the fingers Rossi broke fighting the traitor. Through line clear there, too. Summerset's wife to Summerset to her.

She went out and into her closet. Thinking hell of a day, she grabbed black trousers. She started to reach for a black shirt, sighed, then pulled out a tank in what she thought of as a faded sky blue. It justified, to her mind, the black jacket.

After dragging on the trousers, the tank, she studied her half a million boots.

"You might go with navy."

Her hand slapped for the weapon that wasn't yet there. Then her heart settled back in place as she turned to where Roarke leaned against the doorjamb.

"Jesus, Roarke."

"Navy would play off the black and work well with your shirt."

"Fine. I only have six dozen navy boots."

He stepped in, crossed over, took a pair. Eve turned them over, studied the pristine soles.

"Make that six dozen and one."

He chose a navy belt, offered it.

His suit wasn't navy, wasn't black, but some rich color between. And made his eyes fire.

"You're up early," he said as she slipped the belt into the trousers' loops.

"Not as early as you."

"You didn't sleep well."

"Did anyone?"

"Not likely. Summerset has the travel information."

"I need that."

"He copied you, so you'll have it. They'll all be here by late afternoon."

"All of them, just like that?"

"Yes."

She put on the boots. She didn't think they fit like a glove—feet weren't hands, for God's sake. They fit like boots. Excellent boots.

She carried out the jacket, set it aside, then strapped on her weapon harness.

"I want to talk to Summerset before I go in this morning. I need more details on the incident that killed his wife and Dubois. I read about the explosion—the Dominion HQ, a lot of munitions, equipment, supplies, personnel inside. According to history, the hit was considered a major Underground success, and a turning point, again major, in ending the conflict in Europe."

"But that doesn't tell the story."

"No. Where was he? Where was Potter, and the rest of the team?"

She should've pushed him there last night, she thought. But she'd pulled back. He'd looked ill, so she'd pulled back. And couldn't do that again.

"He's up. I doubt he slept. We could breakfast now, the three of us, in your office."

He waited a beat, then one more.

"Is there any problem with me being there when you talk to him?"

"No. Over a meal just seems . . ." Unofficial. The cop wife, the father figure victim, and Roarke between. "You're probably right. It'll save time. And you weren't thinking of time as much as making him comfortable."

She put on her jacket, met his eyes. "I'm going to make him uncomfortable, Roarke."

"You are, yes. And that can't be helped, can it?"

"It can't. I don't want him leaving the house today. He won't like that."

"Oh well, he won't, not a bit. There will be things he'll want to see to, to prepare for his friends. I'll see they're done and he stays home.

"I can help with this." Eyes on hers, Roarke put a hand on her arm. "I intend to help with this. You need to let me."

"Like I could stop you if I wanted to. And I don't. Ask him to come up."

When they started out, the cat—obviously expecting the usual routine—looked puzzled. Then followed them out.

"I'll see to breakfast."

Eve just nodded. Food wasn't high on her list.

"Keep the coffee coming," she said, and walked to her board.

All those faces now. The actress, the heiress, the thief. And the scientist, the e-man, the dancer.

Then the dead.

Teacher, mechanic, soldier, e-man.

Traitor.

Because it pulled at her, she studied Alice Dormer's ID shot. A pretty blonde with delicate features. Quiet blue eyes, a generous mouth.

She looked, Eve thought, more like a woman who'd bake cookies on Saturday morning rather than one who'd fought and died in war.

Where would Roarke be, she wondered, if Alice had lived? Would Summerset have taken his daughter to Dublin to raise? Would he have been there to save a brutalized, beaten boy, given him a home, a life, a chance?

No way to know.

She turned away when Roarke brought out domed plates.

It did no good for him to know she wondered. It did no good to wonder. It had nothing to do with the investigation.

When he went back for a pot of coffee, she put another chair at the table, then opened the balcony doors.

They could all use the air.

As Roarke brought out the coffee, Summerset walked in.

If he looked more cadaverous than usual, she didn't mention it. Sometimes a shot was just too easy.

"I'm going to record this."

He held up a hand. "There are things you'll ask, about me, background, and so on, I won't speak of on record. I have many reasons," he added, and looked at Roarke.

And Roarke between, she thought again.

"We'll start with that, no record. But then we go on, assuming you want what I want. To identify, capture, and charge the person responsible for Giovanni Rossi's death. To prevent that individual from taking more lives."

"I want what you want."

"Then sit," Roarke ordered. "The pair of you."

He removed the domes himself, then poured the coffee.

Chapter Eight

"When did you get to London? You're not from there," she said when he frowned. "Not from England, not from Ireland. Eastern Europe. I can hear it."

"Yes. There was war. It took my father, my brother. It took my mother's heart, and then her life. I lived, and wanted a different life, so I took the name Kolchek. There are reasons that aren't important to you, for this.

"With those papers, with that name and three years added to my age, I traveled for a time. I was young, clever, angry. In time, the anger faded."

Very precisely, he cut into the omelet on his plate. Eve already knew Roarke had loaded it with cheese and spinach.

"I studied medicine—traditional and holistic. And I made my way to London. I thought to . . . insert myself in King's College, obtain a medical degree."

"Insert yourself?"

He moved a shoulder, elegantly—and it occurred to her that Roarke often made the exact same gesture. "I had certain skills. Why not use them to gain entry to such a prestigious institution? I began there, learned there, started a life there.

"And then war came. Slowly at first. Insidious if you will. Rumbles and dissent, anger, distrust, and more anger. Some had too much, some too little. Some demanded all believe what they believed. Some were from somewhere else, and had no business living, working, breathing, so were demeaned, defiled, attacked.

"It grew and it spread, and the violence erupted until cities were war zones."

"You served as a medic."

"Yes. Ivanna had come to London with her husband and their little boys. And they were caught in the violence. He was killed, and she was recruited by the Underground. And in turn, she recruited me. And I brought Alice into it. Not at first—at first Alice took in Ivanna's children. They were mixed race, and so young. Alice hid them until Ivanna could get them away, to safety."

"But she stayed in London? Ivanna?"

"The war had spread, from Europe to the Americas, beyond. Where and when would they be safe if we didn't stop this hate, this violence?"

"I'm not criticizing her."

He took a breath, then nodded. "No, who'd understand better what it takes to hold back the blood? After the children were away, Alice—she was also clever—she understood what we did, and wanted to take part. We married, and she took part. Then Marjorie, then Cyril, and so on. And we were twelve. We were The Twelve. And in those early years of the twenties, you would say elite covert operatives, given a great deal of autonomy."

"I'm recording now," she said, and he nodded.

"And Potter, Conrad Potter? When did he join your team?"

"In late 2021. He made the twelfth. He had worked in intelligence before, had been in the military, was a police officer. Skilled, experienced. And to my everlasting regret, trusted."

"What happened the night you destroyed the enemy headquarters?"

"We were two teams, as the mission had two parts. Magpie had discovered this HQ when scavenging, and scouting. Mole had learned about a prison where many were being held—some would be transported, others executed."

He paused, ate some omelet. "Most executed, no doubt, as Flame—a small radical group who wanted to burn it all down—had joined with the larger Dominion. They joined, we believed, as the tide was turning. They were losing, and their counterparts in North America had already lost.

"The prison was in Whitechapel. Alice and Hawk would set the explosives in the tunnels of the HQ, get clear, then set them off. Magpie and Shark—Potter—would serve as lookouts and backup. Both Rabbit and Cobra would remain at our HQ for communications. The rest of us would hit the prison. We would wait for the signal, the explosion, and go in."

"What went wrong?"

"Shark left his post. We learned during the trial that he had stockpiled weapons, money, papers. He went in, after Alice and Hawk. He intended to kill them both, take the remote, he'd get clear, set off the charges, vanish. Helped in that escape by alerting the enemy of our plans to take the prison."

He paused, cleared his throat, sipped some water.

"He missed a killing shot with Hawk, and as Hawk tried to fight him off, Alice opened her comms so we heard what was happening. But Hawk, already wounded, already dying, couldn't fight him off. Nor could Alice for long. It was all so quick, as we were rushing back. She made the decision—and he must've seen it in her eyes because he ran."

"She set off the charges."

"Yes. We had a child. We planned to wait until after the war, but we had a child. I know she thought of our child, and she ran after him, but couldn't get clear. And she pushed the remote.

"He'd gotten clear enough, Potter. Injured, but clear enough. Magpie ran to the tunnels. He called out to us, told us which direction Potter had taken, and that he was bleeding. But he'd heard Alice running, and hoped . . . He found her, and pulled her out, but . . ."

"I'm very sorry."

"Yes, of course." He cleared his throat. "It turned the tide, turned back the tide of blood, that night in May 2026. Alice turned the tide. Within a few months, it was over but for a few stubborn pockets, and many of those pockets contained cops and politicians. But people began to rebuild, and to walk on the streets without fear again, children played in parks again."

"And the nine left took an oath."

"We'd been betrayed, not for ideology, you understand? Not for convictions, however wrong. But for money, for the desire to live a life of ease built on corpses. So we swore an oath of loyalty on the sacrifice of those who'd fallen. No matter when, no matter where, if one needed help, the rest would come and give it."

"You went to Dublin."

He arched his eyebrows, looked at the recorder. Eve shut it off.

"I went to Dublin with my daughter, as Kolchek. Alice's grandmother had come from Dublin, and it was Alice's wish to take Marlena to Ireland when there was no war. There was no place for me in London any longer. We lived quietly, a decent enough flat I could afford. After so long, quiet was enough.

"Then, years later, I found a young boy, half beaten to death in an alley. And things changed again. Having this boy—a very angry boy—disturbed the quiet I'd lived in and with for too long. He didn't know it, but I needed the boy as much as he needed me.

"When I killed the man who beat the boy near to death, I did it to save him and my daughter. But it also reminded me I'd had a purpose. I found it again. I found myself again."

"What's on the recorder I have to share with my partner, my commander, with Mira, with whoever assists in this investigation. What's not on it stays here."

"I'm grateful. You can toss gratitude aside," he said before she could speak. "But I'll still give it."

"You have a file on Conrad Potter."

His eyes flickered, then he moved his shoulder again. "Yes."

"I need a copy. It's going to be more detailed and informative than official channels. Did he have a family?"

"No. An only child, and his parents dead by the time he joined the team."

"Lovers?"

"Of course. But none that, after his disgrace, his conviction, communicated with him."

"Possibility of a child?"

"None that I know of. He had no fondness for children."

"Friends outside The Twelve? Potential partners, those he conspired with?"

"He gave no names. He had no loyalty, so I believe he would have. It was for money, Lieutenant. The war was slowing, you could see the ending. Another year—and so much less with what was done that night in May. He saw his chance to take what he'd stolen, scavenged, hidden away, and become someone else. Someone wealthy, perhaps important. Most if not all of us would be dead. I've no doubt he had a knife in the back planned for Magpie, and an assassination for Rabbit and Cobra."

"There would only be one, like on the card."

"It would be the most logical, wouldn't it?"

"How much money, what kind of weapons?"

"He never said, he never broke there. We found some things in his flat that made it clear he'd been amassing funds and weapons, and for a number of years, but not where."

"He would be, what, seventy-eight?"

"I believe. He was about the same age as Kolchek."

"You're actually three years younger." Roarke finally spoke. "And never said."

"Four, precisely. Summerset added a year more. They're only numbers. You're a year younger than we thought, and I'm four younger than it says on my ID. But we are who we are."

As it didn't apply, Eve let that go by as she thought it all through.

"I could've fixed that when you took Summerset. I had enough skill for that even then."

"Not worth the bother."

"When he died," Eve put in, "when Potter died, did you go there? To the prison?"

"For what purpose?"

"To see the body. To see the body of the man responsible for your wife's death."

"I had no desire to see him again, dead or alive, and had other duties."

"Okay, I'm going to need to talk to the others, tonight."

"Understood."

"And you'll stay in the house. You don't leave the house."

She all but heard his spine crack.

"That's absurd. I have any number of errands to—"

"You'll give me a list of them," Roarke told him. "I'll see they're dealt with."

Summerset's frown could have called the thunder. "As if you have time for such things. Or the wit to know how to pick out a ripe melon."

"I pay plenty of people who have time for such things, and know how to pick a bloody melon. I'm buggered if you'll end up like Rossi, so you'll stay here."

"I'm as capable of handling myself as either of you, and have been at that a great deal longer."

"Regardless." Roarke's tone, cool and final, drew a deep, hard line. "You'll give me a list, and the errands will be seen to. The boy still needs you. If you love him, you'll do as he asks."

"That's . . . conniving of you."

"It is. And smart." Eve gave Roarke an approving nod. "He's good at pulling out stuff like that, and it works because he means it. Anyway, if you don't do what the boy asks, the cop will put you in protective custody. You won't like it."

She pushed back, rose. "So go make your list. I'm heading into Central."

Roarke rose, put his hands on her shoulders.

"An early start to a hell of a day. Take care of my cop. I need her, too."

"Don't worry. I'm armed and dangerous."

"That you are." He kissed her.

"I'm leaving early and plan to be back early. I want those interviews. Consider yourself under house arrest," she said to Summerset, and left.

"She had to poke that in, I suppose."

Roarke just smiled, sat again. "Have some more coffee," he suggested. He poured. "You'll want fresh flowers for the guest rooms."

Summerset only sighed. "Yes."

"And a ripe melon."

Summerset laughed. "Actually, yes. Two. And more. It will be a long list."

Eve texted Peabody on the way downtown. It was still shy of seven, but if her partner wasn't up and moving, she'd just have to get up and moving.

> Heading downtown now. I have a lot of new data. Report in asap. Need to brief you and write up this report before my consult with Mira.

She didn't add if Whitney wanted an oral report before she finished her consult with Mira, Peabody needed to give it.

No point giving her partner the jitters this early in the morning.

And while she consulted with Mira, Peabody could start deeper runs on the remainder of The Twelve.

Possibly one of them had been in league with Potter. If not, possibly one of their contacts, sources, lovers, ex-lovers, family members.

And she wanted to contact the prison, satisfy herself there.

He'd been a cop, a treacherous, dirty cop. Maybe he'd come into the team already dirty. Maybe some of his cop friends had been dirty—and part of this.

Sometimes it was just for money, but she wondered.

Why plan to kill the entire team? Easier ways, again, easier ways. Less risky, less destructive.

New York was awake.

She imagined the trio of street LCs she'd spotted on her way to the crime scene the morning before sat in the all-night deli. Night shift workers probably had their blackout shades down, and the day shift was reporting to work, or headed that way.

Some of them rode on the maxibus that farted to a halt at a stop to pick up more.

She caught the sweet and yeasty scent from a bakery that probably had fans blowing that temptation out to the sidewalk.

Because who could resist?

She wondered how you knew a melon was ripe, then shoved that away.

Summerset would stay home, safe behind the gates. He might've gone against her orders, but he'd do as Roarke asked.

Because there was love.

So one worry off her list. She'd check off more when she knew the others were safe in the house behind the gates.

Because one of them was slated to be next. She had no doubt of that. And he wouldn't wait long.

He might have wanted them all in New York, and she'd helped accommodate him there. But behind the gates, the walls, the security.

And if one of them turned out to be part of this, she'd root that out.

She pulled into the garage at Central and headed straight up.

Bring Feeney in—yes, she wanted to do that. But to get things in place first. Her board, she needed that visual. Her book, that documentation. And she needed to write it all out in detail.

Kolchek? She could let that slide. If for some weird reason that crossed into this? She'd find a way. But she couldn't see it.

She went into her office, to the coffee. And with it, began to update her board.

When she sat to do the same with her book, she heard Peabody coming.

"I got here as soon . . . whoa, that's a lot more. Who are— Hey, that's—ah—Marjorie Wright. Two-time Oscar winner. Not a suspect?"

"No, one of your spies. Urban Wars era."

"Holy shit, really? She looks so elegant, and . . . Why is Summerset on there? Is that an ID of him from back when, too? Because he was like dashing. And— Holy shit!"

Peabody's eyes popped wide, and her jaw dropped.

"Summerset's a spy? He was one of the group?"

"You should pack away the 'holy shits' for now because you'll run out of them. These are The Twelve, or were. I've added the code names they used."

"Summerset was Fox. I can see that. You just don't think someone you know could be a spy. Which is part of the deal, sure, but . . . Wow."

"Alice Dormer, Fawn, was his wife."

"His—oh God, oh jeez. That's just really awful. She was so young. I guess I never thought about her being so young. So pretty."

"This is the man responsible. Conrad Potter—Shark. Responsible for her death, the death of Leroy Dubois—Hawk. He was tried for war crimes, and spent over three decades in a prison in the UK. He died five years ago. But there's no way he's not responsible for Rossi.

"Get coffee, take my chair. I have a lot to tell you."

"Did he have family? Potter. An accomplice. Maybe somebody he worked with who went inside for a while, but was released?"

"All good questions. I'm going to start at the beginning. Summerset recognized Rossi."

She worked through it. Even for Peabody she left out Kolchek, and details on Summerset's background that didn't directly apply to the investigation.

Roarke would have called it a matter of respect. She preferred thinking of it as keeping a deal.

"She was a teacher. Sorry," Peabody said. "I can't imagine what it was like for her. For him, for any of them. Being part of something like that, and having someone you trusted, a partner really, turn on you. And he was a cop. It shouldn't make it worse, but it does."

"It does," Eve agreed.

"I'm surprised he lived long enough to stand trial."

"He ran, he hid, but not fast or far enough. Rossi got to him first. And broke these two fingers fighting him."

Eve held up the index and middle finger.

"Where the killer put the card, and the message. It all ties in. But Potter's dead."

"I'm going to contact the prison, get more details on that. Summerset knows the date. November 3, 2056. He contacted the survivors. They're coming to New York today. They'll all be in, at the house by this afternoon."

"*Your* house?"

"It's secure, as secure as it gets. I need to report to Whitney. I need to write this up, send the report to him, to Mira. Then meet with him, consult with Mira."

"What do you want me to cover?"

"Take them one at a time, do deep background. You're going to run into blocks during the Urbans, and some bullshit that'll be cover."

"Summerset, too?"

"No, I've got him. I'd say it's unlikely—but unlikely's not good enough—any of them were working with Potter. Knowing more about them, even small details, will help us with the interviews."

"Us?"

"Until we've got more solid, they're suspects. Low probability, but we interview them with that in mind. Potter never flipped on anyone, so very low on the probability. We'll make it zero."

"I get to interview spies!" With obvious delight, Peabody pressed her hands to the side of her head. "I love my job! I freaking love it!"

"Then go do it. Wait. What time is it in England?"

"Ah . . ."

"Never mind, I'll look it up."

"No, I've got it. It's right there with Scotland, and we have to time it when we touch base with McNab's family. It's, ah . . ." She checked her wrist unit. "Maybe twelve-thirty-ish. I could be off an hour either way."

"At night?"

"No, the other way. They're ahead of us. It's afternoon there."

"Stupid, but currently convenient. Start the background checks. Feed them to me as you get them."

Alone, Eve sat and looked up the prison. It came clear why they called it Five Hells, as it had five buildings. Old stone buildings with guard towers, high walls. Electronic gates and steel doors that looked anachronistic against a place that struck her like it might have held dungeons, torture chambers.

A quick scan of its history told her no dungeons, but they'd had a permanent gallows until the mid-twentieth century.

"Harsh."

She found the name of the warden, and started her struggle through red tape. After a few redirects, two full scans of her identification, verification of same, she shoved her way through to Nial Meedy.

He looked to her eye as stiff and anal as Summerset, in a black suit, a tightly knotted tie. He had patchy gray hair around a thin, pinched face. Pale blue eyes looked back at her, clearly showing both annoyance and impatience.

"Lieutenant, how can we help the New York Police and Security Department?"

"I need information on an inmate. Conrad Potter, life sentence for various war crimes during the Urban Wars."

"Our facility houses six hundred and forty-eight inmates, and a number from that era of conflict."

"At this time, I'm only interested in one. He reportedly died in your facility on November 3, 2056."

"If you're implying negligence or malfeasance—"

"I'm not," she interrupted. "I simply need the details, as they may have some application to a murder investigation in New York."

"I hardly see any application."

Yeah, as stiff and anal as Summerset.

"Conrad Potter was responsible for the deaths of two Underground agents, part of a team he worked with during the Urbans era. He was tried and convicted and imprisoned for those crimes and others. Another member of that team was murdered in New York the night before last. I'm primary. The killer left a message which referred back to that era, with the code names of the other agents."

"I hardly see—"

"I would like information on the man responsible for the deaths of those two agents, as it may apply to the death I'm investigating.

"Got a computer, Mr. Meedy?"

"Certainly."

"Maybe you could take a minute and look him up. I could, if necessary, go through Homeland, Interpol, MI5 or 6, whichever, but that's a lot of time and trouble for both of us."

"One moment, please."

He snapped it out, then put her in a holding pattern.

Hissing between her teeth, she got up, got more coffee. Sat again. Drank some.

Meedy came back on.

"Your information is correct. Conrad Potter, housed in this facility since August of 2026, died on November third of 2056 from gliomatosis cerebri, previously undetected."

"And what is that, exactly?"

"A brain tumor, Lieutenant. It's noted in his file he refused any and all cancer vaccines, which is his right. He was found unresponsive in his quarters, taken to our surgery, where he was pronounced. His body was scanned, the tumor—one of extensive growth—discovered."

"He was pronounced, on-site. Witnessed?"

"As with any death, I viewed the body, signed off, and as the deceased had no family, ordered the cremation."

"I'd like to speak with the prison surgeon regarding the death."

"He was attended by Dr. Martin J. Pierce. Dr. Pierce is no longer on staff."

"Why?"

Meedy let out an audible sigh. "He resigned and relocated."

"Where?"

"You appear to be grasping at straws, Lieutenant. I don't have that information, nor any need for it."

"Okay, how about when? When did he resign and relocate?"

Meedy didn't grind his teeth, but Eve could tell he wanted to.

"One moment."

She played it out in her mind as she went into another holding pattern.

"Dr. Pierce left our staff on November twenty-first of 2056."

She thought: Son of a bitch. "The ashes. Where are Potter's ashes?"

"For pity's sake! Buried, of course. We're not heathens. Unclaimed remains are buried."

"I need them dug up, transported to the lab in New York."

"Lieutenant, I've been patient with your odd line of inquiry, but—"

"No, you haven't, not especially. But I don't care about that. I care about making damn sure Conrad Potter is dead. We can get DNA."

"I have neither the authority nor the inclination to exhume remains for such a tenuous reason. I suggest—"

"I do. I've got the inclination, and I'll get the authority. You'll hear back from me."

She clicked off, sat for ten seconds as it fell into place for her. Then contacted her connection at Interpol.

Inspector Abernathy looked both surprised and a little pleased. She recalled he'd been a stiff one, too. But he'd loosened up considerably by the time they had Cobbe in custody.

"Lieutenant Dallas, what an unexpected surprise. How—"

"Listen, no time for small talk. I'm going to run the highlights. You have to trust me."

"I do?"

"Yeah, you do. I need cremated ashes exhumed and sent to my custody, from the burial site at the prison in Manchester. The one they call Five Hells. Nial Meedy's warden. He's not cooperating."

"This isn't in my purview."

"You can make it your purview."

"And I'd do that because?"

"The ashes are purported to be of a Conrad Potter—life sentence for war crimes, Urbans era. I've got a body in the morgue that tells me those ashes aren't Potter's. I believe I have your war criminal in my city."

"There are checks and balances."

"Yeah, and one of the checks and balances—the doctor who pronounced him—resigned and took off a couple of weeks after he pronounced Potter dead from a brain tumor. One they didn't know he had until he died? I'm not buying it.

"I need the ashes to verify. I'm asking you to find a way to get them to me. It's sure as hell not something I'd ask for unless I needed it. He has a kill list."

She glanced at the board, tried a specific card. "Marjorie Wright's on it."

"Dame Wright? The actress?"

"That's right. She did covert work for the Underground in the Urbans. I imagine you can verify that if you need to."

He said nothing, just studied her for a full ten seconds.

"Let me see what I can do."

"Appreciated. Later."

She got up, paced. It fit. It damn well fit. Not yet explaining who and how the driver connected, but it fit.

She sat again. She needed to write the report, and carefully. She needed to give both Mira and Whitney time to read it and digest it.

And she didn't have a hell of a lot of time herself.

When she'd written it, gave it no more than a cursory check, she sent it off.

She needed thinking time, and couldn't take it.

Instead, she started a search on the prison doctor.

She found a number of individuals by that name, living and dead, adult and child. And a few of those who registered as doctors.

But she found no record of a Martin J. Pierce, doctor, who'd worked at the prison. None who lived or had lived in Manchester, England.

"Because you don't exist anymore. How much did he give you, Pierce? How much to help him fake his death? Enough to wipe out your past, create a new identification, and I just bet, live a damn swanky life as somebody else."

She contacted Feeney. He said, "Yo."

"I need a top-grade search on Martin J. Pierce, a doctor, a prison doctor in Manchester, England. He's wiped off the system, and he'd have done that around November '56 or early '57.

"If you can't find anything, I'll push it on Roarke."

"You trying to hurt my feelings?"

"I need to find the bastard, Feeney."

"That's coming loud and clear. We'll get on it."

"Thanks. Listen, I've got a lot of data on the Rossi murder, the connection to the Urbans. I'll fill you in as soon as I can."

"This Pierce guy in that?"

"I don't know if he goes back to the Urbans, but he's in it now. Can you get somebody up there to do a deep analysis on the security feed from the terminal? On the driver—the face?"

"We haven't hit on that."

"You won't. I want to know if it's fake. A disguise. Prosthetics, masking. He'll have had work done, changed his look, but it's got to be more."

"You got my interest."

"Good. I'll get back to you."

She used the interoffice. "Peabody. Now!"

Her partner came on a run. "I don't have much yet—"

"Later. Contact DeWinter. I need her to stand by."

"She was going to look at the injuries on Rossi, but—"

"I want those, too. I want it all nailed down. But I'm going to send her cremated remains. I need DNA, and as fast as she can get it."

"Whose remains?"

"That's what I need to know. They're supposed to be Potter's. They're not going to be because he's alive and killing in New York."

Once again, Peabody's jaw dropped. "What? How?"

"Read the end of the report I just sent. I've got to get to Mira. Get DeWinter on deck."

"But—"

She waved Peabody off, and rushed out of her office.

Mira would forgive her if she arrived late. But Mira's admin would make her pay for it.

Chapter Nine

SHE ARRIVED WITH FORTY-FIVE SECONDS TO SPARE.

The dragon at Mira's gate turned from her comp screen to give Eve a long, cool look.

"Did you lose anyone in the Urbans?"

The admin blinked, frowned. "I did. A brother."

"I'm consulting with Dr. Mira over a case that goes back to the Urbans. Not here, in Europe, but—"

"It doesn't matter where." She tapped her earpiece. "Lieutenant Dallas is here. Yes, I will. Go right in."

Mira sat at her desk. The department's head shrink, top profiler, and all-around smart woman wore a silky suit in what Eve thought they called turquoise. Her rich brown hair fell in soft curls, a new style. Eve spotted little coral drops at her ears that matched the trio of strands around her neck.

With her soft blue eyes still on her screen, she lifted a hand.

"I'm reading your report a second time. It's fascinating, and tragic. What a horrible loss, in a horrible way, for Summerset."

"Yeah. This dredges it all up again, but . . ."

"No choice. And to be betrayed in this way by a kind of brother." She turned in her chair, looked at Eve. "A man you believe may still be alive."

"I take out the 'may.' It's what clicks for me."

"I understand why. And ask why did he wait so long?"

"I'll ask him when I find him. I figure maybe he didn't find someone corrupt enough to help him. Maybe it took him that long to figure out how to get out. The warden, who's a pain in the ass, says he viewed the body, signed off, ordered the cremation and burial of the ashes."

"You doubt that?"

"Not really. He's a CYA type. But—you're a medical doctor—aren't there ways to simulate death? Especially to a lay person, and one who probably didn't look too close."

"Yes, there are. That would require a great deal of trust from the one being simulated."

"What did he have to lose? He likes risk, he goes for the edge. He thinks he's fucking smart."

"He does. Sit." Mira rose, walked on heels the exact color of her necklace to her AutoChef. Eve knew she'd get tea, and maybe that wasn't so bad considering the amount of coffee she'd consumed before nine hundred hours.

"Conrad Potter. An egoist, a sociopath, and one who kills as much for pleasure as gain. As he has no sense of loyalty, he would have named names at his trial. It may have benefited him, and his own benefit is paramount. Intelligent, a skilled liar, a man also skilled in wearing masks, being whoever he needs to be to win. While he worked for the extremist group, Dominion, as well as the Underground, he had no loyalty to either of them. Ideology isn't part of his makeup."

"Whatever got him more."

Mira handed Eve the delicate cup of tea, took her own, and sat in the twin scoop chair.

"And, I'd say, entertained him more. He played both sides, used one against the other, and it amused him. He stole because he could. Funds, weapons, supplies. Looking to the future. His own. Only his own."

"He could've destroyed the other HQ. The Twelve."

"He may have planned to. Things went wrong. But I believe he saw no purpose, no future there. The wars were ending. Those fringes remained. Dominion, with Flame, looked to burn it all down. Why would he want that? Why stockpile funds and so on if there'll be nothing left?"

"So when Magpie found the HQ, when—what is it—Mole located the prison, he decided this was a way out. Destroy the HQ, break Dominion's back, and take out his team at the same time. That works for me."

"It may have worked for him, but Alice Dormer got in the way. She's the hero of the piece."

"He's had five years to get to his money and the rest. They never got that out of him. Years to change his appearance, and skills in intelligence, in covert ops to use again. Just shake the dust off there."

"If so, he likely targeted Rossi first, as Rossi found him first. And hurt him, physically, enough to prevent his escape."

"Broken fingers. My card between them."

"The killer—whether Potter or an agent of his—wants acknowledgment and a challenge. His ego doesn't allow him to consider you'd best him. He'll complete his mission, and then kill you."

Mira sipped her tea.

"Which you've already concluded."

"I've concluded that's the plan. I'll be screwing up those plans."

"I'm depending on it. Don't underestimate him, Eve. The killer is highly intelligent, a risk seeker, yes, but very skilled. He's organized, well-funded, plans carefully. His plans are convoluted, but he enjoys that. Puzzles that take time to solve, add complications for him, but how clever is he? He loves the complications, the superiority of creating them, rather than the quick, clean, and simple kill."

"Who are you profiling? The killer or Potter?"

Mira shifted, recrossed her excellent legs. "It fits both. Or, if you're right, only has to fit one."

"Potter has all the motivation. A vendetta decades in the making. The others lived full lives, could go where they wanted, do as they pleased. He didn't, couldn't. Because they stopped him.

"The way he killed Rossi—the poison gas for Wasp."

"A deliberate choice. The deliberation would appeal to him. An entertaining death for him."

"He needs a place. He'd want something upscale or at least roomy, wouldn't he, after prison?"

"Very likely."

Tiny pieces, Eve thought. Speculative, but tiny pieces.

"I don't know how long he's been in New York, so I don't have a way to whittle down possibilities. He had to have a place to stash the limo. So maybe he has a place with a garage, or rented a garage.

"I know who he is. I know what he is. But it's not enough."

"You hope to learn more from Summerset's teammates."

"I don't know how much they can tell me, but they'll be where he can't get to them. He'll expect them to come to New York. I think. But he wouldn't expect them to come this soon."

"Don't underestimate him," Mira said again.

"I won't. I don't. Summerset said the last time they were all together was for Rabbit's funeral. Wouldn't he assume they'd all show up for Wasp?"

"Very possibly. Are you planning a trip?"

"Maybe. I'm going to delay releasing the body another day. I want DeWinter's report on the old injuries in any case."

"Because you'd rather he come to you, on your ground."

"I don't think he wants to wait too long. He knows the others are smart, experienced, skilled. Rossi didn't have any warning. But he'll know they will."

"Because he set it up just that way."

Eve nodded. "He did. He could've killed Rossi another way. Lots of other ways that wouldn't have tied to him, or the Urbans. He wants them to know he's coming for them."

"And when it's done, for you?"

"Well, it's not going to get done, so he'll be disappointed."

Eve set the tea aside. "I have to brief Whitney. This has been helpful. I appreciate it."

"Keep me in the loop. I'd like to be more helpful if I can."

"I will." Rising, Eve took another moment. "I have no reason to believe any of the others were part of the betrayal. But I'll send you copies of the interviews, if you have time to go over them. In case I miss something."

"I can't imagine you will, but yes, I'll make time." Mira rose as well. "Be careful with this one, Eve. You, Roarke, all of you. Sharks hunt and kill. When there's blood in the water, they don't stop."

"Then I'll have to make sure the only blood in the water is his."

Since the consult with Mira had given her more to think about, she decided to let it sit in the back of her brain until she'd briefed Whitney.

She took the glides, and pulled out her 'link to look at a text from Peabody.

> DeWinter's on deck. I read the report, and I have to use another Holy Shit!

"Yeah, it's worth one." She shoved the 'link back in her pocket and muttered to herself, "Because the arrogant fuck's alive."

"Language!" A woman on the down glide sent her a look that translated to "tsk-tsk."

"Lady, you're in a cop shop."

That got a humph—an actual humph—before Eve reached the top of her glide.

"Yeah, my language really matters when I've got an escaped war criminal killer in New York." She strode toward Whitney's office, and his admin.

"I requested a meet with the commander after my consult with Dr. Mira. Is he available?"

"They're waiting for you." He also tapped his earpiece. "Dallas is here, sir."

The admin just gestured to the double doors.

She walked in not only to Whitney but to the chief of police.

Tibble, tall and lean in his slate-gray suit, rose from his chair when she entered. He was a dark-complected, cool-eyed man who wore his duties as he did his suit.

Smoothly.

"Lieutenant, the commander has briefed me on your investigation, including your latest theories and findings."

"Yes, sir."

He didn't smile at her response, but a hint of amusement flickered. "No doubt you want to keep these details as contained as possible. I assume you'd trust me to keep the lid on."

"Of course, sir. Absolutely."

"Then why don't we all sit down, and you can reiterate for us why you believe Conrad Potter is not only alive but in New York and is your prime suspect in the Rossi murder."

She preferred staying on her feet, but sat as both Tibble and Whitney did.

"The prison warden states that Potter's sudden death was a result of an undetected brain tumor. He states that he viewed the body in the prison's surgery and signed off on the death, approved the cremation."

"You don't believe him," Whitney said. "Do you believe Warden Meedy conspired with Potter in his escape?"

"I believe he viewed the body, signed off, and ordered the cremation. I don't believe the body he viewed was, in fact, deceased. There are medical methods to simulate death. The doctor, Martin J. Pierce, resigned only a few weeks afterward. I can find no record such an individual existed. I strongly suspect Potter bribed Pierce to aid him in faking his death."

"With what?" Tibble asked.

"Potter was reputed to have amassed funds, weapons, supplies before his capture and imprisonment."

"It's difficult to access those from a prison."

"Sir. He had over thirty years to figure out just how to do that. I believe he found a way, conspired with Pierce. With his take, Pierce then wiped his data, his records, his existence, and created another identity."

"It sounds more like a spy novel than reality."

"Potter is a spy, highly trained, highly intelligent and organized. Dr. Mira's profile terms him a sociopath, a skilled liar, and one who believes himself better, smarter, and more skilled than anyone else. A risk taker who enjoys creating complicated puzzles. He needs to win, and he's had decades to plan his game."

"You have a relationship with one of the targets, with a man whose wife Potter killed. Your card was left on the body of the victim. I have to question if these factors might influence your thinking."

She'd known that was coming since Tibble rose from his chair.

"A facsimile of my card, Chief Tibble. Potter isn't as clever as he thinks. Summerset is a target, as are the remaining members of what was known as The Twelve. But he, and they, are valuable sources in this investigation. Facts influence my thinking, as do the opinions and conclusions of the experts I consult. Dr. Mira's profiles of Rossi's killer and Potter line right up.

"In addition, I've asked Captain Feeney to use EDD's resources to find the prison doctor, or to verify that his data was wiped. I've requested Inspector Abernathy, Interpol, to consider the matter of Potter's death and expedite an exhumation of the ashes so that Dr. DeWinter can determine, through DNA testing, if they are Potter's."

Tibble listened silently through the steps.

"You're putting a lot of time, effort, and resources into this single theory, Lieutenant."

"There were twelve, sir. One was a traitor so there were eleven. One died of natural causes and three have been murdered. So there are seven. Seven who fought and risked and sacrificed. He wants them dead, so yes, sir, I will put all the time, effort, and resources as are available to me into identifying, finding, and capturing him before another life is taken."

Tibble nodded, glanced at Whitney. "You were right, Jack, she makes her case, convoluted as it is. You know, I'm not pleased to have a war criminal in my city bent on murder."

"I'm not real happy about it myself. Sir."

"You'll have to get the bastard, Lieutenant. I may have a string or two to pull to get you that exhumation."

"I—" Before she could finish, her 'link signaled, and Tibble gave her the go-ahead.

"It's Inspector Abernathy."

"Take it."

"Dallas."

"Lieutenant. I tell myself this is lunacy, but doubts niggle."

"Are you getting me the ashes?" And she couldn't help it. She stood, began to pace.

"Understand, I've now put my arse in a sling, and I don't care for my arse in a sling."

"Abernathy."

"I spoke with Warden Meedy. He's a bit of a bell-end, isn't he?"

"If that's Brit for *asshole*, yeah, more than a bit. Are you getting me the ashes?"

"I have an order of exhumation. I have to personally witness the exhumation, take possession of the ashes. Which means going to bloody Manchester, so add that to the pile."

"That's great. Gratitude. How long will it take?"

"I don't believe you understand or appreciate the various channels of bureaucracy that have to be navigated to send exhumed human remains from bloody Manchester to New York."

"We've got red tape on this side of the Atlantic, too. When will I get them?"

He only sighed. "I'm already en route. I expect they'll be in the hands of the special courier by six, who will then transport them to New York."

"Is that six over there? With the planet doing the revolving crap? Or real time?"

"I beg your pardon?"

"Never mind." She'd do the math. "I'm going to give you the name and location for delivery. Dr. Garnet DeWinter," Eve began, and gave him the rest.

"She'll need to receive them personally, and have the proper identification and paperwork."

"She will. You know, this is your guy who broke out of your prison over there killing people over here. But I appreciate your help."

"That's generous of you." Sarcasm dripped. "You'd best not be wrong."

"I'm not wrong, and it's going on your record with Interpol that you assisted in the recapture of a war criminal. It'll be worth a trip to bloody Manchester. I'll be in touch."

When she clicked off, Whitney gave her a steady look, and a hint of smile. "Depending on the type of transportation used, the remains should be with DeWinter between four or five this evening. Barring delays."

"I'll inform her."

"My strings, such as they are, won't need to be pulled." Tibble rose. "I'll speak with Dr. DeWinter, and expedite the necessary bureaucracy on our end."

"Thank you, sir."

"I might question the wisdom of bringing all potential targets into your home, but I've been to your home."

"They'll be safe there, Chief. And accessible."

"Make it so. Commander, keep me updated. Twenty-four/seven on this one."

"You can count on that."

"Lieutenant, I know you'll consider no good deed goes unpunished, but when this breaks, when you have him, you'll be required to do media conferences. International media conferences."

Her stomach just sank. "Yes, sir."

He flashed a grin—rare and brilliant. "No good deed."

When he left, Whitney walked to his window. "You made your case in your report, which Chief Tibble read. He needed to see you make it." He turned back. "You're not wrong on Potter."

"No, sir."

"No, you're not wrong. So go get him. Dismissed."

She walked out feeling as if she'd just passed one of those pop quizzes they tortured you with in school.

Then she pushed that aside and detoured to EDD.

Two trips to the circus within about twenty-four hours was almost more than the average system could bear. To keep hers from shorting out, she turned straight into the dull normal of Feeney's office.

He sat at his desk, his brown tie askew—and the small stain on it, Eve suspected, came from the coffee he swigged.

He wore an expression she'd seen on Roarke. Irritated work mode. Pissed-off e-geek.

"Fucking fucker," he muttered, then spotted her.

"Sorry, bad timing. I'll come back."

He lifted his hand, made a sharp—yes, irritated—come-in gesture. "I'm taking five anyway. Fucking fucker."

"I know I dumped a lot on you, so—"

"How the fuck does some prison sawbones know how to poof, and poof clean as fuck?"

So, Eve realized, he'd taken Pierce himself. A matter of pride.

"He had help. I think help from someone with serious skills, and financial backing."

"I tagged that asshole warden. Merry old England, my ass. Guy's a lazy, stuffed shirt prick."

"Yeah, he is."

"But after a couple rounds I got Pierce's HR file, and his prison ID shot. And still can't find the slippery son of a bitch. But I will," he added, then popped a candied almond.

"I dumped a lot on you," she began again, and he shot a finger at her.

"If I need Roarke, I'll pull on him myself. Got that?"

And she knew prickly geek pride when he snarled at her.

"Got it. I want to fill you in on why I dumped this on you. I need to close the door."

She did so, then crossed over to his desk.

"The victim, Giovanni Rossi, was part of an elite team of covert agents attached to the Underground, with their HQ in London during the Urbans. Though I believe he continued his covert work, in Italy, his murder's tied to the first. Back to the Urbans."

"So you figured, and I agree. The gas canister, the method, and all that."

"Right. I learned last night Summerset was part of that team of covert agents. And why don't you look surprised?"

"A little surprised, maybe. But his background's real smooth." Feeney slid the flat of his hand in the air. "Smooth, with just the right amount of little bumps so nobody'd look twice. No fingerprints to show it's been messed with. Roarke's good. So you gotta figure something's there."

"You did a run on Summerset?"

Shrugging, looking mildly uncomfortable, Feeney picked out another almond. "You're moving in with some rich-ass guy—he was pretty much just some rich-ass guy when you did—who's got this other guy doing like a butler thing? Yeah, I'm going to do some checking."

He jabbed a finger at her. "Didn't you?"

"Yeah, but—"

"I'm figuring, since Roarke's not just some rich-ass guy, he told you about it."

"Some of it. He didn't know all of it, either. I'm going to tell you what I can, and where the investigation stands as of now."

"Okay."

She sat on the edge of his desk, and in the shorthand of partners, filled him in.

"I'm going to say I'm sorry, really goddamn sorry, about Summerset's wife. That's a hell of a thing. I'm going to say it's risky bringing all those targets to one place."

"I know it."

"Riskier for them to stay scattered, so I'd've done the same. They're going to know this guy as well as anyone's gonna. Marjorie Wright. Man, I never saw that coming. I had a picture of her taped inside my locker door at the Academy."

"You— Really?"

"Before Sheila," he added, and looked more nostalgic than embarrassed. "A boy's gotta dream. Anyway, I'm going to give your Potter's alive a probability in the high nineties. Can't give you the hundred. You need that DNA."

"I'll take high nineties. The computer gave me mid-sixties, but I didn't have time to run another after I found out Pierce had poofed."

"That'll up it. But comps don't have a gut. Considering, if I don't get a good scent inside the next hour, I'll tap Roarke. But . . . Potter, how old would he be?"

"Seventy-eight."

Feeney shook his head. "The driver, more like mid to late fifties. I don't know if face work can carve off twenty years. Hell, people'd be getting worked on instead of buying food. I got McNab—he wanted a piece of this—and Callendar working on the face. They should be able to detect makeup, face putty, with enough filters and enhancements. But, well, everybody over forty'd be walking around with putty and all that if it takes two decades off.

"A hire's more likely."

"More likely," she agreed. "To do the pickup, show the card, get Rossi in the limo. But Potter would want to do the kill himself. He'd need to."

"Can't argue with that."

"I'll get out of your way."

"I'm going to find this fucker."

"I'd put money on it." She opened the door just as McNab—Callendar beside him—raised his hand to knock.

"Hey, Dallas, good timing. Cap, we need a minute, okay?"

He did his come-ahead, but not sharp and irritated. "What you got?"

They stepped in, McNab's baggies a screaming green, his airboots canary yellow. Callendar's sported a pattern that made Eve think of some mad witch's garden. On Mars. In contrast her kicks were an almost subtle blue, if you discounted the bright orange laces on the left, the candy pink on the right.

"What we got," McNab began, "is hinky."

"What kind of hinky?"

"Maximum smooth hinky." Callendar answered Feeney, and shoved her hands into two of her many pockets. "We started with the standard OCS, added the combined filters, mostly for shits and giggles, then boosted that with some NL beams."

"Good choice. Did you push on F-10—not the F-8?"

"We went up to that."

McNab picked up the e-speak, and Eve tuned it out before her brain collapsed and died.

When the cross-talk became too much to tune out, Eve lifted her hands. "Dumb it down. In the name of tiny baby Jesus, dumb it down for someone outside your species."

"Too smooth," Callendar said.

"I got that. Maximum smooth hinky."

"I didn't mean that. What we're saying is, the face. Too smooth. It's like faces have flaws, right? Or something. A freckle, a blemish, something. But not this guy."

"He's got a few lines, right?" McNab said. "Eye corners, expression lines, but the smooth is there. You can cover the flaws, get me, with enhancements, but we're not detecting any enhancements, or not enough to show."

"We want to bring in Carmine from the main lab."

"Who's Carmine?" Eve demanded.

"Solid tech," McNab told her. "He's mega solid on flesh, face structure with it. Like he's got a way of detecting if you had a nose job or whatever when you were twenty."

"He's not Harvo, Queen of Hair and Fiber," Callendar put in. "But he could be, say, a prince of skin and flesh. It's hinky, Cap, and we need Carmine. You gotta figure the guy had face work, right? He doesn't pop for us, so he changed his face. Carmine could maybe see more what and where, and find the hinky."

"They say they need Carmine," Feeney said to Eve, "they need Carmine."

"Okay." She didn't like spreading it out, but she needed answers. "Pull him in. I've got to get out of here. Anybody hits anything, tag me."

She escaped.

She needed five minutes, just five minutes of absolute quiet in her office, in her own space—alone. Then another five to let all the information, opinions, questions, and conclusions settle in.

Since she couldn't even think about jamming herself in an elevator, she stuck with the glides.

In the bullpen, Jenkinson wasn't at his desk, so no assault by tie. She saw Quilla huddled with Baxter at his.

She looked at him, Eve noted, as if every word out of his mouth fascinated.

Either it did, or she was damn good playing to a man's ego. And Eve wasn't sure which she hoped it was.

Before Peabody could speak, Eve held up a hand. "Unless it breaks this case open, I need ten."

"It doesn't. I sent you two full backgrounds, and I'm finishing the third."

"Good. I need ten."

She went to her office, to the coffee. And drinking, let the quiet slide over her.

She could wish more fieldwork was required, more angles that took her out, put her on the street. Her last major case involved plenty of that. This one? More a head game.

Easier on the boots, she supposed. But the closet fairy always had another pair waiting.

She walked to her window, drank her coffee while she looked out, scanned her view of New York.

"Where the hell are you? You're out there. I know you're out there. And I'll find you."

Chapter Ten

EVE TOOK HER TEN, THEN SAT TO READ PEABODY'S BACKGROUND REPORTS. She'd started with Alice Dormer first, so Eve did the same.

Not a great deal of data there, as Alice's life had been cut so short. And the life she'd lived seemed usual, even ordinary. No mention, none at all, about her work for the Underground.

A London native—no siblings, parents divorced. Her father died in a fire that may or may not have been arson in the months before the Urbans had been termed war. Her mother left London while Alice remained, continued her career as a teacher. And the mother had died of injuries from a vehicular accident just over a year later.

Her data claimed she married, not a man named Basil Kolchek, but one called Lawrence Summerset, and continued to teach throughout the conflict. She gave birth to a daughter in November of 2025. And died in May 2026 from injuries sustained in a bombing.

Nothing about it being Dominion headquarters. Nothing about her setting the charges herself, giving her life to complete her mission.

Peabody had done good work, finding small details—Alice's education, her residences. Even a mention of the bombed school, and her rescue work there.

But her partner found nothing that added a link in the chain to Potter.

She moved on to Harry Mitchell—Magpie—the thief.

She imagined Roarke would find some common ground there. A street kid, a runaway with a father cited for child abuse, a mother with a couple rounds of rehab.

Not as slick a thief as Roarke, she thought, as Harry had done some small time—as a juvenile, and again as an adult—for his choice of career.

He'd had a younger sister, sixteen to his nineteen when he'd done the second stint. Six months for attempting to pawn a stolen ring. The sister had perished while he'd been inside, a victim of stray bullets fired when she'd walked home from her job as a hotel maid.

And there, the story changed. An early release—compassionate reduction—and employment as a supply clerk.

"Bogus, Harry, bogus. The Underground recruited you straight out of prison when you were vulnerable, angry, grieving. You stole and scouted for them while they had you listed as counting inventory and stocking cans of soup."

According to the data, he'd continued to live in London after the wars, as a photographer. And indeed, Peabody had attached a number of his photos starting with the aftermath and rebuilding after the Urbans.

His photography took him all over Europe.

"So you kept your hand in, too."

He hadn't married until the age of forty-eight, when he became the third husband of a woman of considerable means. They lived in London, had a home in the Lake District and a flat in Florence.

At the age of sixty-three, he traveled primarily with his wife, and continued his photography.

"Retired, maybe, or semi. Unless the well-off wife's in the covert business, too."

She turned to the third report when Peabody sent it.

She found nothing in Iris Arden's background—the Mole—to indicate she was anything but a woman born into a wealthy family who'd grown up privileged, entitled, traveled well and extensively with her family.

She'd grown up in a London mansion, with a full complement of staff—private tutors, then public school. Which meant important and private in England for some reason.

Everything pointed to a young, reckless, live-for-today sort. The parties given and attended even while blood splattered.

She'd inherited the family business after the wars, and had, by all evidence, run it shrewdly, expanded it successfully.

Generous to her charities—one of which she'd founded herself. A school, not, Eve realized, unlike An Didean.

She'd married and divorced in her mid-twenties. Then at thirty-four had married again. Was still married to Sebastian Griggs, a portrait artist. The marriage had produced three children, two of whom worked for the family business. The third had begun to make a name for herself as an artist.

"You could've hidden any additional intelligence work, but I think you said enough. Maybe had enough. And there was the family business to deal with."

Sitting back, she shoved her hands through her hair.

When her 'link signaled, she found a text from Roarke:

> No need to interrupt what I'm sure is a very busy day for you. You should know preparations are in place for company. I should be home by three. If you need or want something else in place, let me know, and I'll see to it. Feed my cop.

She had to laugh at the last bit. He never quit. Plus, it couldn't possibly be time to eat again.

Then she glanced at the time. Sighed.

"How the hell does that happen? How the hell did it get to be noon?"

She didn't have time—okay, didn't want to take time—to feed the cop. And now if she didn't, she'd feel guilty. Which was stupid. It was her stomach.

A candy bar was food, but she realized if today of all days she found the Candy Thief had struck again, she might just implode.

Not worth the risk.

She considered, stared at her AutoChef.

"Okay, okay, fine."

She got up, programmed for a sandwich—ham on rye with hot mustard.

Then she sat, took a bite, and answered the text.

> It is busy, and I'll brief on what I know when I get there. I'll try for about three. Peabody with me to meet the company. I'm sure you've seen to everything that needs to be done. And I'm feeding the cop right now.

"There, done."

And taking another bite of ham on rye, got back to work.

She skimmed through Marjorie Wright's background. Early years, middle-class upbringing. Acting career got started when she was still in her teens, and continued—long and storied. Lots of awards, critical praise, blah blah. Some kudos for charity work, emphasis on environmental issues.

A couple of husbands, a couple of offspring.

And during the Urbans, volunteered in food banks, shelters, lent her voice and image to calls for peace.

Not a single hint she was or had ever been part of a covert group.

She already knew Ivan Draski, as she'd hunted him down after he'd killed a woman on the Staten Island Ferry. The woman, the HSO assassin, who'd butchered Draski's wife and twelve-year-old daughter years before.

The mild-eyed, quiet-voiced middle-aged man, the scientist, the inventor of Lost Time—a device he'd destroyed rather than have it fall into HSO's, or any agency's, hands.

She'd come home to find him sitting in the parlor, drinking coffee, petting the cat. He'd come to turn himself over to her.

And in the end, she'd let him go. She'd let him go, told him to disappear, because if she'd taken him in—done what the job demanded—he'd have been dead within hours.

She'd told him never to come back to New York, but he would. For Summerset, for Rossi, for The Twelve.

She'd deal with it.

She moved on to Cyril Snowden—Cobra. E-whiz, a young, gifted cyber expert with his own IT company before, and supposedly during, the Urbans. Age six when parents divorced. Two half-siblings, one from each parent's remarriage.

Beyond aced it academically, she noted, and got himself a scholarship to Oxford, where he also aced it.

Tried to sign up with the military during the Urbans, but was deemed physically ineligible.

"There's bullshit. Recruited. Big brain, more useful underground."

His data listed him instead as an ambulance driver during the conflict.

After, he'd expanded his business. He and his husband of thirty-two years maintained a home in London, but primarily lived in Sussex. Two children, son, age twenty-nine, daughter, age twenty-seven. One grandchild, female, age ten months, through the daughter.

So that was the crew, she thought, and sat back. Those who'd survived.

She supposed they qualified as motley, and spanned from late fifties to mid-seventies.

Now she had to keep them confined, keep them safe. And find the way to use them to locate Conrad Potter.

She heard Peabody coming, and wished she had a few more minutes to sort out her thinking.

"I think I need a minute," Peabody said. "Ivan Draski."

Eve couldn't claim surprise. She'd trained Peabody herself. If the name hadn't clicked, Eve wouldn't have done her job well.

And she damn well had.

"Close the door." She rose. "Take the chair."

Clearly distressed, Peabody shut the door.

"The name kept trying to click, then when I did the background, the scientist, the murder of his wife and daughter, it did. It's a cold case now because we identified him, but we never found him."

"Because I let him go. I didn't tell you at the time, as I didn't see any reason for you to take any blowback, if it came, for my decision. I let him go," she repeated. "Now I'll tell you why, and you'll need to decide if you can respect that decision. Not only because I let him go, but because he's coming back."

"He killed the woman, a paid assassin, who killed his wife and daughter."

"That wouldn't have been enough for the decision I made. Couldn't have been enough. The courts decide that, not us. The system decides that, and we're only part of the system. But in this case, the system would never have held up. He'd have been dead or abducted before it could."

She laid it out, every detail, from the moment she'd walked in and found him in the parlor with Roarke and Summerset to when she'd walked away.

At the end, Peabody looked down at the hands she'd folded on her knee. "If that got out, you'd have been off the force and charged with accessory after the fact. You risked that to save his life. He saved lives on the ferry that day. If that bomb had gone off— He saved lives, then put his in your hands. And you saved his."

She looked up now. "I hope I'd have the courage to do exactly the same."

"It wasn't courage—"

"Oh, bullshit!" Temper sparking, Peabody shoved up from the chair. "It was fucking courage, and integrity. It was the heart of the goddamn job, and it was right! If I hadn't come to the same decision, I wouldn't deserve the badge."

"That's not—"

"You could've told me." Wound up, Peabody kept going. "You could've trusted me."

"Peabody, trust had nothing to do with it. Absolutely nothing. If I didn't trust you, I'd've come up with some bullshit story because I knew the name would click for you sooner or later."

That didn't dull the anger, or the hurt blended with it, in Peabody's eyes.

"You were protecting me, but I don't want that. Standing up for me, having my back, that's different. I'm your partner. It matters. It has to matter."

"It does matter. I'm not going to say you're wrong, but I did what I thought I needed to do at the time. I made the decision, and didn't give you a choice in it. I'm your partner, Peabody, but I was responsible. You weren't. I'm telling you now because, from this point, we're both responsible."

"Good!" The single word snapped like a whiplash. "We're both responsible. That's how I want it."

"Want it or not, that's how it is. According to the law, when we meet with him, you should arrest him."

"Then I guess I've got enough courage, because I'm sure as hell not going to do that. And I'm pissed off you'd think I would."

If knowing she had to deal with Draski again had kindled a headache, Peabody's outrage sent it flaming.

"You can stop being pissed off about that, because I don't—I didn't. But we're partners, and you need to have the choice."

"Good!" A second lash. "Choice made. And you're just—just stupid if you think there's another detective in that bullpen who wouldn't make the same choice. Not for you—or not just—but because they know the heart of the job."

Eve gave it a moment. "I'm not stupid."

"Okay then."

"Have you finished swearing and snapping at—not only your partner, but your lieutenant?"

"I think so." The hot color fury brought to her cheeks ebbed. "Yeah, pretty much done."

"Then let's go meet with this bunch of spies."

Peabody waited until they'd reached the garage.

"Quilla asked to interview me for her school project, about our current investigation."

Eve said, "No," and got behind the wheel.

"I already told her no, that I couldn't discuss with her details of an ongoing investigation. I said she could pick any closed case I'd worked on."

Peabody strapped in as Eve pulled out of her slot.

"She decided on the Francis Bryce investigation."

"Could've figured. Recent, relevant to her, as the victims were teenage girls. Add Jake and Nadine right there with the first victim."

"Mavis said Avenue A's working on Jenna Harbough's music disc. Her parents gave them a lot of what she'd written and recorded in her room, some she'd written but hadn't actually recorded yet."

Bryce took Jenna's life, Eve thought, but he hadn't taken her dream. Avenue A was making sure of that.

"Mavis told me what she'd heard so far is seriously mag and heading for ult," Peabody continued. "She's going to do some vocals on a couple of them."

She should've figured that, too, Eve realized. It was so very Mavis.

"They're establishing a foundation thing in her name, for scholarships. I guess you know Roarke's putting it on his label, and that cut's going into the foundation, too."

"He mentioned it."

"It means a lot to her family. It doesn't bring her back, nothing can. But it gives life to her music, and she wanted that so much. I'm glad Quilla wanted to bring that into her project.

"We got her justice, and they're giving her the dream. When you're a murder cop, it's the best you can get."

"Plus the murderous little shit's doing a couple rounds of life in a cage," Eve added, "and that's the best we can get."

"There is that."

She looked over at Eve. "We're going to get this one, too. Different motives, different methods, different backgrounds. But Potter and Bryce are, in some ways, the same."

"Arrogant fuckers."

"That's the one. So." Peabody butt-wiggled in her seat. "I'm kind of excited about meeting a bunch of spies. You have to be a little bit excited."

"No, I don't. For one thing, they're potential victims. For another, they're friends of Summerset's."

"Well, I am. I mean, imagine the things they've done and seen, and all that while maintaining a cover. Like being a vid star since you were like seventeen. I guess that's not so much a cover as what she is."

"If you fan-geek over Wright, I'll hurt you. I'll seriously hurt you."

"I can maintain. But think about it, we're going to be talking to a famous actress, to a woman who was born dripping rich then runs a global company that's made her more dripping rich, an expert e-man, a former prima ballerina, a guy who invented a device that conquers time. Which we can't really talk about, but he did that!"

"Don't forget the thief."

"Who's a well-respected photographer. And Summerset. I actually know Summerset, and now I know covert agent Summerset."

"Former."

Peabody pulled her shoulders in like a self-hug. "It's frosty. This part of it's mega frosty supreme. You know the tea Mira drinks—you stock it for her in your office AC—it's the dripping-rich woman's tea."

"Of course it is."

Resigned, Eve drove through the gates.

And saw Ivanna Liski walking arm-in-arm with the woman she recognized from the photos as Marjorie Wright.

"Oh wow!"

"I'm warning you, Peabody. There will be pain."

"Which is why I'm getting it out now. You know, since you pulled me into Homicide, I've met famous actors, I'm actually friends with rock stars, a fabulous designer, a bestselling writer and Oscar winner.

"I'd love my job even if that wasn't true, but that part of it is mega frosty *ex*treme. Whee! Woo! Wow! Okay, fan-geeking complete."

"If you don't want to be limping for the next several days, it better be."

Eve parked, got out while the two women strolled in her direction.

Ivanna, who carried a delicate beauty beside the striking glamour of the woman next to her, smiled. Her eyes, a soft blue, looked directly into Eve's as if searching for something.

"Marjorie, our host, Lieutenant Eve Dallas, and her partner, Detective Delia Peabody."

"Marjorie Wright." She stuck out a hand to shake Eve's. "First, thank you for inviting us into your truly magnificent home. Delighted to meet you. And you, Detective."

She shook Peabody's hand in turn.

"Dame Wright. I admire your work."

"Thank you. God knows there's enough of it. I've been around since the discovery of dirt."

"I'll remind you, Marj, I've got a few years on you."

Laughing, Marjorie threw back her head so her mane of red waves swayed like flames in a breeze. "We're a pair of old girls, Vanna." She draped an arm around Ivanna's shoulders as she looked at Eve. "But not ready, by any means, to be put out to pasture."

"We understand you need to speak with all of us. Harry Mitchell and Iris Arden arrived shortly ago," Ivanna told her. "Summerset is showing them to their rooms. The others are expected very soon."

"And I had the pleasure of meeting your unquestionably delicious husband," Marjorie added. "I admire what he's accomplished. And I'm grateful for what I have every confidence you'll accomplish to bring Gio's killer to justice. He was a very good man, a very good friend, and a quiet hero when the world needed them. I'll help you in any way I can."

"Summerset told me he and Roarke have set up . . . I suppose you'd call it an interview room for you. Marjorie and I are at your disposal."

"If you'd give us a few minutes to set up, I'd like to speak to you first."

Ivanna nodded. "I'll be ready when you need me."

Eve went in just as Roarke walked down the stairs.

"Hello, Peabody. Welcome to . . . interesting times."

"I'll say."

"You met Marjorie, I take it, and saw both her and Ivanna outside?"

Eve flicked her gaze up the stairs. "Yeah. Two more in here?"

"Just getting settled."

"You set up an interview room?"

When he crossed to her, he kissed her. Lightly. "You'd need to cloak your board if you used your office. I thought a sitting room on the top floor—quiet, private—might suit better."

"It doesn't have to be formal, but it needs to be professional. Nothing swank."

He smiled and, unable to help himself, kissed her again.

"Come with me."

He went over to the elevator, gestured them both inside.

"Stairs are fine."

"Quicker and simpler in this case. Interview A," he ordered.

"Are you serious?"

"I reprogrammed it, as I thought you'd find it more professional. Or at least amusing."

She tucked her hands in her pockets. "Sort of both."

"I forgot you had elevators," Peabody commented. "The way they're worked into the walls, you don't really see them. Smooth ride."

"We do what we can."

The elevator didn't open into the room, but the wide hall just outside it. Once again, Roarke gestured.

"Take a look. If you want changes, we'll see about making them."

She stepped in. A big room, a wide view of the back gardens, the grove, the little pond.

A room that maybe edged really, really close to swank on her gauge, but didn't go over the top.

He'd brought in a table. Nothing you'd see in any cop shop's Interview A, not with that gleam of polish on actual wood. And the chairs were dark green leather, generously sized. Rather than dull beige walls, these hit creamy. No two-way mirror, but art she imagined he'd personally selected.

It held a sofa as well, a couple more chairs.

She turned to the large wall screen.

"If you need to display anything there, it's now connected to your command center. AutoChef, friggie." He opened a carved cabinet with gracefully curved legs. "D and C unit." Now he pressed a control that had one sliding out of the wall.

"Frost extreme!" was Peabody's opinion.

"And handy as well. Washroom." He gestured to a door. "You can speak with our guests individually or as a group, whatever works for you."

"One at a time for now. A couple more to come, right?"

"Yes."

"Peabody's been briefed on Ivan Draski and my decision regarding him."

"Ah, well then. I did wonder. Will the room suit you?"

"Yeah. Thanks."

"I think you'll find them interesting individuals. I certainly have on this very brief acquaintance. They're grieving, and they're grateful. The bond with Rossi, and each other, it's strong. It shows.

"When do you want to begin?"

"No time like now. Peabody, pull up the files from my office unit. I'll go get Ivanna."

"You'll start with her? I'll go down for her."

"Okay, save me a trip. And, Roarke, keep an eye on the rest of them. Especially Light-Fingers Harry. This place is full of the swank."

He laughed at that. "The bond, Eve. Harry would hardly steal from the home where Summerset lives. Or, if he's still in the game, from the home of a cop."

"And still."

Shaking his head, Roarke started out. "Ah, nearly forgot. Summerset's planning a dinner for tonight."

"Hey, I can't—"

Roarke waved a hand. "I told him he should have tonight, especially, to reconnect with his friends without the cop and the civilian consultant in the mix."

"Okay then, good."

"I'll send Ivanna up."

"It's kind of swank in here," Peabody commented when he left.

"Yeah, yeah."

"Do you want anything on-screen?"

"Not yet. Maybe not at all. We want the option."

"Got it. How do you want to play this?"

"Straight, and we'll find out if she does the same. Informal interview. She's a target, and she's a source."

"Protect the target, mine the source."

"That's right." Eve walked to the AutoChef, programmed coffee. "That's exactly right."

Chapter Eleven

WHEN IVANNA WALKED IN, SHE GLANCED AROUND, SMILED.

"I'm never not in wonder of this house. So many beautiful spaces. Where do you want me?"

"If you'd just take a seat at the table. I need to record this."

"Of course." Slim, graceful, she walked to one of the leather chairs.

She still wore her wedding ring, Eve noted, a thin band of tiny diamonds that caught the light.

"We've got coffee or tea."

"I'd love some tea, thank you."

"How do you take it?" Peabody asked her.

"Just as it comes." Before she sat, she admired the view out the windows. "Yes, always a wonder. I saw Roarke when he was a boy. Well, a young man," she corrected as she sat. "Shortly after Marlena's murder. The grief, it radiated from him. The grief, the guilt, the rage."

"He hasn't mentioned that."

"He wouldn't have seen me, or noticed me if he had. Or remembered me if he'd done either. I was very good at what I did. I thought of recruiting him, such a clever one, so skilled—and the anger can be a plus.

"Thank you," she said when Peabody brought her tea. "But Summerset needed him, so I let him be. I deleted his file."

"You had a file on Roarke?"

"My agency did."

"And your agency?"

"MI6."

"Ms. Liski—"

"Ivanna, please. You prefer Dallas and Peabody, but we all have connections here. Though I still have connections in my former work, I've retired. There are things about that work I can't and won't tell you. They're above your security clearance. But I believe what you'll ask me here won't apply to any of that."

"You were an agent, a field agent, for MI6?"

"That's correct."

"During the Urbans."

"During the Urbans—and before—I was a dancer, at first in Kyiv. I'd left my home, and Summerset. We were very young, madly in love, as you are when you're very young. But I left to dance, and he stayed. So I danced, and it was my life. I believed it had to be. I met Liev, worked with him. And we loved, we married, and had two children. They were my life, though I went back to the dance. I found a balance.

"You understand."

"Yes."

"And the war spread, and it took him from me. I was asked to use what fame I had amassed, the entrée I had to people and places, to gather information."

"For MI6."

"Yes. Initially as an asset, then as an operative."

"Who recruited you?"

"I can't answer you."

She said it smoothly, sipped her tea. Then set down her cup.

"I can tell you I accepted—anger and grief can be advantages. I trained, and I worked, and I danced. I accepted an assignment to work with the Underground. And in turn, I recruited Summerset. He'd come to London to study medicine, and was working as a medic. He had skills, useful skills, and I could trust him with my life. We weren't what you would call partners, but colleagues."

"And Conrad Potter?"

"A police officer, who'd come into that from military intelligence. He passed all the screenings." Now, as grief showed for the first time, Ivanna squeezed her eyes closed. "What did we miss? How and why did we miss it? I can't say for certain. If he had help on the inside, all of our resources never found it.

"I looked," Ivanna continued as Eve let her set her own pace. "Alice was dear to me, to all of us, as was Leroy. But Alice was so dear to me especially. I looked. He was, I believe, what we call a lone wolf. None of us saw through him, and that is my biggest regret."

She leaned forward. "I trusted him. I trusted him with my life more than once. We all did. We didn't see what was in front of us. I thought him cagey, but this was an advantage. I knew him to be ruthless, but the times called for ruthlessness."

She stopped, shook her head. "But he had no loyalty, and no family. If Alice hadn't given her life, he would have gotten away. I have no doubt he'd have killed Harry. It would provide more cover. And then, caught, tried, he never broke. Never said the name of anyone who might have helped him."

"Because there wasn't anyone," Eve concluded. "Or no one of any importance."

Ivanna nodded. "Yes. He had no one. I can't fathom who he persuaded to kill Gio. I can't fathom who would wait so long, and years after Potter's death, to kill again."

"I have that answer. Conrad Potter isn't dead. He killed Rossi himself, and he plans to do the same with all of you."

"That's not . . ." Holding up both hands, Ivanna sat back. The delicacy of her went steely.

"I've lost a step, haven't I? More than one, I see now. Retired, living my quiet life. Of course, of course. He had no one."

The steel stayed in place as she looked at Eve.

"He'd need someone inside the prison. A doctor."

"That's right."

"The warden."

"I don't think so. That comes across, and clearly, as carelessness. The doctor's in the wind, and has been. Old ID wiped, so he's got a new one. A good one. We're on it."

"I still have contacts and can—"

"If we don't find him in the next . . . eighteen hours, I'll give you the green on that. But not until. He won't know where to find Potter. He can only confirm what I'm already sure of. And pay for it."

"No, he won't know where to find Shark. Still alive," she murmured, "and Gio isn't."

"Tell me things I won't find in background runs, in files. Tell me what he likes, what he doesn't. What he drinks, what he eats."

Ivanna nodded. "Yes, yes, I see. Useful things. Let me think. Let me think back. Understand, we had to be careful about being seen together outside HQ. Summerset and I had a history, so we could meet. And then Alice, of course. I might have lunch or attend an event with Marjorie or Iris due to social circles, but . . .

"Harry is likely a better source for this, but I can tell you he had a sweet tooth, and a particular fondness for Fry's Peppermint Cream bars.

Candy. Three sugars in his tea. His fitness routine was rigid, perhaps to compensate for that sweet tooth. He liked the finer things, fashionable things. Even his casual clothes were higher-end brands."

She paused a moment. "Prison would have been very hard on him I'm happy to say. He considered himself a ladies' man, and could be very charming, very smooth. This, an advantage when the source or asset was female. He was good at what he did. We all were."

"Any attachments?" Peabody asked. "Hobbies, outside interests?"

"He had no family, never spoke of friends. Golf. I recall he commented that the wars had infringed on his golf game. After the explosion, after we understood what he'd done, we searched his flat. He had golf clubs, and the furnishings were top drawer. He'd clearly already removed a great deal in preparation, including his electronics, records, communications."

"You were never able to find those?"

"No. We did track a storage facility outside of London where he had art—art he shouldn't have had—wardrobe, as well as jewelry, a valuable coin collection, another of stamps, and more we learned he'd taken from either people he'd terminated or from homes that had been damaged and were unoccupied."

Ivanna lifted her delicate hands. "We were a unit, and before that night I would have said we knew each other, and well. In Shark's case, I would've been wrong. I was wrong."

"So was the rest of your team, your superiors in the Underground and at MI6."

"Yes, that's true. And none of us can afford to be wrong again."

"If you think of any other details, we'll factor them in. We appreciate the time. If you could send up Ms. Wright."

"Of course. I'm at your disposal for as long as it takes. We all are."

When she walked out, Eve turned to Peabody. "Find out where you can get that candy bar in New York. If you can get it here. And we can start checking golf courses."

"He stole from dead people."

Eve angled her head. "And this offends you more than making them dead?"

"No. Sort of. I'm just saying it's so . . . low. It could be a bad guy, an enemy agent, and Potter's like 007—that's—"

"I know who that is." She'd watched some of the vids with Roarke.

"Okay, license to kill, right, and it's war. But then you take the dead guy's coin collection for personal gain? That's subzero."

"I think we've established Conrad Potter as subzero."

Rising, Eve walked to the window. Yeah, Ivanna had it right. A wonder.

"What she told us fits Mira's profile like a boot."

"It's a glove."

"Not if it's on your foot. And more, we've got candy bars and golf. He's been out for a few years, sure, but he was in a lot longer. You're going to want what you missed. Fashionable high-end wardrobe. If he wants or needs sex, it'd be a high-end LC most likely. We can work all of that."

"We're going to get more. People remember different things. And once they're all together, talking, they'll remember other different things."

"That's exactly right. She didn't like him."

"Sorry?"

"Ivanna, she didn't particularly like Potter back then. Trusted him, respected him, but she didn't really like him."

"I didn't get that, but now that you say it, I do. She was careful how she phrased things."

"Some of that's training."

"Spy training!"

Eve ignored Peabody's delight.

"But she's wired to be polite, discreet on top of that. Ivanna's not the type to just come out and say Potter was an asshole."

"I'll say it." Marjorie glided in. "Conrad was an asshole. Skilled, nearly brilliant, but an absolute prick."

"Care to elaborate?" Eve invited.

"I'd be delighted, especially if you have something stronger than tea or coffee."

"I can make that happen."

"Then, my darling copper, I'd adore a G and T. Gin and tonic," she added.

"Peabody, see if the AC runs to one of those."

"Sure." As she rose, Peabody noticed Marjorie's eyes sparkled, but with tears. "Dame Wright, did something happen?"

"I'm a bit emotional. Ivan and Cyril arrived, and it struck me, and very hard, that we're what's left of us. So a G and T, if you'd be so kind, to fill the crack in my heart."

"I bet telling us how Potter was an asshole will lift your spirits."

Marjorie grinned at Eve, then did that head-toss laugh. "Oh, I'm going to like you. Both of you. And I'm going to flirt outrageously with your gorgeous husband. Do you have one, Detective? A spouse?"

"I've got a guy."

"Is he adorable?"

"I think so."

"Then I'll flirt outrageously with him if I get the chance. That's my wiring. Oh, a thousand blessings on you," she said when Peabody brought her a tall gin and tonic with a slice of lime. "Cheers."

She took a sip, breathed out. "You're quite right about Vanna's wiring. I, on the other hand, have no problem being impolite and indiscreet. If you'd asked her outright if she'd liked Potter, she wouldn't have lied. Not that she can't and won't lie, considering her stellar career, but she won't lie to you. And certainly not about Shark. Bloody hell, I refuse to call him that—those names were ours. I slipped."

She drank again, then set the glass down. "You're recording this?"

"It's necessary."

"I have no issue with that, nor with saying I didn't like Conrad Potter."

She wore diamonds as well, two little hoops of them in one ear, one in the other.

"Did I trust him? Absolutely. We had to trust each other, and I believed he'd earned that trust. But on a more personal level? Wanker. He considered my work—as an actor—barely legitimate. The cinema? Pabulum for the masses. And Cyril, being gay? Earned more than one smirk or look of contempt."

She shrugged. "He was more subtle, more careful with Leroy, who was Black, Iris, mixed race, but you only had to scratch the surface to see the bigotry. And there was a level of that as well for Summerset, Vanna, Ivan, Gio for coming from outside Britain."

"Doesn't sound like a team player."

"Well, he wasn't, was he?" Lifting her glass, Marjorie sipped more of her drink. "He seemed to be, did the work, did it well, collaborated with all of us whenever necessary. Hindsight, Lieutenant. With hindsight, it's clear to see he was more suited to the fringe groups we fought at the end than The Twelve."

"Dame Wright," Peabody began, and Marjorie flashed her a megawatt smile.

"Let's make it Marjorie. We're all just girls spilling the tea."

"Golly. Ah, she means like gossiping," Peabody told Eve. "I wondered, as Ivanna said Potter considered himself a ladies' man, if he ever, well, moved on you."

"Once. It only took once for me to shut that down, as I wasn't the least bit interested. He had more of an eye for Alice, though he never tried anything there—as far as I know—as he was very aware when someone could and would crush him like a bug. Which Summerset could have done, but Alice would've done so first.

"I know he never moved in on Vanna, but everyone knew she was

MI6, so he wouldn't want to cross that line. And he never tried anything with Iris that I know of. But that would've been his bigotry.

"He used women, used sex to pull them in as assets, to gain information. I can't throw stones there, as I did the same myself with men, more than once. But—what's that expression? Ah, I took one for the team. Potter, on the other hand, enjoyed using people.

"Using others, exploiting others, it was necessary. But one didn't have to enjoy it."

Eve ran her through similar questions as she'd asked Ivanna, got similar answers.

Then a little more.

"Oh, he disliked cats. There were a lot of strays and displaced cats on the streets in those days. Potter had an asset who took a couple in, and he complained bitterly about that. Oh, and he was always smooth-shaven. He left a kit at HQ so if we needed to work overnight, he could shave. Obsessive about it."

Sitting back, sipping her drink, she thought back. "A vain man, but I'm a vain woman, so again, no stones thrown. He respected Rabbit—Sylvester. He'd often ask Rabbit to teach him more about explosives, timers. Maybe it was the military bond, I can't be sure. I'd say he found Ivan interesting. He often asked more details about his work, his inventions. And I believe he genuinely liked Harry, as much as he was capable of liking anyone."

She lifted her glass in toast again. "Of course, he'd have killed any or all three of them without hesitation and regret, and we believed he meant to kill Magpie that night. Without Fawn and Magpie giving us the warning, we would have moved on the prison in Whitechapel. Into the trap."

"You were part of the team formed to take down the prison?"

Marjorie smiled at Peabody again. "There's a reason I did most of my own stunts in the trio of action vids I starred in. I was a badass."

"I don't see the 'was.'"

At Eve's comment, the smile became a quick, delighted grin. "See, I knew I'd like you."

"He's alive. Potter. And he killed Giovanni Rossi."

For several moments, Marjorie only stared. Slowly, her deep green eyes hardened like stone. "Of course, the bloody, buggering bastard. Can you tell me how?"

She did, and when she completed the interview, she asked Marjorie to send up Harry Mitchell.

"So we add a bigot who doesn't like cats or facial hair. The superior shit slides into the profile, too."

"He uses—or used—women," Peabody added. "He doesn't respect or value them. The three Marjorie named that he respected, found interesting, or liked? All men."

"White men," Eve said. "And all, with the exception of the interesting Ivan, Brits."

"Wanker."

Eve let out a half laugh, and programmed more coffee.

She turned when she heard footsteps, and thought Harry Mitchell didn't move thief silent like Roarke.

But Ivan Draski stepped into the doorway.

Immediately and instinctively, she shut off her recorder.

"Excuse me. I saw Marjorie and asked if I could come up next. May I speak to you a moment, Lieutenant?"

"My partner has been fully briefed on our previous meeting."

"Oh." He blinked his mild blue eyes. "I see. Well then." He cleared his throat, a harmless-looking man with a round face topped by thinning gray hair. "You very clearly instructed me not to come back to New York, and I feel I agreed, even tacitly gave you my word I would never do so. But I have come back. I took an oath before I gave you my word, and one I couldn't break."

Unclasping his hands, he spread his fingers. "I understand you may be compelled to arrest me, and only ask you wait to do so until I'm able to help you find the traitor who killed my friends. I swear to you I will not resist or attempt to escape."

"Nobody's going to arrest you. That ship sailed over a year ago. We're not going to discuss it or refer to it during this on-the-record interview. Understood?"

"Yes, of course. Thank you. I had to come. I traveled under another name, as I felt it necessary for all parties, but I had to come."

"Also understood. Subject closed, and record on. Please have a seat."

He sat, folded his hands on the table.

"It may be difficult for you to believe," he began, "but I'm very sure Conrad Potter is still alive, that he calculated how to simulate his death and escape. And he himself killed Giovanni."

"Is that so?"

"I'm sure of it. If you'd let me explain how I believe this was accomplished—"

"The ashes buried as Potter are being exhumed and transported to our expert at our lab in New York."

He blinked again, slowly, then smiled. "I should have expected you to see through his ploy. This is hopeful news."

He looked, Eve thought, like someone's uncle who probably raised orchids and had a pair of goldfish. Not at all like a man who'd spent most of his life in covert ops, who invented weapons, one who'd fought, one who'd killed.

"Mr. Draski, this interview will focus on your time with the Underground during the Urbans, and most specifically with the unit known as The Twelve."

"Yes, whatever I can tell you that helps."

"Can I get you coffee, tea?"

He looked at Peabody. "Oh, I would love coffee if it's not too much trouble. Just a bit of cream or milk, if you don't mind. And could I ask, when it's appropriate, if I could express my condolences to Giovanni's family? He made such a happy family, and his loss will be considerable."

"I'll let you know. As part of this Underground unit, you worked closely with Conrad Potter."

"I did, yes. We all did. Synchronization was essential. Trust, essential. While I became trained in combat, in weaponry, my primary role involved science and invention. I had a small, well-equipped lab and work area in our HQ. I often worked and stayed there alone, with my work. I had rudimentary quarters for sleeping when necessary."

"Potter found your work interesting?"

"Thank you very much," he said when Peabody brought him coffee. "He did. He would often come in, ask questions, look over my records."

"What did you make in your lab?"

"Various drugs. To render someone unconscious, to block or blur memory, to cause physical reactions such as nausea, a sudden headache, or other discomforts. Paralytics, poisons, hallucinogens. Medicines as well," he added. "So what could harm, and what could heal."

"And he was interested?"

"He was. And in weapons I worked on. Weapons that used sound or light, or both. Weapons such as—very much like the stunners that are now standard issue for your police department. Weapons that can disable, even kill, from a distance, without a projectile and in relative silence."

"You explained your work to him."

"I did. I found it satisfying to have someone interested. He was older, you see, and experienced. I felt, well, honored he'd take such an interest in my work."

Ivan picked up his coffee. "He used me, and I believe he used whatever he learned from me, from my records, from even my musings, on others. What I created was meant to be used for fighting a war, for ending it. Not for personal reasons, personal gains."

"You spent a lot of time with him. Maybe more one-on-one than the others."

"He also spent time with Sylvester, and now and then with Leroy, with Alice. They were explosives. And Leroy was also a mechanic. Conrad appeared to want to learn more about explosives, about mechanics. And then, I recall Gio mentioning to me that Conrad had wanted a kind of primer on tech. What was current, possible, what might be possible."

Shaking his head, he looked down at his hands. "I thought him brilliant. I thought that as I saw him as a knowledge-seeker. I followed his lead, learned more."

"If you learned more," Peabody put in, "you'd be a better asset to your team."

"Yes, thank you, that was my hope. My wish. I was so young. Iris and I were the youngest, barely twenty. I had a little crush on her, but was far too shy to approach her in that way. Then, before long, we became friends. Good friends, too much like family for crushes."

"When he came into your lab," Eve continued, "did you only talk about your work?"

"Oh no, he was very, ah, personable with me. Older, as I said, and experienced. With women." A smile ghosted around his mouth. "I was shy and not experienced. I felt comfortable asking him about women."

"And what did he say?"

"He advised me to pick one, and have another as what you call a backup? To charm her, flatter her, pretend interest in what she said, to give her trinkets. Nothing of import, just trinkets, and the flattery. If she didn't warm to that . . . He meant . . ."

"I get it."

"If she didn't, ah, respond, well, there was always another. And when the first saw another respond, she would respond as well. This method seemed beyond my reach. And I observed Summerset with Alice, and they had between them what I thought it should be. So I asked him before I tried to experiment with Conrad's method."

"What did he say?"

"I remember so well, because years later, when I met my wife—before she was my wife—it came back so clearly. 'Show her who you are,' is what he told me. 'Don't lie or pretend but show her the respect of giving her who you are. And then, if she accepts, show her how you feel.' This, I found, wasn't above my reach.

"We had love, Summerset and I found love. We held it too briefly, but we had it. I don't think Conrad ever did."

"And besides women?"

"Ah . . . I enjoyed football—soccer for you. To watch, even to play. But he said it was no more than a brawl, for ruffians and the hooligans. Golf was an elegant game. A gentleman's game. I also worked with robotics, and he was interested. He helped me with my hand-to-hand, my knife work. I thought of him as a kind of mentor. I was naive."

"On the night of the explosion, where were you?"

"I was on the prison team, in Whitechapel. We were waiting for the signal—the explosion—to move in. Just before, we heard Alice."

He paused, pressed his fingers to his lips.

"I still hear her," he whispered. "We were meant to be radio silent. If the lookouts saw something, they would signal with clicks. Two to take cover, three to abort. But she came through, screaming. Screaming that Shark killed Hawk. To abort, abort. A trap. We could hear her fighting, and Shark, we could hear.

"Then we heard Shark shouting, 'You'll die. You crazy bitch.' And I think we heard running, but I can't be sure if that's memory or what we learned after. She said, 'No other way.' And Summerset's name. Then the explosion."

"You went to his flat."

"Rabbit, Panther, and Cobra went to his flat."

"You didn't?"

"No, only the three. Too many, too much risk. Fox, Chameleon, and I brought Fawn's body back to HQ. Hawk was too deep in the tunnels, in the rubble to reach, but Panther would alert her handler. Wasp, Magpie, and Mole went on the hunt for Shark."

Eve wound him back, wound him through. Then, as she had before, let him go.

"Add user," Peabody said, "with not only a diverse skill set, but diverse knowledge."

Chapter Twelve

HARRY MITCHELL CAME NEXT, AND THE SMALL, WIRY MAN WITH A FLOP of sandy blond hair still walked on cat's paws.

He shot out a crooked grin. "Been a time since I sat down with coppers." His cockney accent hit a scale so far from Marjorie's they might have come from different planets.

He strutted in, extended a hand to shake. "What I never said to coppers before this? Anything you need from me, you've got it. Gio was a right one. And now Alice and Leroy are back to haunt me. I was on the watch, and the bleeding fuck got by me."

"Have a seat, Mr. Mitchell."

"No 'misters' here. Harry'll do. I taught the bleeding fuck how to pop locks."

"Did you?"

"I did, and how to get through the systems set up against people in my line of living. In those days," he added. "He went out with me a few times on my scouts and scavenges. Made him his first jammer me own self, and

I don't have to tell you where I'd like to jam that jammer, since I'm hearing the cocksucker's still breathing.

"Don't suppose a man could get a pint?"

"Peabody."

Since she knew the story of the bombing, and the story wouldn't change, she bypassed it. "Tell me about him. A quick study?"

"Quick enough. I wouldn't say he could make a good living at the work, but quick enough. Better with strategy, tactics, weapons—and he liked the sharp ones. And the ladies. They didn't have to be sharp ones for him."

"So you spent time with him outside HQ, and off-mission."

"Rabbit gave the green on it, and I didn't mind the company. I've got a rash knowing the company I kept. Embarrassed, you could say. Thanks, Brown Eyes."

He took the pint, and a good gulp of it. "That goes down easy."

"You ever have a pint with Potter?"

"We raised a few. A dark pub, a pint, some toad in the hole or stotty cake sandwiches with ham and pease pudding."

"I assume that's food."

"You Yanks." Shaking his head, Harry drank again.

"I know what stotty cake is. My boyfriend's from Scotland. It's bread, Lieutenant, and makes great sandwiches."

"I'll keep that in mind. So you'd have a pub meal and pint with him. What did you talk about?"

"Not the work. You never know where the ears might be. Or if we did, we used a kind of code. We'd talk about women, as men will do, about how when it was all over, we'd go somewhere hot and sunny."

"Hot and sunny."

"I'd never been out of London at that time. He'd been some places, and he talked about going off to live in the hot and sunny, which sounded just the trick to me."

"Anywhere specific?"

"France was his big one, as he thought it sophisticated. But when it was the hot and sunny, Costa Rica was one. He said there were plenty of expats down there, and a man could live like a prince. But you could still have fair-skinned women who spoke the King's English.

"The man was a prick—I could see that even then—but he knew things. And he always paid for the pint. I wanted to know things, and whatever I stole went for the cause, so I couldn't pay for many pints me own self."

"Did he ever mention any names—his contacts, friends?"

"He was cagey there. If he talked about the work he did before he came on board our train, he was always the smartest in the room, the best in the field. I knew it was bollocks, but he was smart, and I learned as well as taught."

He looked down at his beer. "He bought me a pint not twenty-four hours before he killed two of my friends. Would've killed me if he'd got the chance. Before he betrayed us all.

"'Here's to success, Harry,'" says he. "And I drank to that, drank with him, and what I drank to wasn't what he drank to."

Pausing, he seemed to gather himself.

"I knew that, twenty-four hours later, when I pulled Alice, bleeding, broken, barely living, out of the rubble. And me weeping over her like a baby."

His eyes, hard, shiny with the mix of rage and grief, met Eve's.

"He'd signaled me, you see. Heard something at my eleven o'clock. So I moved from my post, thirty, forty seconds to check. That's when he slipped by me."

He looked up again, and while the rage had dulled, tears sheened his eyes. "He couldn't do for me first, you see, in case HQ signaled. He had to kill Hawk and Fawn, then get out far enough to set off the charges, then he'd know I'd run in, as they hadn't come out. He could do for me then and be off."

"It didn't happen that way."

"Alice changed it. I heard her, but it was garbled some. He'd messed with my comm. But I knew something went wrong. You're never supposed to leave your post, but I knew something was wrong. I signaled Shark, but he didn't answer. Then I started over, and I saw him—didn't know at first it was Shark—running out. So I started to signal, started to run. And it all blew. It all blew, and blowing tossed me back and on my arse.

"I left my post because I trusted him. Then I didn't leave it soon enough to help my friends, or stop the bleeding fuck who killed them."

When she'd finished, she told Harry to ask Roarke to come up.

"We're taking ten before the last interviews."

Peabody's response was "Coffee?"

"Yeah. Coffee." Scrubbing her hands over her face, Eve walked back to the windows. "He's good at this, that's clear. Every one of them had training. They were wired to be suspicious, on guard, to look for tells, but they never saw him for what he was."

"We know what he is." Peabody handed Eve her coffee.

"He's whoever he needs to be in any given situation. That's a skill. But the arrogance . . . Even back then, the arrogance did him in. He's played both sides, and successfully. He has intel from both sides, so he knows what's coming. The burn-it-all-down cells are losing at this point. The risk of one of his contacts on the other side getting captured, flipping on him is growing. Instead of doing the smart thing, taking the money and whatever else he's got and slipping away, he can't resist one more big game."

"And he wanted them dead."

Eve turned to Peabody. "You're damn right. The Underground team, and people he'd worked with in that Dominion HQ. But not just dead, dead because he'd outsmarted all of them. And then he could slip away, be whatever he wanted, whoever he wanted as long as he wanted."

"You were looking for me, Lieutenant?"

Eve turned to Roarke as he came in. "We're taking a break before the last interviews. You're down there with them, and it's your first time meeting most of them. I wanted your impressions."

"They're a fascinating group who've all led interesting lives. And the glue still holds. They're bonded, still a unit, no matter how much time's passed. It's disturbing for them," he added, "to know Potter's still alive, and responsible now for the deaths of three of their number.

"But the glue holds."

Since he didn't want a cup of his own, he took Eve's coffee, had a sip, then handed it back.

"How can I help?"

"Feeney's running on deadline for a search. The prison doctor. I don't want to step on his toes, and it isn't urgent. I can't see Potter sharing any plans with somebody he let live. So we'll either find him, or he's dead.

"Potter's got a place. House, townhouse, fancy apartment. I lean toward the house—more room, more privacy. You'd want both after a few decades in a cage. But fancy apartment? Something like what Nadine has? You've got all the amenities. He likes the finer things, so finer. Problem is he could've had the place for years. Or he could've taken it a few weeks or months ago."

"He'd live alone," Roarke put in.

"Definitely. If he has domestic help, it's droids. No matter how long he's been there, he has a cover in place. Has to have a garage somewhere. Had to stash the limo somewhere, somewhere he could make his alterations."

"We don't have his face," Peabody said. "DeWinter's team can work up a good aged image, but if he's had work—"

"And he has. No question he'd do alterations there, too. Feeney's got some super e-geek working on the driver's face. You can't knock off twenty years or more with face work without it showing some. And there's no way he showed us his real face. He's arrogant, but he's not stupid."

“You’re sure it was Potter and not a hire?” Roarke asked.

“He had to do it himself. That’s who he is. He had to look at the camera and smirk knowing I’d look back.”

“I can contact Feeney and, without stepping on his toes, ask if there’s anything I can do to assist the super e-geek.”

“Maybe, if—” She pulled out her ’link when it signaled. “It’s Feeney. Dallas,” she said. “What you got?”

“I got Mason James Pettibottom aka Martin J. Pierce.”

“Seriously? He went with ‘Pettibottom’?”

“I figure he wanted to keep his initials. Maybe he had some shit monogrammed. He’s living it high in Costa Rica. Got himself a big-ass house, a big-ass boat, a fancy car. Damn good background and ID. Don’t know as I could’ve done better myself.”

“Give me a visual.”

“Coming. Had some face work, got a snazzy goatee. But it’s him.”

When the ID shot came on her ’link, she nodded. “Yeah, it sure as hell is.” She shoved the ’link at Roarke. “Put that on-screen, will you?”

“Hey, Roarke.”

“Feeney. Excellent work, by the way.”

Feeney scratched his fingers through his wiry explosion of hair. “Almost gave you a tug on it, but I had my teeth in it.”

Roarke studied the screen image of a man, tanned, a mane of waving sun-streaked hair, smiling green eyes.

“He looks quite happy, doesn’t he then? I suspect that’s about to change.”

“Fucking A.” She grabbed the ’link back. “Feeney, how about you contact Abernathy, the Interpol guy. He’s maybe in Manchester over there or likely on his way back. Pierce, well, we could waste time and resources getting him extradited, but Abernathy did me a solid on this one, and it’d be easy for him.”

“Wouldn’t mind a trip to Costa Rica, but the fucking paperwork. I’ll tag him.”

"I appreciate this, Feeney. He's a link in the chain, and he may not see it that way, but he's got blood on his hands."

"Breaking a background like this guy set up?" Like a boxer after a long round, Feeney rolled his shoulders. "I need a challenge like that to keep me sharp."

"Nobody sharper. Any progress on the driver's face?"

"The boy's working on it."

"Could he use an assist from Roarke?"

"I'll check in with him after I tag Interpol, see where we stand."

"Okay. I'm going to be in Interview, so you could let Roarke know directly, either way."

"Can do. I keep you up, you keep me up."

"Affirmative."

When she clicked off, she studied the screen. "He does look happy, and yeah, that's about to change. If he knows anything about Potter, they'll get it out of him. He won't, unless Potter slipped up somewhere. Not impossible."

"Unlikely," Roarke said.

"Unlikely. One more thing. Fry's Peppermint Cream."

Roarke sent her an amused look. "You want some candy?"

"Who doesn't? But no, Potter had—and probably has—a thing for them. Can you get them in New York?"

"Of course. And from any number of online venues. It's a popular candy."

"Delivery. Would he go for delivery? Have to think about it. Okay, break's over."

"Should I send up Cyril then? Iris had taken a short lie-down and was just up taking a walk when you asked for me."

"He's fine. We'll take him, her, then round it out with Summerset." She caught Roarke's look. "Being with, talking with, his old unit may have triggered some other detail, something. Like candy, or Potter always being clean-shaven. His strict fitness regimen, his wardrobe. He likes golf."

"Which gives you different avenues to investigate."

"You shouldn't worry about him, too much." Peabody spoke up. "It should help him knowing we're pushing hard on this."

"You're right, of course. I'll send Cyril up. Ah, my impression there? He's taking it all a bit harder than the others."

When Roarke left, Eve turned to Peabody. "Those other avenues."

"High-end barber shops and salons."

"Right. Fancy candy shops, country clubs, and those sports venues that offer indoor golf."

"Upscale men's shops," Peabody continued. "Fitness centers."

"I don't see him going to a gym, but we'll check. More likely he has his own equipment. He's the quiet guy in the neighborhood, or the building. Keeps to himself, but not so much you'd notice. You're riding an elevator with him, he's got a smile, a nod, maybe a word. Polite, a little aloof maybe, but polite. 'Good afternoon, Ms. Smith. Lovely weather today.'"

At Eve's attempt at a poncey British accent, Peabody grinned.

"He'd keep the accent?"

"Most likely. It'd be hard to put on the American for years without risking a slip. And there are plenty of Brits in New York.

"He's got a background story if he needs it. Probably a widower, no kids, retired."

"From what?"

"Something he can slide into," Eve calculated. "From the military, government work, diplomatic service. Just a quiet, polite, well-dressed British gentleman who enjoys a round of golf and a good, close shave."

She turned again when she heard someone approach.

Cyril Snowden, slim, small statured, stepped in. He had large, sad hazel eyes, and skin so white Eve imagined it burning red at the first beam of sunlight. In contrast, his hair was a deep russet brown with well-placed highlights. It flopped over his forehead and ears.

He tried a smile that couldn't reach those sad eyes.

"It's my turn in the barrel, I'm told."

"We'll try not to roll you too hard, Mr. Snowden."

"Cyril, please. I feel almost as if I know you. I've kept up with the lives of my friends," he added. "You're in the life of my friend. You do very good work. I feel . . . It's good to know you're the ones in charge."

"Can I get you some tea?" Peabody offered. "Coffee?"

"Tea would be very nice, thank you. Just a bit of cream, no sugar."

"Have a seat."

Eve sat across from him. "You were one of the cyber operatives for the unit."

"Yes, Wasp and I. We often worked together. Sometimes in tandem, sometimes on separate areas. It's why I wasn't there. I wasn't even there when it happened. Gio was with the prison team with our portables. Eyes and ears, you know. Thank you, Detective."

He took the tea, wrapped both his hands around the warmth of the cup.

"Not as sophisticated or effective as we have now, of course, but very good. I was at HQ with Rabbit, running comms, tracking locations. So I wasn't there, and there was nothing we could do to help. It happened so fast. Fawn turned on her comm, and we could hear . . ."

He closed his eyes. "I hear it still. Her warning us, him cursing her. How she fought. Then the running, then . . . She and Hawk were gone, and there was nothing we could do. Now Gio."

He lifted his tea. "We'd meet once or twice a year, Gio and I. Same line of work, so no harm in it. We had dinner at his home, my husband and I, our children. Met his family. A lovely family."

Eve thought the grief soaked him, so somehow his face lost more color.

"Tell us about Potter, the one you thought you knew."

"Ah well." He sat back, nodding slowly. "Intelligent—very sharp. Experienced. I would have said dedicated to ending the conflict, to restoring order. He liked order."

"Organized?"

"Yes, very. He'd have something to say if someone didn't deal with dishes or tossed a coat or jacket on a chair. He liked things just so. Himself included. Clothes pressed—excellent clothes—hair combed, face shaven, shoes shined. The work—especially Magpie's—caused us to be a bit disheveled. He didn't care for that.

"He could be a bit of a prick."

"Examples?"

"If we were working late in HQ and were lucky enough to score some hot food, someone might bring in fish and chips. Or someone might cook up some soup or stew. And he'd go on about how British cuisine was rubbish. And he'd give the Italians credit for theirs, but the French had it better.

"Not just a flick at what most of us had grown up on, but another at Wasp, you see? And no sort of gratitude, you see, for someone making a meal, or someone managing to bring in enough to feed a dozen."

"Bad feelings? Arguments?"

"Families argue, and so we were. Thought we were," he corrected. "Someone might shut him down there eventually. Marjorie excelled at that. Rabbit never let it go too far. Let a little steam escape, but then put the lid back on."

He sipped his tea, then set it down again, circled the cup.

"He didn't like working with me, or more specifically, working with a gay man. He was careful in what he said, and what he didn't say, but it was there.

"And the women. Four of the finest women, finest soldiers, finest people I've ever known. He didn't think much of them beyond using their sex to gather intel. He misjudged Fawn. That was his mistake. He worked and fought beside her, but he dismissed her."

Tears threatened again. Eve heard them soaking his voice.

"He didn't comprehend her dedication, her ferocity, her incomparable courage."

But those sad eyes filled with pride. "She thwarted him. He planned to kill her, but he didn't. She gave her life, and she stopped him. She saved lives by giving her own. After it was all over, all of it, I never wished anyone harm. There'd been so much harm, so much death. But when I heard Shark was dead, I opened a bottle of champagne. But he's not dead, and another good friend is."

"He liked golf," Eve prompted.

Pulling himself back, he nodded. "Oh yes, that's right. He did. I liked that about him. It seemed to me that talking about the pleasure of hitting a ball with a stick, or running one down a field, of dancing, laughing, anything that spoke of life was hope."

"What else did he like?"

"The theater. He'd make a remark now and then about the cinema—rubbish again. But the theater, serious, important theater, was worthy art. Opera, ballet, worthy. Though he complained that even before the wars, most had stopped dressing appropriately for performances. He expected that when London theaters opened again, it would be even worse.

"Fussy. I thought him fussy. How did I miss it? I can see so many signs now, but I missed all of them."

"Everyone did."

When she let him go, Eve got up again. She needed to move.

"French restaurants."

"Added to the list," Peabody told her. "Along with theater. Serious stuff. Nothing fun or frothy. Opera, ballet. He'd want to indulge, wouldn't he?"

"He would. Maybe the seasonal thing. Good seat. And he'd dress for it. Underestimates women, which would include us. He thinks he's covered his tracks at the prison well enough. Maybe we'll have some questions there, sure, but dead's dead. So that buys us some time."

She paced some more. "DeWinter's going to come through. Feeney's geek is going to come through. And we'll have more. But this is giving us a hell of a good picture."

Iris Arden swept in.

Eve recognized rich and in charge—she'd married Roarke. And that's just what she saw in the woman with creamy golden brown skin, eyes of piercing green. She wore her hair in a short, sleek cap around a face of sharp angles.

Eve imagined she'd changed from her traveling clothes into the silky, silvery pants and flowy top, freshened her makeup.

But even with that, Eve noticed signs of recent tears.

"Lieutenant Dallas, Detective Peabody. I'm told I can get a cocktail for the asking. I'm asking for a very dry vodka martini, two olives. It's been one hell of a day."

"I'll get that for you."

Eve gestured. "Please have a seat."

As she did, Iris opened the handbag she'd carried in, took out a red case, a circular silver dish with a red top. "We're in a private home," she began as she opened the case and took out an herbal cigarette. "So no laws broken. I hope you'll take that hell of a day into consideration and indulge me."

"Go ahead."

She flicked on the silver lighter, drew in, and on a kind of sigh expressed a stream of smoke that smelled—just a little—like Mira's tea.

"I've quit countless times. Truly believed I'd beaten the habit this time. Two years, three months, six days. But then Gio." She inhaled again.

"And now learning, almost worse, that Potter's still alive and responsible for Gio's death. It's crushing. I'm not easily crushed."

She offered Peabody a charming smile as she took the martini glass. "Thank you so much."

She opened the lid on the dish, flicked ashes into it. Then sipped delicately at the martini.

"I may feel human again before we're done. How can I help you? Because I promise you, I'll do whatever I can to help you toss that murdering bastard back in a cell."

"You worked closely with Potter."

"I did. We all did. It's lowering to know that he deceived me. I considered myself, and still do, an excellent judge of character." She sipped again. "He was a very large miss."

"How did you become part of The Twelve?"

"Ah. Let me begin by saying I had a very comfortable childhood. A very pretty childhood. I was very pretty, which adds to it. Some would say spoiled, and I won't disagree. Clouds began to gather. Rumblings of thunder, lightning strikes. Most of this, I remained blissfully unaware of. Then, in a finger snap, the storm broke and I was shipped off to boarding school in the countryside. To safety. I quite detested it."

Taking a long drag, she settled back. "But I began to see and to hear and to pay attention. Some of the other girls had friends or family in the fight. And some lost friends and family. Then, for me, there was a boy. A sweet boy. Not my first kiss, but the first that mattered. He had such strong beliefs about what was right, what was just. When we weren't sneaking off to snog, which we did as often as possible, we talked and talked."

She took another drag, expelled smoke slowly.

"His worldview opened mine. We gave ourselves to each other, fumbling at it, so sweetly, the night before he left for London to fight. He was bound and determined to go, to help restore order and balance."

After one last drag, she stubbed out the cigarette in the little dish. "He was killed less than two weeks later. Barely eighteen."

"What was his name?"

Iris looked up, eyes full of emotion. "How kind of you to ask. John Charles Brooke. Johnny. I decided tears, and mine were copious, weren't enough. I returned to London over my parents' strong objections. But I had turned eighteen and come into the first of my trust. They couldn't stop me. I knew I couldn't fight. The only thing I'd ever shot were clay pigeons—though I was quite good at that. And the London I came back to wasn't the London I'd left.

"The violence, the anger, the restrictions. But of course, there were still places of privilege, parties, gatherings, indulgence. I thought to use that, my place there, to somehow get a sense of things. What was real, what wasn't. Then there was Marjorie."

Iris lifted her glass in a half toast before she drank. "We knew each other a little. We'd met at a party when my parents brought me back for Christmas. So we renewed our acquaintance. Became friends. I had no sense she was feeling me out, but clearly there was enough of Johnny still in my mind and heart that she sensed my willingness, my allegiances. She introduced me to Ivanna at a party. You could have called our conversations, our teas, our luncheons job interviews. I told them about Johnny, and at some point said I wished there was something I could do to help.

"They told me how I could, if I was willing to train, to work, sacrifice, and risk. Not yet nineteen?" Iris laughed. "Of course I was willing. Some of the training was brutal. Hand-to-hand? The delicate ballerina put me down more times than I can count. But primarily, my work was intelligence. And for that, I only had to be what everyone thought I was, what I had been, a spoiled, wealthy party girl, much more concerned about the style of her hair than the state of the world."

She leaned forward. "I was good at it. Bloody brilliant at it. And when

I became part of The Twelve, I had something I never knew I needed. Real purpose. It wasn't just a team for me, it was family. We did important work, we made a difference. We saved lives. But there was a Judas among us. Working with us, eating and drinking with us."

"Tell me about Potter, specifically."

"Sharp. Edgy with it, but sharp. I learned from him, and that still disturbs me. He'd worked in intelligence, so he worked on my skills. He considered me a whore. He didn't say it plainly, but a girl knows. A useful whore. He thought of war as a man's job. But spying, deceit, whoring—useful women's work. He was family. You don't always like all your family. But he taught me well. I trusted him."

She paused a moment to think. "He liked things tidy, and would become annoyed if something was out of place. I tended to kick my shoes off if I came into HQ after a party or assignation. He hated that. He seemed fond of Ivan. I can't say if that was genuine, but he'd often go into the lab with Ivan. He was very dismissive of Cyril, carefully dismissive, but he clearly didn't care to work closely with Cyril."

"Because he's gay," Peabody said.

"Yes. Which seemed counterintuitive, as we were fighting to restore rights for all. I always felt he saw Summerset as, not an enemy, but a competitor. Next to Sylvester, Summerset had the most diverse skill set. The medical knowledge, which was invaluable, but also weaponry, combat, strategy, tactics. He could assist in the cyber work, if necessary. And he certainly knew how to gather intelligence.

"If anything had happened to Sly, it would've been Summerset put in charge of the unit. And that, I believe, was a problem for Potter. He would see himself in command.

"Then there was Alice." Iris laid a hand on her heart. "I loved her. You had to love her. Potter—not love, but desire. And desire not just for herself, but because she loved and was loved by his competitor."

"Did that ever come to a head?"

"If it did, it was away from HQ. I'd say his desire for her cooled considerably when she became pregnant. During that time Alice was off field duty. She worked in HQ or remotely. Then after the birth, she was on leave, tucked safely away with the baby through the winter. She'd only been back a few weeks when we began to plan the mission that would kill her."

"Did you spend time with Potter outside of HQ?"

"During training, yes. Then, of course, we might be teamed up on a mission."

"He had a sweet tooth."

"That's right! I'd forgotten that. The candy . . . Fry's."

"Peppermint Cream."

"Yes, that's the one. For all his complaints about British food, he loved that candy. Oh, he disliked cats in particular. Didn't care for dogs, but actively disliked cats. We had one in HQ for a while, a kind of mascot. I always believed he disposed of it. He never talked about his family. The rest of us did from time to time. Gio and Leroy had wives and children. Ivanna had her boys. I remember Potter saying he considered wives and children a distraction. One couldn't afford distractions in war. And someone said—who was it?—Alice, yes, Alice. She said, 'What do we fight for if not who we love and those who come after us?'"

"What did he say?"

Iris polished off her martini. "He said: 'We fight to win.'"

When Eve let Iris go, she went to the friggie. She pulled out tubes. Pepsi for herself, the diet sort for Peabody.

"We're down to mostly corroboration."

"That last bit?" Peabody cracked her tube. "I thought that was interesting."

"'We fight to win'? Fits his profile, fits the picture we're putting together. We need it, we need all of it. But it's not getting us closer."

"Somebody says every detail matters."

"Yeah. They do." Eve chugged some Pepsi. "A lot of frigging details, and nothing yet that points to where he is or what he looks like."

Eve took another chug as Summerset walked in.

"Lieutenant, Detective. I realize you're putting in a great deal of time and effort. I would only remind you that we have a number of guests who traveled considerable distances today. I'd like to serve dinner in an hour or so.

"You're, of course, welcome, Detective."

"Thanks, but McNab's expecting me."

"I've got work, and I'll need Roarke. Sit down. This shouldn't take long."

"Can I get you something to drink?"

"No, thank you. I'm fine." He looked at Eve. "I don't know what more I can tell you."

"We're going to find out. I've got a list of personality traits, habits, likes, dislikes mined from . . . our guests. Let's see if this sparks any more."

Though she didn't need them, she glanced at her notes.

"A bigot, homophobic, misogynist, organized, intelligent, skilled, dislikes cats, not fond of dogs, demands things stay tidy and in place. Likes the finer things, high-end clothes, French food, Fry's Peppermint Cream."

"How could I have forgotten the candy," Summerset murmured. "He was literally never without it. Three sugars in his tea. No matter how short we were on it."

"So add selfish?"

"I suppose you could."

"He spent time with Harry outside HQ, learning Harry's . . . trade."

"Yes, that's true. But we all tried to learn from each other. He spent time with Ivan in his lab, and so did I. I don't recall Potter spending time with me in my section."

"He considered you the competition."

"Did he?" Summerset's eyebrows lifted. "I suppose that's possible. I would have said while we didn't have any real fondness for each other, we respected each other. I would have been wrong."

"He liked a good, close shave."

"Ah yes, the barber near Piccadilly Circus. Some of the lesser royals were said to frequent it."

"A barber? Not a salon."

"Yes. He told an asset about the barber. I was shadowing them, Potter was working the asset. He mentioned the barber, said not to cheap out, to ask for the full hot shave. Yes, buildings bombed or on fire, people weeping for loved ones, and he never missed a shave. Clothes always neatly pressed. Candy in his pocket, sugar in his tea."

She could see him thinking, remembering.

"What else?"

"He used a bootmaker. Leroy admired his boots once. Potter said he had to find another bootmaker, as his had been bombed out a few weeks before. I believe he dyed his hair."

As he spoke, Summerset tapped a long finger on the table. "There was some gray in it—just a few strands—then there wasn't. He used face cream. Moisturizer. I saw a jar once, and thought it odd and amusing that a man who prided himself on his machismo would use what many still considered a female product."

"So we include vanity. A desire to hold on to his looks, his youth."

"He worked out rigorously and routinely. He was very fit, very strong, and very aware of his exceptional build."

"Is that why you didn't take him on?"

"Excuse me?"

"When he moved on your wife." Because he had, Eve was sure of it.

Summerset gave Eve one long stare, and when she didn't blink, inclined his head. "Alice had handled that situation, and I respected her ability to do so."

"But?"

"I had a word with him."

"Which word?"

"Lieutenant, you are relentless. It can hardly apply—"

"Details matter. And I bet it's a detail Potter remembers."

"Very well. I waited until he was in the shower, then I went in, took his cock in hand, twisted, and sent him to his knees. While he gasped, I told him if he put hands on her again, Alice would surely send him off limping. But there were ways to break what I twisted in my hand, and I'd add that broken cock to his bruised balls.

"Then I left him on his knees with the water running down his face. We never spoke of it again. I'm not proud of it."

"I would be." Peabody shot him double thumbs-up. "Mag move."

"You humiliated him. Bested and humiliated him," Eve added. "He'll have something special planned for you."

In his Summerset way, he looked down his nose. "I trust you'll see he's disappointed."

"That's the plan. If you leave this house before I say go, I won't take your cock in hand. But I will kick every square inch of your bony ass."

"How long?"

"I don't know. An agent from Interpol should soon be scooping up the doctor who helped Potter escape. He may know something. I doubt it, but it's another piece. I know him now, so we work from there. We work the details. One of those details not yet confirmed is the DNA. I know he's alive, but that's the proof."

"You think he posed as the driver. That he's the one who picked Gio up, who showed your card to the camera."

"I know he was."

"Lieutenant, could I see that image again?"

"Peabody."

"Bringing it on-screen."

Summerset rose, walked closer to study the image. "We were all trained, and well, on the art of disguise. But this? This man is in his fifties. Even with face work, even with expert makeup, you can't drop a quarter century, not face-to-face. And Gio was face-to-face."

"We're working on that."

"I wish you, sincerely, good luck. Are we done?"

"For now."

He walked to the door, turned back. "Thank you, both, for your service."

Then walked away.

Chapter Thirteen

EVE PICKED UP HER TUBE, DRANK AGAIN.

"We're both going to write all this up. Different takes maybe. You can do that at home. I'll get you transpo."

"Really? Can I check with McNab? If he's still at Central, they can drop me there. Or pick him up if he's ready."

"Whatever."

"This was a lot, but I think this was the way to do it. Interview one after another. You got overlaps, and that's what everyone remembers. Then you have what one remembers, or some byplay with Potter, what someone else focuses on. Yancy does it with faces, Mira with profiles. But we're sort of building a person. His interior."

"It's a good day's work. It might strain the brain, but it's a good day's work. I'll get your transpo. Go home, take a break, get a meal, then write it up from your angle. I'll write it from mine."

"French restaurants," Peabody began as she rose. "Theater boxes, fitness equipment, barber shops."

"Yeah, we'll hit on that and more tomorrow."

With Peabody off, Eve walked down to her office.

She turned in, stopped, and blinked at her board.

Roarke stepped through the adjoining door.

"You updated my board."

"As best I could. I had the time, and you certainly didn't. So take a moment now." Walking over, he put his arms around her. "You'll have a glass of wine."

"I'll have a glass of wine."

He kissed the top of her head, then walked over to choose a bottle. "And a meal. Take the time to let it all settle."

"Some of it's hindsight with them, but I wonder if some of it wasn't British manners. But they're not all Brits, are they? European manners? They tolerated what they disliked about him. Plenty to dislike."

"Intense and urgent circumstances. You'd need to put personal feelings aside for the greater good." He brought her the wine.

"Summerset twisted his naked dick and threatened to break it. That's pretty fucking personal."

Now Roarke blinked. "That's . . . I can't quite think of the word."

"Scary Roarke tactics—maybe you got some of that from him. Anyway, he didn't mention that in his initial interview. I got it out of him today. Potter put moves on Alice, Alice handled it, and Summerset polished it off."

"If you have more revelations like that, I think we should sit down. I'll get the meal."

"Where's the cat?"

"Busy being fawned over by our guests."

"Figures. I'm going to check in with EDD."

"I did that." He spoke from the kitchen. "We were just finishing up when you came in."

"What've you got?"

"I'll tell you, won't I?"

He came in carrying two domed plates to set them at the table by the open balcony doors.

"Sit," he said, and lifted the domes.

"What is this?"

"Roast beef, Yorkshire pudding, and mushy peas. Very British. No, they're not all Brits, but they worked together in London, so very suitable as a reunion dinner."

"I don't see any pudding."

Roarke pointed, then sat. "And no, I don't know why it's called pudding."

She decided on a bite of the beef first. "Okay, I was going to say that's pretty good, but it's way beyond 'pretty.' What did you finish up?"

"Feeney's man was nearly there. He's more than pretty good himself. He'd determined it wasn't flesh."

"What wasn't?"

"The driver—and I'm convinced along with you it was Potter. The face, the back of the hands. Hands will show age."

"A mask? But—"

"More than a mask. A process. Time-consuming, expensive, meticulous process. The material—a silicone base—has to be blended and formed, thinned and shaped. Measurements must be exact. The machine required to do this, as well as the tinting, is easily ten thousand. The mask is then carefully applied, smoothed, adjusted. If all this is done correctly, painstakingly, it can look quite real for a limited amount of time.

"It doesn't breathe," he explained. "They've yet to formulate a material that does. And it won't feel like skin. While it has the appearance, once you magnify and begin to analyze, it doesn't."

"It could change his face, take the years off?"

"It could, yes, for three or four hours. Five at the very most. After two, discomfort would be an issue."

"He wouldn't take it off in the limo. Too risky."

"And your sweepers would've found traces of it, flaking off during removal."

"Okay, he has to drive to the shuttle station, wait. Sometimes flights are delayed, he has to factor that possibility into his time. Rossi didn't have luggage checked, but he could have. The wit wasn't affected by the gas. He opened the door, saw the body. If there'd still been gas, he should've felt it."

She ate some pudding that wasn't pudding. Also way beyond "pretty."

"Garage. Drive around while Rossi's dying, then take the limo into the garage. You can ditch the mask there, air out the limo. Stick the card in Rossi's fist. Drive to the dump spot. Now you walk away. You've either got a vehicle stashed nearby, or you walk a few blocks, hail a cab."

She picked up her wine. "And the first leg of your mission is complete and successful."

"It will be a mission to him."

"It will. It's more than revenge, though that's part of it. They beat him, Roarke. They won, and that can't be tolerated."

She took a chance on the peas, and rated them sort of all right.

"He said you fight a war to win it. That's it. Not for a cause, not for a country, not for the innocent or the persecuted. Just to win." She went back to the beef. "He lost."

"What can I do? You have to give me a task, an assignment." He reached across the table for her hand. "This is mine as well as yours."

"I know it. You can find where he could've gotten the face machine, and the material. Even with that, we don't know how long he's had it. A couple months, a couple years. But if we can narrow that down . . ."

"I'll start on it, and you'll get a report from EDD, with visuals."

"I need to write up the interviews, then we'll start a lot of cross-references. Fancy French restaurants. You can't eat that every night, so fancy Italian. Or high-end delivery. Prime seats for serious theater, for opera, ballet. High-end men's shops. Probably tailored. Bootmaker.

"Fancy-ass."

She considered Roarke. Though he'd taken off his jacket and tie, rolled up his sleeves, he still looked fancy-ass.

"You could take those. The fancy-ass men's clothes and footwear. He's going to want good materials, good lines, but on the conservative side. He wants to blend, not stick out. Nothing too bright, nothing edgy. Golf. Golf shirts, golf pants, golf shoes."

"I take it he golfs."

"He told everybody he did, bragged about it. He had clubs in his flat. He works out—routinely. I figure him for his own home gym. No pets, he doesn't like them. Especially cats. If he wants sex, he'd hire it. Top-of-the-line there."

She picked up her wine and found it, along with the meal, went a long way to soothing rough edges.

"I think he has a house. Could be an apartment, a townhouse, but I think a house, with garage."

"He'd want the space after so long with so little."

"Yeah, and because he's got a lot of work. He had to store the gas canister. And maybe he has more, and likely does. He had weapons, so storage. No live domestics. They might get nosy. So droids."

"It's a lonely life you're describing."

"Lone wolves aren't lonely. Once his mission's accomplished, he can pick up and build a new life. New ID, new place. Somewhere warm and sunny, that's what he . . . Wait."

"I'm going nowhere."

"He didn't like British food, British weather."

"I dislike having an area of agreement with a murdering war criminal, but—"

"When it was over, he wanted somewhere warm, somewhere sunny. Costa Rica was one place—and that's where Pierce set up."

"Ah, now I follow. And you think he already has that place."

"Why come to New York straight off? He needs time to recoup, to rest, to plan. He needs face work, and a place to recover from it. Warm, sunny, maybe tropical. But somewhere where the rich go to play, because he wants that.

"Where do the rich go to play?"

"Anywhere they like, darling." Then he shrugged. "The Maldives, the Canary Islands—you're not looking for private islands."

"No. He needs restaurants, shops, the face guy."

"Belize. Australia's Gold Coast, French or Italian Rivieras."

"Stop. He goes for French food, he talked about Paris. French Riviera. That's a good start point. He bribed Pierce with enough for solid fake ID and background, a face job, a fancy house and boat. So he's got plenty left. Probably a different name for that. One for there, one for here."

She nudged her plate away. "This is good."

"This time you don't mean the food."

"It was, too. But this is good. This is logical. Get the face work, establish yourself, work on your tan, get some good meals in you. Plan and plan some more. Do your research. Where is everyone, and how do you get to them?

"Take your time. A year, maybe two. No one's looking for you. You're dead."

"But the first strike has to be here, in New York," Roarke continued. "Using Summerset to lure Rossi here, and you into the mix."

"Summerset hurt him, humiliated him, left him naked and blubbering in the shower, so use him to kill his friend. He'll be last on the list, Summerset. The, you know, crescendo. Rossi caught him first, beat him, so he had to die first. The others? I'm sure he has an order and a method to fit. That's organized, tidy, everything in place.

"He wants them here, Roarke. We brought them here."

"And here they're safe, no matter how good he is." Of that, he had not a whisper of doubt. "He's dead, after all, and can't know you've already disproved that."

"Not a hundred percent until the DNA results. But no, he's not dead."

Because he understood his cop, Roarke turned it on her.

"How would you do it? You know him now. How would you do it?"

"I'd find a way to lure one or two of them out. A message from a friend. Keep it to daylight. Just a little catch-up visit with a pal. What's the harm? The others will be harder when that's done, so he'd need leverage. Abduct a family member."

"Their families are secure. I've seen to it."

"Let's make sure of it."

She pushed away from the table.

"He can't get them all that way. If he hadn't left the card, he'd have a better chance of picking them off. But he let us know it went back to The Twelve."

"That wouldn't have been enough. For full revenge," Roarke continued, "for the satisfaction. To win? They had to know why. They all had to know why while it happened. You're ahead of him, Lieutenant."

She looked at Rossi's photos. "You're never ahead when there's a body in the morgue."

He walked to her, stood behind her. He rubbed her shoulders while they both studied the board.

"He could have been free and clear. Living in the warm and sunny, a whole new life with all the French pastries he wanted. Killing's more important to him. Lose the battle, but win the war. That's what this is to him. His personal war game."

"He won't win." Roarke kissed the top of her head. "I'll start on my assignments."

She reached back, covered his hand with hers. "You're a family member. Keep that in mind."

"He won't use me. I can promise you that."

She turned, gripped his face in her hands. "Take an oath on it. They're popular right now."

"I swear on my heart, and that's you, he won't use me."

"Okay. Okay. I need to get started, too."

She dealt with the dishes, as that was part of the deal, then sat at her command center.

Downstairs in the dining room, the remainder of The Twelve gathered. Though he'd prepared the meal himself, and with pleasure, Summerset took Roarke's advice. The droid would serve, clear, and clean.

What had brought them together once more was tragedy, and the grief would wind through again and again. But he could and would prize this time with old friends, good friends, for as long as he had it.

"Well, this is brilliant." After sampling the beef, Marjorie gave Summerset an easy smile. "And where was this brilliance when it was your turn at the pot at HQ?"

"Yet to be born."

"He made a good lamb stew," Harry recalled. "When I could scavenge the makings. Now you, my beauty."

On a laugh, Marjorie waved a hand in the air. "Was rubbish in the kitchen, and still am. I have other talents."

"And always did," Cyril added.

"None of us lack, or lacked, in other talents." Ivanna patted a hand on the back of Cyril's. "And how good it is to sit here and see what each of us has made with those talents."

"You've built a fine life for yourself, Summerset." Iris raised her glass. "After loss, profound loss, you built a life of strength, beauty, purpose. We all have, and that, I think, is a wonder."

"I had a child, and a chance to make a life for her. And when I lost her,

I had the boy. I don't choose to think where or what I might be without the boy."

"So here we are," Marjorie said, "together, after far too long."

"Far too long," Ivan murmured. "I wonder . . . I'm grateful to the lieutenant for allowing me back in New York."

"She's for justice. It runs through her veins like blood. Whatever conflict she deals with, justice will always win." Summerset shook his head. "She knows you need to be here."

"This time. But I wonder, as I don't wish to cause that conflict for her again, if we could meet again. Somewhere. Not in far too long."

"I think that's a marvelous idea. The world's a very big place," Marjorie pointed out. "We'll pick a spot, gather every year or so rather than that far too long."

So they ate, drank, talked about old times and new. It struck Summerset that the old times seemed another life, distant, then like a sheet of glass turned so the sun struck, they were yesterday.

They finished with trifle, then brandy in the parlor.

"Tell me you're not going to feed us like this every night." Marjorie pressed a hand to her stomach. "In my line, I have to keep my figure."

"I'll surprise you. I thought we'll do a buffet for breakfast, so everyone can come and go as they please."

"If it wasn't for the circumstances, I'd feel I was on a lovely, indulgent holiday."

"Behind the gates." Legs stretched out, Harry sipped his brandy. "The old instincts say get out there, hunt the bastard down." He held up a hand before Summerset could speak. "No worries. Leave it to your cop, and right enough. She's a sharp one, she is. There's a look in her eye that tells me if I were still in my old game, she'd have me nicked before I blinked."

"Potter's a different creature," Cyril pointed out. "I know how you feel, Harry. It brings on an itch not having a hand in."

"And being shielded." Ivanna gave Summerset's hand a pat. "Being protected when we once did the protecting. But different times."

"We don't cross her. She has my word."

"She has yours," Iris said, "so she has all of ours." She glanced down when her 'link signaled.

"Oh, it's Darlena, Darlena Corning."

"Oh dear," Marjorie said with a laugh.

"Oh dear, as some of you know. A cousin, for those who don't, who will ring a dozen more times if I don't answer."

"Block video," Summerset told her.

With a nod, Iris put her finger to her lips, and answered.

"Darlena, darling."

"There you are. Or you're not! This bloody 'link's giving me nothing but trouble. The screen works half the time at best. I'd toss it, but it's such a bother to have a new one all set up. They always lose something, don't they?"

"Not if—"

"But, Iris, my favorite cousin, how could you come to New York and not tell me!"

Her eyes flicked to Summerset's, held. "Why would you think I'm in New York?"

"Darling, I spoke with that handsome assistant of yours. I got it out of him—took some work. So very discreet, but he understood I was simply desperate to reach you."

"And why is that?"

"I somehow volunteered to head one of the committees for the holiday gala at the Palace Hotel. I must have your input, Iris, and your presence, of course. I don't know how I let myself get over my head this way, but I've done it again! I'm beseeching you! And since you're right here—"

"Only briefly, Darlie, and I'm actually rather tied up while—"

"Oh, surely you can make just a little time for me? It's dire. I was going to contact Ivanna—she's so clever. But you know her better, so if you could just ask if she might give some time?"

"Ivanna?"

Across the room, Ivanna arched her brows, nodded.

"I suppose I could."

"Oh, that's brilliant! I'm so grateful. You must plan to see her while you're here. We could have lunch tomorrow. My treat! And I could pour out all my woes. Roger's no help at all. He's just 'Why do you stick your oar in, Darlie, when you can't paddle?' Not helpful at all.

"Why are you here? Who are you meeting? Anyone else clever?"

Marjorie held up a hand, pointed to herself.

"As it happens, I'd planned to have a drink with Marjorie. Marjorie Wright."

Darlena squealed. "Oh, good God, Iris, you must bring her. You simply must! If I could add her to the guest list! What a coup! They'll coronate me. Please, please, it's life-and-death for me. You must bring them both to lunch. Chez Robert. They do a superior martini. I'll book a table. Twelve-thirty!"

"Darlie, I can't confirm that. I need to check my schedule, then see if they're available."

"Yes, yes, of course. But I'll book the table because I have absolute faith in you. You never let me down, Iris, no matter what tangle I get into. You're a brick."

"I'll ring you back, one way or the other."

"Pins and needles here. Kiss, kiss!"

Iris clicked off. "It sounded exactly like her, including getting over her head and begging for help."

"A bit convenient, isn't it?"

"Yes, Cyril, more than a bit. But Darlena . . . If he's somehow compromised her."

"We'll take it to the lieutenant." Summerset rose. "Right away."

“Stings a bit.” Harry pushed himself up. “Not to work it ourselves, but here we are, old dogs not able to do our tricks.”

“Mind who you’re calling old,” Marjorie told him as they started upstairs.

Deep in the work, Eve lifted her head when she heard any number of footsteps, and thought: What the hell?

Summerset led the whole damn group into her office.

“I apologize for the interruption,” he said before she could snarl, “but we may have a problem.”

“What kind of problem?”

“My cousin Darlena Corning rang me up.” Iris stepped forward. “It certainly sounded like Darlena. I blocked video, and on her end she complained her ’link wasn’t working properly. That wouldn’t be unusual. She and her husband, Roger, live in New York. She said— Well, I made sure the conversation recorded, so.”

She handed the ’link to Eve as Roarke walked in from his office.

Eve hit replay, listened all the way through.

“And she just happens to contact your assistant, after hours, right? And he tells her you’re in the city?”

“Again, not unusual for Darlena. But . . .”

“Coincidence equals bollocks.”

“That’s one way to put it.”

“She brought up Ivanna, and then you told her Marjorie was in New York.”

“That’s on me,” Marjorie said.

“And do you tend to come to your cousin’s rescue?”

“She has a good heart, a good and generous heart. And a very chaotic brain. So yes, and I’m concerned. If she didn’t contact me on her own, he may have forced her. He may have hurt her. He may—”

“You’d have heard it in her voice.” Eve cut off the rising worry. “He hit on you next because you’re a woman, and therefore less. Less bright, less cautious, less capable. Your cousin calls, you help. That's your pattern. He's using your pattern."

"But my cousin . . ."

"We'll check on her. What's the address?"

"I—I need to go through my address book."

"I have it. Roger and Darlena Corning," Roarke said. "It's not far."

"Bring a car around," Eve told Summerset. "Not mine. If he's watching, he'd make it. What kind of building?"

"Luxury high-rise," Roarke told her.

"Yours?"

"As it happens."

"Handy. Underground parking?"

"Yes."

"Fancy car," she said to Summerset. "And not one of Roarke's usuals." As she swung on her jacket, she turned to Iris. "If she contacts you again, tell her you left a v-mail for Ivanna, and Marjorie's checking her schedule.

"How far?" she asked Roarke.

"Five minutes."

"Keep her talking as long as you can."

"This isn't a problem with Darlena."

"Good. Stay in the house. Let's go."

"Thinks on her feet, that one." Harry picked up the cat, who'd followed them up. "We could've used her back in the day."

"I'm happy to make use of her now." Marjorie laid a hand on Iris's arm. "If he has Darlena, he needs her until we confirm. But I think the lieutenant's right, darling. Darlena would never pull off that act."

Eve took one look at the low-slung bold red sports car and gave Summerset points. If you were trying to go unnoticed, it was the last vehicle you'd pick.

So they'd go unnoticed for that reason alone.

"We didn't have anyone on Corning."

"She's actually a third cousin." Roarke took the wheel.

"Third cousin. How do people keep track? But he knew about her. She didn't make the contact. Not a single waver in her voice, no hesitations. Just plowed right through."

"He could've lifted her 'link, fed recordings of her voice into a simulator. Complicated, but he appears to like the complicated."

He slid right into the underground parking of a steel and glass tower.

"He could have a place here, minutes from the house. But it doesn't fit. Too many people coming and going, no garage, not enough room to work."

"Penthouse B for the Cornings."

The elevator required a swipe for that level. Roarke took one, suspiciously blank, out of his pocket, and accessed the floor.

"Do they have a vehicle?"

"Ah." He pulled out his PPC. "A 2061 black Majestic. Four-door sedan."

"We're here making inquiries about an accident involving same. Quiet building."

"I swiped in express."

"Still more handy."

When the doors opened, she stepped into a wide hallway carpeted in quiet blue with walls of the palest of pale golds. Flowers, fresh and bride-white, stood on a polished table. Their rich scent followed her down the hallway to Penthouse B.

Top-of-the-line security, she noted. Palm plate, swipe code, security cam. Eve pressed the buzzer.

And recognized Darlena Corning's voice through the intercom.

"Yes? Corning residence."

"Ms. Corning." Eve held up her badge. "NYPSD. If we could have a word."

"Goodness gracious! The police! Roger, it's the police!"

Locks thumped before the door opened to a woman in a stylish black cocktail dress with every blond hair in place. Her eyes, more gray than blue, held a kind of giddy anticipation.

"Has there been a burglary? An assault? A murder! Roger!"

"No, ma'am. If we could step inside?"

"Of course, of course."

Like the woman, the entranceway and the living area beyond had everything in place. A man, his tie loosened, his feet in house skids, wandered in with two snifters of brandy.

"Oh, company."

"They're the police! I called you."

"Did you? My, my, Darlie, will I have to make your bail?"

"Don't be silly." But she giggled. "You should sit down."

"We'll only take a moment of your time. You own a 2061 four-door black Majestic sedan?"

"Is that what it is? Roger?"

"Yes. We do."

"A vehicle of that description was involved in an accident about an hour ago on Third Avenue."

"Oh goodness! While we were having dinner with friends. We only just returned home. We didn't drive at all, did we, Roger? There would be cocktails and wine, so we took a cab there and back again. Baritello's."

Eve nearly followed up with the standard questions, but cut things off. "We appreciate that information. Did you use your 'link this evening, Ms. Corning?"

"My 'link. How odd you'd ask. I misplaced it sometime today. So annoying. I honestly think someone stole it!"

"She's always misplacing her 'link," Roger said.

"Maybe we could help with that. Do you remember where you last used it?"

"I do! I had brunch today with a dear friend at Czarina's. Their blinis are lighter than air! Another dear friend rang me up just as I was going in. I arranged a salon date with her for . . . How can I remember! It's on my 'link! Then I set the 'link down on the table. Or put it back in my bag. I'm not sure. But when I changed bags for our dinner, it wasn't there!"

"We'll see what we can do. We appreciate the time."

"I do hope you can locate my 'link. Such a bother getting a new one."

She was still talking when the door shut behind Eve and Roarke.

Chapter Fourteen

"GO AHEAD AND TEXT SUMMERSET THE COUSIN'S ALL CLEAR. TELL THEM to stay where they are."

"I think they're aware of that already."

"Hammer it home. Chez Robert. Yours?"

"It's not, no."

"The handy had to end sometime. Chez—French, right? Like saying *Ro-bare* for *Robert*'s French."

"It is."

"He couldn't resist. He was capable with weaponry," she continued when they reached the garage and the car, "but he wasn't a sniper, a sharpshooter. And he'd have lost a lot of that skill in prison. A few years to re-hone, yeah, but that's not how he plans to take them out."

"He may have hoped for all three, but could hardly count on it."

"He would think that way. Women. One goes to the john, they all go. I can't figure that one out myself. And he brought in Ivanna, and that's a little nudge to add Marjorie. He knows Ivanna's in New York. And we'll check with this assistant, but if he learned Iris was, he'd assume the rest."

"Taking three at once," Roarke continued. "And what he'd consider the weakest? He could take more time with the rest."

"They'd be shaken, and angry, and they'd sure as hell lose any trust in me."

"But none of that's going to happen."

"No, it's not."

But she had to figure out what he planned in order to subvert those plans.

"He can't use the gas again unless he rigs it to take out the whole restaurant, or at least the section they're sitting in. He books the table so he'd know that."

"Disguised again, some poison in their drinks."

"Possible. But fancy French place?"

"They'd know their waitstaff. Explosive."

"That's top of my list. Remote or timer. Timer makes more sense." She considered it as they drove through the gates. "He'd want to be close, but not that close. If he can't see them to set off the charge, a timer works better."

"How will you handle it?"

"Working that out."

"You'll include me." He pulled up, turned to her. "I'm very fond of Ivanna, and I've also grown fond of the rest."

"You're already in the mix I'm working out." She breathed a sigh as they got out of the car. "And I don't see a way of pushing them out of it."

"You're not letting them go to the restaurant."

"Oh, hell no. But as much as it doesn't sit all the way right, I have to keep them informed."

Starting now, she thought as they went up the stairs.

It didn't surprise her to find them all waiting in her office. It struck her as weird, but not as a surprise. Some on the sofa, some at the table, and Harry and the cat enjoying her sleep chair.

At least they hadn't taken over her command center.

Iris got to her feet. "You're absolutely sure she—"

"We had a conversation," Eve interrupted. "She's under no duress. She misplaced her 'link earlier today."

"He lifted it," Harry said. "I showed him how it's done."

Iris sent him a weary look. "It wouldn't take any particular skill with Darlie."

"You need to check with your assistant."

"I did while you were gone. He did take an after-hours call from her, or believing it Darlena. I didn't specifically instruct him not to tell her I was in New York, so it didn't take much pleading for him to tell her."

"Then that checks. But if she'd wanted to speak to you, why didn't she contact you directly? Why go through your assistant?"

"I . . . I'm slipping. I will say it wouldn't be impossible for her to go that route. Click his number first, as I've asked her to when I'm working. She remembers about half the time."

"Don't bring that up when you call to confirm."

"I'm going to confirm?"

"We're going in the field?"

Eve turned to Marjorie. "You are not."

"It does sting." With a sigh, Marjorie lifted the coffee that came after the brandy.

"You'll confirm. The three of you to meet her, Chez Robert. You can't make it until thirteen hundred, and have to leave by fifteen hundred. You've got a holo-meeting shortly after."

"I see, add details and make him work for it a little."

"Don't contact yet. Roarke, I need an interior of the restaurant, and an idea of their security. And what we have across the street."

He sat at her command center and got to work. Summerset poured him coffee, then took a cup to Eve.

"Yeah, great." She drank; she paced.

"He wants to take all three of you together. He's not that solid a marksman."

"Close range, good enough," Summerset told her. "Or with a covering fire. But no, he was no sniper. Leroy was our best. Iris right along with him."

"He needs to get in there, but won't be in there at thirteen hundred. Can't get close enough to poison the drinks, especially three at once."

"Happy thought," Iris murmured.

"A boomer's the way. You just have to be close enough to see it, hear it, have that satisfaction. But you have to get in to place it."

"He might have done already."

She glanced over at Ivan, who shrugged.

"Anticipate the enemy, he'd say to me. Set the trap, then wait to spring it."

"Security," Roarke said. "Decent enough, but not tight or layered."

She pointed to the screen. "Harry. Could he get through that?"

After setting the cat aside, Harry rose for a closer look. "If he couldn't, I wasted my time on him."

She pulled out her communicator, ordered surveillance on the restaurant.

"If he tries tonight, we'll spot him," she said. "And we'll take him."

Could it be that easy? she asked herself. Would he make so major a mistake, one so simply exploited?

"Restaurant interior," Roarke said, "front of the house on-screen."

Hands in pockets, Eve rocked back on her heels as she studied the setup. Tables—two- and four-tops, booths, a bar, a host station, stairway leading down to restrooms.

"Nothing with a street view. Okay. No interior cams. He could plan to place one, if he wants to watch.

"Do you want back of the house? Kitchen, storage? Wine cellar, lockers, and so on?"

"He won't bother with that, but I need to see."

So she studied the kitchen—blinding white and stainless steel. The counters, the racks, the tools, and all the rest.

"If he wanted to take down the whole place, sure, set charges throughout. Kitchen, cellar, one at the bar, under a table, under a booth. But he doesn't want that. That brings in anti-terrorism—too much attention."

"One small charge." Ivan spoke quietly. "A blast radius of eight to ten feet."

"Agreed," Eve said. "Minimal collateral damage, and too bad for them. Keep it contained. Unless he places a camera, he'll go with a timer. No point in the remote when you can't see.

"Roarke, street view."

"On-screen."

"Okay, okay. A pair of restaurants, outdoor seating. Couple of shops with windows. Mixed residential and commercial above. If he had sniper skills, I'd look at the roof or the residential windows. But that's a no. Add he can't be sure to get all three. But he'll be there, and it'll be across the street where he has a view."

She turned to Iris. "Make contact, text it. Thirteen hundred arrival."

"Have to leave by three. Got it."

She sent the text, and the response came quickly.

"God, even this sounds just like her. 'Brilliant! Though I'd so hoped you'd come with me after lunch to help me buy a new 'link! I'm such a dolt about these things, and always get talked into something that never works properly. Maybe I can drag Marjorie or Ivanna off to help me. Mad to see you and catch up, even for so short a time. Until tomorrow! Kiss, kiss.'"

"All right. I don't want to call in the bomb squad on this. They tend to generate a lot of attention." She looked at Roarke. "Can you rig a sniffer?"

"I can, of course, but no need, as we already have more than one."

"Great. Let's go sniff, in case he has already planted it."

"And if he's on his way to do so, you'll take him down."

"That's the bonus round."

"And if it is already planted," Summerset began, "and activated?"

"I'll deactivate it." Roarke rose. "I had a very good teacher. Give me a moment, Lieutenant, to fetch the sniffer."

"I'll get it. I'll get it," Summerset repeated before Roarke could speak. And walked out.

"Allow him to worry about you." Ivanna let out a sigh. "Allow us all to do so. Being together like this, after so long, it brings back memories. The memories make it difficult to sit passively while others take the risks."

"You took the risks," Eve reminded her. "And more than your share. You've taken another by coming here. Now it's our job. Roarke, is the restaurant still open?"

"Likely they take reservations until nine, and people will linger. But it may not be when we get there, as it's Lower East Side."

"Let's cover that." She pulled out her 'link, tagged APA Cher Reo.

Though Reo wore a baggy T-shirt, had her froth of blond hair messily bundled up, Eve concluded: Still working.

"I need a warrant."

"So I assume, as I didn't think you'd called to chat."

"I'm good. How are you? Great. There, I chatted."

"Dallas, I'm buried here."

"Yeah? Me, too. More chat. Done. I have probable cause to believe there's an incendiary device planted, or about to be planted, at Chez Robert, a restaurant on the Lower East Side."

"Have you contacted the boomers?"

"No. The attention drawn would hamper my investigation, and warn off the perpetrator. I need a warrant to enter the restaurant should it be closed, and to search for said device.

"Conrad Potter, convicted war criminal—Urbans. I have evidence indicating he faked his own death, escaped prison in England. Interpol is picking up, or in the process of picking up, his accomplice, the prison doctor, in Costa Rica. Potter is responsible for the murder of Giovanni Rossi."

"The limo hit."

"Affirmative. Potter has a kill list. He plans to check off three more names tomorrow. I can feed you all of it, Reo, but I'd sort of like to take care of this bomb."

"I'll get you the warrant, then you feed me frigging all of it."

"I'll send you everything I have." She glanced over as Roarke came back in from his office. He wore his suit jacket again, she noted, and assumed he had a weapon somewhere on him.

Summerset stepped in behind him with another pot of coffee and a tray of cookies.

"I have more to write up, and you'll get that when I do."

"Make sure of it. I want to be up to date and prepped when you bag him. And I'm not great. The boss and two colleagues are down with a stomach virus. While I've escaped that, so far, I've got work up my ass."

"Sorry. Good luck. See, more chat. Later. Let's go," she said to Roarke.

When they left, Marjorie poured herself another cup of coffee. "I like the girl more and more. Just no bollocks about her."

"She can be, and often is, stunningly rude." After topping off his own coffee, Summerset sat. "Honest, not to but beyond a fault, brilliant in her way and her focus, which does not include social niceties. Unflinchingly loyal to those who have earned her loyalty. And terrifyingly brave.

"She once stepped in front of a stream to spare me. I had not earned her loyalty. I had not. Yet she did so without hesitation."

Reaching over, Ivanna took his hand. "He won't best her, *miy druh*. He won't best either of them."

"If he harms them, either of them, he will not live." He said it calmly, coolly, with absolute certainty. "Not this time. Not again. I swear that to all of you."

Marjorie set down her coffee, walked over to lay her hand over theirs. "That's an oath we'll all take with you."

And one by one they laid their hands, and swore it.

As Roarke drove, Eve sent the files to Reo.

"They're going to get restless," Roarke warned her.

"I can't help that." Then she scrubbed her hands over her face, into her hair. "I know that. I feel that, but they'll have to suck it up. And I know if I don't take Potter soon, it's going to be a problem."

"Let me handle that. You'll just order or threaten."

"You've got something better?"

"I do, yes. Guilt. Why would you add to the lieutenant's work? Why would you fracture her focus when she needs her focus? Losing her focus could cause her to make a mistake, and be hurt. Why would you add to her worries, and to mine?"

"Jesus. That's good. It's mean in a twisted way that makes it meaner."

"Passive-aggressive may not be an honorable choice, but it'll work." He glanced over. "I'll handle them, my word on it."

"All yours. And here's my warrant. I'm going to check in with the surveillance team, and let them know we're moving in. By the way, don't draw the weapon you hooked on before we left the house unless there's no choice."

"Which weapon?"

Eve just closed her eyes a moment. "Any and all."

She contacted the team on Chez Robert, then sat back, considered.

"Restaurant's just closing. No single male went in or out since they've been on it. If I were going to break in to plant a bomb—or rig toxic gas—I'd wait a couple more hours. Give the neighborhood time to settle in for the night."

"Or you move in directly so it looks as though you're an employee who forgot something. Look harried instead of furtive. Go in, switch on the lights—nothing to hide here—plant the device, then leave the way you came."

"Huh. Well, you'd be the break-in expert. Drive past it, park about a block away. We'll give it a few minutes. Better it's closed," she said half to herself. "No need to go in, stir anybody up. 'Hey, just checking for explosives.' No media reports to scare him off."

He cruised by the restaurant.

"And if he hasn't already planted it?"

"I come back in the morning."

"We come back in the morning," he corrected, and slid along the curb.

"I can pull in a boomer for it."

"We come back," he repeated. "And again, no doubt, sometime before thirteen hundred."

No point in nudging him back, she thought. And no good reason. "I'll have men placed, soft clothes, in the restaurant, the other restaurants, the shops, on the street an hour prior. I'll need more to cover the roofs, just in case. We'll check if any single male has rented any of the residential or commercial spaces with a view of the target. Say in the last six months. Longer than that doesn't make sense, even for him."

"I agree there. While he must have considerable funds, they aren't unlimited. He risks the whole operation if he squanders what he has."

"You'd also be the expert on money, but I'd already gotten to that one. Let's take a walk. Wait."

She pulled out her signaling 'link. "It's Abernathy. Dallas," she said.

"We have Pierce in custody. I have to say, it was remarkably easy."

"Good work. I've got a few questions I'd like you to work into your interview."

His face, his voice, radiated haughty. "I believe we know how to conduct an interview, Lieutenant."

"I'm not questioning that, Abernathy, but we've got some movement on this end. It's doubtful Pierce knows anything that could apply here, but I don't want to assume. I'll send you the questions."

"Very well, since I appreciate the tip on Pierce. Now I'm going to get a few hours of sleep before we escort Pierce back to London. It's been one brute of a day."

"Tell me about it," Eve muttered as she pocketed her 'link. "Let's take that walk."

"He should've shown by now if he was doing what I'd have done." Roarke got out, joined Eve on the sidewalk. And took her hand. "Just in case," he said. "We're an ordinary couple taking a stroll on a lovely September evening."

"Right."

She took out her communicator, told the team they were moving in.

"No sign of him." She pocketed the comm. "I'm turning on my recorder. We'll go straight in. Record on. Dallas, Lieutenant Eve, and expert civilian consultant Roarke."

She gave Roarke a nod at the entrance as she read in the details of the warrant.

"I've bypassed the alarm," he added, "so as not to cause undue attention."

And slick, silent, and smooth, they were in.

Eve hit the lights; Roarke took out the explosive detector.

They worked front to back, sweeping the tables, the bar, the booths while the indicator remained green and silent.

"Maybe he's got another way," Eve began.

At a back corner booth, it chirped, turned red.

"And there we have it."

Handing the detector to Eve, Roarke took out a penlight, crouched down. "Interesting."

"That's not a word I like when attached to a bomb."

She got down with him, twisted to look under the table. "Timer, right?

Set to go off in thirteen hours, thirty-six minutes, forty-six seconds and counting. Give them time to sit and settle, maybe order a drink, wait for the cousin. How the hell did he get past the team and set this a half hour later than he'd said in the first contact?"

"He set the timer remotely. And there's a backup to detonate by remote."

"Well Jesus. Fuck. Get out of there. I'll bring in the bomb squad."

"No need, give us a minute."

"If he's watching the place, he could just set the goddamn thing off. Your face is on top of it. I like your face."

He glanced toward her, smiled. "Thank you, darling. I'm very fond of yours. This is an old device. Urban Wars era. I learned on one of these bastards. Hold this on it, will you?"

While she held the light, watched the minute go from thirty-six to thirty-five, he got out tools. She didn't know what the hell he did with them, but wished he wouldn't.

"Listen, Roarke—"

"Shh. It has a nice but faint hum. I need to hear it. I thought, after all this time, you'd trust me."

"I do, but . . . that's the guilt crap, isn't it?"

"Mmm. There now." He set some sort of housing down. "You'll want to bag all this. You should run back, get your field kit."

"I'm not going anywhere, Ace. And if you think I'd leave you here with a fucking bomb, you hurt my feelings."

"A good attempt at the guilt crap."

His long, clever fingers drew out some wires. She wanted those fingers whole and attached to his hands.

"He does like to complicate things, the right prick, so we're not falling for that, are we now?"

Another minute clicked by. She remembered what the master told her in dojo training, and tried breathing through her toes.

"Ah, there you are. Not as clever as he thinks, is he then. Not as clever by far."

"They can respond within four minutes."

"And he'll know they have."

More wires, and a look in his eye that warned her he was about to do something. She started to ask him what, then decided to save her breath while she had it.

"A simple ploy, unnecessary booby-trap, and . . ." He clipped two wires at once. "Done."

The timer froze at thirteen hours, thirty-one minutes, thirty-eight seconds.

"Can I get a 'well done'?"

"Can he reactivate it? Remote it?"

"Absolutely not."

Instead of words, she pulled him to her under the table and kissed him, hard and long.

"Don't touch anything else until I get my kit and we seal up. I'll call, have it picked up. Nonemergency, silent, unmarked."

She crab-walked back, rose, then jogged away.

Roarke stayed as he was another minute, studying the device.

"Clever," he murmured. "But no, not as clever as he thinks."

Within thirty minutes, they were on their way home.

"There'll be prints on it, ones that aren't yours. Sure, he could've sealed up, but why bother? I'll check tomorrow who had that table, get a description. He had to do it today—yesterday," she corrected, as it had gone past midnight.

"Risks and complications, sure, but he'd have no reason to place it before that. He had lunch or dinner there, at that table. And at thirteen hundred tomorrow, he'll be somewhere close enough to see it blow, or hear it, witness the immediate aftermath."

"It'll be a disappointment to him," Roarke commented.

"So will finding his ass back in a cage. Listen, if they're all still up, I need you to take them."

"Where would you like me to take them?"

"Don't get me started."

They breezed through the gates where the house stood against the night sky, windows burning with light. And right now, not the sanctuary she'd grown to crave, but a safe house.

There was a difference.

"I have to write this up so Peabody, Whitney, Reo, Mira, all of them are fully updated in the morning. Update the board. Have five minutes to think. So I need you to keep on the expert consultant, civilian, and brief all of them."

"I can do that." He parked at the front entrance, then shifted to her. "Forty minutes. We take forty minutes more for this, then it shuts down for the night."

"It's a lot to write up."

"Happily, you're not only good at what you do but efficient. Forty minutes," he repeated, and got out of the car.

She decided she could probably do it in forty, if everyone left her the hell alone. And if it took longer, she'd renegotiate. The man understood negotiations.

They walked in, started for the stairs.

"They're all still up there," she said darkly. "Spread out in my office."

"I'll deal with it."

And he would, she thought. He had a way of dealing with annoyances and inconveniences. With people, who often amounted to the same thing.

Just as she imagined, they were all spread out in her office, in her space, with coffee, and cookies, and conversation.

How did people find so damn much to talk about?

To cut off questions, as all turned to her and Roarke, Eve took the lead.

"The situation's handled. Roarke's going to bring you up to date."

"Why don't we use my office so the lieutenant can write her report?" As he gestured, they rose as a unit, and Eve went straight to her command center.

She opened operations.

Summerset placed an oversized cup of black coffee and a plate of cookies at her elbow. "Caffeine and sugar. You appear to thrive on them."

"They do the job."

"So do you, Lieutenant."

He followed the others into the adjoining office, then shut the door.

Eve took the first of her forty minutes to absorb the solitude, the quiet. Then got to work.

Thirty-nine minutes later, Roarke came in.

"What? Do you set an alarm?"

"Do I need to?" After a glance at her board, he nodded. "You've updated, and wouldn't be standing here staring at your board if you hadn't sent off your report."

"Upper East for Rossi, Lower East for the bomb. He's got a place on the West Side."

"Because it's more complicated."

"Affirmative. He's got his own vehicle. Public transpo wouldn't cut it. He's got a garage."

"You've had at least some of those five minutes of thinking time. As well as coffee and some of Summerset's exceptional shortbread biscuits."

"Cookies on this side of the Atlantic, pal."

"I'm an Irishman currently surrounded by Brits."

"And where are they?"

"Gone to bed, as we're about to."

He took her hand to lead her away from the board, and out of the room.

Chapter Fifteen

"How'd they take it?"

"Like the professionals they are. And with considerable mining for details. They want to see the recording. And before you say no, which is your first instinct as it was mine, these are people who worked with the kind of device we deactivated."

"You deactivated. I held the goddamn light. I'll think about it. I'll think about it because they did work with that type of device, and because—active or not, and who can be sure which—they are pros."

When she walked into the bedroom and saw the cat sprawled on the bed, she immediately felt better. But winding through the better, she was embarrassed to realize, was a strong thread of resentment.

She pointed at him. "He didn't give me the time of day— Why did I say that? How's a cat supposed to tell you the time? God, I hate saying things that make no sense. I'm surprised he's not bunking with one of them."

"They're an entertaining and attentive novelty. You're home."

Home, she thought. Sanctuary or safe house, it was still home. And that's where they were. A couple hours before, they'd been one wrong move away from a very nasty death.

She gave Roarke one long look, then put her hands on his shoulders. She boosted herself up, wrapped her legs around his waist, and locked her mouth to his.

"I had caffeine and sugar." Revved and ready, she nipped her teeth along his throat. "We could've been pink mist, but we're not. And I still like your face."

"I'll need to deactivate forty-year-old bombs more often."

"Solid negative there." She went back to his mouth as he dropped them both on the bed.

The cat gave one low growl of annoyance as he rolled away and leaped off the bed.

"Serves him right. And why is it whenever I'm in a hurry, you're wearing too many clothes?"

"So are you, plus you're still armed. But we'll take care of that."

It didn't take him long to release her weapon harness, strip that away. It took her longer to tug him out of his jacket as his mouth, his hands, distracted her. While she struggled with his shirt, he had hers off so quickly it might not have been there in the first place.

Now, with her blood running hot, her pulse thumping fast, he drew up her legs to pull off her boots.

"Nearly there."

"Come here, come here."

She dragged him back to her, just to feel the weight, the shape of him over her, the taste, the heat of his mouth on hers.

All so real, so warm. So alive.

So his hands stroked down her, taking that pleasure, down the long torso, the narrow hips, those endless legs.

If he burned for her, she'd kindled the flame, and it spread as he took his mouth over flesh and bone and muscle.

His warrior, his heart, his abiding passion.

She stripped off his shirt; he peeled away her tank. And they were flesh to flesh, body to body, heart to heart while the kiss took on a wildness that raced through both of them.

When his mouth found her breast, she arched under him. On strangled cries of pleasure and impatience, she fought with his belt.

Take more. Take me. Take all.

Those clever fingers found her first, found her hot and wet and sent her flying. Even as she flew, he drove into her so that pleasure, dark and desperate, slammed into release, then release into even more pleasure.

Once again, she locked her legs around him. Body quaking, need building impossibly again, she took his face in her hands. Looking into those vivid blue eyes, she saw the same need, the same heart, the same unity.

"I love you."

"A ghrá."

With his eyes on hers, he let himself fall into her.

She didn't remember dropping into sleep, but she woke in gloomy light with the sky window overhead running with rain. The cat curled at her back, and the bed beside her was empty.

Already at work, she thought, but not yet sitting across the room with the screen scrolling on mute. She missed that, the routine of that, but at the moment, routine had gone to hell.

She got up, checked the time, and decided she had enough of it for a quick, solid workout.

She grabbed coffee first, let it smack away the last dregs of fatigue. She pulled on gym shorts, a sports tank, running shoes. A couple of miles, she thought as she got in the elevator, get the heart pumping. Some weights to wake up muscles.

Then more coffee.

Downstairs, she turned toward the gym.

And stopped short when she found Marjorie and Iris doing curls.

Her first thought was that though they had about thirty years on her, they were in damn good shape. Her second: What the hell were they doing in her space?

They stopped when they saw her. Marjorie shot out that vid-star smile. "Good morning! Another early riser—and we have the excuse of getting our body clocks on New York time."

Iris put her weights back on the rack. "We're in your way."

Eve thought: Yes. But said, "No, that's—"

"We thought we'd be out before anyone else was stirring." Marjorie racked her weights. "One has to stay in tune if one insists on doing stunts. And since I enjoy making the occasional action vid, I'm honor bound. I see you have a new model of sparring droid. Mine's considerably older, and should be updated. How do you like this one?"

First, she tried to imagine the middle-aged woman going at it with the droid, one fabricated as a muscular male of about thirty-five.

"Ah, I haven't tried it yet. I broke the last one."

Marjorie's brows winged up. "Sparring?"

"I was a little pissed off."

"Impressive."

Iris handed Marjorie a tube of water. "We'll get out of your way. We just need to stretch it out."

"How about we finish with some yoga, Iris? Could we use your very Zen dojo for that, Lieutenant?"

"Sure. Ah, there are programs."

"I have my own." Marjorie tapped a finger to her temple as they left.

Eve stood a minute to make sure they kept going. She couldn't remember ever having that much conversation or pulling out that many manners ten minutes after rolling out of bed.

To compensate she put herself through a hard, sweaty three-mile run, then another session with weights. She might have used the dojo for a little yoga herself, but for all she knew, they'd still be in there.

Doing sun salutations, or meditating.

She stretched where she was, then headed straight back to the bedroom.

Roarke sat, the cat across his lap. The screen scrolled on mute as he did whatever he did on a tablet. But routine took another detour as he wore black jeans and a blue T-shirt that turned his eyes to blue lasers.

"Where's your suit?"

"Taking the day off."

"You're taking the day off?"

"The suit is. I'll be working from home until I join you at Chez Robert."

"Oh."

It actually helped knowing he'd be around for a while, keeping their guests contained.

She grabbed more coffee. "Two of them were down there, the vid star and the tea queen. In skimpy skin shorts and sports bras."

"I see."

"They're pretty ripped. I had to talk to them, and pretend I didn't want them to go away so I could work out."

"A challenging start to your day."

"Tell me about it." She headed in to shower.

When she came back, he had plates under domes, more coffee waiting, and the cat banished to the floor.

"Even with the conversation, the workout, I'm ahead of schedule. I'm going in early again."

When she sat, he took off the domes, revealed pancakes, bacon, fruit.

The world got considerably brighter.

She immediately swamped the pancakes in syrup.

"I'll coordinate with you, but I need to refine the op, get a team briefed. I'm going to bring Lowenbaum in."

"You think you'll need SWAT?"

"Potter's a professional, too. The more coverage, the better. If we can box him in today, take him, it's done. Turn him over to the Brits—not the ones staying here. They all go home."

"And all's right with the world."

"Except for Rossi and his family, yeah. Can't make all right with their world, but we can bring them justice." She shoveled in pancakes. "About letting them all see the record from last night? If we miss Potter today, I'll green-light that. It may trigger something that can help. If we get him, there's no need."

"Fair enough."

"What were you working on?"

"Not working so much as checking. The Great House Project. It's winding up."

"So Peabody said, but with a lot more words. They're spending the weekend there."

"There's still some work. They could move in altogether if they wanted." With the tablet set aside, he ate with her. "It's finish work, punch out work primarily. But they want the big moment. The weekend's a trial run."

"You made it run. I know you made it run smoother and faster than it would have. They appreciate it."

"I've enjoyed it. The project itself, and the working with friends."

As he enjoyed sharing breakfast with his wife and speaking, for a few minutes, of happier things.

"Which reminds me," he added, "the chair for Number Two will be ready by official move-in."

"That's good. Did I tell you Jake's moving in with Nadine?"

"Yes, you mentioned it. And so did Jake, when I saw him at An Didean—he's taken an interest in one of the students. Gee's got a rather masterful way with a guitar. Jake and Nadine seem very happy."

"It's happening everywhere. It's weird."

Stuffed with pancakes, she got up and faced her closet.

"It's an op, a major op. I'm wearing black."

Because she said it like a challenge, he had to smile.

"It's a bit cooler today, and rainy. Go for the leather jacket. You have a black one that's very thin and flexible leather."

"How am I supposed to know which one that is?"

He held up a hand, then wary of the cat, took the plates to stow inside the AutoChef cabinet. Shut the door.

He went into her closet and directly to a black jacket.

"This one."

Simple, she noted, no fuss. Good pockets. And she did have a weakness for leather. "What's the symbol on the buttons. Flowers?"

"Four-leaf clovers. For luck. You might want those lug-soled boots. Good traction if you have to run down your bad guy."

"He's pushing eighty. I think I can take him."

But she went for the boots, and a black shirt, black trousers.

"Not those, darling." He took the trousers, exchanged them for another pair. "Those were indigo. You'll want true black."

"Black should just be black."

They both heard the crash from the bedroom.

"Bugger it."

When they pushed out, the cat stretched up inside the open cabinet, happily licking syrup off a plate.

The dome sat on the floor where it had fallen.

"He opened it," Eve said. "He opened the damn door."

"I'm impressed. I'm bloody well impressed. And yet."

Roarke strode over, plucked up the cat. "I'll put a lock on it if needs must," he told the cat, and set him down.

Unconcerned, Galahad licked syrup off his paws. His bicolored eyes zeroed in on Eve's, and were full of delight.

Amused, she dressed.

"I expect to be on scene by twelve-fifteen," she told Roarke. "If you want to go in with us, be at Central by noon. Otherwise, I'll give you a location."

"I'll let you know."

"If he contacts Iris again . . . she knows how to play it. But I want to know about it."

"I'll make sure of it."

As she loaded her pockets, he walked to her. "Take very good care of my cop today."

"You'll be there for part of it, so take care of my gazillionaire, expert consultant, bomb deactivator."

"Then we have a deal." He kissed her. "I'll see you in a few hours."

She glanced at the cat as she started out. "He's thinking about doing it again."

"Are you now, mate?" she heard Roarke say. "Are you really?"

She was barely through the gates when Whitney tagged her.

"Sir."

"My office, as soon as you get to Central."

"I'm on my way in now, Commander."

"Good. So am I."

When he clicked off, she winced.

Just over a minute later, it was Mira.

"Dr. Mira."

"I'd like to meet with you this morning regarding your investigation."

"I'm on my way in, and meeting with the commander. I can come to your office after that."

"I'll come to you. I'd like to see your board."

So much, Eve thought when she ended the call, for getting an early start on the op. After some calculations, she sent a group text to her bullpen.

If it's not hot, drop it. Operation briefing zero-eight-thirty. Peabody, send last night's report to all and book a conference room.

She sent a request for Lowenbaum to attend, then considering her time crunch, shot off more to Berenski, DeWinter, and the boomer citing the urgency on receiving their findings on prints, DNA, and bomb analysis.

And driving through the rain, avoiding idiots who lost all ability to drive at the first drop, she planned her op.

When she arrived at Central, she rode the elevator straight up to Whitney's office. As others got on, got off, she shared space with a street LC who looked like she'd had a nasty scuffle with a colleague or client, a pair of uniforms arguing baseball, and an undercover cop sporting a black eye and chowing down on a breakfast taco.

Whitney's admin had yet to arrive, but the commander's doors stood open. He said, "Come."

Eve knew tired and annoyed when she looked at it, as she often felt the same way.

"Sit." When she hesitated, he pointed to a chair. "Sit."

She sat.

"Make this clear, Lieutenant. You suspected an explosive device had been planted somewhere on the premises of a restaurant on the Lower East Side, and rather than alerting the bomb squad, obtained a warrant to enter and search."

"Yes, sir. I—"

He cut her off with a look. "You and the civilian consultant entered the building with the civilian's explosive scanner, located the device. Upon doing so, you did not move to a safe distance and contact the division manned and equipped to secure and deactivate incendiary devices, but allowed the civilian to risk his life and yours by attempting to do so."

"Yes, sir, with one qualification."

"Qualification. What did I miss, Lieutenant?"

"The civilian identified the device as Urban Wars era, and assured me he could and would deactivate the device. While the civilian might have risked his own life, he would never have risked mine. He would not risk mine."

Whitney drew breath in and out his nose. "As simple as that?"

"As certain as that. If Potter had been watching the target, we risked alerting him by calling in an explosives team. The probability he was, was low, sir, but not zero."

"I'll remind you you've yet to conclusively establish that Potter is the suspect, that he is still alive."

"I messaged Dr. DeWinter this morning expressing the urgency of that confirmation. There's a high probability his prints will be on the device. I've also messaged Chief Berenski on the urgency of that confirmation."

"Pierce is in custody. Has he made a statement?"

"Not as of my last contact with Inspector Abernathy. Pierce is set to be extradited and transported to London this morning. There are things I can control, Commander, and things I can't."

"Get in line," Whitney muttered.

"I'm consulting with Dr. Mira shortly, and plan to brief my squad on an op to take Potter this afternoon. He'll be there, he'll be close. I've requested Lieutenant Lowenbaum attend."

"You haven't been given clearance for this op."

"No, sir. If you could attend—"

"Oh, I'll be there." He took another breath. "Dallas, you're exceptional police. You run your division with skill and sense, and your instincts are solid. But Potter, if it is Potter, pulled you into this investigation, and he's playing with you."

"Understood, sir, absolutely and completely. But the fact is . . ." Screw it, she decided. "Permission to speak frankly."

"By all means."

"He's fucking up. He firmly believes he's smarter than any of the targets, than me, than the NYPSD. And his vision is narrow while his methods are unnecessarily complicated. He thinks of them as a puzzle only he can solve. And it's stupid. The use of the cousin of one of the targets? We disproved that in about ten minutes. He should've expected us to check, but he didn't. He believes we think he's dead so we're down some rabbit hole.

"He fully expects those three women to just—just la-de-da their way into that restaurant today. He killed one of their friends, someone they went through a war with, and they'll just stroll into a ladies' lunch? He doesn't understand them or respect them. Or me. He's so focused on taking them out so they're just check marks on a list."

When she finished, Whitney inclined his head.

"He managed to escape from a maximum-security prison, fake his death, and access considerable funds before coming to New York and executing a trained agent."

"I didn't say he was stupid, Commander. His methods are. If he'd just killed Rossi, he could have walked away and focused on the next. But he couldn't leave it at that. And there's the stupid."

"I want those confirmations. Until we have them, you're pursuing an unsub. The prints aren't enough, if there are prints. He might have handled it during the wars. Which you've considered."

"Yes, sir. It would up the probability, but we need the DNA to confirm."

"Where's the briefing?"

"Peabody's booking a conference room."

"I'll be there. Dismissed. Dallas," he said as she got up and started out. "How did Roarke learn to deactivate an Urban Wars–era bomb?"

"Summerset taught him."

"Summerset—" Whitney rubbed his eyes. "Never mind. Go."

She went, jogging down glides this time. She had an hour before the briefing, so some time to prep. On the jog, she texted Feeney, informing him and inviting him in.

She headed straight to her office, intended to hit her AC for coffee, then get down to it. Get some of it organized before she met with Mira.

And found Mira already in her office, sitting at her desk, studying the board.

"You haven't been able to update your board since you clocked out yesterday."

"No."

"And want to get to that, and other matters. I want a few minutes first."

"I'm briefing at eight-thirty if you'd like to attend."

"I'll adjust my schedule." She rose so they both stood facing the board. "He's not rational."

"I clued into that."

"What he's attempted to do this afternoon, the way he's attempted it, is foolish."

"I said fucked-up and stupid."

"All of that. When he fails, when he realizes he's failed, his next move will be more irrational, and more dangerous."

"That's why I want to bag him today. He'll be there."

"No question," Mira agreed. "But irrational, foolish, fucked-up, stupid, doesn't discount cunning, Eve. And after today, if he slips through, you'll be on his kill list."

"I figured I already was, just low on it. I need coffee. Do you want coffee or tea?"

"I'll take the coffee."

Mira walked over and sat on the very edge of Eve's visitor's chair in her pretty russet-colored sheath. With it she wore a triple strand of pearls, some sort of russet-colored studs with tiny pearl drops, and sky-high heels that swirled russet and pearly white.

"Take the desk," Eve told her.

"I'm fine. I'm not sure you were on the list before this. Thanks." She took the coffee. "He had no need to kill you when he believed he'd best you. He'd have enjoyed your failure, and the guilt you'd have felt for the death of Summerset, as well as the others."

"Roarke?"

"He'd have the satisfaction of Roarke's guilt and grief. All that power and money, and he'd lose a father figure and, now that you're on that list, a wife. While he's incapable of understanding love, he fully understands guilt and grief. Not feeling them, but knowing others do.

"You took a considerable risk last night."

"Calculated, weighed. Would Roarke have let me hold the light if he couldn't deactivate the bomb?"

"No. But he's not infallible."

"He hasn't missed yet. We have a good chance of getting Potter today, before anyone else is hurt, because Roarke didn't miss. And the way Potter's set this up—"

"Foolishly complicated, easily dismissed. He considers you and the targets the foolish ones. He'll do at least some recalculation after today."

"I plan for him to recalculate in a cage."

"I'd like to sit in when you interview him. You will interview him?"

"He murdered in New York. The Brits will extradite him, but I'll get my shot."

"I'll get out of your way, and come back for the briefing. Again, don't underestimate him, Eve."

"I never underestimate a killer."

She took the next fifteen to organize for the briefing before she heard Peabody's boots coming.

"Conference room's booked. I turn my back for a few hours, and you're defusing a fricking bomb."

"Roarke deactivated."

"And still. Feeney tagged McNab as we were coming in. He wants him and Callendar at the briefing. They'll man an EDD van, help work the comms, and be on scene if you need eyes and ears."

"Good." She handed Peabody a disc. "Set this up, and start putting up a board. Updated."

"On it. You should know Carmine—the lab guy—is working on something with Yancy. He thinks together they can get some sort of idea what was under the mask. Something about face shape, bone structure. Eyes, ears, and whatever."

"They think they can get a face?"

"Sounds like a long shot, but Carmine's got his teeth in it, and Feeney's giving him the go."

"Can't hurt. Set us up. I'll be there in five."

"Conference room one."

Eve took the five to update her own board, then walked into the bullpen. And into Jenkinson's tie with bright yellow, orange-beaked rubber ducks swimming on frothy blue bubbles in tiny tubs.

"I can't even begin," she said.

"You're messing with bombs, and you don't call, you don't write?"

"You're on call now. And you know what? Soft clothes, but wear that terrifying tie. Nobody's going to think you're a cop."

"That's just another way to kick their asses into a cage."

Maybe he was right, she thought. She didn't want him to be right, but maybe.

She walked out of the bullpen—and nearly into Garnet DeWinter. Another sheath, this time pale green and worn with candy-pink skyscrapers.

She'd changed her hair—people were always doing that—so some of her natural curls framed her damn near perfect face.

"I didn't need the reminder to do my work."

"Did you get the DNA?"

"I went into the lab early, after working late."

Eve echoed Whitney. "Get in line. Walk and talk. Did you get the DNA? I've got a briefing on an op, and Whitney wants confirmation."

"I'm very good at my work, and have considerable of it that doesn't apply to your investigation."

"I wouldn't have asked for you if you weren't good at your work. Look, DeWinter, this asshole planned to blow up three women, and anybody else within about ten feet, this afternoon. I spent part of my night holding a fucking flashlight so Roarke could deactivate a bomb and stop that from happening.

"Quit your carping, and tell me if you got the DNA."

"I wouldn't have taken the time to come here if I hadn't. The remains were not Conrad Potter's, but the remains of one Trevor Kimball, age fifty-eight, who according to his records self-terminated—a bedsheet hanging—in the same prison as Potter three days prior.

"There were not sufficient remains to match an adult male of his height, his weight."

"Pierce divvied them up."

"That's for you to determine. In the meantime—"

"Thank you." Eve held out a hand.

DeWinter frowned at the hand, then sighed, shook it. "You're welcome. We are on the same team, Dallas."

"I'm aware. He's a very bad guy, DeWinter."

"So many are."

"You could've just sent the report instead of coming in."

"I was a little pissed off."

"Again, get in line."

"Yes, but that seems to be your natural state of being."

"It helps catch the very bad guys. How do you walk around all day in those shoes?"

"Stylishly." With that, DeWinter turned on her skyscraper heels and walked stylishly away.

In her lug-soled boots, Eve went into the conference room.

Chapter Sixteen

PEABODY HAD FINISHED THE BULK OF THE SETUP. EVE WALKED OVER TO help complete the board.

"He'd know the whole group's in New York now."

Eve nodded. "He knew they'd come. He knows they're here now, but not where. Ivanna has electronic surveillance on her apartment, so we'll know if he tries there. But he hasn't so far."

"He could waste his time trying to find them at hotels."

"If they weren't with us, they'd have rented a house. All together. He can waste his time trying to find that. He thinks he can lure the women out with a lunch date. He doesn't give them any credit for brains."

"Us, either," Peabody said.

"Us, either. DeWinter confirmed DNA. Not Potter."

"XL!"

"Excel at what?"

"No, XL. Excellent. And Abernathy has the prison doctor."

"He's not going to know dick, but he's going to find out what it's like on the other side of a cage."

Feeney walked in, nodded at the board. "Moving right along. You know, those old boomers can do some serious damage."

"Now this one can't and won't." She pulled out her signaling 'link. "Berenski, text. Bitch, bitch, whine, whine, bitch. Fingerprints on housing, on timer, etc., etc., confirmed as Potter's. And a bitch to cap it off."

She replaced her 'link. "DNA confirmed as not Potter's."

"Moving right along," Feeney repeated. Hands on hips, he studied the board. "Lab rat and Yancy are working on the face."

"Peabody told me."

"They may just pull it off. Not before the op, but it'll look fine in the file. You'll take him in the box before they haul him back to England?"

"For Rossi, yeah, for the bomb."

"Good. Is that Roarke's coffee in there?"

"No," Peabody told him. "But I can make that happen. If?"

"Shit, go ahead." Eve stepped back, scanned the board as her detectives started coming in. "Get coffee, take a seat. The commander and Dr. Mira are sitting in. We'll wait for them."

McNab bounced in, wearing neon-blue baggies and a shirt that held the solar system. Some of the stars gleamed and Saturn's rings sparkled.

"Callendar got held up, but she'll be here. I smell real coffee." He made a beeline for the AutoChef.

When Lowenbaum came in, wearing sensible black, Eve crossed over to have a word with him before Whitney and Mira arrived.

Then she walked back to stand between the screen and the board.

"Chatter off. The target is Conrad Potter. The remains purported to be his are not, but the partial remains of another inmate. Dr. DeWinter confirmed this morning. The prints on the explosive device have been confirmed as his. Potter is seventy-eight. Caucasian male, five-ten. At the time of his imaginary death, one hundred and sixty-three pounds. We don't have his current face.

"If you read the file, you know his background. He was, in London during the Urbans, a skilled operative, a double agent who betrayed his team and killed two of them. He was captured, tried, and convicted and served the last few decades in max security in Manchester, England.

"His accomplice in faking his death and his escape is now in custody. Potter is also responsible for the death, here in New York, of Giovanni Rossi, another member of The Twelve, Potter's Underground team. He used an Urbans-era gas to kill Rossi."

She skimmed through the details, gave a brief nutshell of the targets housed in her home, and moved on to the contact the night before.

"He again used an Urbans-era device, incendiary, planting it under the table he'd booked."

"Does he think the women he targeted are lamebrains?" Callendar wondered.

"Yeah, he does. Had this device worked as he planned, he would have killed the three women and anyone else within approximately a ten-foot radius."

"Collateral damage," Baxter muttered.

"Which wouldn't concern him at all. This is his war. It's retribution, sure, but it's also finishing his mission. And that was to eliminate the entire team.

"If you haven't read Dr. Mira's profile, do so. He doesn't take the simple way, considers himself too clever for simple. He considers the layers of complications and unnecessary steps a puzzle the opposition can't solve."

From his seat, Santiago pointed to the board. "Wrong about that."

"Damn right. While he's had a few years since his escape to sharpen his skills, they're not as sharp as he believes. He won't resist being in the area, having a view of the target area today. Thirteen hundred for their arrival, fifteen minutes more to detonation. There are multiple areas where he can find that view. We need to cover as many as possible.

"Peabody, on-screen. The target, here."

"He'd like to be inside," Jenkinson said. "Watch his work. But unless he's a serious fuckhead . . ."

"He won't be," Eve finished. "Across the street's most probable. Plenty of good views. My information says he's not a sniper. But he may want that bird's-eye. Lieutenant Lowenbaum's team will sweep and man the rooftops. DS Jenkinson and Detective Reineke will cover this restaurant."

One by one she assigned teams while Peabody worked the screen.

"He works alone, he'll be alone. Just a well-dressed man browsing a shop, having a bite to eat, taking a walk. But he will, almost certainly, be armed. He will, following patterns, very likely be armed with an Urbans-era weapon."

Eve scanned the room. "He had a stockpile; he's using it. I'm running rentals on the residential and commercial spaces above street level. If he snagged one, it would be within months, as he couldn't be sure of this step until his targets were in New York. He's got money, but his funds have limits."

"And that neighborhood don't come cheap," Carmichael pointed out.

"As he has some B and E skills, we'll sweep any empty unit, make sure he hasn't set up shop. EDD will monitor comms and the street. Questions."

She fielded them.

"Commander Whitney, are we a go?"

"You're a go."

"Be ready to roll at noon. If anyone catches a case—"

"I'll see it's covered," Whitney said.

"Thank you, Commander. Peabody and I will be in the field. Peabody, with me. Keep the conference room," she added as they started out. "We'll break it down when we have him."

"It's a lot of area to cover. With binocs, he could hole up in any building on that side of the block."

"He could, and he might." Without hesitation, she chose the glides. "But he's a risk taker. He'll want to be close, close enough to hear the bang."

Fast-walking on the glides, she glanced at Peabody. "What do people do when there's a boom?"

"Scream, panic, run."

"He put a cam in the back of the limo so he could watch Rossi die. None in the restaurant, but he'll want to watch that panic, hear the screams."

They took the clanging metal stairs to the garage.

"That's not going to happen." As they crossed to the car, Peabody caught her breath. "What does he do next?"

"We watch for someone who reacts to nothing at thirteen-fifteen." Eve got behind the wheel. "Easiest for us if he's set up in one of the restaurants or shops. But you're right, a lot more area to cover than that. Check the in-dash incoming for those search results."

"Okay, first up, commercial and residential units rented within the last six months." Peabody slid her gaze toward Eve. "Not as bad as I figured, but a lot."

"Prioritize with leaseholders, male, over the age of sixty. Street-view units."

"That'll whittle it some. More than some."

"While that's working, we look at empty units. Street views."

"I'm transferring this to my PPC, and yours, so we both have it mobile. And happily, people like the neighborhood, only fourteen unrented street-facing units on the block."

"Combine those with the other filtered results. We'll take it building by building."

After congratulating herself on finding a street spot, Eve parked at the head of the block. While the distance equaled low probability for her, they had to cover it.

They pulled out the super and got started.

By the third building, they'd eliminated a sizable chunk.

"Some nice spaces. None of the recently rented came close to our guy. I thought we might have something with the one in the last building. Had the age range, the height and weight close enough. Until you got there and he's babysitting his toddler grandkid who lives in the same building."

"And he had a cat. Potter hates cats."

"Couple of empty units that could work."

"With no sign anyone's been in there, no tampering with the locks. What have we got here?"

"Two vacant two-bedroom units, street facing. Two occupied with leaseholders that fit our parameters."

"Let's get the super."

The super, a dark-skinned woman with improbable blond hair worn in waist-length coils, gave Eve the wide eyes.

"Oh my God, it's you! It's you. Who's dead? Somebody's been murdered? I saw the vid. It was wild."

"No one's dead, Ms. Oglebee. We're—"

Oglebee sucked in air, and her eyes went wider. "We've got clones?"

"No, ma'am. You could help in an area of an investigation."

"Bet your ass I will. Sorry, that's rude! I'm a little, you know, aback. Who'd say no to Dallas and Peabody?"

"We'd like to look through two empty units. Peabody?"

"Units 5-A and 3-C."

"Oh my God, are you looking for your own place? You're busting up with Roarke?" She slapped a hand on her heart. "Don't do it!"

"I'm not. This is part of an investigation. If we could look through those units, and if you could tell us more about the occupants of . . ."

"Units 5-C and 2-A."

"Are they suspects? Holy hell!"

"This is a standard inquiry," Peabody put in. "Unit 2-A is a Jared Cross."

"Sure it is. Good-looking gentleman, moved in about six weeks ago. And what happens not two weeks later? A woman half his age moves in with him, her and her dog. One of those dogs about the size of your hand. Cute little guy though."

"So he doesn't live alone?"

"Not anymore. Good-looking, and he's got some . . ." She rubbed her fingers together. "Not like Roarke, but he's got some, all right. Pushing seventy if he hasn't already pushed it, and her maybe half that. And a couple days ago, he takes her off to the Olympus Resort, and that takes . . ."

Fingers rubbed.

"Me, I'm not going off-planet for love or money, but they're off."

"And 5-C?" Peabody asked. "Claude Roster?"

"Poor guy. His wife left him for her yoga instructor. Thirty years married, and that's it for you, buddy. Moved in about three months ago. His daughter helped him. She and her man and their kids visit him, get him out of the apartment. They brought him the sweetest little kitten a few weeks ago so he'd have company."

She offered a brilliant smile. "Am I helping?"

"Yes, thanks. Those fall outside our area of investigation. If we could see the empty units."

"Absolutely. I've got my pass swipe right here." She patted her pocket.

"I have a master," Eve said. "If it's all the same to you, we'd like to take a look on our own."

"Oh, well, sure." Oglebee's disappointment flooded the area. "It's all official and everything, right?"

"Yes, ma'am. We appreciate your time and cooperation."

"Is there going to be another vid?" she called out.

Since she could feel Eve's inner shudder, Peabody glanced back. Smiled. "They're working on it."

"Can't wait!"

"Think of it this way," Peabody began as they started up the stairs. "We got a lot out of her because she saw the vid."

"I'm trying not to think about it at all. Women, dogs, cats, family. Potter likes complications, but no way he could build that kind of cover in a matter of weeks or months. And he works alone."

"Can't argue there."

Eve turned into the hallway. "Good soundproofing, clean, good security on the apartments."

She mastered through at 3-C.

"And a really nice space again." Peabody walked in, turned a circle. "Nice, street-facing windows. Without the rain, there'd be lots of natural light."

As she was more interested in the view, Eve walked to the front windows. "Prime spot. He wouldn't need binocs from here. Might use them to get a closer look."

"They must've just painted the place."

"Yeah, I can smell it." She went back to the door, crouched down to examine the locks. "Top-of-the-line. He may have gotten his hands on a master, otherwise, there's no sign of circumventing them."

"I'll say the painters couldn't have finished more than a day ago. Breaking in after hours, maybe, but the building has cams, too, and tight security."

"Go give Oglebee a thrill. Ask her to let you scan the security feed for the last forty-eight, find out when the painters finished, and if either of the units have applications in. I'll go through here, and if you're not back, you can meet me at the one on five."

Alone, Eve walked through over shining floors with the smell of fresh paint everywhere. She found every surface immaculate. Including the kitchen, bathroom, and the tiny powder room drains.

When her 'link signaled, she scanned an incoming from Nadine. The intrepid reporter had managed to amass considerable data on Potter, which Eve already had.

But she'd managed to track down one of the cops—female—who'd served with Potter.

> Interview attached, but to summarize, DCI Gemma Standish, a young constable at the time she was on the cops with Potter, describes him as—and I quote—a right prick. Heavy-handed with suspects and prisoners. She doesn't recall him having any particular friends in the unit, no one who'd buy him a pint or socialize with him after hours. A loner. He treated all female officers with overt disrespect, often referring to them as Cunt Coppers.

"Yeah, that sums him up."

Eve secured the apartment, and took the stairs up.

On five, she repeated the routine. Here the walls needed that fresh paint, and she spotted a number of holes where someone had hung art. Clean enough, she judged, but not pristine.

Unlike on three, these windows held a thin film of dust inside and some street grime outside.

Still, she thought, another prime view of Chez Robert.

And more recently vacated, she concluded, than 3-C.

Peabody confirmed when she joined Eve.

"Tenants moved out of this one just two days ago. They bought a house. Painters are coming in today, she hopes. It's not publicly advertised yet, and won't be until they paint, deep clean, and inspect. Nothing on the security feed, Dallas. Couple of lone males coming in or going out, but none in the right age frame. And she identified one as a tenant, the other as a frequent visitor. She sure knows her building."

"All right. Let's move on. Nadine sent some data," Eve added as they started out. "Most just confirms what we already know about him. She also dug up a female officer on the job with him back then. No friends, a loner who referred to women officers as Cunt Coppers."

Peabody hissed out a breath. "I really, seriously don't like this asshole."

"You're not alone there. It adds more weight to the lone wolf, no friends, associates, long-term accomplices. He's on his own, and that's how he likes it."

Building by building, floor by floor, they worked the block.

"None of the newer tenants fit," Peabody said. "No sign on security feeds of him entering buildings with vacancies. In any case, it's easier—and a hell of a lot cheaper—to get a table right out here."

On the way back, Peabody stopped at the first restaurant. "Book a table for like one, maybe twelve-thirty, but probably one, take your seat. Order yourself a nice Cobb salad, maybe a glass of wine. Front-row seat. And in the inevitable confusion after, you walk away."

"Easier. Simpler. And that's why it doesn't slide in smooth for me. Let's go across the street, find out who booked the bomb booth."

Though the restaurant wasn't yet open, Eve's badge got them in. The manager, a fussy little man with jet-black hair and a blond goatee, blended concerned with annoyed.

"We open at noon, and we're eighty-eight percent booked through the lunch shift. We've barely begun our prep."

"Then the quicker you help us out, the quicker you can get back to it. We need to know who booked that back corner booth yesterday."

He sighed, a huge huff from the gut. "At what time?"

"At any time."

He mumbled, grumbled, fussed with his facial hair, and finally brought up the previous day's bookings on the station screen.

"Noon for Ms. Johnstone-Trevor and party. As she's a frequent guest and never lingers over ninety minutes, we took a two-thirty booking. Mr. Pouncy, party of three."

"Is the server here?"

"Of course! We're in lunch prep."

"Get her."

"Officer—"

"Lieutenant."

"Whatever. This is adversely affecting our schedule, and that can affect our service. Poor reviews can lower our rating and damage our reputation."

"Get her fast."

"Melinda!" He lifted his hands, fingers facing backwards. Wiggled them.

The server—early twenties, curvy, big smile, auburn hair back in a smooth tail—hurried right over.

"These are the police. They have questions."

Wide brown eyes showed alarm. "Oh!"

"For you, not about you," Eve qualified. "You handled that booth yesterday?"

She glanced back. "Yes, that's my table."

"Can you describe your two-thirty?"

"Oh, sure. Um, two men, one woman. Brothers. They took Mom out for lunch. They were both really sweet to her, and the older one—"

"How old?"

"About . . . maybe forty? He paid, and he tipped well."

Eve glanced back at the manager. "Who handled the dinner service?"

"Oh, I did," Melinda said. "I worked a double. There's a stomach virus going around."

"We're short-staffed," Mr. Fussy said, mouth pursed. "So if that's all."

"It's not. Tell me about that table, dinner service."

"Sure. I had a seven-thirty. It was supposed to be a party of six."

"Supposed to be?"

"That's right. With a seven-thirty booking, party of six, we wouldn't do a turnover. The single arrived right at seven thirty, and said his family would be coming along. Joked how they were always a bit late. He ordered a bottle of Charman's sparkling water and a gin fizz."

"Describe him."

"Well, older, you know, grandfather-type old. Very distinguished, I guess. Beautiful suit. Dark hair, with the temple gray. Distinguished."

"Was he carrying anything?"

"Oh right, yeah. A really mag leather man bag."

"What did he do?"

"Well, he took his time with the cocktail. I saw him checking his watch a couple times. I refilled his water glass. I guess it was about seven-forty-five or so when I started over to ask if he wanted another cocktail, but noticed he was on his 'link."

"The rest of his party never arrived."

"No. He got up really quickly, put some cash on the table to cover the drinks, and a nice tip, too. He said there'd been a family emergency and he rushed out."

"What name did he use to book?"

Scowling now, the manager checked. "C. S. Urban."

"He just can't resist," Eve murmured. "Melinda, if I could have your full name, your contact information, I'm going to send a police artist to work with you."

"Really? Did he do something? He was so nice."

"He's not, and if you see him again, keep your distance. Contact me." Eve dug out a card.

"I insist you allow us to get back to our work."

Eve spared him one long, cool look, and had the satisfaction of watching his bristle turn to a wither.

"We appreciate your cooperation, Melinda. The police artist will be in touch."

Peabody waited until they walked out. "That guy's a dick. I'd hate to work for somebody who's that big a dick. Potter planted the bomb before he contacted Iris. What if she'd said she couldn't make it?"

"They're lamebrained women, remember? He played the odds in his view of women. He could always come back and retrieve the device. Or hell, blow it up because he was pissed they didn't bite."

"I think he might have done that." As if she felt a chill, Peabody rubbed her arms. "Just let it go off."

"I wouldn't bet against it. See if you can get Yancy to hook up with the server. If he's too involved with this find-the-face project, ask him who's next best and tap them.

"Let's get back to Central. I don't want to be on the street on this block where he could spot us when he gets here."

They went, and Eve grabbed coffee, wrote it all up, sent it all out.

She had the map up on her screen again when Roarke came in.

"You're a little early. That's helpful. Let me catch you up."

When she had, quickly, efficiently, he nodded.

"The facing restaurants, particularly the sidewalk tables, are prime spots. Which is why you're worried he'll go somewhere else."

"I can't put cops in every building on the block. But he's not expecting cops. He's expecting three women. He *should* be at one of those tables. There's no indication he's cased any of the units, vacant or otherwise, and every indication he hasn't."

"But."

"But. Still, it's barely raining now, and the sidewalk areas have cover."

"You've done everything you can to box him in. Now it has to play out."

"His server was about twenty-four, pretty as it gets. He'd have blown her to hell without a second's regret. Just a casualty of his war. He'll be armed today, with something from his stockpile."

"Something easily concealed. Most likely an Urbans-era handgun. Semiauto, quick-release holster. And likely a secondary, a clutch piece."

She'd calculated the same, and that calculation formed a weight in her gut.

"A stunner on full can do some damage, but bullets fly, Roarke. They fly and they ricochet, and they can rip holes in a dozen people in a matter of seconds."

He heard her concern, brushed a hand down her arm. "And not everyone has a magic coat."

"For all we know the son of a bitch carries hand grenades in his pockets. It's not possible to clear a whole block of civilians, the businesses, the apartments, the streets and sidewalks. I don't want any casualties, not on my team, and not with civilians who just happen to get in the way. We need to close that box."

"Then that's what we'll do."

"Are you wearing Thin Shield?"

He opened his light jacket to show her.

"Okay. Time to move out."

In the bullpen she gathered with the team again.

"There are a handful of unoccupied units along the block, and no sign of illegal entry. No sign he's cased any of them. The probability reads he'd choose his view from one of the restaurants or shops, or just time it so he's on the street when it's set to blow. I'm going to emphasize again. He will be armed, most likely an Urbans-era handgun, potentially more than one weapon."

She paused, felt that weight in her belly.

"Protect and serve. Protect and serve the civilians, and each other. You all know your positions. Feeney, Peabody, Roarke, and I ride with you. He knows our faces.

"Now let's go get this fucker."

Chapter Seventeen

EVE CONSIDERED THE RAIN, STEADY BUT THIN, ANOTHER KIND OF SHIELD. It made bigger idiots out of drivers, but it encouraged the pedestrian population to either hurry on their way or stay indoors.

Feeney parked the van a half block from Chez Robert, and Eve huddled in front of the screens in the back and their various street views.

Watching, watching, she checked in with Lowenbaum.

"We're in position," he told her. "All clear."

"Roger that."

On-screen, she watched members of her team move toward their positions from various locations, scouting the block as they went.

"Give me a view of Chez Robert. I can't see him going in there, but."

As McNab added the angle, Feeney climbed in the back. "Got about fifteen minutes." Pulling the bag of candied almonds out of his pocket, he offered them around. "If he wants one of those front-row seats?" Feeney nodded toward the sidewalk dining views. "Booking at thirteen hundred's probable, and we're sliding past that. Got a few empty tables."

He shook his head, crunched an almond. "Why people want to eat outside with the traffic noise and rain clogging the air beats me."

"Urban treat." Callendar shrugged. "And see, that woman's got a little dog on her lap. They won't let you do that inside."

"I won't start on eating lunch with a dog on your lap."

"That guy." Eve tapped the screen. "Right height range, right weight range. Close in there."

This time Roarke handled it.

"Nice suit, umbrella. Clean-shaven, appearance closer to sixty, but he's done that before. Heading into the men's shop. Baxter, check the man coming in your location."

"Copy."

"Got a couple, male, female, getting out of at cab at 186. Can't get a good angle on them," McNab told her. "Sharing a big umbrella."

Eve shifted her focus as Baxter spoke in her ear.

"No go. Assistant manager back from lunch break."

"Copy."

She watched the couple go to the residential door, saw the woman take out a swipe, glance up at the man, laugh, and pat his arm as they walked in out of the rain.

Works alone, she thought. But.

She'd seen the lights on in the empty fifth-floor unit. As the privacy screen was off, she'd also seen the ladder, the figures in white coveralls.

Painters.

She kept her eye out for the lights to go on in 3-C.

"Another possible," Callendar said. "Black suit, black umbrella. Got facial hair."

"He likes disguises. Jenkinson, coming in at your three o'clock."

"Got him. Going straight to a table, younger guy already there. Shaking hands."

"Yeah, I see." He works alone, she thought again. But, but, but. "Keep an eye on him."

While Jenkinson kept an eye, and Eve scanned screens, Potter—under the name Jamison Brockstone—stepped out of the elevator on the third floor of 186. The real estate agent, one Brendita—"just call me Dita"—Havanara, continued her pitch.

"As you can see, a well-maintained, secure building in a lovely, active neighborhood. Easy walking to shops, restaurants."

She led him down to 3-C. "As I told you, apartments here turn over very quickly. I'm sorry your wife couldn't make it today."

"So is she." He lifted his hands. "It's only the sniffles, but Alice is very cautious."

"And with this rain. In any case, palm plate, door cam, and as you hear—or rather don't—excellent soundproofing."

She opened the door, and he listened with half an ear as she hyped the space, the privacy screening throughout, the flooring.

"Let me get the lights. So gloomy today."

"No, I'd like to see it as is, in the gloom first, if you don't mind."

He wandered, as if interested in the space, the screening, the flooring. All he cared about was the view of Chez Robert.

And it was perfect, of course.

He'd planned to watch from the restaurant on the street, but this? So much better. More a private moment, to cherish, to savor. He'd had to scramble a bit when he'd seen the listing, but worth it.

So worth it.

"The kitchen area."

She went on about counters, cabinets, appliances.

"Do you cook, Mr. Brockstone?"

He laughed as if such a question was foolish. "Not at all. My wife handles such things. It's often reservations," he added with a wink. "But she's quite a good cook when she puts her mind to it."

"She should love cooking here. It's a wonderful space for entertaining. For family evenings. Do you have children?"

He despised the little brats, but made up a son, a daughter, and three adorable grandchildren on the spot.

"Lovely! You'll see the second bedroom is a good space. For guests, for grands spending the night, and of course, an excellent home office or multipurpose space."

He tolerated the tour—he had time, still had time. Made approving comments or noises about the main suite with its windows—and the street view—its en suite, the double closets.

The surprise bonus, according to Dita, of a closet holding a combination washer/dryer.

"Not all the units have this, so there are laundry facilities, along with storage areas, on the basement level. The storage facility is an additional monthly fee."

"Of course."

"Is there anything I've missed? Do you have any questions?"

"Actually, I'd very much like to contact my wife, take her on a virtual tour. Then we can discuss—just the two of us, if you don't mind."

He very much wanted to be alone to enjoy his moment. If she objected, well, he could slit her throat. But he supposed he'd avoid the mess and be shocked at the explosion with her.

"That's an excellent idea. As I said, these apartments don't stay on the market long. Since you indicated, when I told you about the vacancy—not yet listed!—on five, you'd like to see it, too, why don't I meet you up there when you're done? 5-A. Remember, they are painting this afternoon, but if you and your wife want a look?"

"Perfect. I'll just walk through with Alice. It shouldn't take more than ten minutes or so, then I'll come up."

"5-A."

"5-A." He beamed smiles. "Ten minutes. Fifteen if Alice is chatty."

When she finally shut the door behind her, Potter moved straight to the window. Then checked his wrist unit. "Five minutes, thirty-two seconds."

They'd be at the table now. He was sorry he'd missed seeing them arrive, but he'd had to pretend interest in closets and double sinks and a ridiculous laundry machine.

But he could imagine, oh so well.

And up here, alone, he could cheer, right out loud (good soundproofing) when the bomb blew those bitches to bits and pieces.

For fun, he sent Iris a quick text from her cousin's 'link.

> Darling! So sorry, running late! This rain. I'll be rushing in, wet and frazzled, in five minutes! Kiss, kiss.

The response came moments later.

> No worries. We're having a glass of wine and catching up without you.

Smiling, he slipped the 'link back into his pocket. "Enjoy your glass of wine. It's your last."

In the van, Eve checked her own 'link. "He contacted Iris, said he's running late. Or her cousin is. Goddamn it, no sign of him."

No light in 3-C, painters still moving around in 5-A.

"He's here, I know he's here."

She looked at the view of 186.

"Lights on in 5-A. Painters in there. Shit, what if he's posing as a worker up there? I'm going in. I'm going to check."

"He knows your face," Roarke reminded her.

"Right." She plucked the bucket rain cap off Callendar's head. "This'll work. Peabody, give me two minutes inside, then follow. I'm checking 5-A, then we'll hit 3-C on the way out if it's a bust."

"You got three minutes, forty-eight seconds till it doesn't blow."

"Got it. All teams, Peabody and I are doing a check of 186. Give me two minutes inside," she repeated.

She went out the back, and hunching over as if bothered by the rain, walked the quarter block to 186.

"Want company, LT?" Jenkinson said in her ear as she passed.

"Peabody's behind me in two."

She mastered in, scanned the small lobby, then took the elevator to five.

On five, she scanned the hall, then walked straight to 5-A.

One hand resting on her weapon, she mastered in.

And into blasting music and the thick smell of paint.

Two figures in white hooded coveralls and breathing masks manned sprayers on either side of the living area.

One, obviously female by the way the coveralls fit, spotted her, turned off her sprayer.

"Jeez, Denny, we got another one. Do for you?"

Eve held up her badge, and since she couldn't see the second painter's face, kept the other hand on her weapon. "Turn off the music. Take off the masks."

"What the what?" The female slapped a pocket, and whatever device blasted music. The second pushed up his mask.

Since he couldn't have been more than thirty, Eve relaxed slightly.

"We're supposed to be here," he told her.

"Just the two of you painting this unit?"

"Us and Ned. He's cutting in the bedrooms."

"Stay where you are," she said, and moved in the direction he'd pointed.

In one of the spare bedrooms, the man, with an ebony hand, rock steady, painted a line ruler straight at the top of the ceiling. Since he was easily six-four in his paint-splattered kicks, he reached his target without a ladder.

She backed out, walked to where the painters stood, both slurping from tubes.

"Counting down from thirty," Roarke said in her ear.

"5-C's clear," she responded. "Sorry to interrupt," she said, then stopped on her way to the door.

"What other one? You said you had another one?"

"Another one what? Oh right, person coming in. The lady."

She gestured to what Eve remembered was the main bedroom just as a woman came out.

"Please don't start the sprayers again until my client arrives and I show him through. It's already . . . Hello," she said to Eve. "Can I help you?"

She recognized the suit, the slice of face she'd seen glance up and laugh. At a man shielded by an umbrella.

Showing the apartment. A client.

"You came in with a man about fifteen minutes ago. Where is he?"

"Excuse me, I have exclusive rights on this unit until it's advertised. Who are you?"

She yanked out her badge. "Where the hell is he?"

"Well, for heaven's sakes! Mr. Brockstone should be on his way up to view this apartment."

"Where is he *now*?"

"On his way up, didn't I just say?"

"3-C. Son of a bitch! All teams, all teams. Subject is in the building, 3-C. Cover the exits. I'm heading down."

She pulled open the door just as Peabody turned to run for the stairs.

As the Realtor stepped out of the bedroom in 5-A, Potter stood by the window. "Five, four, three, two, one!"

For an instant, his heart was full of joy, of triumph. He even pumped a fist in the air.

And nothing happened.

No blast of sound. No one on the street stopped, no cars braked at the sound of an explosion. No one ran screaming out of Chez Robert.

Furious, he jabbed the remote in his pocket.

Nothing.

And in that next instant, as fury turned to fear, he knew.

They'd set him up. Somehow.

He ran.

He flashed back to the night, decades before, when he'd been forced to run. His legs didn't move as fast now, but they wouldn't take him.

They wouldn't take him. He'd kill them all first.

Eve pounded down to three with Peabody on her heels. The door to 3-C hung open.

"Clear it, clear it fast. Black suit," she shouted at her team as she and Peabody cleared. "Box him in. He's running."

And so did she, down the steps as Santiago and Carmichael ran up.

"He didn't come this way. He didn't come out the front," Carmichael told her.

"Clear the basement level!"

Alarms went off.

"Fire exit. Goddamn it."

She launched herself over the railing, hit the floor, then streaked toward the back. She looked right, left, and saw him running across the intersection at the end of the block.

She shouted orders, locations, directions as she raced through rain that had decided to come back with a vengeance.

Though she had to dodge umbrellas and people who weren't looking where the hell they were going, she cut the distance in half before he looked over his shoulder and spotted her.

Then he did exactly what she'd feared. He pulled out a gun.

She felt the impact of the bullet on her shoulder, a light punch. And kept going.

Her own weapon in hand, she was still yards away when he planted, changed tactic.

With a wild grin he aimed not at Eve but at two women, oblivious as they walked arm in arm under an umbrella and chattered away.

She was fast, but not as fast as a bullet. With no choice, she flung herself in front of the women. She felt the impact again along her ribs, and a quick, hot sting as the women, shrieking, fell on the wet pavement.

One of them wrapped an arm around her leg and started screaming for help. For the police.

"Lady, lady, I'm a cop. I'm in pursuit."

And losing him, losing him in the rain.

The woman kept screaming, and before Eve could pull free, a good Samaritan built like a maxibus got in her face.

"I saw what you did. You knocked these ladies down."

"We're cops, we're cops. In pursuit." Panting, Santiago ran up, waving his badge. "An armed suspect. Go, Dallas, go!"

She went, but when Roarke cut across her path from the north, she knew they'd lost him.

"No sign of him the way I came," Roarke told her. "Feeney's circling in the van, and your BOLO went out."

Breathing hard, a drenched Santiago caught up. "I used to steal bases like they were candy, but fucking A, Dallas. You'd've had him, you'd have had him if those civilians hadn't gotten in the way. And let's hear it for Thin Shield."

"He fired on you?"

"Twice," Santiago said to Roarke. "Second time he aimed for the civilians. Bastard. Dallas knocked them down to spare them a bullet, then they tangled her up just long enough."

"We lost him. All this, and we still lost him."

She pressed her fingers against the sting on the edge of her right ribs. And they came back bloody.

"Well, shit."

"You're hit."

Roarke dragged up her shirt.

"Hey, hey, we're on the freaking street."

"Shut up. It didn't penetrate." Relief trembled through him as he examined the wound. "A graze, not a pleasant one, but shallow."

"I could've told you. It hit the lining. I felt it. I guess it caught me a little when I had to jump in front of those idiot women."

Roarke tapped his earbud as she dragged her shirt back down. "Feeney, we need the van at our location. The lieutenant's wounded."

"Don't say that!" Appalled, she shoved at his arm. "I'm not wounded. I'm scratched. I need these blocks canvassed, I need to see security feeds from door cams. I need—"

"To tell your very efficient team what you need them to do while you're getting that wound treated."

If she could've torn out her hair—or better, his—she'd have done it.

"I'm not going to the hospital for this. That's ridiculous."

"We'll see what the MTs have to say."

Santiago cleared his throat. "Say! How about we get started on the canvass? Here's Carmichael now."

"Was that gunfire?" Carmichael demanded. "I thought I heard—Dallas, you're bleeding."

"White male, seventy-eight. Looks late sixties, approximately five-ten, a hundred and sixty, blond, collar-length hair, black suit, white shirt, blue tie. Heading west on foot when I lost him."

Peabody jogged up. "I took over the civilians from Santiago. All handled. Did I hear— Dallas, you're bleeding."

Eve ignored her, along with the chatter in her ear from various team members. "Everybody, shut the hell up! There's a glide-cart on the next corner, talk to the operator. Canvass the block, then split with the rest of the team. West, north, south. I couldn't see which direction he took. I want McNab and Callendar on door cams."

"Your ride, Lieutenant," Roarke said as the van pulled up.

"Goddamn it, I'm in charge of this clusterfuck of an op. He has a vehicle, and if he used it, he could already be in it. I want patrols sweeping, looking for single male drivers in late-model, luxury vehicles.

"He's armed—handgun, and may have more weapons in a vehicle. He won't hesitate to fire. Get started. Crap," she added as an MT van pulled up behind Feeney.

"We got it, Loo," Santiago assured her.

She started to turn to the EDD van, but Roarke steered her to the MTs. "If it's nothing, as you insist, this won't take long."

Eve took one look at the MTs. Male, twenties, blue-streaked blond hair in a tight topknot. Female, forties, cool eyed, brown hair in a short braid.

She addressed the female. "No painkillers. Don't come near me with that shit, clear? It's a scratch."

"Why don't we have a look?"

Sitting in the back of the van, Eve lifted her shirt.

"More a gash, short and shallow. Let's clean it up." Those cool eyes met Eve's. "It's gonna hurt."

"No painkillers."

The MT didn't lie. It stung like fire. To take her mind off it, Eve snapped out more orders to the team.

They cleaned it up, closed it up—which hurt more than the cleanout. When the MT loaded a pressure syringe, Eve put a hand on her weapon.

"For infection. You're not going to do a follow-up, are you?"

"No."

"Shouldn't have a problem, but keep an eye for redness, for heat. Change the bandage in twelve, and keep the physical activity down to moderate for twenty-four to thirty-six."

"Got it. Thanks. Ow," she added as the pressure syringe gave her one more jolt.

When she got out of the van, Feeney stood on the sidewalk. He took a long look. "Too bad about the shirt."

"Yeah."

"We got him on some door cams. Got him turning, got the weapon in his hand. Fired twice."

"Jacket took all the first one."

"We got you jumping in front of the two civilians, and the tumble. How he caught you some? Pure bad luck. The jacket shifted just enough on the jump. You hadn't moved, the woman on the right woulda been down, bleeding from a bullet in the gut."

He paused, kept his eyes on hers.

"Just a graze. They fixed it."

"Okay. What he did, he headed north at the corner, and got his head straight enough to move outside of cam range. We lost him. The team's canvassing for wits, and we brought in some uniforms, but we lost him. That's the fact."

"I know it. I watched him walk into 186. I watched him go in."

"With the woman. Arm-in-freaking-arm. We missed it. He duped us. That's another fact."

"He wouldn't have gone into any building with a cam," Roarke pointed out. "Or you wouldn't have lost him. So a vehicle. He had one, got to it, or caught a cab. Or if panicked—"

"Subway, maxibus," Eve finished. "Where there are more cams. We'll check that, but he had a car somewhere close enough. It's raining, why walk, why take a cab that can, eventually, be traced?"

Frustrated, she shoved her fingers through her hair. "I need to talk to the woman, the Realtor."

"Brendita Havanara," Feeney told her. "Jenkinson took her, got her statement. He's got her contacts."

"That's something, at least." She stood in the rain, scanning the street and the people moving along under umbrellas.

"A guy pulls out a handgun and fires, and people just go about their business."

"New York." Feeney shrugged. "We got some who thought it was a vid shoot. And plenty who didn't notice a damn thing. It's rainy, it's noisy. Just a couple bangs."

"We'll finish the canvass, then debrief at Central. But he's gone. He slipped right through."

He'd run like he hadn't in decades. West, north, then east, lungs screaming, legs burning. He cursed the fact he'd parked three blocks east of his target—then in a panic had run in the wrong direction.

When he reached the lot, the car, he slid down in the seat while his breath whistled in and out. He pulled off the blond wig. With trembling fingers, he pinched the tinted film from his eyes that turned them blue. Then removed the appliance that gave him a slight but noticeable overbite.

Just precautions. More a kind of costume, he'd thought, almost for the fun of it. He thanked God he'd taken the time for them.

He took off his tie, shrugged out of the suit jacket. His hands still shook as he unbuttoned his collar, rolled up his shirtsleeves.

He got a tube of water from the in-dash AC, and relieved his desert-dry throat.

His heart continued to pound as he backed the car out of its slot. He had to back up again, reposition the car when he stopped too far away to reach the autopay. Then he nearly hit it, and had to stop, wait to gain some control.

He held up his 'link, waited for the comp.

> *Your account has been charged forty-five dollars, and is verified and cleared. Drive safely and enjoy the rest of your day.*

"Fuck you," he muttered, then carefully eased out of the lot.

He drove east. He needed to drive well clear of any canvass area. Basic evasion techniques. He knew what to do, but couldn't find his calm.

The bitches had set him up. Somehow, some way.

And somehow, some way, the cop bitch had located the bomb and deactivated it.

She'd nearly had him! It seemed impossible, but she'd been right on his heels. He'd gotten two good shots off. He'd hit her, he knew it. Protective gear.

As he paused at a light, he felt himself begin to settle again.

He should've gone for a head shot.

She'd jumped right in front of the women he'd aimed at to distract her. Probably considered herself a bloody hero.

Bloody idiot, more like it.

She'd chased him down the sidewalk as if he were a common criminal! There was nothing common about Conrad Potter.

She'd have to pay for humiliating him, for ruining his day. He should be celebrating. He should be heading home to toast his success with the bottle of champagne he had chilling.

The finest French champagne.

Now he was driving around in the goddamn rain with his bladder throbbing with the need to empty.

Oh, she'd pay. They all would.

He pulled the candy, his Fry's Peppermint Cream, out of his pocket. Its sweetness, and that bite of peppermint, soothed.

They all thought of themselves as heroes. Well, he knew just the way to make them prove it.

He knew exactly how to lure them out.

He'd thought to save this for the last of them, for Summerset. He'd just push the plan up in order, and—why not?—give the heroes a choice of who would stand as sacrifice.

Yes, let them prove themselves heroes. And he'd prove, at last, he was better than all of them.

Back at Central, hoping to avoid any more comments, Eve changed her shirt. After pulling on the plain gray T-shirt, she shoved the ruined one in the recycler.

When she came out of the locker room and started down to the conference room, Whitney got off the elevator.

"Lieutenant."

"Commander."

"You were injured during the op?"

"A minor injury, sir, and treated."

"Very well. I'm attending this debrief to learn what went wrong. And how one of my officers was injured when the suspect opened fire with an illegal weapon on a public street."

"Yes, sir."

Head throbbing, wound stinging, she walked into the conference room where the team already gathered.

"Take your seats," she ordered. "Conrad Potter remains at large. The operation to capture him failed. Each one of you performed your duties during same. The failure is my responsibility."

"Bullshit."

"Detective Sergeant—"

"You can write me up if you want, but I'll say it again. That's bullshit, LT. You weren't the only one who saw him go into 186. The motherfucker walked right by me. McNab says he saw him on-screen."

"I did. The description was off, and he was with the woman—like they were a couple. It didn't ring."

"Saw him myself," Feeney put in, "and maybe should've known better, but he slipped by me, too."

"I was in charge of the op. The op failed. It's on me."

"No excuses," Baxter said, "but reasons. We were covering a block, in the rain, looking for a man who worked in intelligence, knows how to change his appearance and slide through. And that's what he did.

"This time."

"You knew he'd be there," Carmichael added. "You were right. He ran. He's spooked now."

"And more dangerous because of it," Eve pointed out. "At this point—"

"Lieutenant," Whitney interrupted. "Why did you enter building 186?"

"Other than the sidewalk service, it had the best view of the target. And two unoccupied street-facing units. One had a painting crew working. It seemed unlikely, as time ticked down, he would use the sidewalk restaurants, and more possible he might have infiltrated the painting crew. I went in to check it out, cleared the crew, and discovered the Realtor, the woman who'd walked in with what turned out to be Potter posing as a prospective tenant. She'd left him alone in 3-C.

"I alerted the team. One minute the other way, Commander, we'd have boxed him in. He was already on the run when Detectives Peabody, Carmichael, and Santiago arrived. I ordered Peabody to clear 3-C, and Carmichael and Santiago to check the basement area. The emergency exit alarm sounded, and I pursued in that direction."

"Sir, Carmichael and I made the snap decision for her to clear the basement area, and for me to back up the lieutenant. I thought I was fast."

He shook his head. "I got nothing. I couldn't catch up to her, was still well behind when Potter fired on her, then fired again when the lieutenant jumped in front of two female civilians. I didn't know she was hit."

"I wasn't hit," Eve began, but Whitney pointed at her.

"Continue, Detective."

"One of the females grabbed the lieutenant's leg, and a male civilian rushed over and confronted the lieutenant. When I reached them, I told the LT to go—I'd lost sight of Potter—and I ascertained neither of the female civilians had been wounded. At that time, Detective Peabody arrived, and I left her to handle that situation and continued after the lieutenant.

"She'd reached the next corner, and Roarke had come in from the north. At that time, I noted my lieutenant was bleeding along the right side of her torso."

"Is that accurate, Lieutenant?"

"Yes, sir. We have some door cam footage of Potter as he fled, and have determined he turned north at the corner, then moved out of camera range. With the rain, visibility wasn't optimum, but we have enough. With that, with the artist's rendering from other witnesses, and the work in EDD, we should have enough for a current likeness."

"And the Realtor?"

"I took her statement, Commander," Jenkinson told him. "She's who she says she is. Potter, using the name Jamison Brockstone, contacted her about seeing 3-C. It had been well-advertised. He and his wife were to meet her at her office. She ran a standard background, as is her company's policy, and he checked out. He arrived alone, claiming the wife wasn't feeling well, and they shared a cab to 186. Then used his large umbrella to the entrance doors.

"They toured the apartment, and he asked if he could do a virtual tour, alone, for his wife so they could discuss. He was to meet her in the other unoccupied unit when he'd finished. She states it was nearly thirteen-fifteen when she left him."

"He cut it close."

"Sure as hell did. Sir."

Nodding, Whitney got to his feet. "Write it up, Dallas, and get me a damn face."

"Sir."

When he walked out, Eve started to speak.

"I got something to say."

"Jenkinson, that doesn't surprise me."

"We don't appreciate you taking it on for him getting by us."

"Jenkinson—"

"If we'd bagged him, would you take all the credit? Hell no, you wouldn't, so don't treat us like we're assholes who don't know the job. Plus, the motherfucking fucker fucking shot you."

"At. Shot at." Recognizing if she didn't cut this angle off, she'd have a mutiny on her hands, she held one up. "Okay, we all did the job, and he still got away from us. Feel better?"

"No, but at least that's not bullshit."

"Somebody get me some damn coffee, and we'll go over it point by point. Then everyone write up their part of it and have those reports on my desk by end of shift."

Roarke got her the coffee, and smoothly pressed a blocker into her palm. "Take it, you're in pain. Take it," he murmured, "or I'll sic Jenkinson on you."

She took it.

Chapter Eighteen

SHE COULDN'T DENY THE BLOCKER HELPED—SO SHE WOULDN'T MENTION it. But it helped get her through the rest of the debrief. It helped keep her mind clear to write up her report, in detail. Then to read and review others that came in.

Then Yancy rapped on her doorjamb.

"Tell me something good and you can have real coffee."

"For real coffee I'd make something up, but I've got something good."

She jerked a thumb at her AC.

He went straight for it. Peabody would've called him a frosty-looker with his pretty face, curling black mop, dreamy eyes. Eve considered him a genius as a police artist, and a damn solid cop.

He set a folder on her desk.

"I've got good descriptions from the server, from the Realtor—which correspond with the shop cams on his run. And another—we're still working on the mask peel, but I've worked up another, and I think it's close.

"And one more," he said as she opened the folder. "A kind of combination, with a lot of comp input, using the other three."

She looked at the first two, matching the server's, the Realtor's respectively.

"The gray temples don't work. He's too vain for gray, especially since he came full gray out of prison. I think the cheekbones are too sharp—that's enhancement."

"I'm going to agree."

"He doesn't have an overbite like this in the second. And that's bound to be a wig. Little bit of jowls going here, too. The little scar in the left eyebrow. And no, too vain."

"Same chapter, same page."

"This one, the one you and the e-geek are working on."

"It's not a hundred percent."

"But it's closer. He had his eyes done. He got bags under them, lines around them in prison. Nose work. Rossi busted it good on the capture, and it stayed crooked. Had it straightened, thinned it some. Cheekbones, sharp but not like in sketch one. Not as prominent. Chin's more square—he'd go for that. Took prison and about a decade off."

She studied the next. "Yeah, yeah, I see where you're going here. This is useful. Shows how he can morph with appliances, enhancements, skin and eye color changes. But it's still the same man. As the driver, with the mask deal, bigger change. Two decades off. But he hasn't used that again. Maybe he doesn't have the necessary to create another. Or he has to save it until he really needs it."

"Worth a cup of the real?"

"Oh yeah."

"I heard you got shot. You don't look like you got shot."

"Because I didn't. I got shot at. People leave off the *at*. Number three. This is him."

"It's not a hundred percent."

"I get that, Yancy. I get that, but it's him."

"We're still working it. It's fascinating. We get more, you get more."

"You get more, I get more, you get another hit of real."

"Hold you to it. I'm heading back to EDD."

"It's end of shift."

"Fascinating," he repeated, and smiled his frosty smile. "Figured you'd want hard copies, and now?" He pulled out his 'link. "You've got them on your unit."

"Appreciate it."

She added them to her report, sent them with her notes to the bullpen.

Then she added them to her board. And tapped the third sketch.

Dark hair, dark eyes, skin smooth under them, brows thick and dark over them. Slim, straight nose, hard-lined mouth. A nice hint of cheekbones, a square jaw.

"There you are. You had some luck today, but I'm going to make sure your luck changes."

She went out to the bullpen, and wasn't surprised to see Roarke sitting at a desk working on his PPC.

"Heads-up. I've just sent you Detective Yancy's images. The third's the winner, in my opinion, but you have them all to show around. Officer Carmichael, I need you to select uniforms coming on shift to begin circulating these images. On the street. I'm sending out a list of high-end men's shops, barber shops, bootmakers. Uniforms can start on those tonight.

"Any detectives not on another investigation, pick that up in the morning. Add in high-end licensed companion agencies. If he wants sex, he won't hire it off the street. I want client lists where we can get them. For the barbers we're looking for regulars who want the hot towel shave. He can't use appliances or enhancements for that.

"Peabody, we're going to start refining those lists to areas and sectors. Roarke, unless you're applying for a job at Central, with me."

"Dallas." Peabody trotted after her. "We didn't get him, but the op wasn't a failure."

"How do you figure?"

"Nobody blew up, nobody died, and we have more than we did going into it. He ran. He had to run, like he had to run during the Urbans. He's going to remember what happened then. And be afraid. We didn't get him, but we will."

Eve considered Peabody's summary accurate enough.

But.

"He's going to escalate. He has to. And whatever it is he has in mind to do, it won't be pretty. We'll get him, but we have to make sure we get him before he does what comes next."

Roarke joined her on the glides. "You're a target now."

"I always was. You knew that. I may have moved up on the list, but I always was."

Irritated, unable to say what she needed to say on the glides, she shoved her hands in her pockets.

"Knowing is one thing, even a bit abstract, isn't it?"

His tone, light and conversational, had the hands in her pockets balling into fists.

"The reality of you bleeding on the corner of First and Third is a different matter."

"We knew he'd be armed. We knew it would be old-school. He's freaking old-school. And it's not the first time I've done some bleeding on a corner."

"And unlikely the last," he added as they got off the glides, pushed through the door to the garage.

The clang of her boots on the stairs matched the return clang of the headache at the base of her skull.

"Let's clear this up. I get you were upset that he opened up on me."

"Do you now?"

"Yeah, now, then, later. I get it. But you can't step on my authority on an op, especially in front of my team."

"You'll have to excuse me for demanding medical attention when my wife's been shot."

"At, at, at! Shot at!"

"I believe, technically, when a bullet makes contact with flesh, it's shot. 'At' is a miss."

"It barely did, and that's not the point."

"It's a very sharp point for me."

She knew that tone, the icy cool one, that meant there was a burning temper under it. And as her own rose to match it, she stopped at the car.

"I said I get it, and I do, but an op isn't one of your meetings where you're in charge. I'd lost the bastard, and I had to redeploy the team to search mode, and not stop to worry about a scratch."

"A gash," he corrected in that same frosty tone. "Be accurate. And one you got by jumping in front of civilians."

"Damn right. That's the job! What would you have done?"

"I hope I would've done the same."

"Hope, my ass. You'd have done exactly the same because that's who you are. I know you, goddamn it. I know I don't have a couple holes in me because you came up with this."

She opened her jacket to the Thin Shield.

"And you came up with this because somebody put a hole in me a few years back. And I have this." She slapped her hand on the car. "This vehicle that looks like nothing much but can withstand most anything short of a nuclear blast. And, hell, maybe that. I have this ride because some asshole blew my previous ride up. Those are big fucking deals, but you can't protect me twenty-four/seven. And you can't order me around on an op I'm leading!"

He waited a beat. "I have to disagree with that last bit. When my wife is bleeding from a bullet wound—a wound caused by a bullet is a bullet wound," he said before she could snarl at him, "under those circumstances, I am duly authorized to call for medical attention."

He waited another beat.

"It's in the Marriage Rules."

She opened her mouth, closed it again. Turned a circle, pulled on her hair. Hoisted by her own petard, she thought. Whatever the fucking fuck a petard was.

"You yanked up my shirt in front of Santiago."

And that statement, her ridiculous and somehow endearing embarrassment, simply evaporated his anger.

"And if I'd been standing at First and Third, bleeding, what might you have done?"

She hissed out a breath. "Shit. Shit. Shit. I'd have done the same damn thing. Okay, okay, but . . . No, fuck it. Look, I'm—"

He stepped to her, touched a finger to her lips. "You feel obliged to apologize now. Don't. I don't want an apology, and none is warranted in any case. Lieutenant Dallas, my darling Eve, I don't want to change you. I'm madly, wildly, completely in love with the woman who'd use her own body to shield others. With the woman who, even while wounded, is embarrassed Santiago saw a part of her midriff.

"I love who and what you are, every glorious and frustrating bit of it. And I was terrified. Now I want credit for not doing this when I very much needed to, on that corner, in front of Santiago."

He gathered her in, held on. "There you are," he murmured.

She held on, too. "I appreciate the restraint."

When he laughed, she drew back to cup his face in her hands. "What you just said, about loving every glorious, frustrating bit? Same goes. I don't want to change you, either."

She pressed her lips to his.

"But I bet, if you got shot at in one of your meetings, and I came pushing in, pulled up your shirt, and demanded medical aid, you'd be a little pissed."

"Should that ever happen, we'll test your theory."

"Okay. You drive. I've been shot."

She tossed him a grin as she got in the car. And shaking his head, he slid behind the wheel.

"So anyway, what's a petard?"

Laughing again, he glanced over. "I so clearly see where that one comes from. Your Marriage Rules hoisted you, didn't they now? It's a small bomb."

"How the hell do you get hoisted on a bomb? See, these things make no sense."

"Shakespeare would disagree."

"What the hell does he know?"

Leaning over, he kissed her.

"I've sent you a list," he told her, "on the machine and materials Potter would need to create the skin mask. Both legitimate and black-market venues. It's not long, considering."

"That's good. Another angle."

As he drove, she pulled out her PPC. "We're going to start a search on houses, with garages, purchased or rented within the last year. Gotta start somewhere. We can cross-reference with the barbers, possibly the men's stores, bootmakers."

Reaching over, Roarke squeezed her hand. "And yes, there you are."

She worked, picking through the steps to open her command center's operations from her PPC, to then coordinate the search between command and her mobile.

"Could be a townhouse, and he rents a garage. Have to factor it. He could have rented or bought it two years ago. Three, four. He could've formed a shell company, or manufactured a spouse on the lease, the deed, like he did with the Realtor."

"You have his face now."

"Yeah, or close enough. It's going to help. It may help pin where he got the face-making machine. And if we can pin down where he gets those fancy shaves . . ."

Frowning, she reached over, rubbed his cheek. "You're pretty smooth. Do you get those?"

"I don't, no. I dislike having someone run a naked blade along my throat."

"Good thinking. But he gets them. Old-school again. Old-school. A lot of tech advances since he went inside. He'd have kept up as much as he could, but . . . Still, he fabricated that mask. But the gas, the bomb, the gun. His vehicle . . . Wouldn't he want something that's been around? I don't mean the actual vehicle, but the type. Old, respected brand. Familiar. Something with status. It'll be loaded—lots of new tech and additions since the Urbans—but a make that speaks to him.

"Did he have a vehicle back then?"

"I'm sure our guests will know."

"Yeah." She closed her eyes a moment. "Yeah, yeah. I'm going to have to brief them on all this, aren't I?"

"Not only because they deserve to know, but because they're useful."

"Useful," she repeated, as the gates of home slid open. "They're useful."

But she thought she might need another blocker to get through it.

Despite the guests, when they walked in, Summerset loomed in his black suit. Not unlike, Eve realized, the suit Potter had worn when he'd shot *at* her.

The cat sat at his feet, then rose, stretched, before walking over to ribbon through her legs, then through Roarke's.

"Briefing, my office in ten. Everyone."

"Very well. There was a brief bulletin regarding an unidentified male deploying an illegal weapon in the East Village this afternoon."

"Ten minutes," Eve repeated, and went up the stairs.

"She's a bit out of sorts," Roarke told him. "She'll explain."

"There's a bit of blood on her trousers."

"You always had a sharp eye. She'll explain that as well. Or I will. Where are our guests?"

"Scattered about. I'll bring them up."

When Roarke joined Eve, she stood updating her board. The cat stretched out on her sleep chair.

"Why don't I check on your search? I may be able to filter and refine."

"It'll probably need a lot of both if I want to find him this decade."

"You're discouraged, and you shouldn't be."

"I'll get over it."

"You identified him, proved he faked his own death, established his motive, brought his kill list to a safe location. Located a bomb, saw it deactivated. You saved lives. And now you have the face he bought himself."

She'd pat herself on the back for all that later. Because . . .

"He's going to escalate. I don't know how, when, but the way he aimed at those civilians today?" She stepped back from the board. "I saw his face, the look on it. He wanted to distract and delay me, yeah, but it was more. He enjoyed the idea of it, like he was back in the past. In a street war. It was a tactic, sure, and it worked. But it was more.

"If we don't find him soon, stop him soon, someone's going to die. It won't be one of The Twelve. He can't get to them as long as they're here. He'll pick someone else, someone he can get to. He won't count the risk. He lives for the risk."

Hands in pockets, she circled the board. "Someone he can get to. Potentially use to get to them, or me. Or you," she said, turning to him. "You're in it, too. You're Summerset's, you're mine, and he knows it. And you're a big, shiny risk."

"Is that what's worrying you? I can promise you, he won't get to me. Should he try, he'll not only fail, but you'll have him."

"I don't think he will." She scrubbed her hands over her face. "It's too direct, and he'd know how covered you are. For a risk-taker, he's still a coward. Direct confrontation, not so much. Duplicity, betrayal, that's his style. But I'm allowed to worry some. Marriage Rules."

"Of course. I'm refining this here and there, then I'm opening a bottle of wine. Or, considering our guests, two bottles."

"I'm working."

"And a glass of wine hasn't impaired you before. It may relax you enough to open a new channel."

"I could use a new damn channel."

When he finished refining, he went into the kitchen, and Eve sat to scan the search results as they trickled in.

He came back with a tray holding a platter of various cheeses, thin crackers, olives. Little plates, little napkins.

"You're always feeding people."

"We both went hungry often enough as children. So we know, or should, that hunger can distract, cause the mind to stay unfocused. And food, well, it can open those channels."

He set the food on the table, opened her terrace doors to air washed clean by the day's rain.

By the time he'd opened the bottles, Summerset led the others in.

"No one goes hungry around here." Harry started toward the table, then stopped. He walked closer to the board.

"Why, that's Potter, isn't it? Bloody hell, that's some good work he had done, but I'm damned if that's not the raving bastard Conrad Potter."

"Which one?" Eve got up, walked over.

"This one here." He tapped the third. "It's the eyes. Barely a line showing, and there should be, but I know those eyes."

Beside him, Marjorie nodded. "With all four up here this way, I can see him in all of them. But I'd have walked right by one and two. The fourth, maybe I'd've felt some tingle. But this one?"

"You'd have looked twice," Iris finished. "I'm not sure I would have, but that's my lack. I've been out of the game too long. I see him now."

She turned to Eve. "Have you?"

"Yeah, I got a look, but of this one. The third is the work of EDD, the lab, and a police artist. They've been using a program and probabilities to go under the mask he wore when he got Rossi."

"Well done then." Ivanna laid a hand on Marjorie's shoulder as she took a long look. "I agree, not only excellent face work, but his eyes. And, in my opinion, how he'd wish to look. Younger, thinner, straighter nose, a bit more cheekbones, the square line of the jaw. Enough of a change it would elude face recognition programs, and more classically handsome than his own."

"I see the tricks on the others now," Marjorie added. "Some of which I taught him myself. Change the bite, which changes the shape of the mouth, cheek line, jaw. Add a little flaw, or the perfect touch of gray. Vary eye color, skin color, hair color, style, and length. Fill in lines or add them."

"You saw him today."

Eve looked over at Summerset. "That's right, and we lost him."

"Have some wine," Roarke said, "and the lieutenant will fill you in. Eve." He handed her a glass already poured.

"Fine. Get what you want, then have a seat."

She took them through it, reminding herself they did have a right to know. And maybe they'd see some angle she'd missed.

Was still missing.

"Using the Realtor, someone legitimate, as cover." Ivanna nodded. "Yes, I can see that. He'd have killed her if she'd gotten in the way or if his ruse with her had cracked."

"He wanted to be alone to watch us die," Marjorie added. "No reason she couldn't stay, be shocked with him—and smarter that way. But he wanted to savor in private."

“He was lucky with the rain. A pity.” Summerset stared down into his wineglass, then lifted his gaze to Eve’s. “You pursued.”

“We pursued. It was necessary to clear 3-C, which Peabody did. And to clear the basement level, which Detective Carmichael did. I had the lead, so I pursued. He did, in fact, exit by the emergency door, then fled west. He drew an old-school handgun and fired.”

Ivan, quiet in a corner, blinked. “He shot at you.”

“I was wearing protection, which I assume he realized. He then aimed at a pair of female civilians.”

“Yes, of course he would.”

Eve narrowed her eyes at Summerset. “Elaborate.”

“He had no issue with collateral damage. The mission, he believed, took priority over lives. Any lives,” he added. “All lives.”

“Enemy blood, allied blood, innocent blood, same color, and to win the war, you’ll have to spill some.” Harry nodded. “He said that to me once over a pint. Seems like I pointed out we were fighting to save lives, and he just said, added a shrug to it, ‘War kills, and the big picture? Win the war. Whatever it takes, whoever it takes.’”

“Were they injured?” Iris asked. “The women?”

“No, but the tactic worked, and I lost him. We canvassed the area—”

“Eve.” Roarke spoke softly. “You shouldn’t censor your report.”

Summerset understood immediately. “You were injured. You shielded them. He shot you.”

“I was wearing protection,” she repeated. “It was, and is, my job to protect civilians. I sustained a minor injury, which has been treated.”

“He knew you would.”

Summerset got to his feet. Eve realized she’d never seen him pace before. It made him almost human.

“He would have studied you, researched you. Know your enemy. Anticipate, act. He knew you’d stop the pursuit long enough to shield the civilians. And he’d use that to get away.”

"I guess I could've put the mission first priority, and let him shoot someone."

"That's hardly what I meant, and you're well aware of it," Summerset snapped right back at her. "You're sniping because you're justifiably angry he got away from you. You had no choice, he gave you no choice. He knew it."

"He was never very good with a handgun." When the cat jumped into his lap, Harry stroked. "I'd say he hasn't gotten any better. Otherwise, he'd have gone for you and a head shot. He went for the women—two, so bigger target—hoping you'd get in the way, and knowing if he hit one of them, you'd have to stop, help. He did it because he's a poor shot and a coward who doesn't give one ripe shit."

"I agree with all of that." Ivanna let out a sigh. "He went into the military, I believe, because he envisioned having power over others. Giving orders more than receiving them. He went into intelligence, as he appreciated the idea of deception, of using the enemy's weakness and secrets against them. Then into the cops again for the power and authority. He joined us to benefit from both sides, as he had no allegiance."

"And to profit," Iris added.

"And to profit. It's all very clear in hindsight, but in the fog of war, we believed him one of us."

"You went into that particular building," Marjorie reminded Eve. "Why?"

"As I said, he might have infiltrated the painting crew."

"There were other buildings with a view of the restaurant, but you broke off from your team to check that one. Only that one. You had a feeling in the belly."

Eve started to speak, stopped. She sipped some wine, thought it through. Roarke had it right. No point in censoring the briefing.

"That building afforded the best view, and offered two units, vacant, he could potentially use. And where he could . . . savor. You said that. I had a feeling about that building, those two units when Peabody and I went through in the morning."

She drank again.

"I didn't listen to my gut, not enough. We had to cover the area, and I had to stay off the street because he'd recognize me. If I'd listened to my gut, I'd have stationed myself in 3-C and another officer in 5-A.

"And I'd have him in the box right now."

"You had to cover the area." Ivan spoke again. "Because he could have chosen any of those locations. Any of them. And he would certainly be armed, which put civilian lives at risk. You chose the most logical, broad-based strategy."

"And I missed."

"Well, bugger, that never happens to anyone, ever," Harry commented.

With a smile, Marjorie lifted her glass. "What does your gut tell you now?"

"He has a place, a detached house with a garage. On the West Side. The house is bigger than he needs, but he has to have the space, the freedom of space. It'll be in a good neighborhood, convenient to high-end shops and restaurants, probably near enough to a food shop that carries the candy he likes."

"Couldn't get that in prison, could he?" Marjorie nodded. "He'd want his peppermint creams. What else?"

As she spoke, sipped at the wine, Eve circled the board again.

"He uses an old-school but high-end barber. Most likely gets that fancy shave once or twice a week. We're working that now. He has a tailor, a bootmaker. He's not as well-funded as he was when he started, but he needs the high-end. He won't go back."

Can't go back, Eve thought.

"He's stuck in the past, not only because of the mission, which is kill all of you, and me after he's done that. Before if need be. But because that's when he had power and control."

"Too much of both," Iris murmured. "Hindsight. Is anything more frustrating than hindsight?"

"He has a vehicle," Eve continued. "A major, long-term brand. A brand that's been around a long time. Fully loaded, luxury vehicle, but not flashy. Black, dark gray, dark blue. Nothing sporty. Dignified. He has his own fitness equipment. No fitness center, too many people. He keeps to himself, but not so much it has people saying just that. He failed today, so he'll escalate. He'll try something complicated, put another life or lives on the line."

She turned to the board, looked at his face.

"He's a killer, and the wars fed that need. He didn't get that rush of satisfaction today, that hunger wasn't sated. He didn't get to savor, and instead had to run. Had to run the way he did decades ago. He's afraid, and the fear makes him angry. He needs to find something, do something so he gets that rush, and blows off the fear with success."

Eve paused, then added, "He has to teach us all a lesson. Show us he's better than we are."

"You know him very well." Marjorie drank. "How do we find him?"

"Working on it," Eve muttered. "Working on it."

Chapter Nineteen

SHE WANTED TO GET TO WORK, BUT PEOPLE SAT AROUND, DRINKING wine, eating cheese. Talking.

Maybe she didn't have the finest social skills—no maybe there—but this wasn't a party. Sure, the talk was case related, but they weren't cops. And the way Marjorie and Ivanna had their heads together, they might've been talking about shoes. Or hairstyles. Or whatever the hell.

Wrap it up, Eve thought. Move them out.

"That's all I can tell you for now," she began.

"We've had a lovely day." Marjorie rose. "Despite the circumstances. It's difficult not to enjoy gathering with good friends in such a beautiful home. Iris held some virtual meetings, I read an interesting script. We made use of the pool, the game room. I still say you cheated, Harry."

"You'll never prove it, Red."

"Rematch," Cyril demanded.

"Anytime, mate."

"I'm looking forward to the kotleta po Kyivsky Summerset's promised us for dinner. It's been a lovely, bittersweet reunion, and only strengthened the bond forged so long ago."

"Good, that's good. Now, I need to—"

"And that's enough of that," Marjorie interrupted. "Put us to work."

"Ah—"

"You have seven intelligence operatives at your disposal, all with a vested interest in locating Conrad Potter, in making bloody well sure he's put back where he belongs."

"Or ends up in the ground," Cyril muttered.

"I'd not shed a tear. But my point is we're useful. Use us. We have here decades of experience. We have skills, and those of us who need to can blow the dust off those skills quickly enough."

"We may be twice your age, Lieutenant," Summerset put in, "but in this case, that's our advantage."

"You know him," Ivanna said. "That's clear, and impressive. But you haven't interacted with him, worked with him, fought with him as we have."

"Thirty-odd years ago," Eve pointed out.

"As you said," Iris reminded her, "he's stuck in the past. We are his past."

"You're looking for a location." Cyril rose, topped off his wine. "Single-family, with garage. You say the west side of the city. You conclude that, I take it, since he's struck on the opposite side. He'd want that distance. Though it would be simpler for him to scout and select his spots if he had his HQ closer to the area, he'd believe you'd assume that and concentrate your efforts there. I agree with your conclusion. West."

"Looking for his car," Harry continued, and scratched Galahad behind the ears. "Would be a car—not a lorry, not a van. Sedan. Black first choice. Possible on gray or dark blue. And you're right about the make. It's like . . . lineage. He'd want what was around before he went inside."

"Mercedes, BMW, Bentley, or Cadillac. Not only for performance and style," Summerset added, "but the longevity of the brand."

"Not the Bentley." Ivan offered an apologetic smile. "He'd enjoy the status, but he considered British-made shite, or so he said. And, excuse me, but that make's more unusual on this side of the pond, and he needs to blend more. To be admired, envied, but also to blend."

"Quite right." Summerset nodded. "You're quite right. We're not victims, Lieutenant. We're not marks."

"We're weapons," Marjorie finished. "Use us."

Regulations and logic pushed her in one direction. Instinct pushed her in the other. If she'd put more weight on instinct than logic, procedure, Potter would be in custody.

Going with instinct, she turned to Roarke. "Can you set them up in the comp lab?"

"I can."

"Get something to eat. Lay off the wine. Cyril, Summerset, on the house, west side. Entire west side. Marjorie, Ivanna, the house, east. Iris, house, central. Ivan, Harry, vehicle.

"Start with the most probable, then work back. Townhomes, warehouses." She looked at Harry. "Top sedans, all-terrains. He needed time to set up, establish himself, learn the city. Go back eighteen months. Two years if nothing hits. He couldn't wait longer than that to start."

"Yes, you know him," Marjorie murmured.

"He had to use private transportation to smuggle the weapons to New York."

She spared Summerset a glance. "I'm aware."

"Yes, of course."

"I want results as they come. Go, eat dinner. Whatever the hell kotleta po something is."

"Ukrainian," Summerset said, and rose.

"I'll have the lab set up for you when you're done," Roarke told them as they made their way out. "You made the right choice," he said to Eve.

"It'll keep them occupied anyway."

"Marjorie made a solid case."

"Okay, yeah." She pressed her fingers to her eyes. "I don't want them to feel like victims." She dropped her hands. "And I sure as hell don't want them to be victims."

"You need food, and we'll get started."

"I don't want Ukrainian. I want pizza. I should get pizza. I've been shot."

"Oh, again now you've been 'shot,' not 'at.'"

"You made such a big deal out of it, I should be able to use it awhile."

"Then rather than sitting at your command center with a slice in one hand while you work, you'll sit at the table and eat. Since you've been shot."

"That's the petard deal again."

He kissed her cheek and said, "Boom."

But it would give her time to think, and time for her own search to push out some results.

She fed the cat while he got the pizza. Then sat with a slice and a Pepsi.

"I need successful, high-end smugglers who have good private transpo, connections in Britain and New York, and a rep for keeping their mouths shut."

"I'll see what I can do."

"Financials—"

"Ah." Lifting a finger, he glanced up. "I hear music."

"He may, likely did, stash some solid cash with the weapons. But that's running money, not millions. So he had an account somewhere. Somewhere they don't blink if you stuff in those millions. Somewhere they don't look too hard at where it comes from."

"I'll see what I can do," he repeated. "We are talking three decades, and as he was in prison, that account would have remained open, and likely untouched for the majority of that time. But . . ."

"Yeah, he found a way to access it."

"Them," Roarke corrected. "Not only foolish to put all in one account, but it wouldn't fit his profile, would it? At least two—depending on how much he had. I'd assume three, in various locations."

"He had enough e-skills, enough time, to work a way. Get access to a comp. Pierce could've been helpful there. And if Abernathy would tag me back, I'd know."

"So a transfer of considerable roughly five years back. That's a thread to pull."

"I should've asked you to pull it before."

"Been a bit busy the last few days, haven't we? Don't diminish what you've accomplished." He put another slice on her plate.

"Why do people say going down a rabbit hole?"

"Well now, there's a segue. A reference to *Alice in Wonderland.* The White Rabbit. She went down after him."

"Right. Right. That sort of makes sense. Maybe I went down the rabbit hole."

"And if you hadn't, you wouldn't know Potter is alive, and the seven downstairs wouldn't be enjoying what translates to chicken Kiev. You're talking about his puzzles, Eve, and putting them back together again your way."

"He's still ahead of me."

"I'd wager heavily not for long."

"How long's the problem. He's planning something, or he's already got it in the works."

Potter had taken the next step in his plan even while Eve debriefed her team at Central.

Once he'd calmed himself, he understood he could use the rain. He changed out of his wet suit and into more casual clothes, added a black mac, and as a precaution, a gray wig.

He disliked the gray, but for this mission, he wanted to look old, and harmless. Thinking just that, he added a few lines to his face, softened his jawline.

Harmless, he decided as he studied the result. Just someone's harmless grandfather out in the rain.

He'd planned to do this—his crescendo—at night. A streetwalker, a woman alone. But this would be so much more invigorating, so much more effective.

He took what he needed to the garage, to the car, then drove out once again in the rain.

Driving carefully, he hummed to himself. He'd scouted the area before when selecting the best dump spot for Rossi. It hadn't suited that need, but would suit his current purpose very well.

And it was nearly as far away from his HQ as he could get and remain on the island of Manhattan.

It took time, but he ordered himself not to lose patience. His gaze ticked right and left. He'd been smart to use the rain! Fewer pedestrians, and all of them rushing along, paying no attention to what happened around them.

Busy, busy.

And so would he be busy, very soon.

The little park he'd cased before with all the sticky-fingered, shrieking children was deserted now. No watchful nannies or parents. There, the empty building, and no workers replacing windows, no workers' trucks parked today.

He made use of the short alleyway beside it, checked the time.

Yes, yes, perfect. School's out and most of the little buggers on their way home. He needed a young one, but not so young a parent or nanny walked with them.

He needed one who trailed behind, a bad little boy or girl who'd had to stay after school. Or a good one who'd had some ridiculous activity.

But who lived close enough to walk home. Alone.

Ten minutes, fifteen. He watched schoolchildren hurry by, but in twos or threes, or even bigger groups.

Fifteen minutes, twenty. And the impatience began crawling through him like hissing snakes.

The next pair that walked by. The very next, he promised himself. He'd grab the smallest of the two. And the other?

He had his knife.

Then, positioned in the wet gloom at the side of the building, he saw his target.

Alone, splashing along in puddles, wearing a bright yellow mac. A red backpack, and some sort of case—musical instrument—in his hand.

Leaning heavily on the cane he'd brought as a prop, Potter stepped into view.

"Young man? Could you help me?"

Potter put on his most harmless smile as the boy glanced over.

"Oh! There she is now!"

As the boy turned his head to look where Potter pointed, Potter jabbed the pressure syringe on the side of his neck.

With barely a sound, the boy went limp.

Potter simply took his weight, kicked the case into the alley. He rolled the unconscious boy into the trunk, slammed it shut.

Pleased, flushed with success, he began the drive back uptown. He calculated the boy would be out at least two hours, giving him plenty of time to do what he needed to do.

Twenty minutes later, as Potter crept along in crosstown traffic, Devin McReedy's mother, more annoyed than concerned, began calling Devin's friends.

She'd told him to come straight home after orchestra practice, but sometimes . . .

Ten minutes later, concern edged out annoyance.

She paced, window to window, sure she'd see her oldest coming down the sidewalk any minute.

Five minutes later, she looked back at her youngest, cuddled up on the sofa watching an animated vid on-screen. She and her husband had taken turns with him through the night. A night they'd all spent primarily in the bathroom as the poor kid suffered with the stupid stomach bug going around.

She walked over to lay a hand on his forehead. Cool.

"I feel better," Silas told her, and gave her the smile she loved. "I'm hungry."

An excellent sign, she thought. Devin had had the same bug a couple of days before. Twenty-four-hour deal.

"You look lots better. I have to run out, just two minutes. And when I come back, I'll fix you a snack."

"Peanut butter cheesies?"

"Peanut butter cheesies. You stay right here. Don't answer the door."

"Mom! I know!"

"I know you know. Two minutes."

She grabbed an umbrella, hurried out.

To offset the grinding worry, she told herself she was giving Devin the what-for when she found him. Probably taking a swing or a slide in the park in the damn rain.

"Oh, you're in for it, my man."

But her stomach stayed knotted, and panic tickled at her throat.

When she saw the violin case at the mouth of the alley, her knees gave way.

By then, Devin, ankles and wrists zip-tied, lay unconscious in the windowless basement storage room while Potter completed his preparations.

A little more time, he thought, and the remains of The Twelve were in for a big surprise.

* * *

With coffee, Eve worked at her command center. Roarke had set up the group in the comp lab and now worked on his part in his office.

As initial results came in, she dug into them. Eliminated or put on a potentials list.

She cross-checked those with the potentials list from season ticket holders for opera and ballet.

When her 'link signaled, she read ABERNATHY.

"Finally." She snatched it up. "Dallas. What the fuck—I've tagged you a half dozen times."

"And I had nothing to tell you. We got a confession out of Pierce—he broke fast and easy. But he knows little to nothing regarding Potter, nothing that advances your investigation."

"How about I judge what advances my investigation? How'd he get the payoff?"

"Potter transferred ten million—in five-million installments—to an offshore account Pierce opened on his instructions. He used Pierce's personal comp to make the transfer, which, on Potter's instructions, he then destroyed. Potter, with Pierce's help, used the prison's own bloody equipment to fabricate Pierce's new ID and background."

Wincing, Abernathy rubbed at the back of his neck. "I need a vacation. Pierce executed the plan, gave Potter the drug, brought the warden in to verify the death. He brought Potter out of it, smuggled him out of prison in his own shagging car."

Abernathy sighed. "He's lucky Potter didn't kill him on the spot."

"He still needed him."

"You're right, and Pierce saw it through. Used some ashes from another dead inmate, sealed it up, labeled it, saw it buried. Potter had given him the name of a doctor who'd match the ID—just a few changes. We'd pull her in, but she's been dead two years. And with a fresh new look and ID, and a fat account, Pierce headed to Costa Rica."

"Where did the funds come from? Transferred from where?"

"We're trying to run that down. Pierce doesn't know. He'd have spilled it all if he did. Potter didn't tell him where he was going, what he was planning. Why would he? Pierce, and he got sloppy with it, tried to claim he believed Potter was an unjustly persecuted war hero. That's bollocks, but a man has to try."

"I want to see the interview recording."

"Considering all, I'm sending it to you. We included your questions, Lieutenant, and this is what we have. And the fact is, if Potter had told him anything—"

"It would be bollocks," Eve finished. "I still want to see it."

"I'll send it. We greatly appreciate your help. Interpol is also on the hunt for Conrad Potter."

"I don't care who gets him first, as long as he's got."

"If you'd pass on any updates—"

"As soon as I can. I'm up to my neck. Dallas out."

She sat back, gulped some coffee. As more results came in from Roarke's comp lab, she thought: They're efficient. And got back to work.

She surfaced again when Roarke entered her office. With a first aid kit.

"I already had medical treatment."

"You're about to get more. I'm changing the bandage, putting a topical on it, as I know full well it's hurting you again. You're taking a blocker as well. And for being a good girl—"

"Seriously?"

"Seriously, I'll tell you what I know so far."

"This isn't something to screw around with. I've got a couple of maybes on my cross-checks."

"Neither is a gunshot wound anything to screw around with."

To solve the matter, he lifted her shirt.

"Don't you get tired of playing Nurse Nancy?"

"I can't begin." He eased the bandage away. "No sign of infection," he said, and laid a hand, gently, on it. "No heat. See?"

"I'd pop you one but you're so pretty."

"Here now." He spread on the topical.

The pain she'd ignored eased off.

"Okay, good. Why do I need the blocker?"

"For the headache, for the knots in your shoulders, for the pain in your neck."

"Right now you're the pain in my neck."

"And I walked straight into it." He finished the fresh bandage, handed her a blocker.

"What do you know?"

He sat on the edge of her command center, commandeered her coffee. "A former associate has a colleague who heard of a competitor—"

"Just say smugglers."

"My word was there would be no names given, and no record of the conversation."

"Agreed. Classic anonymous tip if needed."

"After a check of files, which the competitor of the colleague of the associate—former—keeps unknown to his clients, transportation was booked, sixteen months ago, under the name Carson Wells. The man who traveled from Calais to a small island off the coast of Maine—"

"Maine?"

Roarke held up a hand. "A place sometimes used by the competitor for this sort of transportation. The passenger matches the third sketch, or closely enough. The client is remembered for having three large crates, electronic equipment, and considerable luggage, for requesting a bottle of French wine and escargot for the flight."

"You're not kidding me."

"I'm not, no. The passenger had an SUV waiting. The pilot doesn't remember make or model, but helped load the crates and so on into the

SUV. The client paid cash rather than a wire transfer. He paid in full, and the competitor went on his way."

"He drives down from the coast of Maine—SUV's probably gone by now. He wouldn't keep it. He's already got the house."

She rose, paced. "He needs somewhere to go, to stay. Sixteen months ago. Sixteen. That's right in there. He bought or rented the house remotely. We'll factor that in now. He had to hire someone to help him unload when he got there."

"Or he bought a couple of droids. He needs the house maintained."

"And wouldn't have live domestics. This is good. A timeline. We can use this. And I can add it into my cross-checks. We add the timeline to check on the barbers and so on."

"For now? The financials. Starting in the Urbans era with his birth name—challenging."

"And?"

"He likes complications, and has some skill. Some records simply don't exist any longer from that period, as war will make things sketchy. But those that do? Two accounts under his name so far. Moderate, in the range you'd expect. A third, and very well buried, under—you'll like this—Feeding Frenzy Productions."

"Sharks."

"Exactly. While the records are full of gaps, what I did find was considerably more than moderate. Its value today? Round and about twelve million."

"A hell of a lot more than he'd make in the military or working for the cops."

"It is, yes. Gaps, as I said, months when no records exist, but I did find those that included five- and six-figure deposits. Then, nothing."

"What do you mean nothing?"

"No account. Closed. Gone. No record of withdrawal or transfer, which may fall into one of those gaps. I tried another tack, picking back from Pierce's account. Complications. Whatever Potter lacks, he has excellent skills in hiding funds, no doubt laundering it, creating identities, backgrounds, mixing the bogus with the genuine."

"Tell me you're better."

"Well now, false modesty's so tedious, isn't it?" He smiled, tapped a finger to the shallow dent in her chin. "It took some work, but Pierce's payoff came from a numbered account, which bounced through two others before it landed."

"Did you get a name, any kind of contact?"

"Bogus again, but with some persistence, I tracked one of those accounts back to Feeding Frenzy Productions. And in backtracking, circling, persisting, I found yet one more account. The name on that—tucked into the Caymans—matches the name he gave the Realtor today."

"Which is bogus."

"It is, yes. But I can tell you Potter came out of prison, after the payoff, with twenty-eight million and change, and whatever cash he might have secreted away. Those accounts have been active all this time, so growing."

"He'd have been stealing and taking payoffs for years. Probably before the Urbans."

"Very likely. I have the names for you, the addresses and contacts given. None are in New York, but may, with persistence, give you more. The accounts themselves, beginning five years ago, have records of withdrawals and transfers."

Shifting around her, he programmed more coffee for both of them.

"I suspect he paid the cosmetic surgeon in cash. He transferred a million to an account in Bath—that's England—under a week after his escape. Zeroed it out only days later."

"Got the face work, paid, took the rest in cash for himself."

"Another transfer within the month. He bought a flat in Paris. My analysis says he used primarily cash for expenses, one or two small withdrawals, and lived there about two years. Sold the flat—made a tidy profit there. I imagine he used that profit, and another transfer, for the villa on the French Riviera. Saint-Tropez. Which he sold, again at a profit, eighteen months ago."

"That's a trail. Those are dots to connect."

"They are, yes. But from that point, complications I haven't yet unraveled. He zeroed out two of the accounts, hasn't touched the third I found. And wherever he put those funds I've yet to find."

"Cash? How much would he have?"

"Not counting the six million or so in the untouched account, taking out the smuggler's as well as what he laid out the last few years? Maybe eighteen. Possibly twenty."

"Million. But he didn't pay cash for the place here."

"Highly unlikely. Even if he's renting it . . . and previous pattern is buying. If it is a house, as you believe, one with a garage."

"With top-of-the-line security, in a good neighborhood, upscale. Nothing that needed repairs—he's not having a crew in there."

"If it's a purchase?" Roarke shrugged. "Depending on the square footage and a myriad of other factors? Three million to easily five times that."

"Not the low or high end. Double, maybe triple the three. And he had to buy a car, droids, furniture."

She pushed up to pace. "From Manchester to the Bath place, to Paris, to the Riviera, to Calais, to Maine, and finally to New York. That's a goddamn solid trail, with a timeline, and we'll find something on it."

She turned back to him. "You're way ahead of Interpol."

"Well now." He sipped some coffee. "It wouldn't be the first time."

"Bet. Get me the names he used. I'll dig into them, check them with what I've got on fancy theater. You said he's good at forging IDs, backgrounds, but why keep generating them? Why not use one already established, like he did today? Nobody's looking for Conrad Potter because

Conrad Potter's dead. He's got a new face, a new life. Maybe he's using one of his previous IDs in New York."

"Possible."

"But he likes the complicated. Yeah, yeah. Still, worth looking there. This is good, Roarke. This is really damn good."

"We do what we can."

"Go do some more of it." But she grabbed two fistfuls of his shirt first, yanked him to her, kissed him with enthusiasm. "I'll pick it up here."

The boy slept twice as long as Potter expected. Initially concerned—he didn't want to spend time looking for an alternate—he checked the boy's breathing, his pulse.

He'd wake soon enough, and the extra hours simply gave Potter more time to complete this stage of the mission.

He'd gone through the boy's backpack and all the contents, including the tablet. With the bait's name, he did some research on the family.

Father, Roland McReedy; mother, Kim Cho; younger brother, Silas. McReedy, human resources manager; Cho, paralegal.

Maybe if the mother had stayed home rather than taking a man's job, her kid wouldn't be drooling on the basement floor.

Two kids and she was probably giving her boss blow jobs under his desk instead of cleaning the house.

Made him sick.

He'd set up the camera, so he watched the boy on the monitor while he ate—salmon en croûte, roasted fingerling potatoes, and green beans with shallots. He enjoyed a single glass of Pouilly-Fuissé, perfectly chilled, and finished the meal with coffee.

And the boy began to stir.

Excellent timing, he thought, and left the dishes for the droid to deal with.

He didn't bother with a disguise. Devin McReedy wouldn't describe him. After all, dead boys tell no tales.

He unlocked the basement door, went down into the media room he rarely used but enjoyed having. He bypassed the door—also locked, and secured by his retinal scan—to his workshop, and unlocked the next door into the storage area.

He'd cleared that out some time ago, in preparation for the finale of his mission.

It stood empty now, but for the boy on the floor, the recorder, a bucket, a single chair, and the cameras he'd installed that covered the whole of the room.

No windows, no identifying features. Just walls painted bright white, and a floor of fake wood planks.

Potter walked over, sat in the chair as the boy moaned, shifted.

As he moaned again, and said: "Mom. Mom."

"Mom's not here. And if you want to see her again, you'll do exactly what I tell you."

Chapter Twenty

DEVIN FELT SICK, SORT OF LIKE WHEN HE'D HAD THE BUG. BUT NOW HIS head hurt really bad, and he was awful thirsty. He shivered with cold, then when he opened his eyes and saw the man, he screamed.

It was a bad dream, so his mom and dad would come. They'd come and hug him and tell him it was a bad dream.

In the dream, the man held a gun, like in the old vids his dad liked, and had eyes mean like a monster's.

"Mom! Mom! Mom!"

"I said she's not here! You shut up. You stop that yelling or I'll shoot you in the leg."

Devin choked back the next scream, but couldn't stop the tears. "I want my mom. I want my dad."

"Then you'll do exactly what I say. If you don't, I'll kill you. Then I'll go kill your mom—she's Kim, your dad, Roland, and your little brother, Silas. I'll cut them up into little pieces, then set your house on fire."

As the boy sobbed, Potter smiled.

"Is that what you want me to do? Is it! *Is it?*"

"No, no, please, mister. Please, please! I just wanna go home now."

"You're not going home, Devin. You'll never go home again unless you do exactly what I tell you. Say exactly what I tell you to say."

"I'm—I'm cold."

"Fuck your cold! And stop your sniveling or I'll give you something to snivel about."

Potter rose, stepped over, bent down, and gave the smooth young cheek a hard slap. "Want more?"

Shaking his head, choking on sobs, Devin tried to curl into a ball.

In his whole life, no one had ever struck him. No adult had ever, ever shouted the f-word at him.

The bad dream was real. Monsters were real even though his parents told him they weren't.

Potter went back to the chair.

"Now, once you do and say what you're told, you'll stay here while I run an errand. At that time, I'll free your ankles so if you need to urinate or vomit while I'm away, you'll use the bucket. If you urinate or vomit on my nice, clean floor, I'll punish you on my return. Do you understand?"

With his chin tucked into his chest, Devin nodded.

"Look at me when I speak to you, disrespectful brat. And say: 'Yes, sir, I understand, sir!'"

Fearing another slap—or worse—Devin looked up at the monster. "Yes, sir, I understand, sir."

"Very good. Now, let's begin."

It took more than an hour because the boy kept fumbling. Potter had to get the brat some water when his voice turned to a croak. And tissues, as the snot running out of his nose was disgusting.

But he finally had what he wanted. And after some editing, he'd have perfection.

He considered just putting a bullet in the boy's ear and finishing it. But he'd need the brat for the follow-up.

So he walked over with the clippers. "Try to run, scream, I'll break your leg. Then I'll go to your house and use these on your mum. Do you understand?"

"Yes, sir. I understand, sir."

Potter's smile spread. "Very good."

He clipped the ankle tie. "Use the bucket if necessary."

"Can I please go home, sir?"

"When I get back from my errand. I told you, what you said was a trap for a very bad person. Once that's taken care of, you can go home."

Potter shut the door, locked it.

He went upstairs to edit the recording, and glanced at the monitor.

The boy did use the bucket to urinate, but fumbled that, too. Some dribbled down his pants, some hit the floor.

The droid would deal with it. Later.

It didn't surprise him to see the boy hobble to the door, try to pull it open.

"Tried to run, so earned the bullet in the brain I was giving him anyway."

Still, he considered the disobedience warranted some pain first. And maybe, just maybe, he'd kill the boy's family after all. At some point.

All those years locked away he'd forgotten just how satisfying taking a life could be. He'd had to be so careful to follow the rules, even when he'd been free again.

The mission came first.

Satisfied with the recording—perfection—he walked up to the bedroom level, and into the room where he kept his wigs, facial enhancements, putty, alternate wardrobe, and all the rest.

Though he doubted he'd need one, he selected his persona.

The red wig with the ridiculous stub of a pigtail. A larger nose, prominently hooked. Though rarely used—he hated the feel of facial hair—he added a dramatically pointed goatee that matched the wig, and bushy eyebrows.

Meticulously, he gave himself a scatter of freckles, then a few more. A large stud earring, left ear. A bit of padding around the waist. Pressed jeans, a white collared shirt that would show the temporary tattoo he affixed on his left biceps.

He added an army-green canvas satchel, slung it over his shoulder.

And examined himself in the triple-glass, full-length mirror.

"There now, thanks to Chameleon's tutelage, your own mother wouldn't recognize you. Not that the selfish bitch ever would if she still lived."

Which she didn't.

She'd deserted him and his sad sack of a father. God knew why he'd bothered to track her down after he'd joined the military.

Maybe to kill her.

But she'd already been dead—dead by her own hand.

He shook that away. No matter now.

On the way out, he checked the monitor again. The boy was curled in a corner, crying. His hands, tied together, bled a bit.

Tried to beat down the door. Pathetic.

Potter shut down the droid, then went out through the garage.

He drove south, then east, parked. He walked to the bus terminal he'd earmarked. He'd already checked the schedule, so simply strolled around to the bus leaving for East Washington at eleven.

He bought a ticket—cash, to Boston—then filed out with others heading north. Just another hapless slob taking a bus trip.

Then he peeled off—found the correct bus.

He slipped inside, fixed the 'link to the underside of a seat in the middle of the bus.

Just as he walked back to the front, a uniformed driver stepped up.

Potter thought about the knife in his right boot.

"Hey, man, you want to board early, I need to see your ticket."

Potter affected an American accent. "Early? But we're leaving in like, you know, five minutes."

"Closer to twenty."

"But—is this the bus to Boston?"

"East Washington, pal."

"Jeez, wrong bus. Sorry!"

Potter scrambled off, hurried away. Then made a turn, strolled easily back to his car. He could track the bus on the in-dash, make certain it left on time.

He'd set the message to send at twenty-three-fifteen.

By the time they managed to trace the source—and he hadn't made that easy—the bus would be well on its way.

And the idiot cop would chase it down while he sat in his lovely house, having a brandy.

He hoped she didn't have an accident on the chase. He really wanted the pleasure of killing her.

Eve felt herself starting to flag, and pushed through the fatigue. She'd gone down the damn rabbit hole again—no choice—only to hit dead ends on the first two names Roarke gave her.

She had to admit, Potter did have a knack for creating very solid IDs and backgrounds. When you picked at the threads, they fell apart.

But it took a lot of picking first.

She sat back, gave herself a minute to let her brain coast.

"You need sleep."

She didn't jolt—too tired for it.

"I've got another hour in me. Did you get anything else?"

"A bit, after some hard pulling. Still not a direct link to a New York location."

"Maybe check in on the others?"

"I'll do that. But we're calling it at midnight. That gives you about forty-five."

Since she'd expected him to push for now, she took the forty-five. "You can tell them to call it then, too. We've got all this, and the other angles to work tomorrow. We're closer. A lot closer."

As she spoke, her 'link signaled. "Relayed from my office. It's on twenty-four/seven until . . . It's him. Display says THE TWELVE. I need you to—"

He'd already pulled out his PPC. "Triangulate. Trace. Ten seconds to set it up. And done."

With his other hand, he took out his 'link, signaled Summerset. "They should hear this."

She answered. "Dallas."

Eve Dallas. The computer-generated voice jumped a bit. *Listen carefully. This message is for you. It is for Mole, Panther, Chameleon, Owl, Magpie, Cobra, Fox. All who remain of The Twelve, all of whom are responsible for the imprisonment and death of Shark.*

> *The time has come to pay. The time has come to choose. Will you hide behind the false mask of hero, or show yourselves to be the cowards you are?*

The video unblocked, and she saw the boy.

"Jesus Christ, he's got a kid. On-screen."

She heard the others come in, heard the exclamations.

"Quiet!" she ordered.

"Tell them your name." Not comp-generated now, but the hollow sound of computer-disguised.

"I'm—I'm Devin. Devin McReedy."

"How old are you, Devin?"

"Nine. I'm nine."

Eyes on the screen, Eve used the keyboard to run Devin McReedy, age nine, New York. And saw the Amber Alert.

"What's going to happen to you, Devin?"

"You—you—" Tears tracked down his face. "You're going to kill me with the gas, so I can't breathe and I die. I don't want to! Please. I didn't do anything bad! I was just—"

"Devin? Remember what we discussed. Say what I tell you, no more. Or I'll have to hurt you. Again. Do you understand?"

"Yes, sir. I understand, sir."

"Now, what has to happen so I don't kill you with the gas? So you don't die?"

"Somebody has to take my place. Um, um. Owl or Mole or Fox or . . . I can't remember all the names. I can't!"

"Or Chameleon or Cobra or Magpie or Panther. Or Eve Dallas. And what will happen when one of them takes your place?"

"I can go home. You promised, I can go home and you won't hurt my mom or my dad or my brother."

"How old are you again, Devin?"

"Nine. I'm nine."

"Just nine years old. So young! So innocent! So defenseless! What do you say, heroes? Is your miserable life worth more than this boy's? Decide, choose which of you will trade lives. I will contact Eve Dallas again at precisely noon tomorrow. If you attempt to stall, or negotiate, he loses a finger, and the price goes up to two lives for his."

On-screen, the boy curled up, sobbing.

"At that time you will receive specific instructions. Follow them, precisely, or he loses a hand, and the price goes up to three lives. Fail, and he dies, and I take another. Payment is due."

The transmission ended.

"On the turnpike, heading south," Roarke told her.

"No, he's not. He's not. That's a ploy, misdirection. How fast is he traveling, what's the last mile marker?"

"He's been at a steady sixty, and sticking to the right-hand lane."

"A truck, a bus. He's not on it."

But she contacted Whitney.

"Commander, urgent situation. I need roadblocks, southbound turnpike."

She whipped through the details.

"Five minutes," Whitney said, and clicked off.

"He'll do it." Marjorie rubbed a hand on her heart. "He'll do exactly what he said to that child."

"Quiet."

She tagged Peabody.

"Don't talk, listen. He's got a kid. Devin McReedy, age nine. Amber Alert's been out since just after four." She reeled off an address. "Get there, find out who's handling it, talk to the family. Details. Get them all. Then get here, you and McNab. Have him contact Feeney. And you contact the rest of the bullpen.

"Everybody here by six hundred hours for a full briefing."

"I've got it. Goddamn bastard!"

"Get the details and relay them."

She clicked off. "Computer, replay message received from The Twelve."

"Lieutenant," Summerset began.

"Quiet. I fucking mean it. The screen's jittering some. Bouncing some. Not a smooth ride. Computer, get me buses leaving New York, southbound—fuck, what time, what time?"

Unable to compute.

"You shut up, too. Message received, twenty-three-fifteen."

"At the rate of speed," Roarke calculated, "allowing for time to get on the turnpike, the mile marker at the first trace . . . About eleven."

"Computer, buses leaving New York, southbound, between twenty-two-thirty and twenty-three hundred. Give me departure location, destination."

Acknowledged. Working . . .

"If I could speak."

"Not yet," she snapped at Summerset. "Freeze screen."

While the computer began listing buses, Eve moved closer to the screen.

"That's it, that's the one. Eleven o'clock bus, nonstop to East Washington. Departing from the East Side terminal. Roarke."

"I'll give Whitney the information."

"Get this screen to enhance. I want to see that back wall closer, better. Can you sharpen it?"

"I can do that." Cyril stepped forward. "If I may."

"Do it, just do it. Yeah, more. That's the ceiling line there. You can just see it. Low ceiling. Maybe seven and a half feet. No window. It's a basement. Kid's in a basement room."

"And terrified. I will speak!" Summerset snapped it out. "I will not sit safe in this house while he torments, tortures, and kills that child. Someone's child. I will not put my life above his. I will not risk it."

"So what? You'll be the trade?" Furious, she rounded on him. "How, with that big stick up your ass, do you find room to shove your head in with it?"

"Well, that's a good one," Harry murmured. "I'm stealing it."

"You can save your insults."

"I've got plenty, but I'm going to say I gave you credit for more brains than this. But you're broken brick stupid if you think he lets that kid live two minutes after he kills you, or any of you."

"You can't be sure—"

"She's right." Ivanna put a hand on Summerset's arm. "He'd never let the boy live. He took a child because it would shake all of us to our core, and you more than anyone. He doesn't plan to let the child live."

"No." Summerset put a hand over hers. "No, of course he doesn't. But I'm not as easy to kill as he believes. I could—"

"You will not do a damn thing unless I tell you to do a damn thing."

"You have no authority to—"

"Fuck yeah, I do. I'll slam you in lockup before you can blink. Material witness. I'll put every one of you in lockup if I have to. Jesus Christ, did you hear him?" she demanded. "Did you listen? He's so egotistical he thinks we still believe he's dead. He doesn't know how close we are because—egotistical. Narcissist. Goddamn psychopath.

"He's pissed. He's so pissed he missed this afternoon that he goes right out and snags a kid. Grabbed him up."

She began to pace again. "Still raining some when the alert went out, and that had to take a while. Used the rain for cover. Kid walking home from school alone in the rain. I need the report. Details. Nine—probably not far to walk, lives in the neighborhood. Lower East, that's pattern."

When Summerset started to speak again, Roarke held up a warning hand, shook his head.

"He should've cooled off, taken a day or two, but he couldn't. Grabs the kid. Kid that age would put up a stink most likely. Maybe lured, but more probably, knocked him out. Quick jab, toss him in the car, and drive home."

"That doesn't—"

Now Roarke held up a hand to Iris. "She's working it."

"Drive home, straight into the garage. Haul the kid down to the basement because that's a fucking basement. Zip-tie him. Prep the room? No, no, already prepped. Grabbing the kid today, impulse, but he already had the room, the gas, the idea. Just for one of you. Now the kid's bait, and he's switched to this method."

"We factor in basement," Roarke said.

"And that'll narrow it. Maybe a full basement, a lower-level apartment or whatever. Maybe just below-level storage, but basement. Basement, attached garage. No other way."

"If I may." Now Marjorie lifted a hand. "It's possible, isn't it, the child's in a garage. A rented garage."

"No, floor's wood—probably fake wood, but wood—and how many rented garages have full soundproofing? He can't risk holding a screaming kid, and why wouldn't he scream, unless Potter's sure he couldn't be heard?"

"I'm going to agree. For what it's worth," Harry said. "He needs the ease of entry. He puts a cam in to watch, sure, but something goes wrong, he's running off to a rental? No, it's all in one place. His place."

"Lieutenant." Ivan cleared his throat. "If he plans to use gas, as with Giovanni, he would want the space fully sealed. He would then require a mask and a way of dissipating the gas—after. It's a fairly large space from what we could see, so he'd need more than one canister to be . . . to be sure."

"All right. What does that tell you?"

"The house is large enough for his purposes. This basement area, a secure area for his weapons, another area for his, ah, costumes? He learned from me, so may have a small lab to make drugs, such as may have been used on the boy. A living space, of course, and I believe he would keep that main area clear of any of this. On the risk someone might come to the door, or he has a delivery, that sort of thing. I would also try a two- to three-story home, with basement."

"Okay. Do that. All of you do that. If you need sleep, take it. Two-hour shifts."

Then she turned to Summerset. "By noon tomorrow, I'll have him in a box. He made mistakes. The boy's just the latest one. He has to keep the kid alive for the follow-up at noon. Show him off again, scared and crying. Instead, the kid'll be home with his family."

"You can't be wrong. How would we live with it? How would any of us live with it?"

"I'm not wrong. Go find me a basement."

Roarke waited until they'd left the room.

"Well done. You gave them exactly what they needed. The straightforward, the matter-of-fact. Confidence."

"I'm not wrong," she said again. "Because I can't be."

He went to her, laid his hands on her shoulders, met her eyes. "You're not wrong. But you were before."

"When? About what?"

"When you said he was a step ahead of you. He's not. He still thinks he's anonymous, an unsub, and his pains to conceal his identity are wasted, time-consuming. So he's fallen behind, and has no idea what's coming."

Rubbing her shoulders, he pressed his lips to her forehead. "You won't do two-hour shifts. You need sleep, but you won't take it."

"I'll take a booster if I need it. But right now? Sending that message? He's given me a strong second wind. And it's going to blow him back to hell."

Her communicator signaled.

"Commander."

"We have the bus, and the 'link he used, as well as a description from the driver. Male, Caucasian, sixties, red hair and beard. The detectives in charge of the McReedy investigation have a description of a Caucasian male, gray hair, clean-shaven, black raincoat standing in the alleyway where the boy's mother found his violin case. Between a building, currently vacant, and a black car. 'Car' is the best the wit could do."

"They're both Potter. I have Peabody and McNab with the parents now. They'll bring any further information here, sir. I have the remaining Twelve in Roarke's comp lab. They've given me several possibilities on Potter's location and his vehicle. I'm bringing in the rest of my detectives here, at oh-six hundred. Sooner if we hit."

"I'll be there at oh-six hundred. Contact me if sooner. Narrow down those possibilities, Dallas."

"Yes, sir."

"I'll work here," Roarke told her. "I'll take the auxiliary."

"Stick with the financials. That's another angle. Money, house, vehicle." She shoved at her hair. "He won't have the car and the house under the same ID, that's too simple for him. But there's got to be some overlap with the accounts. He needs a driver's license, vehicle registration, background that'll pass if he gets in a fender bender, deals with any traffic stop. He doesn't want to bother, have to remember grabbing that license every time he uses the car."

"And the IDs he's created are too good for one-offs."

"Right." Funds flush, she remembered, but not unlimited. "I'm going to push on the car. If they don't narrow the potentials on the house in an hour, ninety minutes, we shift and focus there."

Something would give, she thought. Something would break.

They worked in near silence. She heard Roarke mutter or curse now and then, and his mutters and curses leaned harder into the Irish.

She tried not to think of Devin McReedy, of the fear in his weeping eyes, the terror in his voice.

Why were there so many luxury vehicles in New York? The wit said black, but she couldn't discount dark blue or gray.

Devin's voice played back in her head.

"He edited the recording."

"Hmm. He did, of course."

"Because it had to be perfect. It wasn't quite seamless, but close. He took that time. Status, top-of-the-line. If it's French food and design at the top for him, and the Italians after, who makes the best vehicles?"

Deciding he could use a short break, since she'd distracted him anyway, Roarke got more coffee. "I like to think I do."

"You weren't making them pre-Urbans. And he's not putting money in your pocket. You're Summerset's. What nationality? Think like him."

"Ah, I see. For status and longevity and so on. Add he's from Europe. Germany."

"Okay. I'm pushing German makes up."

Her 'link signaled. "Peabody."

"We're leaving the McReedys' now. I've got the report from the detectives who caught the case, and Devin's parents couldn't tell us much more. They're holding on by a thread, and the thread's really thin."

"Go by Central, pick up helmets. He might try for a head shot this time. And a battering ram."

"Bollocks to that," Roarke said.

"Battering ram's a backup."

"How close are we to finding him?"

"Getting closer. Take a booster if you need it. It's going to be a long night."

She clicked off, rolled her stiff shoulders.

"You could take an hour on the sleep chair."

"I'm good. I'm still good."

"You get so pale."

"I'm good," she repeated.

Time to take a hard look at the far-too-many German luxury cars registered in New York.

She lost track of time as she searched, whittled, added, or deleted.

Roarke's 'link signaled.

"Peabody and McNab at the gate. I've let them through. Summerset will let them in."

"Good. I need to move."

She rose, rolled her shoulders, circled her neck. After adding her current list of cars to the board, she paced.

"Are you getting anywhere?"

"I might be."

"Passed ninety minutes. I lost track."

"Give them a bit longer. You've McNab to add in now."

"Yeah. An hour more."

She checked the time. Ten hours, eight minutes until noon.

"Twelve. It's noon because it's twelve. He should've given us less time, but he had to hit that mark."

"That slipped by me, and of course, you're right." He crossed to her, held out a cookie. "A bit of fuel."

"What kind of cookie is that?"

"Oatmeal."

"Oatmeal in cookies should be illegal." She stuffed it in anyway. "Next thing, it'll be spinach."

"Actually—"

"Don't tell me. I don't want to know."

She turned as she heard the clomp and prance.

They came in carrying boxes. Peabody in black didn't particularly surprise her. But she wouldn't have believed McNab owned any black. The shirt had a lot of black-on-black swirls and symbols, and the airboots sported dark red and black stripes.

But the baggies looked almost normal until you considered the shocked-face emoji on the belt buckle.

"Helmets," Peabody said. "Battering ram."

"Put those anywhere. McNab, computer lab. Summerset and the rest of them will bring you up to speed."

"I'm there." McNab's pretty face hardened like stone. "Somebody uses a kid like this? He's going down, he's going down hard. Booster or high-octane coffee, She-Body. Not both."

"It was just that one time. Where do you want me?" she asked Eve.

"I've got a list of lower probability vehicles, a culled list of seasonal theater tickets, and a list of Potter's known—so far—aliases. You can use your PPC, cross-check. A wit says the car's black, but—"

"Yeah, can't be sure. I'm going for the coffee instead of the boost."

After she programmed her coffee, Peabody sat at the table.

And all three got back to work.

Chapter Twenty-one

At the end of the hour, Eve swiveled in her chair. "Status, Peabody?"

"I've got it down to five."

"Better than me. I'm at eight. Okay." She pressed her fingers to her gritty eyes. "We're going to switch it up. Computer lab takes the cars, we take the locations. Fresh—well, not fresh. Different eyes. Roarke?"

He waved her away. "Sticking. May have something."

Less than nine hours now, she noted. And that second wind had died. Resigned to taking a booster, she started to rise.

"And there you are! Bloody bastard, I fucking see you now."

"You got it?"

"This one's important, as he buried it deep. Not much in it, just under four million. I might've missed."

"Four million," Peabody said as she pushed up and struggled back a yawn. "Not much? Shows the rich are really different."

"Name," Eve demanded.

"There's the other thing. Two names on this account. Reginald and Alicia King."

"Alicia—close to Alice. He's still obsessed. Wait, wait, I saw that name. Alicia King."

"It's in mine! Wait, wait!" Peabody rushed back to the table and her PPC. "I got it, I got it! A 2060 Mercedes EQE, black, registered to Alicia King, 154 Riverside Drive.

"Jesus!"

Eve started to tag McNab, then heard his bounce, and the others coming behind him.

"We've got three solid that hit—"

"Reginald and/or Alicia King, 154 Riverside Drive."

"That's one of them. Hell, yeah!"

"Peabody, call in the team. Add Officer Carmichael. I want him and five of his best. McNab, tag Feeney and Callendar. They're here. Now."

She yanked out her communicator.

"Commander. We've got him. I'm calling the team in now."

"On my way. Good work."

"It's good," Eve said as she pocketed her comm. "But not good enough until Potter's in cuffs."

"And the boy."

She turned to Summerset. "In a couple hours. Three tops, the boy's home with his family. His safety's priority."

"How many do we expect? How many police officers?"

"Ah . . ." Her brain, back in business, still couldn't quite do the math.

"Including the three here," Roarke said, "seventeen. Eighteen with Whitney."

"Sounds right. Why?"

"They'll need chairs and something to eat."

"That's where you get it from," she said to Roarke. "Fine, but make it fast. They can eat while I brief them. Roarke, get me the house, exterior visuals, blueprints."

"Already on that."

"Lieutenant. I know you need time to plan your op. When you have him in custody . . ." Marjorie looked at the others. "We need to see him. We don't need to speak with him, and won't interfere in any way, but we need to see him."

"Need to lay eyes on him." Nodding, Harry gave Marjorie's hand a squeeze. "And it'd sure bloody well suit me if he lays his on us."

They'd earned it, Eve thought. Earned the justice of that and the closure.

"I can make that happen. When we have him, Roarke will contact Summerset. He can arrange your transportation to Central. I'll clear you for Observation."

"Your visual's on-screen."

She walked back. "Yeah, good-sized two-story house, with full basement and attached two-car garage. Nice water view's wasted on this asshole. Gated entrance to keep the riff from raffing on that water view. Not much grounds, the house takes most of the lot. But that's good for him. He doesn't need a big yard. That's just maintenance.

"Front door, side doors, south and north, big glass doors on the river side main entrance, and a walkout from that end of the basement. Second-story deck with double doors—that'll be the primary. I'm going to need you and the EDD team to take out all the alarms, cams, locks."

"Understood. I'll access the schematics for the security system."

"He'll have made some of his own adjustments," Cyril told him.

"Also understood. We can work through it. Blueprints coming up."

"There." As she moved closer, Eve pointed. "Storage area, southeast corner of the basement. That's where he's keeping the kid. No windows, only one door."

"Poor little boy," Iris murmured. "It's been hours for him now."

"Just a couple more. Roarke, can you dig up the description from when the house was last listed?"

"If you give me a minute."

"Take your time. We've got time now. There's a good-sized bedroom with bath on the main level, but the biggie, the main with the larger bath and that access to the deck, is on the second. Got a fireplace. He'd take that for himself. Three more rooms up there and another bath. One room listed as a bedroom, but it's smaller."

"Good size for an office," Peabody commented.

"Yeah, good place to put in a command center, his e-toys. This one here, walk-in closet. Maybe the costumes. And the third, smaller closet, but roomy enough. Why waste it?"

"Armory."

"Mmm-hmm." Still studying the blueprints, she nodded at Roarke. "He'll have weapons stashed throughout the house, monitors, too. But he needs those rooms for his work and security. Fitness room, basement level. Another room with a door down there. Maybe a lab. Kitchen and lounge area main, dining room main. I bet he sits all by himself in the dining room and eats his French food."

"Here's your last listing. On-screen."

"Okay. He put the money he got for the villa and more into this one. See there? Storage area, fabricated wood plank flooring, lower level. I guess it's too fancy to call a basement. Media room, fitness room, bedroom, same level. Full bath down there, fully equipped kitchenette.

"And look there. Fully secured—door cams, alarm system, palm plates, and so on. Even gives the name of the security system. That's yours."

"It is indeed." Roarke smiled at her. "That makes it simple for a change."

"He'll have more," Summerset warned. "Interior cams, locks, alarms, booby traps."

"Yes. We'll account for them, won't we, Ian?"

"Bet your ass and mine on that."

"This boy's good." Cyril gave McNab a slap on the back. "If you ever decide to work in the public sector, you're hired."

"Thanks. EDD and New York, that's home. Can I get a fizzy from the kitchen AC, LT? I could use a hit of the sweet."

"Get what you need."

"I'll see to breakfast. I could use some help with the chairs, a table."

She gave Summerset a little credit for moving the civilians out. Then focused on the screen.

She saw how it would work—had to allow for complications, but she saw how it would work.

Feeney got there first. He looked like he'd slept in his clothes—but that was usual.

He took a look at the board, then moved to stand beside Eve, studied the screen.

"That's his hole? Big, fancy one."

"Yeah. A few decades in a cage makes you want some space."

"He won't have it much longer. The kid there?"

She nodded when he pointed to the storage room. "Yeah. That's where he did the recording. No reason to move him."

"He didn't plan on letting the boy out of there breathing."

"No. But he has to keep him going until noon for the follow-up."

Feeney checked the time. "We'll have the kid home in time for his breakfast. Got the security system?"

"Roarke's working that. It's one of his."

Feeney grinned. "Ain't that sweet?"

When he leaned over Roarke's shoulder, and they began to talk e, Eve left them to get more coffee.

No booster, she decided. Too close to go time, and she'd found yet another wind. This one, a gale.

She caught the smell of food as Summerset and his friends carried in the domes, plates.

Galahad caught it, too, and he padded in, looking innocent.

"More coming now," Roarke said.

"Yes. I'll see to it." Summerset went out, and minutes later, Baxter and Trueheart came in.

"I knew we could count on you." Scanning the table, Baxter rubbed his hands together.

"Can I pour you some coffee, Detectives?"

"Ms. Wright." Baxter laid a hand on his heart. "I fell in love with you when I saw *This Side of Morning*."

Laughing, she reached out to take his hand. "You couldn't have been six when I played Eloise. And that vid's hardly appropriate for a child."

"I was twelve the first time I saw it after I figured out how to shut down parental controls. It was love, and no woman yet has met that standard."

Callendar popped in. "Breakfast! Woo!"

"Let me make introductions," Marjorie began, and continued as the others straggled in.

"Get food," Eve called out, still working on the details. "Eat. We're just waiting on the commander. Jesus, Jenkinson, Potter could see that tie from space."

"I'll tuck it into the shirt till we have him, Loo." And grinning, he fluttered it. "I wore it special. See? A big rat in a little cage."

A big, glowing, purple rat, Eve noted, in a glittery silver cage. And both on a field of emerald green.

"I see. If I look much longer, I may go blind, but I see. Commander," she added when Whitney came in. "Please, help yourself to some food, some coffee."

"I will." But first, he walked to The Twelve, saying each name as he shook hands. "It's an honor to meet you all. Though Summerset and I have met many times before, let me take this opportunity to thank you, all of you, for your service to your country, and to the world.

"Let me also extend condolences for the loss of your friend. We will bring Conrad Potter to justice. Lieutenant, you have the floor."

"Yes, sir. As you're all aware, this afternoon, Conrad Potter abducted this child. On-screen, Peabody. Devin McReedy, age nine. We have full confidence Devin is being held at this location on Riverside Drive, in this area of that location.

"The safety of Devin McReedy is first priority. When EDD has cleared our way and confirms the boy's location, and Potter's, we move in, and move in unison, and in silence."

She gestured to the back of the room. "Helmets in those boxes. Everybody wears one. As we know from earlier today—yesterday," she corrected, "he has illegal weapons and will fire. He has combat skills and is likely to resist or try to flee. Multiple weapons, and he very likely has some areas of the house booby-trapped.

"Remember, we move in, in unison, in silence, and with care. Baxter, Trueheart, south entrance, Jenkinson, Reineke, north. Santiago, Officer Carmichael, rear—clear the main level, secure any weapons found. An officer on the rear to block any attempt of escape from the doors leading to the deck or the basement walkout. One each on the side doors."

"Did I get demoted?" Detective Carmichael asked.

"No. When we go in the front—that's Roarke, as he'll deal with any last security, and myself—Detectives Peabody, Carmichael, and Callendar will go in behind Santiago and Officer Carmichael. Peabody's team goes directly to the basement steps, located here."

She highlighted on-screen. "Down, through this area to this door. If EDD hasn't already disengaged the interior security and the locks on this door, you'll have Callendar. If electronic, she'll disengage. If not. You've got the battering ram."

"Dallas—"

Eve held up a finger when Peabody started to object. "He's going to want his mother. He's nine and he's scared shitless. We don't know if Potter's hurt him just for the hell of it. He's priority one. You have a way with victims, and with children. I want women to get to him first, as he'll feel safer with women sooner.

"You get in, signal me. You get him out to safety, and call for medical assistance. When you're certain he's secure, contact his parents, give them his location. Peabody, I need you to stay with him. He'll need someone to stay with him until his parents get there, or if needed, to the hospital."

"I get it. I'll stick with him."

"Officers Shelby and Donovan, you will take the attached garage, clear it, and disable the vehicle inside, secure any weapons you find. Secure that interior doorway. Detectives Carmichael and Callendar will also sweep the basement area for weapons once the child is safe."

"Leaving a few of us out here, kid."

"No, getting to you. I need you and McNab in the van or on the ground with a mobile until you're certain there are no electronic traps the rest of us could walk into. More, that the boy would walk into before he's all the way out. At that time, you will signal, then take whatever entrance is most optimal. If he gets by me, gets by Roarke, secure the doors, box him in. Take him."

"Well covered, Lieutenant." Whitney drew her attention. "I trust you don't expect me to remain in the clear throughout this operation."

She had intended to have him remain in the van with the excuse of running comms. But she knew that look. "Which position would best suit you, Commander?"

"Correct question. I'll go in the front, behind you and Roarke. Up the stairs and begin to clear the third floor with you.

"He won't get by you, or Roarke, but if he does, he'd still have to get by me. You haven't addressed possible explosives or gas."

"We have sniffers for explosives. I don't expect to find any set to blow. He's not going to blow up the house. He's got millions invested in it, and money matters to him. For gas, every field kit has a breather. Everyone takes a breather. He does intend to fill that storage room with the same substance that killed Rossi. He will rig that by remote, but I don't believe he will until after noon tomorrow."

She glanced back where the remainder of The Twelve sat. "He doesn't want to kill any of his targets quickly. He wants them to suffer, wants to taunt them. And he'll want to watch. He won't engage the gas until he has one of his targets, and the boy locked in, so he can see and hear his former teammates agonize over the dying boy."

"You're very right." Ivan nodded. "Yes, he'd feel a triumph in that."

"The only thing he's going to feel is bitter disappointment. Any questions, ask them now. Then we suit up. EDD team, the Commander, Peabody, me in the EDD van. Everyone else—crap. Roarke, do we have a van?"

"It'll be out front."

"Everybody else in that. Jenkinson drives."

When she'd wrapped up, Roarke brought her bacon and eggs tucked between toasted bread. "You can eat in the van if necessary, but eat. Do this for me."

"Okay, okay." She grabbed a helmet, tucked it under her arm, then took a bite. "God, God, that's good. We'll get there before sunup. Another advantage. Put on the jacket with the Thin Shield, grab a helmet. Do that for me."

He put on his jacket, took a helmet as he looked toward The Twelve. And Summerset.

"You'll know when we have him."

"And when we do," Eve added, "get some sleep. It'll be at least a couple of hours before I bring him into Interview, probably closer to four.

There are things to work out, so get some sleep. Someone will contact you when it's time to come into Central."

"Will you," Summerset asked, "get any sleep?"

"Depends on the things to work out."

When they sat alone, Ivanna put a hand over Summerset's. "She's outlined a very good plan. And yes, even very good plans can go astray. We'll trust this one won't."

"More usually I learn what she's faced down—or they have—when I deal with the blood on her clothes. It's different, and difficult, to know from the beginning."

"And different, and difficult for us, even at this point in our lives," Marjorie said, "to be the ones sitting and waiting."

"There's very fine equipment in the lab here." Cyril looked from face to face. "It's possible, with a bit of this and more of that, I could hook into the mobile equipment. We can't be there, but we could see as it happens."

"What are we waiting for?"

As Marjorie rose, the others rose with her.

The drive didn't take long. When they parked out of the gate's camera range, Roarke got to work.

"The trick is to shut down the camera without alerting the system. And it's an excellent system."

"You'd know," Eve said.

"I would, and it has layers to foil someone doing precisely what I'm doing. Can't just backdoor work-around it," he said, more to the other e-geeks. "And no drilling the tunnel, no sliding down the pole. It's a peel, you see, skin by skin, all while doing the cloning."

"I'm seeing it." McNab hunkered closer.

"Are you going to inchworm it?" Callendar asked.

"I am."

"Well, shit, watch that trip wire."

Roarke nodded at Feeney. "No worries. I have it." He'd designed it, after all.

"And son of a bitch." Feeney shook his head. "They're down. The system reads green, but they're down."

"For sixty minutes, and not a second more."

Eve set her wrist unit to sixty minutes while he melted through the gate locks.

"Exterior house cams."

"I've got the locks," Feeney said, and his hound-dog eyes gleamed. "Yeah, I see it, I got it. Couple minutes."

"McNab, get me a read on how many and where in the house."

"On that. No shields there. Guess he didn't figure anyone would get this far. Two heat sources, and you can see, Dallas, just where you figured. Both horizontal. No movement."

"Then we're moving. We're go," Eve ordered. "On foot, comms open, all teams, go."

They moved quick and quiet through the dark, keeping low. Spreading out. A breeze off the river trickled through the air as Eve watched them peel off to their positions, and headed toward the front doors.

"Exterior locks down," Feeney said in her ear. "Moving to interior. Different system on the basement doors. Prioritizing there."

"Too easy," Roarke muttered. "Feeney, do a U-turn and slide."

"Copy that. Yeah, tricky bastard. Little booby-trap, secondary alarm. Another minute."

"Everybody hold," Eve ordered. "Hold positions."

A line of sweat trickled down her back as she held.

"You're clear! Moving to interior."

"Go for entry, all positions."

She nodded at Roarke, glanced back at Whitney.

Roarke went in high, she went in low. Whitney swept behind them.

* * *

"They're in," Harry said in the computer lab. "A lick and a split. If I'd had your boy back in my day, Summerset, oh, the fun we'd've had."

"They're moving upstairs. There's barely any light," Iris pointed out.

"Detective Peabody and her team are in the back." Marjorie watched the different views on-screen. "Some trouble at the inside door."

"They'll get through." Ivan kept his hands clasped together like a man at prayer. "They have to. That little boy . . ."

"Locks still engaged here, Cap."

"Working it," he told Callendar. "Don't use the ram. Don't use the ram till they've got the target. It's coming. It's . . . clear."

"I see that."

Peabody scanned the stairs. "Pitch-dark basement level."

"I've got you." Callendar switched on a flash. She swept it, and her weapon, side to side as they went down.

With the blueprints and Eve's orders in her head, Peabody moved toward the storage room as all three women cleared as they went.

"Door lock still engaged," Peabody said.

"Different system, got a seal and a runner. Going to take time, fuck it, by remote."

"I can get it on-site, Cap." Callendar holstered her weapon, pulled out her reader. "I can get it. You've got the seal down. I'm on the runner."

"Trapdoor! You see it?"

"Yeah, yeah." Now sweat beaded on Callendar's forehead as she took slow, steady breaths. "It's got a trigger, Cap. He could have it triggered to release gas and kill the kid. Or—"

"Don't pull the trigger."

"Callendar?" Eve said. "Do you need assistance?"

"No, I got it. I got it. The first read's a decoy."

"That's right. Circle back," Feeney told her.

"Reassessing, rereading. We're clear!"

Peabody shoved through the door and into strong light.

The boy lying in the center of the bare room opened his eyes. She saw the scream in them and held up her badge. "It's okay, Devin. We're the police. We're here to help."

"I want my mom! I want my mom! I want my dad!"

"Got your back," Carmichael murmured and slipped out the door to guard.

"I talked to your mom and dad." Peabody spoke softly as she lowered down to Devin. "I'm going to cut off these ties on your wrists. I bet they hurt."

"I couldn't get them off. I couldn't, and I tried and tried."

"I can see that." His wrists were raw and bloody where he'd pulled, where they'd dug in. The bruises on his hands told her he'd beaten them against the door. "But look, now they're gone."

On a sob, he threw himself into Peabody's arms. "Don't let him come back. Don't let him kill me and my mom and my dad and my brother."

"We won't." Callendar crouched down and pulled a small tube of juice from one of her many pockets. "Here you go. Don't drink too fast, just take sips, okay?"

He sipped, he slurped, then he sobbed. "He hit me in the face, and it hurt! He made me pee in a bucket and I got pee on my pants."

"We're not going to worry about that now. Everything's okay now." Because he burrowed into her, Peabody stroked his hair, then picked him up. "We're going to take you outside and call your mom and dad. Carmichael?"

"Basement level's clear. Stairs clear. I've got the lead."

"I'm on your six," Callendar said.

"We're clear, Dallas. Taking Devin out to the van via the walkout. Minor injuries from the zip ties. I'll tell the MTs to come in silent."

Chapter Twenty-two

WHILE IN THE COMPUTER LAB THERE WERE TEARS AND CHEERS, EVE clicked twice to signal she copied.

They'd cleared the third floor, sweeping his wardrobe, his office. She'd noted the lock system on one of the closet doors.

Armory. That could wait.

With the boy clear, out of danger, she paused outside the main bedroom doors.

Holding up a hand, Roarke crouched down to examine, then scan the locks. When the scanner blinked red, he tapped out a quick message.

Electric charge activated on handle. One minute.

With a nod, she waited.

It took him the minute, and a few seconds more before his scanner blinked green.

Rising, he slid it into his pocket, signaled clear.

Fast, she mouthed to Roarke. *Lights*, to the commander.

They burst in; the lights flashed on full in the wide room with its river view. Raven-black hair sleep-tousled, dark eyes wide, Potter jerked up in bed. Dawn trickled gently in the windows as he swung a weapon toward them.

Eve's stream hit center mass, and even on low, had him jittering. The gun dropped from his hand, hit the side of the bed, then thudded to the floor.

"Police." She rushed forward. "Hands up."

Though his hands still shook, he yanked another weapon from under the pillow. Closing in, Eve struck his gun hand with her left and just batted it away. He tried to roll, and she had the satisfaction of grabbing him by the collar and hearing something rip.

As she dragged him out of bed, he flailed. His head cracked against one side of her ribs, his trembling fist connected with the other side.

"Give it up, Potter. You're bagged." Rolling him onto the floor, she cuffed him. "Conrad Potter, you're under arrest for the murder of Giovanni Rossi, a human being. For the kidnapping and unlawful imprisonment of Devin McReedy, a minor child. For the attempted murder by explosive device of Marjorie Wright, Ivanna Liski, and Iris Arden. Boy, this is fun. For the—"

"Let me take him, Lieutenant." Roarke nudged her aside. "You're bleeding again."

"What?" She looked down, saw the red seeping into the gray shirt. "Crap."

"No strenuous physical activity for twenty-four hours," Roarke reminded her.

"It wasn't that strenuous. Additional charges, you treasonous fuck, include possession of illegal weapons. Firing an illegal weapon, assault on an officer by firing an illegal weapon. Attempting to fire two illegal weapons at a police officer. Oh, almost forgot, threatening to maim and execute a minor child."

Because it had—hell!—started to sting again, she pressed a hand to the wound.

"There's more, but that'll do for now. Oh, and just a comment. Black silk pajamas? Really? Though I'm grateful you covered your tiny, useless dick so none of us have to be exposed to it."

"You ignorant bitch! You whoring cunt! You should be dead!"

"Hurt." Eve held up her bloody fingers. "Not dead."

In response, Roarke turned out of the range of the recorders, and delivered a single, short-armed jab to Potter's kidneys as he hauled him to his feet.

On a choking sound, Potter paled, and his already weakened legs gave way at the knees.

Eve simply shot Roarke a warning glare. But in the doorway, Jenkinson, just arrived, grinned. And untucked his tie.

"We got him from here."

"Read him his rights. House skids beside the bed. Somebody grab them for him."

"I've got them." Whitney bent to pick them up. "And I'll arrange his transport to Central, his booking, and a stay in maximum holding until you're ready for him."

The commander looked around the elegant room with its lovely view as Reineke joined Jenkinson to perp-walk a sagging Potter away.

"He's had his last night in the lap of luxury, but you and your team still have work to do here. Good job." Holstering his weapon, he gave a nod of satisfaction. "Damn good job."

Whitney paused in the doorway. "Go have the MTs close that wound before you start."

"Sir, I—"

"That's an order, Lieutenant."

"Yes, sir." She waited until he'd walked away. "Damn it."

"Don't be a baby about it." Roarke took her arm to lead her out.

"I need to set things in motion here first. And you shouldn't have punched him."

"Yes, I certainly should have."

"That's the sort of thing that gives cops a bad name."

"I'm not a cop," he reminded her. "And I'm only human."

"Yeah, yeah. All right, boys and girls." She paused halfway down the steps to relay orders, and, pushing a hand over her face, inadvertently smeared blood on her cheek. "Take this place apart. Any explosives, canisters, chemicals, call in the appropriate units to handle. Confiscate, log, and secure all weapons and ammo. EDD, you've got the electronics. Peabody—where the hell is Peabody?"

"She's with the kid and the MTs," Callendar told her. "Good call sending the girls in for him, Dallas. He's bonded to Peabody like glue."

"She can stick with him as long as he needs. Have the parents been notified?"

"We did that as soon as we got him out. They're on their way."

"Good. Everybody get to work. I'll be back in five. Ten," she corrected as she had to make some contacts of her own. "Roarke, let Summerset and the rest know this part of the mission, accomplished."

In the computer lab, they stood, linked with Ivan's hand gripping Iris's, and Cyril's arm around her waist, his hand on Summerset's shoulder. Ivanna had Summerset's hand in her right, Marjorie's in her left, and Marjorie held Harry's.

"That was brilliant." Tears clogged Marjorie's throat, thickened her voice. "That was bloody brilliant."

"I wish Gio could've seen it," Ivan murmured.

Harry nodded. "So say we all."

Summerset took out his 'link when it signaled. "Roarke, of course."

"Should we move out of here before you answer?" Cyril asked him.

"No. The boy and I don't lie to each other."

When he answered, Roarke lifted his eyebrows. "Ah, I see. So you already know."

"We needed to bear witness."

"Of course. Go get some sleep. It'll be some time yet."

"Tell the lieutenant . . . well done."

"I will. I'll send a driver when it's time, so you'll all come at once and together."

"Thank you for that. From all of us."

When Summerset replaced his 'link, Marjorie sighed.

"You know, I believe I could sleep now."

"So say we all," Harry repeated, and made them laugh.

As they shut down, started out, Summerset picked up the cat. "They won't be home for a while, my friend. You can settle in with me."

Eve spoke to the boy, but didn't push. Peabody remained his anchor until his parents arrived, younger brother in tow, and all rushed to the MT truck.

As tears and gratitude flowed, and the kid was all but smothered in hugs, she left it to Peabody, stepped out of the van.

She made her first contact. "Reo, we got Potter. Let me roll through the many charges here in New York. Have you got anybody there who can carve their way through international laws and all that?"

"As a matter of fact." Reo stood in a robe, her hair still dripping from a shower. "I think I know where you're going, and was going there myself."

"That'll save time. Abernathy—Interpol—he's my next contact. They'll start working the extradition. I've got some ideas on that, and I want to know if we have weight."

"I'm all ears."

They confiscated twenty-three handguns, ten AR-47s, four M16s, silencers, bump stocks, body armor, an assortment of knives in the second-floor armory.

And enough ammunition to start a war.

He'd rigged two canisters of gas in the air vents of the storage room and had another six to spare. In the basement, he'd stockpiled the C-4, the grenades, along with chargers, timers in a workshop set up to make more.

And a lab where he made and stored a variety of drugs, paralytics, hallucinogens, poisons, anesthetics.

With sweepers, explosives teams, hazmat teams in place, Eve left Feeney and his e-team in charge.

In the van, Roarke at the wheel now and the rest of her team in the ridiculously plush back, Eve let her shoulders finally relax.

"He wouldn't have stopped with them. It wouldn't have been enough. After he'd killed the rest of The Twelve, me, maybe you," she said to Roarke, then glanced in the back at Peabody, "maybe you, he'd have picked more targets. Anybody still alive who'd had any part in his incarceration."

"Their families," Roarke added. "He'd have felt more power, more triumph with every kill. He'd have spent the rest of his life waging his personal war."

"Now he'll spend it back in a cage." Jenkinson tapped his tie. "Just like this. And since we're all friends here, nice sneaky punch."

"I enjoyed it."

"Enough of that. I still say you shouldn't have had my cops' rides taken down to Central."

"Simpler this way."

"Only you'd think that." But she'd let it go as they could all use this time as a team. "You could've gotten some sleep at home."

"I will when you will."

"It's still going to take me a while to set things up for interview."

"I'll find a way to occupy myself."

He always did, she thought, and let that go, too. And since they were just that, a team, she shifted and spent the rest of the drive laying out her strategy for interview. And beyond.

"You know what I like about you, boss?" Jenkinson got out of the van in the garage. "You got mean smarts. Mean's just mean, smart's just smart. But together, you got something."

When they piled in the elevator, Roarke did something to the controls. "Nonstop."

"You're not supposed to do that."

"I like he did," Reineke commented. "Wish I could figure out how he did it."

"No." Eve said it flatly, and stepped off as soon as they reached Homicide. "Peabody, we don't need the conference room. Why don't you go break that down? You could give her a hand, since you need to occupy yourself."

"Happy to."

Roarke walked off with Peabody; the rest of the bullpen scattered to desks and cubes. Craving coffee, Eve went into her office to find Reo at her desk.

"Give me good news."

"I believe I have some, which is why I'm enjoying your coffee and I'm not sitting in that horrible chair."

"Sit wherever you want. Gimme."

Crossing her legs, swiveling gently side to side in Eve's desk chair, Reo smiled. She wore a deep blue suit, and either that or satisfaction made her blue eyes sparkle.

"It's not finalized, not set in stone, but I know when a deal's going to happen. And the fact is, there's considerable agreement for your solution on the other side."

Eve satisfied her coffee craving.

"There's blood on your shirt. Yours or his?"

"Mine, but it's fine. Has he asked for a lawyer, a legal rep?"

"No."

"That's always advantage us, but either way. Mira?"

"I contacted her after Abernathy. She's in."

"Another advantage us."

"He will, as we all know, have to serve out his sentence—life, no parole—where those previous crimes were committed."

Eve just gulped more coffee. "And?"

"Even with extradition in the works, you'd have full authority to interview him here for crimes committed here. We, of course, have an absolute right to try and, unquestionably given the evidence, convict him of those crimes. And those crimes carry an equally heavy weight."

Eve went for more coffee. "And?"

"As I said, I know when a deal's going to go through. This will. The rest is up to you."

"I want the rest. I can make it happen. I'm going to call him up soon, get started."

"When's the last time you slept?"

"I honestly can't tell you. But I've hit some point where that just seems irrelevant. I want to wrap him, so we're going to wrap him. Then I'll sleep."

She went straight to the conference room. "Tag Summerset, let him know we're bringing Potter up inside an hour."

"Is it set?" Peabody asked.

"Reo's confident, so we'll be confident. Let Mira know. And Whitney. I'll book the interview room."

"Already done," Peabody told her. "We've got A. I really don't have to be good cop?"

"Be as mean as you want. But smart mean."

"They'll be on their way as soon as possible." Roarke pocketed his 'link. "Go do what you need to, both of you. I'll finish this."

She went back to her office, ordered uniforms to bring Potter to Interview A, cleared the group to come to Homicide and go into Observation.

She wanted a shower, but she'd already used the spare shirt in her locker, so one more thing to let go.

Instead she sat a moment, in the quiet, and looked at her board.

Before she slept, she thought, she'd contact Rossi's family, let them know Potter was in custody. And she was bound and determined to inform them of his payment for Rossi's death.

"It won't go unanswered."

Though she had no investigative need for it, she added Devin McReedy's photo to her board.

"It won't go unanswered."

She wanted cold, so programmed for a Pepsi, and guzzled half the tube before she heard the click of heels. Not Reo, she decided. Mira.

And Mira had dressed for the occasion in a severe dark suit and single strand of pearls.

"You're so pale," Mira said. "And there's blood on your shirt."

"I'm good. My bloodstream's a hundred percent caffeine, but I'm good. He's on his way up."

With a nod, Mira looked at the board. "That's the boy he took. Poor little guy had a rough go."

"Potter had the gas rigged, so it would've been a lot rougher. And Potter's going to pay for it."

"It's set then?"

"Reo says it's going to go through. Obviously I don't need a confession on the kid—though I want one. And I'll get one on Rossi. We'll do our part, and the Brits better do theirs. That's Reo now," she said when she heard the next set of heels.

Reo stepped in, smiled. "Done. Some paperwork, but done. My boss and Tibble gave it the last push."

"Then let's go seal the deal."

"The boss wanted to handle this part," Reo told her as they walked, "but he agreed with your tactics. Potter thinks women are inferior."

"He's coming into the find-out portion of the program. Peabody."

"With you."

Eve paused when she saw Roarke in the corridor.

"Summerset and friends are on their way up. I'll show them to Observation. Whitney and Tibble are already there."

"Tibble's in Observation?"

"He is. I won't wish the four of you luck, as you don't need it. I'll just say, finish him."

"Count on it."

They walked to Interview A, and Eve opened the door.

She enjoyed the site of Potter in an orange jumpsuit—a far cry from silk pajamas. And the wrist and leg shackles added a nice finish.

"Record on. Dallas, Lieutenant Eve, entering Interview with Potter, Conrad. Also entering, Peabody, Detective Delia, Reo, APA Cher, Mira, Dr. Charlotte."

"What is this?" Dark eyes full of derision, he sneered. "A fashion show?"

Eve just reeled off the various case numbers and sat.

She set the file she carried at her elbow, as did the other women as they took their seats.

"Mr. Potter, you've been charged with a number of serious crimes, including murder in the first. Were you read and do you understand your rights and obligations in these matters?"

"I understand them perfectly." This time, he smirked—as he had at the camera on the night of Rossi's murder. "I've spent considerable time studying law."

"I guess you had plenty of time for that during your incarceration in Manchester, England. Due to your knowledge and study, are you waiving your right to legal representation during this interview?"

"I am my legal representation. And this interview is bollocks. I see you brought your sidekick, and . . . APA?"

"Assistant prosecuting attorney," Reo supplied.

"How often do you sleep with your boss?"

"I haven't, thanks for asking. Office romances are so messy, and his husband wouldn't approve."

"A preoccupation with sex is understandable," Mira commented. "You had no conjugal visits during your lengthy incarceration."

"And we have the shrink, a woman pretending to be a doctor instead of tending to her own family."

With a cool smile, Mira opened her file, made a note.

"Now that we're all properly introduced," Eve said, "let's talk about the murder of Giovanni Rossi."

Potter started to wave a hand in dismissal, but couldn't manage the insouciance with the chains.

"Are these necessary, ladies? Are you not able to defend yourselves?"

"I think I managed that just fine when I put you and your silk pajamas down. The shackles stay. Giovanni Rossi."

"What about him?"

"Did you contact Giovanni Rossi, posing as Lawrence Summerset of New York, both former Underground team members, in order to lure Mr. Rossi to this city?"

"He'd hardly have come if I'd sent up a flare, and one does miss one's old compatriots."

"You had established yourself in New York, in the residence on Riverside Drive, as Reginald King."

"It flows, doesn't it?" This time instead of his hand, he just waved his fingers. "*Reginald* for royal, and of course, king."

"*Reginald* comes from the Latin *Reginaldus*, which stems from *regina*. Meaning queen."

He bared his teeth at Reo. "Don't be absurd."

"Queen King. Funny." Peabody shifted to Mira. "Would choosing a name like that indicate delusions of grandeur? Because what I'm looking at in here sure doesn't come off royal."

"Not delusions as much as a deep and obsessive need to prove himself superior."

"I have no need to prove what is."

"We can sort all that out later." And keep pissing him off, Eve thought. "He's used a lot of names, and there's probably a treasure trove of psychological issues in them, but for now, Mr. Potter, you communicated—we were able to access that communication from your electronics. Posing as his old friend, you asked Mr. Rossi to come to New York, and with this message, included tickets for his travel. You instructed him that he would be met upon his arrival."

"A common courtesy. Didn't your mother teach you manners? Oh, that's right, you have no mother on record." Eyes lively, he bared his teeth again. "No wonder you are what you are."

"But enough about me," Eve said easily. "Then, disguised as a driver, you met Mr. Rossi upon his arrival in New York. Nice work on the mask, by the way. It took our techs a few hours to analyze, extrapolate, whatever, to peel it away and come up with this."

She slid the sketch out of her file. "Pretty good likeness."

Shock rippled over his face, and anger had color flaring into it. But he shrugged.

"Technology is easily manipulated to achieve desired results."

"You'd know. You hated Rossi, wanted him dead. Wanted them all dead. Wasp, Fox, Panther, Mole, Owl, Magpie, Cobra, Chameleon. The remainder of The Twelve, the Underground unit that fought Dominion and other violent fringe groups during the Urbans."

"One doesn't hate what's beneath them. One only feels contempt."

"Sure. They make up the unit you betrayed. The people, along with Leroy Dubois, whom you murdered, and Alice Dormer, who stopped you, who sacrificed her life to stop you. You spent decades in prison plotting and planning your escape for one primary purpose. To kill them all."

"I had a purpose. Fawn prevented the full completion of that purpose."

"Because she was able to warn her team of your betrayal, stopping the ambush set up to kill them all. So you had to run."

"Retreat," he corrected.

"You didn't get far. Rossi found you. Wasp might have beaten you to death if Fox hadn't stopped him."

Eve angled her head, smiled just a little.

"Which was worse for your twisted ego? I wonder. Being caught and beaten, or being spared more beating by another you felt contempt for? I bet it's a tough call."

"I'd have handled Wasp. I'd have handled both of them."

"But you didn't. Rossi busted your nose, your jaw, cracked a few of your ribs. Bruised your kidneys."

She glanced up from the medical report in the file.

"I bet you were pissing blood for a week."

"You're a crude, ignorant female."

"I can't argue with the 'crude.' Then, thanks to The Twelve, you ended up in Manchester, in Five Hells. It took you decades, and then the only way you could *handle* Rossi was through deception."

"It's all he's got," Peabody commented. "Lies, deceit, masks, wigs. Oh, and the face work so he could massage his gigantic ego and look younger. When it comes to a one-on-one fight? Just another pussy."

"You're nothing but an underling serving under a bitch who's trying to be a man."

"That's Lieutenant Bitch to you, asshole," Peabody snapped back as she rose, leaned forward. "You're on that side of the table. Shackled. The ovaries on this side are a hell of a lot tougher than your tiny, shriveled balls."

"The day will come when I'm not shackled. And I'll kill you. Slowly."

"Oh. Shiver." With an eye roll and fake shudder, Peabody sat again.

"We can add threatening an officer—on record—to the charges."

He turned his head to smirk at Eve. "Your charges are shite. Even if you could prove them, they're shite. So fuck your charges. I'd say fuck you, all of you, but none of you are my type."

"We're all grateful for that small blessing," Reo commented before Eve continued.

"You drove Rossi in a limo you'd previously stolen—"

"Speculation!"

"Which you had modified," Eve continued. "And using a canister of phosphine—which you'd also stolen and hidden during the Urbans—filled the passenger area with said poison gas. While you watched Rossi fight to escape, choke, convulse, die through the camera you'd installed."

"No proof. None whatsoever."

"We found additional canisters, same poison, same era, same canister type, in your residence."

"Circumstantial."

"Wow." Reo gave a quick laugh. "You should've studied a lot harder. And that doesn't even touch on the fact your prints are on the explosive device planted under the table in Chez Robert, or the fact that Devin McReedy was held captive in a locked room in your basement."

"With another canister rigged to fill that room with poison gas," Peabody added. "Or Devin's hair found in the trunk of the car parked in your garage. The recording you forced him to make, which you then edited and sent from a mobile device."

"I was going to get to all of that," Eve complained. "I'm taking things in order. But since we're there. We tracked the 'link and recording, identified the bus, and the driver ID'd you—or the red wig and beard you wore, and which we again found in your residence. And, of course, we have Devin. You didn't bother with a disguise after you had him in that room because you were never going to let him leave that room alive."

"Bollocks and shite and of no consequence. I could have shot the boy in the head and tossed him at your feet and it wouldn't matter a bloody damn."

"Just how do you figure that?"

"I'll be extradited. Nothing I've done here matters at all."

"I see." And she did. She shot a look at Reo, and to her credit, Reo shot back one of concern and worry before she spoke.

"We can fight it."

"You'll lose." Sitting back, Potter spread his fingers. "You didn't think ahead, did you? None of you. If that bomb had gone off and killed those three whores and half a dozen besides, you could do nothing. If I'd lured one or more of the rest into that room with the boy and killed them all?"

He shrugged. "Nothing. Impunity. I'm serving life, and, oh yes, they'll insist on extradition."

"You got out once, you figure you'll get out again. And fulfill your purpose."

He only smiled as Eve looked at Mira.

"He'll certainly try. He's failed twice. He despises—we'll call them The Twelve. He despises them for what they are, what they stood for, the lives they've led while his has been locked away. They're responsible for his loss of freedom, for the wasted years. There must be . . . would you call it restitution, Mr. Potter?"

"Retribution."

"You put my card in Rossi's hand because I'm not only a woman trying to be a man, but one who's achieved rank in what you consider a man's job. But more, because I connect to Fox, to one of The Twelve. That was just too good to pass up. You'd beat me, humiliate me, killing him and the rest in the process. Bonus round. And once you'd accomplished that, you could live as whoever you wanted, wherever you wanted."

"The game's not over." His eyes—and there wasn't madness in them as much as fervor—bored into Eve's. "Skill and savvy adjusts."

"Maybe, but we figured out you were alive, that the prison doctor—who's in custody, by the way—accepted a substantial sum from you to help you fake your death and escape. We were onto you very quickly."

"So you say. It doesn't matter." The angry color that rose into his cheeks belied that. "Nothing I've done on this side of the Atlantic outweighs the rest. You'll have to turn me over." She leered at Reo. "Even the empty-headed blonde knows it."

"You'll still be in prison," Reo said.

"I'm sure it soothes you to think so."

Eve slapped a hand on the table. "You murdered Giovanni Rossi."

"What of it?"

"You watched him die, left his body under the underpass, and walked away."

"It wasn't a long walk. A few blocks to where I'd left my car. It's outrageous what parking costs in this city."

"You admit it? You sit here and admit to the premeditated murder of Giovanni Rossi?"

Potter leaned forward. "I boast about it. He walked right up to me in the terminal, looked right at me, and didn't know me. He settled right into the limousine, sipped some wine. This man who hunted me, who bloodied me, a man who worked for decades in intelligence, handed me his bags so I could stow them in the boot, and walked into his own death. I enjoyed every moment. I savored it."

"You have no remorse," Mira murmured.

"Retribution needs no remorse."

Chapter Twenty-three

In Observation, Harry hissed out a breath.

"He's just a git after all. For all he's done, and would've done, he's just a bloody git, and she has him cold."

"She sees him," Marjorie murmured. "She sees him as I can only wish we had."

From behind her, Summerset laid a hand on her shoulder. "We see him now."

"And she's not nearly done with him," Roarke commented. "No, not nearly done."

He was enjoying himself now, Eve could see it. And she played it.

With just a touch of frustration in her voice, just a hint of anger, she continued.

"Do you admit to making and planting the explosive device in Chez Robert with the purpose of murdering Iris Arden, Marjorie Wright, and Ivanna Liski?"

"It was an excellent plan. Complex, and God knows they're simple women. It was perfectly staged. They should have been sitting there, drinking their frivolous cocktails, waiting for the ridiculous cousin when the bomb went off."

"While you were in apartment 3-C across the street, watching."

"A fortunate turn, seeing that advertisement. Otherwise, I'd have sat at a table under an awning in the rain. But I realized quickly something had gone wrong.

"You interfered."

"I interfered, and you ran."

"Retreated. You, girl, may have gotten lucky with the explosive, but you obviously know nothing about tactics or strategies."

"I know running when I see it, but we'll say 'retreat' if that blows up your skirt. Your retreat included taking a shot at me—with an illegal weapon."

"Illegality hardly matters."

"And when you missed, you aimed and fired that weapon at two female civilians."

He just shrugged. "Needs must. You're like them, The Pathetic Twelve. Always concerned about civilians, innocents. War is death. And death doesn't separate the innocent. By firing at them, I stopped you."

For the first time he frowned. "And hit you. I'd swear it. But you had body armor, I suppose. Still, it stopped you, and I completed my retreat."

"Only to, a short time later, abduct Devin McReedy. He was on his way home from school. You must have scouted that area previously, known about the park, the school, the alley and empty building."

He sighed, adult to slow-witted child.

"Of course I did. Preparation is key to success. If the boy hadn't been alone, if his mother had done her parental duties, I couldn't have taken him. She bears the blame."

"You complete prick." When Peabody shoved up from her chair, Eve held up a hand.

"Easy, Detective."

"He's sitting there blaming the mother for somehow allowing him to drug a child, dump an unconscious child into the trunk of his car. To zip-tie the kid's wrists and ankles and dump him in a locked storage room."

"Emotions, you see?" Visibly amused, Potter shook his head. "The female runs on emotions rather than logic. The softhearted man does the same."

"I'll show you emotions." Peabody balled a fist, and Eve pushed quickly to her feet.

"Take it down, Peabody."

"Lieutenant, I carried that kid out of that basement, sat with him while the MTs treated the wounds on his wrists, his ankles. Held him while he cried."

"Have one of your own then," Potter suggested. "And be a mother to it instead of pretending a sidearm and badge make you as good as a man."

Eve put a hand on Peabody's shoulder as if restraining her.

"Take it down, Detective," Eve repeated. "He's bitchy because his mother ditched him when he was a kid."

"You shut up about that."

"Hey, I get it. No mother on record here." Eve tapped her chest. "Maybe Devin's mom should've walked him home from school—orchestra practice," she added. "He plays the violin, which his mom found in its case in the alley. Guess he dropped it when you grabbed him."

She walked around the table, gave a long look through the two-way glass before she turned again.

"But since none of it matters . . . I have to say it took some guts to let Pierce dose you back in Five Hells, make you essentially dead."

"He's a greedy man, an unhappy-in-his-circumstances man. It pays to know your tools, and I knew he wanted that second payment. He wouldn't get it until I was clear."

"Risky though, still risky. But you're a man who takes risks to get what he wants. Gotta admire that." As if chatting, she eased a hip onto the table on his side.

"You took your time after. Accessed your hidden funds somehow or other, got your face work. Took some time to refresh. Where'd you go? I bet France. Say . . . a flat in Paris, then a villa on the French Riviera. How about Saint-Tropez?

"I research, too," she said when his surgically chiseled jaw hardened. "You go for French food, another reason you chose Chez Robert for your kill trap."

"The coquilles Saint Jacques is excellent there."

"I bet. You had to enjoy freedom after all those years in a cage. And had to plan. Logically. But with complexity, too. No simple, direct methods. Not your style. I think I get why New York. You had a little thing for Alice Dormer, but she was married to Summerset, and didn't return that little thing."

"I assure you, had I pressed the matter, she would have. And she had no business remaining in the unit after giving birth."

"Mom thing again," Eve said casually. "I bet you'll mine that one, Dr. Mira."

"Oh, I already am."

"Figured. But the point is, Summerset's in New York, and as it happened, a second target on your kill list, Ivanna Liski. They've been friends since childhood. Pre-Urbans friends who worked and fought together when war broke out."

"A talented dancer. That should've been enough for her, as obviously her fatherless children weren't. And Fox? Some skills, certainly, but he should have kept his wife out of the fray. Wasp at least did that much."

"But with two in New York . . . No, wait." Shaking her head, she pushed off the table. "I almost missed it, again! On the slim chance something went wrong, or you were found out after you'd completed your mission, your purpose, it would end just like this."

She turned around, met his eyes. "Where nothing you did here would matter. One murder—Rossi's—seven with all of them. More with collateral damage in the restaurant, Devin McReedy . . . You weren't going to let him go, were you?"

"Of course not. Leave no witnesses." He tapped a finger on the table. "Logic."

"Logic. So you kill all of them, the kid, whoever went down in the bombing. And whoever else was useful or got in the way, like me, the two female civilians on the street. It wouldn't matter. If someone got lucky enough to catch you, or you got unlucky enough to get caught, there'd be no price for any of it. You're back in Manchester like none of that happened."

"You've chosen this career, I suppose you call it. You should know the laws and rules better."

"Yeah. Yeah. It looks that way."

Pulling out her 'link, Reo rose. "I'm sorry. I have to take this."

"Reo, APA Cher, exiting Interview."

"He can't get away with this, Lieutenant."

"Watch me," he told Peabody.

"Mr. Potter," Mira began, "do you feel your retribution entitles you to take these lives?"

"As many as necessary. Wars aren't just to be fought, but to be won."

"This is, for you, war?"

"It's my war."

Nodding, she made another note in her file.

"Lieutenant."

"Peabody, I don't like it, but we have what we have. At least we have his statements, his full admission. You thought this out, Potter, I'll give you that. Since it's what we have, we're going to go over the details for the record."

"It would be a pleasure to rub your nose into it."

She took him through it, point by point, step-by-step. And yes, she could see he enjoyed it. She let his insults, his smugness roll off her as she got every tiny detail on record.

She paused when Reo came back.

"Reo, APA Cher, reentering Interview. Reo, Mr. Potter's providing us with details. We're nearly done."

"Go ahead, finish." Reo sat, folded her hands.

"Failure weighs heavy, doesn't it?"

She shot him a look, hard and hot, but said nothing.

"To continue?"

Eve didn't have to lead him through it, a few prompts here and there, but he relayed details, bragged enthusiastically.

"I believe that covers it," he finished.

"Nearly, yeah. You knew they'd all come. The remainder of The Twelve."

"Of course. As I said, we took an oath—one for all, all for one, nonsense. And they took another after Hawk and Fawn fell. Rossi told me himself, when he confronted me after my capture. A sacred oath, he called it. The foolish man believed it would shame me. A sacred oath, if one needed help, he had only to ask and they would all come. A bond that would never break, he said. Now he's dead, by my hand, because he answered that call. Kept that oath."

"You used loyalty as a weapon."

"Everything is a weapon."

"Okay, we got it all, on record."

"Which is worth the price of piss. I'd like to go back now. I'd enjoy a nap before my travels."

"I guess we did disturb your sleep. Mira?"

"Mr. Potter is legally sane. He is an intelligent, organized psychopath who fully intends to complete his kill list by any means necessary. The loss of human life means nothing to him, only a means to his stated goals. The mission, his mission, is sacrosanct. If he is able to escape prison—"

"When," Potter corrected.

"He will continue his war, endangering any in his path, until he kills those who remain of The Twelve. He will also attempt to kill the four of us in this room for standing against him."

"You'll never see it coming. Enjoy living in fear."

"You're right, Peabody," Eve commented, "tiny balls, complete prick. Reo? Your end?"

"Yes, I have some paperwork here."

"Extradition. Boo-hoo."

Without sparing a glance toward Potter, Reo held out the papers to Eve.

"That's your deal," Eve told her.

"I insist. Do what Roarke suggested."

"Passing the buck, you Yanks say." Another sneer. "Typical."

Eve scanned the papers, then laid them on the table.

"Conrad Potter, you have confessed, on record and of your own volition, to the premeditated murder of Giovanni Rossi, to the attempted murder of Marjorie Wright, Iris Arden, and Ivanna Liski, to the possession of illegal weapons, of banned toxic gas, of explosives. You have further confessed to the firing of an illegal weapon upon a police officer and civilians, to the drugging, abduction, imprisonment, and assault against the minor child Devin McReedy.

"You have stated the intention to commit murder if circumstances allow you freedom to do so.

"For these crimes and intentions, you will not be tried in the state of New York, or serve any sentence here. You will be extradited—"

"You lose."

"You will be extradited, you festering, puss-seeping boil on the ass of humanity—"

"Sticks and stones."

"From the city of New York directly to the off-planet, maximum-security prison of Omega."

"You lying bitch!" He tried to stand, but the shackles kept him in a hunch.

"Where you'll spend the rest of your miserable, shit stain of a life, with no possibility of parole—"

"I'll kill you first! Every fucking one of you!"

"In a concrete cage. This relocation is authorized and agreed upon, due to your crimes committed in New York City, by the British government and the goddamn United States of America.

"You'll never step foot on planet Earth again, you pathetic fuck. You'll never complete your mission, you flaming pile of puke. You'll die on a rock in space, and you'll always know women brought you down. Starting with Alice Dormer. You couldn't take her life, but she gave it to save others. You'll never understand that kind of courage or loyalty or sacrifice.

"Now I'll speak for Alice and the rest of The Twelve. You're done."

"I want a lawyer."

"Sure. One will be provided for you, as you're broke. Did I mention we found and froze all your accounts? You got nothing, you are nothing."

"I won't go. I can't be forced into an off-planet prison."

"I'd say wanna bet, but you've got nothing to put up. They beat you."

She went to the door. Signaled to the uniforms outside. "He's feeling frisky."

"We got him, LT."

Since she'd chosen two of the burliest, she didn't doubt it.

She turned to the glass, signaled. Then took a breath as they unshackled a struggling Potter. "Interview end." Then grinned. "Nice job. Girls. You don't want to miss this part."

She walked out behind Potter, then stood as The Twelve filed out of Observation.

He tried to lunge when he saw them, when they stood joined together.

Wild red color stained his face as he struggled against the two uniforms. "I'll kill you all! And your families. Your children. Their children. Dead. All dead. I swear it!"

Harry stepped forward. "We decided I should speak for all of us, just to add to what the lieutenant said, and it was bloody eloquent."

He held up his middle finger.

"Now we'll never speak again."

"Secure him," Eve ordered.

"I'll come back for you," he shouted at Eve as they dragged him away. "I'll listen to you scream as I cut out your heart."

"What was that you said in there before, Peabody? Oh yeah. Shiver."

"He'll live the rest of his life," Mira said, "plotting, planning, and burning inside. He'll never get through the rage, and it will eat at him, every day."

"Good to know. Really good to know."

"The world's a better place without him on it. I'll complete my report."

"Thank you, Dr. Mira."

"And I'll let the people who need to know that it's done. And tied in a big, shiny bow. Some days, work is just a joy," Reo added.

"You got that right." Eve turned to Peabody. "Bad Peabody."

"It was invigorating! I wasn't really going to punch him though, except in my mind."

"I know. Bad Peabody did good. Contact the McReedys, let them know he's going away, and where. Then go home, get some sleep."

"I'll write it up."

"No, I'll write it up. Go sleep. That's an order. Don't make me punch you."

She walked over to where Roarke, Whitney, and Tibble waited with The Twelve.

"Chief Tibble, Commander Whitney, thank you for your help in arranging the transfer to off-planet."

"Politics can sometimes come in handy," Tibble said. "In this case, it wasn't a hard sell. He escaped British authorities and subsequently murdered an Italian citizen, attempted to kill British citizens, a New York police lieutenant, and abducted a minor child.

"He's going exactly where he needs to go. Agreement all around. Excellent work, Lieutenant. To all."

"Thank you, sir."

He turned, shook hands with The Twelve. "Again, it was an honor and privilege to meet you."

As he left, Whitney stepped to Eve. "Go home, sleep. I'll write it up."

"Sir, I—"

"That's an order, Lieutenant. Don't make me punch you."

"Yes, sir. Thank you. It's just that—"

She stopped herself when his eyes narrowed.

"Thank you, Commander. Before I go off duty, I would like to contact Mr. Rossi's widow and inform her and her family. I'd like to break down my board."

"Go ahead, then get out."

"Lieutenant Dallas. Eve." Marjorie reached out for Eve's hand. "We owe you."

"You don't. You were part of it, all of you. We wouldn't have wrapped him so quick or so tight without you."

"Can I say you ladies kicked his ass in there?"

Eve nodded at Harry. "You can say that."

"We'd like to stay tonight," Ivanna told her. "If you'd allow us to impose on your hospitality one more night. We'd like to stay together one more night. We'll leave tomorrow for Giovanni's memorial."

"It's fine. No problem. Roarke, I'll be maybe another hour. You can go home with them."

"I'm with you. But I'll see to their transportation."

"Have a drink with us at least before we go tomorrow."

"Sure," she told Cyril. "I'll see you back at the house. I need to finish up."

She stopped in the bullpen first. "Good work," she told her squad. "Excellent work."

"He screamed like a girl. We could hear him."

She jabbed a finger at Jenkinson. "Don't insult girls."

In her office, she stood, looked at her board. "It didn't go unanswered."

She started to sit to contact Rossi's family, then stopped when she heard footsteps. Not familiar in her hallway.

Then frowned when Summerset came to the doorway.

"A word, please."

"A quick one. I've got orders."

"I want to thank you." He sighed a gust of air. "Don't put on that face."

"It's my face. I'm always wearing it."

"I'm not thanking you for doing your job, which you would dismiss. I'm thanking you for what you said at the end of your interview about my wife. About Alice."

"I said what was true. Truth doesn't need thanks, either."

"Truth matters, and when spoken matters more. She would have liked you a great deal. She was a warrior, too."

He glanced down. "There's blood on your shirt."

"It's from before."

"I'll see to it. We'll have spaghetti and meatballs tonight, for Giovanni. If you're not overly tired by then, I hope you'll join us."

He walked away before she answered, or could think how to answer.

Instead, she finished the work, then went out to see Roarke sitting at Peabody's desk.

"Done," she told him. "Jenkinson, you and your tie have the wheel. I'm going home."

"We got it." He, very deliberately, fluttered his tie so that she walked out on an eye roll.

"They were impressed," Roarke told her.

"With what, the interview?"

"With how you handled it. Tibble had told them what was happening, the transfer. It took the edge off. I won't say they enjoyed it—although some parts, yes."

"He was just so . . . do they say 'cocksure' because it's a man thing?"

"I refuse to answer that. You got your color back in there, skewering him." He rubbed his knuckles down her cheek. "You're losing it again now."

"Just need some sleep. A shower. A really long, hot shower, then sleep. Peabody was fierce."

"She was."

"Mira and Reo really played him."

"The four of you bonded—one purpose. And it was impressive."

"Teamwork. He was so proud of it, the idea he'd worked out that nothing he did here would matter. 'Kill, maim, destroy, so what? Can't hold it against me.'"

"And you proved otherwise."

"The law did. The system worked—both sides of the ocean."

By the time they made it to the garage, it started blurring a little. But it satisfied that she could still see the shock on Potter's face when she'd lowered the boom.

"A boom's a noise."

"It is indeed." He opened the passenger door, all but poured her into it.

"Then why do you lower it?"

"A boom on a ship. You raise and lower it."

"That's stupid. I wish I hadn't thought it."

Adoring her, he walked to the driver's side, got behind the wheel.

"Spaghetti and meatballs," she muttered.

"After you've slept."

"Yeah, no. Summerset said spaghetti and meatballs, and we should eat with them. I dunno."

"After you've slept, I think you'd enjoy it. They're, as I've said, an enjoyable bunch."

"Maybe. Is he going to Italy, too?"

"Summerset?" He glanced over as he drove, noted she was nearly under. "Of course. They were mates."

"Just you and me tomorrow."

"Tomorrow, and a few days more, you and me."

"Nice. Been busy. Miss you and me."

She dropped into sleep so he took her limp hand, brought it to his lips. And kept it pressed there for several seconds.

You and me, he thought. Even when it's not just, it's you and me.

He drove home, where he intended to sleep with his exhausted wife until spaghetti and meatballs.

About the Author

Bruce Wilder

J. D. ROBB is the pseudonym for #1 *New York Times* bestselling author Nora Roberts. She is the author of more than 240 novels, including the futuristic suspense In Death series. There are more than 500 million copies of her books in print.